# 32AA

...........

# 32AA

Michelle Cunnah

AVON
TRADE

*An Imprint of HarperCollinsPublishers*

HarperCollins books may be purchased for education, business, or sales promotional use. For information please write: Special Markets Department, HarperCollins Publishers Inc., 10 East 53rd Street, New York, NY 10022.

FIRST EDITION

*Designed by Elizabeth M. Glover*

Library of Congress Cataloging-in-Publication Data

Cunnah, Michelle.
  32AA / by Michelle Cunnah.
    p. cm.
ISBN 0-06-056012-6
1. British—New York (State)—New York—Fiction. 2. New York (N.Y.)—Fiction.
3. Young women—Fiction. I. Title: Thirty-two double A. II. Title.

PR6103.U5A613 2003
823'.92—dc21            2003049593

03 04 05 06 07 JTC/RRD 10 9 8 7 6 5 4 3 2 1

............................................................................

Prologue

## LIFE GOALS
Emmeline Beaufort Taylor
Age 13
*(after attending first George Michael concert)*

1. Develop breasts, like other girls. Mum says I'm a slow starter. Plus, bigger boobs are not important compared to Human Rights and World Peace.

2. Marry George Michael.

3. Have George Michael's babies.

4. While being perfect, glamorous, pop star wife (with adequate boobs) and wonderful mother, will also effortlessly juggle career as top businesswoman and ambassador for Human Rights and World Peace.

5. Have wonderful house in Kensington, Chelsea, or similar, providing perfect setting for pop star parties (Elton John and David Bowie will drop in daily for coffee).

6. Have wonderful weekend retreat near Windsor or Balmoral, or similar, so that Her Majesty (or other appropriate royal family member) and international diplomats can visit to discuss progress on Human Rights and World Peace.

7. Change name. To be named for Emmeline Pankhurst, famous British suffragette of Victorian era, is depressing, as am not a stone-throwing, letter-box-burning radical. Think my name encourages Mum to have false hope. Madonna would be a good name for me. Or maybe Cher . . .

## LIFE GOALS
### Madonna Beaufort Taylor
### Age 16
*(during really boring class on atomic chemistry)*

1. Not marry Chris Stevenson, gorgeous, blue-eyed, blond-haired jock, as have just discovered that he is taking Susan Grayson to senior prom instead of me. Apparently, Chris and me are "just good pals." Just good pals? I don't need any more friends. I want a boyfriend!

2. Stop obsessing over the fact that Susan Grayson is perfect goddesslike senior with breasts, hips, and always gets the boys that I want to date. Best friend Rachel says I should stop obsessing over lack of breasts, too—I must not feel pressured to conform to society's stereotypical ideals of the female form.

3. Change name. Madonna is not a good choice. Class peers love to joke about this and fall frequently to floor in hysterical laughing fits, after checking out my lack of boobs and un-Madonna-like physique.

4. Meet Jon Bon Jovi (kind father has bought me birthday gift of tickets for concert at Madison Square Garden).

5. Marry Jon Bon Jovi. Much better looking. Much kinder person than Chris. Plus, am sure my George Michael phase was just puppy love, not like true love I feel for Jon.

6. Have Jon Bon Jovi's babies.

7. Live happily ever after with Jon in New Jersey (in nice part of New Jersey, obviously, as will be married to rich pop star), while (also obviously) working for Human Rights and World Peace!

### LIFE GOALS
### Emma Beaufort Taylor
### Age 29

1. Get promotion and become woman of independent means with great career prospects. This will please hard-to-please, strongly feminist, but ultimately loving mother, who considers men good for only one thing (but only after you explain to them exact location of female eroge-nous zones). Plus, will be able to afford multiple pairs of Manolo Blahnik shoes.

2. Meet successful, perfect, handsome boyfriend, thereby pleasing capitalistic but ultimately loving plastic-surgeon father. Because boyfriend is already perfect, father and his partners will not constantly offer plastic surgery proce-dures as birthday/Christmas gifts for him.

3. Get engaged to above-mentioned successful boyfriend, thereby pleasing self. Plus, it will prove that not only am I multifaceted, slut-in-bedroom, Martha-Stewart-in-kitchen type, but also nurturing, caring mother-of-future-children type.

4. Have great apartment in SoHo, Greenwich Village, or similar, plus weekend home in the Hamptons.

5. ~~Maybe I should take up Dad's offer to have Uncle Derek do my breast implants.~~
   Maybe not. Not only am I scared witless of elective sur-gery and dangers of implants, but also best friends Rachel and Tish have a good point. Surely a mature relationship

is based on mutual attraction, respect, etc., and not the size of one's mammary glands? Besides, the thought of "Uncle Derek" (Dad's best friend and partner) finally getting his hands on my boobs is not attractive. Suspect he's been after them for years.

6. Do not give up best friends just because am happily ensconced in perfect relationship, thereby having no time for best friends.

7. Make monthly donations (obviously need to concentrate on career to earn more money) to assist World Peace and Human Rights.

# 1

*Birthday Girl?*

## TO DO
### *(before birthday next year)*

1. ~~Stick notes on refrigerator, coffee machine and all mirrors (because that way he's *bound* to get message) to remind Adam about my forthcoming birthday.~~

2. ~~Send Adam many e-mails to remind him about my forthcoming birthday.~~

3. ~~Talk incessantly and at length about my forthcoming birthday.~~

4. *Forgive darling Adam.* (Tiffany's ring is, after all, Tiffany's ring! Y-e-s!)

**6 A.M.**

I open my eyes and blearily check the radio alarm as Robert Plant (a god among men) sings to me that he's got a whole lotta love. Yes! It's Friday. It's June 28. It's my *birthday*. My *thirtieth birthday!*

Wonder what gifts I'll get from darling Adam, lovely friends, and odd-but-caring family . . . Of course, gifts are not important, not at all when compared with greater issues such as World Peace and Human Rights. But still would be nice to get gifts . . . Tiffany's ring, maybe . . .

Anyway. Am I depressed at the onslaught of middle age? *No!* Am I obsessing that the best years of my carefree youth are over? *Not me!* Am I unhappy to see the end of my twentysomething years? *Not a chance!* Am I carefully scanning the mirror each day for signs of lines? *You bet.*

It's crazy, you know? But I *yearn* for a few mature lines around my eyes. Now that I'm thirty, people will *have* to take me more seriously.

I can't *wait* to start the day! Because today is a day filled with exciting possibilities. Three, actually.

1. *The Promotion. Should* find out today. The interview, last week, went very well. I think that William Cougan (CEO) and Jacintha Bridges (Director of Human Resources) were impressed that the Kitty Krunch *and* Perfect Pantyhose campaigns were my ideas. Although they did seem to think that Adam was responsible. Strange . . .

2. *The Party.* With Adam and wonderful friends. I'm *sure* they like him more, now that they know him a bit better . . .

3. *The Proposal.* At least, I think Adam's going to propose. I'm *sure* he's going to propose. Yes, definitely . . .

As Bob (as I familiarly refer to Mr. Plant) croons that he's going to give me all of his love, I want to give Adam all of *mine,* so I snuggle back toward him. If I wiggle just a little, he'll know I'm ready for some early-morning, birthday romance. Can't be too obvious about it, because Adam thinks there's nothing more of a turn-off than a woman who initiates sex. That's men for you.

Oh, I know that's a bit old-fashioned, but he's an old-fashioned sort of guy about some things. Although his firm belief that women should always wear modest skirts is a bit unfortunate for me. Being four feet, eleven inches tall means that my legs are not very long and modest skirts turn them into six-inch matchsticks. This is not a good look for me. Although Adam does have a penchant for stockings and garter belts . . .

As I wriggle further to his side of the bed, all I meet are empty spaces and no Adam. The crumpled pillow holds the dent of his head, but not his, you know, actual head. And the covers are cold. *Where is he?*

*Of course.* He must be making me breakfast in bed! I'm a bit disappointed about the fading possibility of some early-morning sex, because he's been very distracted and tired over the last few weeks. I wonder if he needs to go see his doctor? I hear that Viagra does wonders for the male sex drive. Anyway, after a leisurely breakfast in bed, maybe he won't be so tired. Maybe he'll reach over and kiss me, then . . .

I sigh and dive back under the comforter for an extra few luxurious minutes before Adam returns with my birthday feast. Hmmm . . . I'll eat strawberries straight from his hand, and take bites of croissant in between kisses . . . One thing will lead to another and we'll have lovely, romantic sex. Adam, bathed in the afterglow of love, will magically produce a small jeweler's box from Tiffany's and beg me to marry him . . .

Oh. *Perfect!* The radio station's playing doubles. More Led Zeppelin. Bob is now telling me that *I will be his!*

Hope Adam doesn't mind that I switched the radio to classic rock, instead of the classic classical he prefers . . .

**7 A.M.**

Radio has clicked off and I've just realized that I don't hear any noise coming from the kitchen of our small (but tastefully lovely) apartment, so I'm getting up.

My hand lingers briefly on my ratty old bathrobe, then I spurn it in favor of the new cream silk robe Adam gave to me. Although the old robe is comfortable and familiar, it is not a particularly good look for me. No, the cream silk is definitely the right choice. I slip quickly into the bathroom to rinse my mouth with mouthwash—morning breath is so unromantic.

*Oh, God, my hair.* Albert Einstein on a bad hair day! Must do something about it before Adam sees me . . .

I pad over the beautifully refinished wood floor and into the living room. God, you can say what you like about Adam (all good, of course, because he's completely wonderful), the man has great taste! Tish says his taste is flawless, and she's an interior designer so she knows what she's talking about.

As I glance around at all the creams and whites in the sun-filled apartment, I shiver slightly at the coldness of the décor. But still, I'm happy to leave it to him. I really am. I mean, my idea of interior design is to buy things that catch my eye. I could be, oh, anywhere—at a flea market, walking in a street market—and something will leap out at me and I'll immediately know that I want to buy it.

But, as Adam has pointed out to me on several occasions, I don't give any thought to where it would go, or whether it will fit in with the rest of the scheme. Take that beautiful lacquered Indian bureau I bought. I thought it would be the perfect addition to our bedroom—you know—give it a splash of color as a relief from all the creams and whites. But Adam was right. I mean, he did actually *like* it. Just not in his apartment. So I gave it to Tish for her birthday and she loves it. So that's good, isn't it?

I'm hugely disappointed because the cream and white kitchen with stainless steel appliances (the latest in good taste) is completely Adamless. The coffeepot is gleaming with clean emptiness. The whole kitchen gleams with clean emptiness, not a crumb or a stray strawberry to be seen.

Where is he?

He can't have forgotten . . . Can he?

As my brain refuses to deal with this possibility, I suddenly *know* were he is. He's just gone to get my favorite breakfast in the world—an egg and sausage biscuit! Of course! *That's it.* Yes it is. My stomach grumbles at the thought of food as I reject the alternative option. That he *really has* forgotten.

No. *Not possible.* I've been talking about it for weeks.

Tonight, we're having dinner at Adam's favorite restaurant, La Trattoria. And after he proposes (and I am *almost sure* he's going to propose—why else would he be so distant? Gotta be nerves), and after we toast each other with champagne, we're off to Chez Nous. My friends Sylvester and David are closing the restaurant for the whole evening, just so they can host my party. How nice is that?

But where the hell is Adam? Not that I'm worried or anything . . .

As I see the white envelope propped against the toaster, the telephone rings and I grab it. *Adam!* Darling *Adam.* See? He *hasn't* forgotten my birthday after all.

"Hello," I say.

"Good morning, my name is John. Am I speaking with Miss Emmeline Taylor?"

Oh *fuck.* I really hate these people.

I am convinced that telemarketers exist just to torture me. Whenever I move, it takes them less than two weeks to track me down. They are the *bane* of my *existence.* I *wish* I'd checked the Caller ID.

However, in recent months I have developed several cunning ways to thwart their attempts to extract money from me. Adam thinks it's childish, but I find it hard to just say no and hang up.

I quickly decide on my strategy for today.

"*Non,*" I say, with probably the worst attempt ever at a French accent.

Why do these bloody people never ask for Adam?

"*Je viens vous parler au sujet de mon fils,*" I say, with complete conviction. "*J'ai vu faire cela à plusieurs ouvriers.*"

"Do you speak English, ma'am?"

"*Ja hoor. Ik neem dit.*" (No, I am not calling John a whore.)

"Is there anyone in the house who speaks English?"

"*Kde jsou toalety?*"

"Er, thank you for your time, ma'am."

"*Obuv!*"

No, I do not speak multiple European languages, but I picked up some handy phrases from summer vacations in France, the Netherlands, and the Czech Republic. This is the translation of our conversation.

ME: "I'm coming to speak to you about my son. I have seen several workmen do that."

JOHN: "Do you speak English, ma'am?"

ME: "Yes, of course. I'll take this."

JOHN: "Is there anyone in the house who speaks English?"

ME: "Where are the toilets?"

JOHN: "Er, thank you for your time, ma'am."

ME: "Shoe shop!"

After all, it is totally necessary to be able to ask directions to rest rooms and shoe shops when visiting a foreign country.

And the phone rings again, immediately. John and his buddies will not catch me out twice in one morning, I think, checking the Caller ID.

Not John. Not Adam, either.

"Happy birthday, darling Emma," Peri, my stepmom, burbles down the telephone.

"Thanks, Peri," I say, trying not to sound disappointed.

"Did you get our cards? There's one from me and Daddy—"

Yes, I'm thirty years old and Peri still insists I call my father "Daddy."

"—and one each from Jack Junior and Joe Junior—they made the cards in art class last week. Miss Zolowski says they have real talent for their age—she's very excited about the abstract paintings they did for her yesterday, although she was a little upset when Joe Junior painted Charlene Gordon's hair with rhododendron red . . ."

I phase out Peri as she burbles on about the terrible twosome-twinsome. Call me hardhearted if you like, but the criminal antics of my three-year-old half brothers do not amuse me. On account of having been their victim on more occasions that I care to recall. I'm totally with poor Charlene Gordon on this one.

Unfortunately, Peri believes that the path to child genius involves allowing the twins to do whatever they like. Apparently, disciplining children in any shape or form curtails their development. I don't know if they have child prodigy qualities, but I do know that they are the most badly behaved kids I've ever encountered. Of course, I *do* love them. They are my half brothers, after all. I just prefer to love them from a distance.

Last time I visited them, Joe Junior peed in my purse and Jack Junior fed my car keys to the garbage disposal. The purse was *ruined* (was DKNY—a bargain from the outlets— okay, so last year's fashion, but that's entirely beside the point because it was a very nice purse). I mean, could you imagine using a purse again after it had been peed in? Fortunately, best friend Tish drove over to bring me my spare set of car keys.

"So we'll see you and Adam on the Fourth of July?"

I really hope the twins behave. You see, Adam's meeting my family for the first time.

"And don't worry about a bathing suit—I've bought you a darling little bikini from the new boutique in town. Oops, that was meant to be a surprise—don't worry, Daddy and I have some other gifts for you—I can't *wait* until you open them."

Oh God, I really don't want to spend Independence Day in a chosen-by-Peri bikini. I'm practically flat-chested, you see. And skinny. And you might think that this sounds perfect. You might think I'd be happy with my Gwyneth Paltrow physique (except she's taller and has larger breasts), but I'm not. When dressed in nothing more than underwear, I am self-consciously aware of my feminine attributes. Or rather, my lack of them.

"We're *so* looking forward to meeting Adam," Peri says. "It'll be great, all the family together for the holiday."

I wonder if I can come up with an excuse not to go? I want Adam to meet them, of course, but maybe it would be better if he met Peri and Dad without the twins first.

"Now, Emma, I have another lovely surprise for you. I wasn't going to tell you, but I'm just *so happy!*" Peri shrieks with excitement and I have to hold the telephone slightly away from my ear.

"I'm just so delighted! You'll never guess who's coming. Go on, see if you can guess."

Guilty for trying to avoid Peri and her demon brood, I realize that if I try to get out of this, she will be hurt. And I really don't want to hurt her. She's only ten years older than me and has always made such an effort to be friendly and include me in Dad's life (older sister syndrome—thank God not mother syndrome). Especially since the twins were born.

I wonder, again, how Dad could have married two such different women, from two different continents. One (my mother) a top, radical, feminist barrister in London. The other (Peri) a receptionist from New Jersey. Not that there's anything wrong with being a receptionist, because it's a very worthwhile job. Not that there's anything wrong with *New Jersey,* either (after all, Jon Bon Jovi lives there, so that's good, isn't it?). I'm *very glad* I got the chance to live in New Jersey with Dad. My mother (ever one for equal rights) made sure I spent equal time living with Dad. Although it has to be said that he was barely married to my mother long enough for the ink to dry on the marriage certificate (she was back in London before she even realized that she'd brought rather more back from the States with her than she'd bargained for—me).

I realize that Peri's side of the phone line has gone unusually quiet as she waits for me to guess the identity of the mystery guest. Oh, God, I hope it's not Uncle Derek. Or Norbert.

"Er, Uncle Derek? Norbert?" I pray I'm wrong. Uncle Derek, Dad's partner, apparently a complete whiz with a scalpel and a pair of implants, has a disconcerting habit of talking to my breasts instead of to me. And although I'm sure his interest is purely professional, I can't quite rid myself of the idea that Uncle Derek enjoys his work more than is usual. How would he feel if I spoke to his penis?

And Norbert, a junior partner (also a breast man), is a complete bore. He's convinced he's irresistible to the entire female population. But why does he feel the need to point out the smallness of my breasts whenever I meet him? I don't ask men how long their penises are, then recommend penis extensions if they're anything under eight inches.

"Guess again," Peri grunts with her gusty laughter. And then, "Emma, just give me a moment, will you? The boys are smashing eggs on the kitchen floor . . . Joe Junior, raw egg is not good for you . . ."

As Peri rescues my half brother from near death by salmonella, I suddenly remember the envelope I'm holding. It says *E.* on the envelope. It's for me! From Adam! Everything's fine, just like I thought. It's got to be part of my birthday surprise. Maybe it's a magical mystery tour, you know, "Meet me at the café on the corner and all will be revealed."

I rip it open and pull out the neatly folded sheet of paper, scrabbling at it with excitement. And then my heart sinks into my feet as I read it.

*Breakfast meeting with important client. See you later, A.*

What meeting? Which client? As Adam's assistant, I keep his office diary and I would have remembered, *Breakfast meeting with important client. See you later, A.* Especially today of all days. And it doesn't even say *Love, A.,* with kisses. You'd think he'd remember to add a few X's to the bottom of the note, wouldn't you?

I can't help the very bad feeling that's congealing in the pit of my stomach. Am I obsessing? I think I *am* obsessing. I take a deep breath and try not to assume the worst, but it's hard. I always assume the worst, because that's usually the real deal, so I'm just preparing myself in advance for disappointment.

Rachel says it's my English half coming out and she is one smart cookie. She has a doctorate in biochemistry, or genetic engineering, or something scientifically brilliant. Anyway, she's scarily clever, and if she says that my English half is insecure and that it worries compulsively, then I figure it must be right.

"Darling, I have to go," Peri splutters down the phone. "Oh God, Joe Junior just puked on the kitchen floor. Does salmonella show that quickly? I don't think it does, but you can't be too careful. I'd better call the pediatrician, just to make sure. See you on Thursday. Oh, and happy birthday again."

I hang up the receiver as the panic attack starts to build, moving up from my stomach to my throat. What if Adam's getting tired of me? *Breathe, breathe, in-out, in-out.*

Oh, God. *What's if he's having an affair?*

I wonder if it's too early to call Tish or Rachel? Think I'll call Tish. Rachel will only tell me to stop being pathetic and needy. Okay, it's now seven thirty. Tish will be having breakfast in Rufus's Organic Deli on Washington, in a bid to finally make Rufus notice her and fall madly in love with her after three years of breakfasts in his deli. So I speed dial her cell phone.

Friend Tish (shared an apartment with her for four years until I moved in with Adam three months ago) sings "Happy Birthday to You" to me.

"Tish, Ithinkadamforgotmybirthday," I gasp into the receiver. "He was gone before I woke up. He left me a note. Do you think he's trying to subliminally send me messages that he wants to finish with me, or do you think he's just nervous about proposing?" I can't quite bring myself to utter my suspicions about an Adam–another woman affair.

"Honey, slow down. Tell me exactly what happened."

I spend the next ten minutes going through my angst, and Tish spends the following ten minutes telling me that I'm overreacting and that everything will be fine, there must be a logical explanation for his apparent amnesia. I feel a bit better. I really do. At least I think I do . . .

"Wear the Donna Karan pantsuit," Tish tells me. "It will give you confidence. It absolutely screams 'I am a capable, intelligent woman who is totally going to be a great account manager.' Stylish, discreet, yet not boring. Wear the four-inch Manolo Blahniks and take the Prada briefcase Rachel bought you last Christmas. And don't overdo the makeup. Keep it simple."

"This is great," I tell her. And it is. Tish always knows what to wear for whatever occasion. It's that designer eye of hers again—totally infallible.

"So, how's it going with Rufus?"

"Oh, same as usual," she tells me cheerfully, and I know that means she barely said hello, just gave him her order and sank into tongue-tied embarrassment.

Tish, at thirty-five, is a young Sophia Loren (and will look gorgeous as an older Sophia Loren when she's seventy). Men line up in droves at the door of her Interior Design store in Hoboken, but does she ever date them?

No. For the last three years she has pined over Rufus O'Leary, a big, brooding Irishman. Rufus is a nice guy, but he's not exactly the type to spout poetry at you and sweep you off your feet (more the type to spout organic bean sprouts and offer you today's special menu). Alas, the poetry and feet-sweeping are exactly what Tish is waiting for.

"Well, I've got to go," she says, and what she really means is, "Oh, here comes Rufus I must get out before he speaks to me and I make an idiot of myself."

I haven't told her yet that Sylvester and David have invited

Rufus to the party (Rufus does, after all, provide the restaurant with the most wonderful organic produce). I feel guilty about this, but Sylvester made me promise not to tell Tish. He says that if we tell her, she'll only obsess and be nervous for longer, and there's no point needlessly torturing her. Besides which, by the time we've managed to pour a couple of glasses of Chardonnay into her, she'll be more relaxed and confident enough to finally speak to him.

I wonder why Adam's so off sex . . .

Oh shit. 8 A.M. already. But I don't care. You see, I accidentally found Adam's latest Visa statement. When I say "accidentally," I mean that I found it while sneakily rummaging through the contents of his bedside table in my quest to find evidence of an affair. And there it is—on his statement! A *twenty-five-thousand-dollar* purchase at Tiffany's. *Twenty-five thousand dollars.*

From *Tiffany's!*

My engagement ring! *Y-e-s!*

. . . . . . . . . . . . . . . .

**4:30 P.M.**

I am hiding in the ladies' bathroom.

It is a very nice bathroom, with art deco mirrors, lots of silk ivy plants and beautiful terra-cotta tiles everywhere, but the aesthetics fail to impress me.

I am gripping the cold marble counter and concentrating furiously on the artfully arranged faux flora, because if I don't, I will cry, and the after-cry look is not a good one for me. Squinty eyes and blotchy red skin are what crying does for me.

I wonder if I can hide in here until everyone else has gone home?

## 2

........................................................................................................

# Bad to Worse

## TO DO

1. Hide in ladies' bathroom. *Forever.*

It happened on Fifth Avenue.

I should have known it was a sign of bad things to come!

A group of workmen on coffee break whistle and call after me as I saunter past on my way to work, and of course I am so delighted (because even workmen usually ignore me) that I preen and hold up my head as I attempt a seductive sashay.

I have to say, with the help of a well-padded bra, this Donna Karan suit boldly gives me curves where no other suit has given me curves before.

*Looking good, baby,* I think to myself.

I am *hot!*

So I slip immediately into daydream mode, imagining that men everywhere will be so enraptured by this goddesslike vision, madness and mayhem will ensue. Fender benders and innocent pedestrian injuries all down Fifth Avenue as men ogle *me* instead of watching the traffic.

And then, because I am so busy recreating myself in Aphrodite's image (and, it has to be said, imagining how great *the Tiffany's ring* will look on my finger), I step into a manhole cover and *poof,* just like that, off comes the heel of my Manolo. This is a sure sign of impending disaster.

I *love* these shoes.

I have nurtured and protected these shoes *for three whole years*. I keep them in their box, complete with shoe stands, so that they don't lose their shape. They were a rare personal Christmas gift from my mother. She usually buys me politically correct gifts, like sponsoring children in third world countries in my name—which is completely admirable and much more worthy than an expensive pair of shoes. But I still *love* these shoes.

And I *cannot afford to buy another pair.* Well, not yet, anyway. Unless my promotion comes with a good pay raise.

I should have worn my sneakers to walk the ten blocks to work, then changed in the lobby like I usually do. But today I made an exception because it's my birthday. Plus, the sneakers look *terrible* with the Donna Karan suit.

At this point (after the humiliation of a group of high school students on a school trip sniggering at my demise), I should just turn around and go home to bed to eat Häagen-Dazs ice cream, and play air guitar along with Jimmy Page. Instead (spurred on by the promise of a Tiffany's box) I push boldly forward and make an emergency stop at Payless Shoes. Result: a pair of very nice sling backs with mock snakeskin finish for the bargain price of twenty bucks—black, of course.

When I finally arrive at work (amazingly, I am only twenty minutes late) Bud, the security guard, opens the door for me and tells me "not to worry," that "these things happen." And Angie, the bulldog receptionist from the Deepest Pit of Hell, is *not nasty* to me. She isn't actually nice, either, but she doesn't say a word about my lateness. Not a snide remark about how some of us manage to get out of bed with the alarm. She just raises an evil eyebrow (her resemblance to Cruella De Vil is uncanny—funny I'd never noticed that before) and gives me a pitiful smile.

This in itself is usually enough to set all my internal alarm bells ringing. But when everyone else in my department

gives me the same pitiful smile, accompanied by gentle in-
quiries about how I feel, and telling me not to worry, that
"these things happen," I just assume that it's because I'm
thirty.

I smugly imagine that they all fear I am about to have
some sort of midlife crisis, on account of the fact that they
are all in their twenties and haven't yet had the liberating experience of looking the big Three-O squarely in the face.
*Bloody cowards.* Their time will come.

But the oddest thing about today is Adam, conspicuous by
his absence. Apart from a couple of meetings in his office
diary, there's nothing to suggest that he'll be out all day, and
by three in the afternoon I am starting to panic. My fertile
imagination takes full control of my brain, as I conjure up all
kinds of horrific scenarios, each one more bloody than the
last.

Maybe he was mugged (oh, no! My ring). Maybe he
choked on his coddled egg during his early breakfast meeting, and because I wasn't there, no one knew how to perform
the Heimlich maneuver. Oh, no! Suffocated by a coddled
egg, how awful! Or he could have been the innocent victim
of a gangland-style drive-by shooting. I imagine his crumpled body, broken and bleeding on the sidewalk as he gasps
my name. Or maybe he was hit by a cab, because the driver
was distracted by my morning goddess impression on Fifth
Avenue . . .

Oh God, I can just see it now. Me, pale and wan (but obviously in a beautiful kind of way) in the ER, being com-
forted by a George Clooney lookalike as he tells me that
Adam, despite grievous horrible wounds to his poor body,
confessed his love for me shortly before wheezing his last
breath . . .

And it would all be *my fault* for distracting the cabdrivers
in such a shameful way!

But I don't guess the most obvious reason for his inexpli-
cable absence.

*He is avoiding me.*

When he finally saunters into the office (the picture of good health, not a hair out of place or bandage to be seen), he barely looks at me as he passes my cubicle and asks me to step into his office. So I do. Butterfly wings flapping madly in my stomach.

This is what happens next.

"Please sit down, Emmeline," he says from his leather swivel chair, placing clasped hands on his huge, mahogany desk. And then he smiles, and his perfectly white teeth (regularly touched up with his bleaching kit) contrast healthily with his tan (hours on the tanning bed at his gym). He is truly one of the most handsome men I've ever set eyes on. And while I am inwardly rejoicing that all his body parts are intact and imagining what beautiful children we will have, he clears his throat several times and fiddles with a paper clip.

He doesn't say, "Happy birthday." He doesn't say, "Congratulations, you got the job." No Tiffany's box magically appears on his desk, either. I know we're at work and have to maintain a professional distance, but he's even more "me boss you secretary" than usual.

And then I'm scared, really scared, that the feeling of impending doom that I've had since I got out of bed this morning is for real, and not just me obsessing.

"I didn't get it, did I?" I ask in a small voice, willing him to contradict me. But he doesn't. After long, agonizing seconds, he looks at me for the first time. But he still can't meet my eyes.

"No," he says, finally. "You, er, didn't. Not this time."

And then he looks back down at the paper clip, and he is obviously nervous, which is odd. Unnatural. He is usually the epitome of comfort in his own environment.

I swallow the lump of disappointment and try to be calm and reasonable. But I *deserve* that job. I worked so hard to prove myself and I thought I'd succeeded.

"Why not?" I ask, clutching the seat of my chair, which is

much lower down than Adam's, so I have to look up at him to get this bad news.

"I'd be great with my own accounts—you know how much input I gave to the Kitty Krunch and Perfect Pantyhose campaigns," I say, pleased that my voice is more assertive than I feel. And then, "Who *did* get it, then?"

"It was felt that Lou Russo should be appointed. On this occasion. But not by me, of course," Adam stresses, then gives a guilty little laugh.

This is the icing on the cake. I must be hallucinating. I would rather Angie of the Cruella eyebrows beat me to a job than Lou Russo.

"He only spent last summer here for work experience. How could they choose *him* instead of *me?* Don't you remember how useless he was?" I know I sound whiny and a bit bitchy, but I can't help it.

Lou Russo is twenty-two years old and probably needs to shave once a week, max. He is also a nasty little boy who made my life last summer a living hell. Because he was given the title of Trainee Junior Account Manager, working for Johnny Cray (my boss before Adam), and also because he was a soon-to-be Ivy League graduate (paid for by Daddy's money), he took great delight in thinking up all manner of meaningless, menial tasks for me, the Brainless Secretary, to do.

My favorite was the constant request for coffee. He sat much closer to the coffee cubicle than me, but he found it amusing to watch me trot back and forth when I really had better things to do. The thing I couldn't figure out was why he *wanted* to watch me trot back and forth—my cleavage is definitely not of the bouncing variety.

"But *how come* he got it instead of me? I'm experienced—I've been working on your accounts for five months now, and I come up with great ideas. Why would William Cougan pass me over? What did he say to you?" I know I'm babbling, but I can't seem to switch off my mouth.

"Oh, you know, usual reasons," Adam mumbles. "Lou has a good degree from a prestigious school."

He then proceeds to mutilate another paper clip and I am confused, because I know that Lou got a very mediocre degree, because, apart from the fact that Tracey the secretary in Human Resources told me so, Lou is a very mediocre person with no imagination.

"I have a degree, too," I tell him. "In fact, I have two degrees. I graduated with honors. Last month. You came to my graduation, remember?"

I originally studied English Literature in London.

Now, a degree in English literature is all very well. If you want me to explain Shakespeare's use of imagery or if you want a reasonably accurate translation of Chaucer, I'm your woman. But English literature degrees don't seem to hold much sway in this company. Which is precisely why I put myself to the trouble of taking another degree—this time in business studies. At a great deal of inconvenience to myself and my loved ones, because it meant nighttime classes. Plus, I paid for it myself, which meant less cash donations for Human Rights and World Peace. And obviously excluded the possibility of Manolo Blahnik shoes.

"And my degree is better than his," I tell Adam, now indignant that I have been passed over for such a pathetic reason. "In fact, *both* of my degrees are better than his *one* degree, so it can't be the degree issue. Come on. Give me some more to work with, here."

*Maybe I'm too old*, I worry, chewing on my bottom lip.

"Oh, you know, er," Adam bumbles on heartily in a too-jovial tone, and I feel sorry for him again. This is not his fault. It cannot be a pleasant task, breaking such bad news to your significant other.

"William's always on the look out for fresh, enthusiastic new blood."

So that *is* it. I *am* too old! And here I am fondly imagining that my life will begin at thirty.

"It's nothing personal. The management just feels that you might not be quite ready for this—maybe in six months' time. Just bide your time, darli—Emma," he says, and I think that he's very distracted if he nearly called me "darling" at work. And he's calling me "Emma," instead of "Emmeline." This is not a good sign . . .

"Just keep your head down and come up with some more wonderful ideas, and I'm sure you'll get it."

And then the telephone rings and Adam grasps it like a life jacket on a sinking ship. I'm still not really taking in the news he's just given me. Or the fact that he really has forgotten my birthday.

"Hello. Er, yes. Yes, of course." He eyes me surreptitiously, his face slightly flushed.

He keeps glancing across as he's talking, very uncomfortable that he is taking this phone call while I am in the room. Which smells of dead rat.

"No, not yet. She's here with me now. Yes. Me too. Byeee."

And as he's mumbling into the telephone, I'm getting an even stronger smell of dead rat. This is all wrong. And Adam *only* ever says "byeee" to me. It is our special good-bye phrase. I feel my heart sinking further into my mock snake-skin shoes.

Abruptly, he gets to his feet and grasps his garment bag.

And then I actually *notice* that he's holding his garment bag and I am even more confused. This cannot be right.

"Adam, where are you going? Why do you need luggage?"

"I'm sure I told you I'd be away this weekend," he tells me in his best "let's be reasonable" voice.

"No, you didn't. I'd have remembered."

"I'm sure I did," he says, stalking across the office to retrieve the lovely leather briefcase that I bought him for our three-months-together anniversary. "It's a business weekend. Mainly meetings and golf. It'll be boring, but frankly, we have to keep the clients happy."

I don't believe this. He *can't* have forgotten all the plans we've made. And I am about to open my mouth to tell him so when the telephone rings again, and Adam lunges for it with an apologetic, relieved smile.

"It's for you." He frowns a few moments later as he passes me the receiver. "Your mother."

"Happy birthday, Emmeline."

My mother, like Adam, insists on using my full name at all times—I think she still hopes that I'll turn into a radical feminist. I mean, of course I believe in women's rights, but not to the point where I'm committing felonies and getting thrown into prison.

"I wouldn't usually call you at work, but George and I are off to the country for the weekend with the Smythe-Joneses—we're doing a protest march on Sunday against fox hunting, and what with the time difference between England and the States, I thought I'd catch you now."

"Thanks, Julia," I tell her as I anxiously watch Adam shuffle a sheaf of papers (my mother thinks that family labels are outdated and has insisted that I call her Julia instead of Mum since my sixteenth birthday).

"Darling, I've sent you a card with details of your birthday present. I thought I'd make this one something special, seeing as thirty is such a landmark," she tells me, and I wonder if she's bought me another pair of shoes.

It's amazing, isn't it? I've just been told that I've been passed over for promotion for no good reason whatsoever, my boyfriend seems to be suffering from amnesia regarding birthday plans, and all I can think about are new shoes.

"You'll love it," my mother tells me in a no-nonsense, Mrs. Thatcher voice. "You've bought some goats for a village in Uganda to help the Msoze family become self-sufficient. I've sent them your name and address, I'm sure you'll receive a lovely letter from them soon. Well, got to go—it's eight in the evening and we want to get to the hotel in time for a late supper. I'll call you next week to let you know how it went—bye, darling."

In the meantime, Adam has just about made it out of the door and looks positively disappointed when I put down the receiver. Tough. He has some talking to do.

"You know how much I hate these things." He tries to cajole me. "But work is work. Oh, review the Burgoyne file over the weekend, will you? See if you can come up with some ideas for the new advertising campaign—their CEO isn't keen on the stuff we've already suggested. And I've left you a list of e-mails to be deleted from my computer."

My mind clicks and whirrs with disbelief.

"I have to go, Emma, or I'll miss my flight." He smiles, his teeth positively glittering, and before I can draw breath, he disappears out of the door. See? See? Again *Emma* instead of *Emmeline*.

And then he reappears again, two seconds later.

"Oh, and do remind your mother that personal calls during working hours are frowned upon."

Trust Adam to turn the situation around and find fault with me.

"Yes, I know," I tell him, finding my tongue. "But I think they'd make an exception for a girl getting an international call from her mother, on her thirtieth birthday. Don't you?"

And his smile falters ever so slightly, and then he gives me the full beam of his perfect teeth.

"Well, I know that, silly."

See? See? He's just called me silly. He's forgetting about work/personal life boundaries again. This is not good.

"I didn't want to mention it because I thought you were a bit oversensitive about not being in your twenties anymore."

Nice recovery, but I'm not buying it.

"Adam, I've talked about nothing else for weeks. Haven't you been listening? What about our plans for dinner? What about my birthday party? Everyone's expecting you to *be* there."

*Particularly me*, I think. And then another thought occurs to me. *What about that entry on his Visa statement?*

"Keep your voice down," he says, glancing furtively around the main office to check for eavesdroppers.

No one at work knows that we are an item. According to Adam, William Cougan disapproves of personal relationships in his workforce, although Jacintha Bridges from Human Resources and Guy Pirelli from Marketing have just got engaged, and William doesn't seem to mind *their* personal relationship. In fact, I did hear on the grapevine that he's offered them the use of his luxury home in the Bahamas for the honeymoon. But they don't work together like Adam and me. I suppose that does make a difference, Adam being my boss and everything.

"Emmeline, your friends don't like me," Adam tells me in a reasonable tone, as if I am a fractious child making unreasonable demands, and this annoys me intensely because there is nothing unreasonable about me wanting him there for my birthday celebrations.

"Tom and Katy are touchy-feely hippies who think that anyone who votes Republican must be from Pluto. Rachel makes snide remarks, Tish barely even speaks to me, and David flirts with me, which pisses off Sylvester, who just scowls at me. Which makes me very uncomfortable."

Is this true? I just thought it was because they didn't know him very well. Although I do know that David thinks Adam's a bit of a hunk, because he mentions this quite a lot.

"Anyway." Adam glows brightly at me. "I'll bring you back a beautiful little something from my trip."

But I thought he'd already bought me a beautiful little something. From Tiffany's.

"We'll have a fabulous celebration at La Trattoria next week, to make up for me missing the fun. Because I'm not going to have fun, you know, it's all business this weekend. Boring and humdrum. Well then, have a good time tonight—gotta dash. See you Monday night."

And then he truly is gone.

And with complete incomprehension, I sink into Adam's

lushly comfortable chair, inhaling the smell of the expensive leather and trying to make sense out of the strange conversation I've just had with him.

I am so miserable I can't feel anything, so I pick up the list of business e-mails Adam asked me to delete and turn to his computer. He was so anxious to escape me, he has forgotten to exit his *private* e-mail. And despite the fact that I am numb with misery, I cannot resist the urge to peek at his private e-mail. And I discover two very interesting facts.

1. Adam got the credit, and a very fat bonus, for his work on the Kitty Krunch and Perfect Pantyhose accounts. Okay, he *is* Director of Advertising, so as the top dog he gets the credit, but there is no mention in this e-mail of the fact that I did a lot of the work for him.

2. Adam *didn't* recommend me for the promotion. He recommended *against* me getting it. There it is, in black and white, almost word for word what he said to me. My lack of experience, blah, blah, ending with the possibility of a review in six months.

Oh God! What about the Tiffany's box? It's obviously for someone else. *It's for another woman.*

Adam's telephone rings again and I nearly don't pick up. What could be more important than my breaking heart? How could he do this to me? Why has he done this to me? Who is she?

And while my thoughts whirl chaotically, I pick up the receiver.

"Emily, this is Stella Burgoyne. Put Adam on."

I hit my forehead with the base of my palm. The last thing I need is Stella Burgoyne, CEO of Burgoyne's Fine Paper Products. Stella, the curse of the conference table. Stella "I-can-get-you-fired" Burgoyne. Definitely a man's woman. This woman has met me no less than six times and she still gets my name wrong, but I cannot afford to make an enemy of her and so I am nice (but ironic—just my little joke).

"I'm sorry, Stella," I say, with saccharine sweetness, knowing full well that she prefers to be addressed as Ms. Burgoyne by minions such as myself. "Adam's gone for the weekend. Can I take a message?"

And if she wants revenge for my having had the audacity to call her Stella, she could not deliver a more crushing blow.

"No, Emily," she gushes, swiftly moving in for the kill. "I'm meeting Adam at the airport for our little rendezvous— I just wanted to be sure he left on time. The Bahamas are so beautiful at any time of year, don't you think? Gotta run, or Adam will think I've stood him up."

And with a tinkling little laugh, just to rub salt in the wound that is my bleeding heart, she hangs up.

I take a good look at myself in the art deco mirror. For once, no one would mistake me for being younger than my years because I am stooped and defeated, the air of world-weary misery surrounding me is palpable.

How did our relationship disintegrate so quickly?

# 3

## When Emma Met Adam

If someone were to ask me now how Adam and I met, I would have to say that it started with a death.

And a pair of ripped pantyhose.

I wish it had started with something more romantic—like a kiss. Yes, a kiss definitely sounds much more appealing—a romantic tale to tell to our children and grandchildren in the years to come . . .

Oh, God, how *can* I tell our children and grandchildren in the years to come? Our love is *doomed* . . . I should have *guessed* that the death thing was definitely not a good sign. I should have *known* it could never work for us . . . But I was blinded by my image of the perfect boyfriend. Obsessed with my stupid list of what I thought I should achieve by age thirty.

And lust, of course.

This is what happened.

Adam came to work at Cougan & Cray a year ago (apparently a whiz kid, head hunted from Sezuma Advertising, our chief competitor). And the moment he sauntered into the office, with his blond good looks and Peter Pan boyishness (and immaculately cut Armani suit), the entire female workforce (and some of the male) fell as slaves at his feet.

Me included.

The second I set eyes on him, I just knew that I wanted him, that I had to *have* him. He was perfect. My dad and Peri would love him. My friends would love him. Julia would appreciate his aesthetic, athletic male beauty and ask me if he was any good in bed.

So *I* would love him.

And besides, Adam was *the* perfect candidate for my Goals by Thirty list, and time was running out.

I fell hard.

And so the whispered speculation started. Is he married? Is he dating? (Is he gay?) Is there a significant other? Fortunately for me, because of my friendship with Tracey in Human Resources (she is the central point for all gossip and speculation), I was able to get the scoop on him.

Single. *And straight.* Y-e-s! Y-e-s!

Apparently, he'd been involved in a long relationship with some girl from a good Boston family, but she'd practically ditched him at the altar. She found true love with a street artist from South Street Seaport. (Word has it that he could juggle knives and eat fire like you wouldn't believe. I think I saw him once.)

Stupid, *stupid* girl. *Poor,* poor Adam and his broken heart.

But *lucky* me.

I fondly imagined myself listening to his tale of heartbreak with understanding and sympathy. And then, when he'd talked out his grief, I would soothe his wounds with the balm of my kindness and beauty. He would forget all about his cheating, WASP fiancée and fall in love with me . . .

Adam was a dream come true—*my* dream come true. Tall, gorgeous, successful, sexy. And with a loft apartment in Greenwich Village, too. *Thank you, God!*

From that day forward I made it my mission in life to look as fabulous as possible every day. You would not believe how much money I spent on new outfits to tempt him. Or how early I had to get up in the morning to get ready for work. I rode the elevator at the times I knew *he* would ride the elevator (after having carefully watched him to ascertain this information). I visited the coffee cubicle whenever I thought *he* would get the urge for liquid refreshment. But it seemed that all, alas, was in vain. Although charming and polite whenever our paths happened to cross, he would smile and say, "Hello, how are you?" in the same manner as he would say, "Hello, how are you?" to the rest of the smitten workforce.

I was a desperate woman. So desperate, in fact, that I began to accidentally-coincidentally visit the ladies' room at the same time as *he* got the call of nature. (Yes, I know this is sad, but I was getting to the point of losing hope.)

I was so anxious to make some sort of breakthrough with him, and so mesmerized by his handsome face, that on one occasion I nearly followed him into the men's room. When he paused at the door and turned to me, I thought, *Hel-lo, here we go,* and gave him my best beaming smile (all the while mentally thanking my dad for insisting on expensive orthodontic treatment). But instead of asking me out for dinner, he pointed at the MEN sign on the door, smiled right back at me and said, "You sure you want to do this?"

God, I nearly *died*.

From that moment on, I left him to ride the elevator, drink coffee, and visit the bathroom alone, ashamed and embarrassed that I'd been such a fool. Plus, my face would flush strawberry red whenever he was near, and this is not a good look for me. So I avoided him like the plague.

And just when I'd completely given up on ever making any progress with Adam, Lady Luck smiled on me. My boss, Johnny Cray Senior, did, in fact, die.

Now this may sound very hardhearted and callous of me, feeling lucky at the death of my boss, but Johnny Cray Senior lived a full and active life. He passed away while having a *very good time* on honeymoon with wife number four (a pretty, blonde, twenty-eight-year-old ex-cheerleader, Babette). And although I was (obviously) sad to learn of his passing, Johnny Senior was eighty-four and died of a mid-orgasmic heart attack. Apparently, in his excitement, he'd forgotten to take his heart medication. But still, what a fabulous exit!

If I had to select my own time and method of death, I would *choose* this particular fashion to depart the mortal coil. Can't you just see my obituary?

> Ms. Emmeline Beaufort Taylor (women's rights activist and campaigner for Human Rights and World Peace), age ninety-eight and spinster by choice, departed this life while cruising the Greek islands with her close, personal friend, Hans Schwarz (male model), age twenty.
>
> "She vas ze most beautiful woman in the world—ze best lover I ever had," said the distraught Mr. Schwarz, as he sobbed over her grave.
>
> It is rumored that Ms. Taylor will posthumously receive the Nobel Peace Prize for her many humanitarian works.

Of course, I *was* very sad about poor Johnny. I'd been his secretary for two years and had developed a tolerant fondness for the way he could never remember my name (he called me babe—he called all women babe). Yes, I remember *well* the affectionate way he would pat my butt whenever I forgot that he liked to do this and got too close when taking him coffee . . .

So how can this possibly have any relevance to my romance with Adam? This is what happened next.

It is the day of Johnny's memorial service and all the staff at Cougan & Cray are expected to attend. Because Johnny was a prominent member of the community, it's taking place at St. Thomas's Church on Fifth Avenue (opposite Nine West). I am wearing a simple black shift dress (Jones New York), with a black blazer (also Jones New York).

This is a very good look for me.

The black brings out the blonde highlights in my short, artfully tousled hair. Plus, my grandmother's pearls, at my neck and in my ears, enhance the creaminess of my skin. I'm also wearing my favorite shoes—Manolo Blahnik four-inch heels, to give me added height and to enhance my small but well-formed ankles.

William Cougan, CEO, has ordered limousines to transport us all to the church as a mark of respect for the late Mr. Cray (one of the founding fathers of our esteemed company). These limousines will arrive in approximately three minutes. Nearly everyone else has gone downstairs and I have just discovered the most enormous rip in my pantyhose.

I cannot attend a somber, serious service while inappropriately sporting a run large enough to accommodate the entire New York City Fire Department, and although I have emergency spares in my desk, I have no time to make a quick trip to the ladies' room to change. My only options are to either (a) change at my desk (not good if some last-minute straggler walks by), or (b) slip into the late Mr. Cray's office and do the deed in there.

Plan B is good. I swiftly check the vicinity and slip inside, closing the door behind me.

Just as I have my dress up around my waist and the new pantyhose half way up my legs, the door opens. I freeze as I see Adam in the doorway, and he freezes as he sees rather more of me than he expected. And then I remember the panties that I am wearing today. Tish gave them to me as a joke. They are (obviously) clean. They are also black, with large red letters that say PRESS THIS BUTTON, with an arrow pointing down in the unmistakable direction of my clitoris. These panties are my way of wishing good old Johnny a final *bon voyage,* since he was so very fond of my butt. But I hadn't intended to share the joke with anyone else.

So what do I do now? Do I apologize? Do I ask to be excused? Do I continue my mission as if nothing has happened? Do I wait for him to do the gentlemanly thing and leave? In the end I do nothing. I am like a statue, immortalized in this very unattractive pose, because my heart is pounding right out of my chest and I'm sure my whole body is flushing bright red.

Instead of leaving, Adam smiles a wolfish smile as he gives me the once-over.

"Hel-lo," he says, as he leans against the doorframe and crosses his arms over his very manly chest, and I'm not sure if I should be embarrassed or pleased, because it's obvious that he likes what he sees.

"Need any help?" He grins, and I realize that I am *still* standing here half dressed and making no move to finish donning my new pantyhose.

"Pantyhose can be such a pain, don't you think? I prefer stockings."

Does he, indeed? I make a mental note of this to file away for future reference. He's definitely interested. I would have to be blind not to notice the way he is eating me with his eyes.

"Er, did you want anything in particular?" I ask.

*Like me, for instance? On the desk? Now?* But obviously I don't say that.

"Maybe later."

This man is flirting with me. At least I think he's flirting with me. Y-e-s!

"The limousines are here. Everyone is downstairs. I thought you'd got lost so I came to find you."

He came to look for *me?* For *me* in particular? Better and better. He noticed I wasn't with everyone else. Y-e-s! This is *excellent.*

"Oh, good," I say, mentally kicking myself for sounding like an idiot, as I pull up the pantyhose and smooth down my skirt, in what I think is a very slick, matter-of-fact motion. "That was very thoughtful of you."

Yuck. Can I really not find anything more scintillating to say? I have an English degree, for God's sake. Surely I can put together a couple of relatively coherent sentences?

"All finished?" He raises a Sean Connery eyebrow at me and I have to brush past him to get through the door, because he makes no move to get out of my way.

"Nice panties," he breathes in my ear as I pass, and I can barely stop myself from shuddering with sexual heat.

"Thank you," I tell him, primly, because it's not good to sound *too* eager. And then, because I can't resist, "It took me ages to choose just the right ones this morning."

I feel his eyes on me as we walk down the hall to the elevator. They are burning into my back. I imagine them watching my ass, so I immediately sashay in what I hope is an alluring fashion.

"Shall I press the button?" he innocently asks as we get into the elevator, and I blush, because there is no way I can possibly miss his meaning.

"I miss this," he says, as he presses *G*.

I have no idea what he means. *Sex?* He misses *sex?* Oh, I can certainly help him out with this. I instantly have this very erotic image of Adam pressing *my G*. Ooh.

"Riding together in the elevator."

Oh, not sex. He misses me in the elevator! He did notice, then. *Yes!* All was not in vain, after all. All that time I thought he didn't see me, he was watching me, waiting for the right moment . . .

"You don't call, you don't write . . ." he tells me, leaning right in toward me, and I can't help a girly giggle.

"Actually, I came to find you so that we could talk," he tells me, taking a step back as the elevator doors open. "We're going to be working very closely together. I'm taking over from Johnny Cray."

Oh, this day just gets better and better. It's like winning the *love* lottery. Although everyone thought Grady Thomas would get promoted . . .

"Adam Blakestock," he says, holding out his hand.

Like I don't already know this? I know rather a lot more about you, Adam Blakestock, than you think (thanks to Tracey in Human Resources). But I don't say this, of course. I just stand there like a goldfish opening and closing my mouth before I remember that he's still waiting for me to shake his hand.

"I'm—" I hold out my hand.

"Emmeline Beaufort Taylor," he finishes for me, looking right into my eyes as he takes my hand in a much warmer way than boss/secretary requires.

"But everyone calls you Emma. I think I'll call you Emmeline. Goes with the sexy English accent," he says, and winks at me in a way that suggests "later."

He's my boss. And he knows my name. (Although I'm not very fond of Emmeline, it's really sweet he wants to have a special name for me.) He thinks I'm sexy and he obviously can't wait to get inside my panties. Hallelujah!

And while I mentally thank Mr. Handel for his chorus, I find myself being gently led to the waiting limousine with Adam's hand guiding my trembling (lust-induced) elbow.

The service is very moving. The church is packed, and I hope that as many people come to my memorial service. I am sitting right at the front of the church because Adam, as the new Director of Advertising, is sitting at the front. And he insisted that I sit with him. I have, after all, just lost my boss of two years and am therefore practically a family member.

As we sit on the pew, mere feet away from Johnny's (thankfully sealed) coffin, I am breathlessly aware of Adam's proximity as his thigh brushes frequently against mine, and as his arm brushes frequently against my breast. This is very bad of me. I should not be thinking lustful thoughts while sitting in the House of God. And this is, after all, a funeral. I glance around to take my mind off Adam.

Babette Cray, the newlywed widow, is beautiful in the shortest, lowest-cut black number I've ever seen at a funeral, and is weeping copiously (but prettily) into her handkerchief. As her blonde hair falls over her bowed face, the handsome man by her side puts his arm around her shoulder to hold her up. She can barely stand, poor thing, she is so overwhelmed by grief.

It's so sad. To lose one's husband on one's honeymoon must be such a devastating blow. To have found true love, even if it is with an octogenarian nearly sixty years your senior, and then to have it snatched away, *poof*, just like that, before the ink is dry on the marriage certificate.

I wonder what it's like, having sex with a man old enough to be your grandfather? I imagine both my dearly departed grandfathers and can't help but shudder at the thought of either of them having sex with a woman younger than me. But still, poor Babette *is* visibly crushed.

There must have been more to Johnny that met the eye, because he was certainly no oil painting.

I am quite overcome by emotion and feel my eyes fill with tears. And then Adam pushes a crisp linen handkerchief into my hand.

"Thank you," I whisper. Then add, "It's just so sad. Mrs. Cray is so beautiful. So brave. So alone."

"And *so* rich," Adam whispers back, which I think is a little callous of him. "Emmeline Beaufort Taylor, you are *so* sentimental. The grieving widow has a luxury apartment overlooking Central Park, plus five million dollars. That's enough to ease anyone's pain, don't you think?"

Oh. That's a lot of money. I can't even imagine what five million dollars *looks* like, never mind actually *having* it. The cynical part of me thinks (only briefly, because having bitchy thoughts in the House of God is also not good) that Babette got a very good deal, after being a wife for only a day.

But, I remind myself, I like Babette Cray very much and refuse to have horrible, gold-digger thoughts about her. On the few occasions we met when she and Johnny were dating, she was very nice to me—not at all snooty or condescending to the hired help. And she also took great care of Johnny— several times she came to the office to bring his heart medication when he'd left it at home. What a shame he forgot to take it before his wedding night.

"Good old Johnny might have been a little off the wall," Adam says, "but he was no fool. She's more likely weeping because the prenuptial agreement is so watertight her lawyer can't find any cracks. You see the slick guy with her? That's her lawyer."

"No. Really?"

"Thank God he didn't leave her any shares in the company. That would have been a disaster."

I wonder, briefly, at Adam's display of cynicism, but remember that he recently had his heart broken. That's why he's bitter. But I will help him overcome . . .

After the service, Babette is the first to exit the church. Despite the cruel January wind, she stands by the open door to personally thank everyone for coming. I think she really did love Johnny, no matter what anyone else thinks.

"Mrs. Cray," I say, when it is my turn to speak to her. "I'm so sorry for your loss. If there's anything I can do . . ."

"Thank you," Babette says, fresh tears springing to her eyes. She takes hold of my hands, which surprises me, because I don't know her that well. And then she shocks me even more when she hugs me like a long-lost friend.

"Johnny was very fond of you," she tells me between sobs. "He said you were the best secretary he ever had."

This is stunning news. I didn't think that Johnny even knew my name. Oh, how *sweet*. What a *lovely* man. I'm so overcome by warm thoughts of Johnny that fresh tears course down my cheeks, ruining my makeup.

"Would—would you like me to pack his personal effects at the office?" I ask her. It's the least I can do to save the poor woman even more pain.

"Oh, I should never have married him," she wails. "If only we'd stayed just friends, this would never have happened. He'd still be alive . . ."

I am dying (forgive the pun) to ask more, but don't feel that this is my business.

"I thought he was just old-fashioned, wanting to wait until

our wedding night to consummate our love. If only he'd told me that his doctor had warned him against having sex . . . And now he's dead and it's *all* my fault . . ."

Oh. This is more information than I wanted, but I pat her back in a comforting way.

"You mustn't blame yourself," I tell her. "Johnny obviously loved you and wanted to have . . ." Have what? I grope for the right words. "He wanted to have a special night with you because he loved you so much."

"Yes. Yes he did love me. At least I have that to hold on to," she tells me, straightening and wiping away her tears.

"We'll all miss him," I say, as Adam guides me firmly away.

"Bit pointless, Emmeline," Adam tells me as he steers me down the church steps. "You know, Babette can't help your career."

How cynical of him. He obviously needs *me* to restore his faith in womankind.

"I like her," I tell him. "I just feel so sorry for her. She really did love him, you know."

"You really are a tender-hearted little thing, aren't you?" Adam says, smiling rather condescendingly down at me. "I know exactly what you need to make you feel better."

Adam takes me for a very long lunch, during which he plies me with delicious delicacies and very good wine. To get to know me, and, of course, to forge a bond between us to establish our working relationship. And to help me cope with my grief for losing Johnny.

We don't make it back to work that afternoon.

As I'm about to get into the cab he's hailed for me, he leans forward and kisses me full on the mouth.

No tongues are involved.

*Damn.*


On the first day of our life together (in the office, of course) Adam calls a staff meeting. And as he is telling his account managers about his expectations, I cannot help think about my own expectations as his foot accidentally finds my leg and he rubs my ankle with it.

Ooh . . . This is really nice, but I mustn't read too much into it. Just in case he's a serial-flirter-with-secretaries, rather than a man interested in me, personally. He is my boss, after all. I dreamily allow myself to replay the moment he kissed me last night . . .

And when he is instructing his team that he wants fresh, new ideas for the possible new Perfect Pantyhose account (only if they like our fresh, new ideas), just as I am hoping for another kiss from Adam in the not-too-distant future (but with tongues this time), *I* have a fresh, new idea. I have an epiphany. It comes to me in a blinding flash.

*I have a plan for the Perfect Pantyhose account.*

Now, I've had lots of great ideas for other accounts we've dealt with, but Johnny wasn't interested in his secretary having ideas about anything other than typing his letters and making his coffee. Obviously the butt patting figured in there, too.

But I don't know how receptive Adam will be to a Secretary with Ideas. Before I ask him, I decide that it would be better if I show him rather than tell him, and I begin to plan my campaign.

For the next two days, I work like a demon, in between flirting with Adam and working late with Adam. Although mentally undressing me with his eyes, he doesn't try to put his lustful thoughts into action. Neither does he attempt to kiss me. I think he's waiting for the right moment, once we've got to know each other a little better. So while all this flirty, pre-seduction game is in progress, and me actually doing any secretarial work, I work on my portfolio.

But first I need some photos. I find a great on-line photo library. I search for the types of photos I have in mind. When you use a photo from a photo library, the price you pay for it varies accordingly to the photographer, whether it is for television, or billboards, or magazines, and is also dictated by the number of copies in the print run. So, with costs in mind, I am careful to try and find midprice photos. This will show that not only will I make a great account manager, but that I am also thrifty and thinking about the company's money.

On the third day, just as everyone is leaving for the day, I present my portfolio to Adam. This is what I have come up with.

1. Image of hippopotamus with ass to camera, head turned around to look at camera, mouth wide revealing large teeth and almost-smile. Have (obviously on computer) added pantyhose, plus caption: "Do you think these pantyhose make my ass look firmer?"

2. Image of two ducks (obviously one male, one female), fondly nuzzling each other. One is wearing pantyhose, thereby creating new, hourglass female duck figure. Caption from other duck's point of view reads: "I'm Quackers Over You."

3. Image of Vietnamese potbellied pig, duplicated. On one picture, potbellied pig is featured minus potbelly because of fabulous control-panel pantyhose. Caption beneath both pictures reads: "Before and After."

4. Image of mother hen with sweet little brood of chicks. Caption beneath reads: "On your feet all day running after your brood? Get some support with Perfect Pantyhose."

I'm so anxious as Adam looks through my portfolio that I nearly forget to breathe. What if he doesn't like it? What if he hates it? What if he thinks I'm a complete idiot?

"Emmeline, I love it! You're a genius!" He smiles sexily at me, and I remember to breathe again.

And before I know it, he's asking me all sorts of questions

about my portfolio, and then he's *all over me like a rash*. This time, with tongues, and hands, and everything.

Before we go too far, Adam locks his office door.

Hmmm. Heavenly.

I am very glad that Johnny's desk has been replaced. It would have been very strange (and somehow morbid) to have sex on a dead man's desk.


Over the next few weeks, Adam and I become very close, but not to the point where we tell anyone about "us." I mean, I do see his point about us working together as boss and secretary. It would be okay, though, if we were working in the same company but not actually *together,* as it were.

One night, as we're lying in his bed in his lovely loft apartment, Adam tells me about the cruel Sabrina Sheffield. His ex. And he is obviously in so much pain that I alternately want to whack her for having toyed with his tender heart, or to thank her for leaving me a clear playing field.

Apparently, her family and his have been friends going way back and it was always expected that the two of them would marry. To keep all that lovely WASP blood (and money) in the family, I suppose. I wonder if I should tell Adam that Sheffield is a city in the north of England, and used to be famous for its steel and coal. I have a vision of the perfect Sabrina's great-great-grandfather coming off his shift, covered in coal dust. And then reality bites.

Her family probably *owned* the coal mine. And the steel factories. *Bastard plutocrats,* making their nouveau riche fortunes by the sweat and toil of near-slave labor by the working classes. I realize this might be a little over the top, so I keep it to myself and resent her privately.

And as the days turn into weeks, I decide that Adam really is becoming my proper boyfriend, rather than just an affair, and I think that it's time for him to meet my friends. I take him to Chez Nous for dinner.

I don't think Rachel likes him much, but then she's hard to please.

"So what do you think of him?" I ask her.

"I hope he's great in bed," she says.

Typical Rachel. She'll warm to him in time.

But Tish thinks he's a nice guy, because I ask her, repeatedly, if she thinks he's a nice guy.

"Will you stop obsessing?" she says. "It doesn't matter what anyone else thinks of him—you're the one who loves him, and that's all that's important."

Adam does seem a little threatened by Sylvester and David. But I think that's because he's not used to gay men and will relax once he knows them better. Plus, David flirting with him does not help. But Katy and Tom really enjoyed discussing opposing politics with him, so that's encouraging, isn't it?

Actually, I didn't realize until now that Adam is a Republican, but I don't hold it against him. We're all entitled to our own views, even if they *are* misguided.

So, really, the only tiny fly in the ointment is this: Adam gets a little upset that I have to work on my business degree. I need to study for my finals, so I can't spend every night at his apartment working on client accounts, followed by lovely, lovely sex with him. And he doesn't want to stay at my apartment, because I share with Tish. Plus, his apartment is much more convenient for the office.

But I don't want the love of my life to feel neglected, so while I am stressing about how to reassure him, I come up with a great idea for another client. For Kitty Krunch.

This is what I propose:

Several supermodels (I was thinking maybe Kate, Naomi, Chandra, and a few of their friends) all dressed in sexy Catwoman-style outfits, complete with spiky black heels. I picture them crawling on the floor, in the manner of sex kittens (which, of course, they are), until they are distracted by the call of Kitty Krunch. Famous male model type such as

Fabio will pour Kitty Krunch into gold (-plated, not solid) bowls. And as the supermodel kitties purr and munch happily on Kitty Krunch, Fabio will stroke their lovely hair as they eat. *Ta-da.*

Adam *loves* this proposal too. He loves it so much, he buys me a lovely gray suit from Bloomingdale's, because it caught his eye and he thought of me. How great is that? It's a very nice suit, but the color is a little drab for me and the skirt is too long. But I wear it to work anyway, to show Adam that I appreciate his kind gesture.

And I'm really glad that I did. That evening, as we are having dinner at Adam's favorite restaurant, La Trattoria, he tells me that he has a proposal of his own.

He's going to ask me to marry him!

This is what I've been waiting for.

"Emmeline," he says, reaching for my hand across the table.

*Here it comes.* Although I was secretly hoping for the one-knee approach, complete with small Tiffany's box.

"Will you—will you move in with me?"

Not exactly what I am expecting, but it is a move in the right direction, don't you think? If we live together, full time, he'll soon realize how perfect we are together.

But he doesn't actually say that he loves me. I think he does love me, though, because why else would he ask me to move in with him?

"Yes, Adam," I say. "I will."

I think he just needs time.


Oh, if only I'd known then what I know now. But how easy it is to be wise with the advantage of hindsight.

# 4

········································································

# The Five-Month Itch

## TO DO

1. Meditate. "I do not need bigger boobs—ohm. I shall not pander to society's (men's) perception of the perfect breast size—ohm."

2. Maybe *should* think about breast implants.

3. Repeat after me: "I am at one with my boobs—ohm. They are fine—ohm. Adam is a bastard ionic bonder—ohm."

I pace up and down the restroom for a while to stop myself crying. Exercise generates endorphins, which make you feel better, so if I pace briskly for a few minutes, surely I'll feel better?

But I don't, and I can't stay in here forever. I must formulate a plan . . .

Until now I've always harbored a furtive, grudging respect for Prince Charles. Not to take anything away from poor, beautiful Diana (may she rest in peace), but to me there was always something rather noble about the heir to the Kingdom (or is it politically correctly a queendom at the moment? I must ask Julia) rejecting youth and beauty in favor of true love, for the older, much less attractive Camilla Parker Bowles. Not that I think Camilla isn't attractive, of course, because I think she definitely is. And I do hear that she's a very charming, witty person—and perfect looks aren't everything.

But now that my prince is cheating on me with an older (although, I have to admit, a very attractive but scathingly bitchy) woman, my sympathy is waning sharply.

*And Stella wears a C cup.*

And I don't know what to do.

I don't know what to think.

I rub my aching temples as I pace for a bit longer to give the endorphins time to work, and try to reason this through. (I.e., lie to myself. I am in denial—but at least *I know* that I am in denial. Which is good.)

Is Stella just being her usual bitch self and tormenting me with false images of her and Adam cozying up together on Bahamian beaches? Or is she really sleeping with my boyfriend? I wish it's the former. I don't want to believe that Adam has betrayed me.

But he has betrayed me, hasn't he? What about my ideas that he passed off as his own? (And what about that huge bonus he got for them?) And, the sneaky little voice of reason in my head reminds me, what about his e-mail to William Cougan? The one in which Adam definitely doesn't recommend me for the promotion. Plus, that little voice tortures me even more, there's that bloody *Visa* statement! I mean, it's *obvious*, isn't it? It's completely *obvious*, even to my poor demented brain, that the Tiffany whatever is not for me. Because it's *obviously* for Man-Stealing Bitch Stella!

Last night, when Adam was out at a business dinner (oh God, I bet he was with Stella), I was so happily checking out my list of Goals by Thirty, thinking I was well on my way to achieving most of them. How could I have been so blind?

Oh, I just don't know what to think, but the pacing seems to have worked, so I stop.

*Think, Emma, think clearly,* I tell my reflection. Okay. Here we go. For several minutes (double checking once again that I am alone in the bathroom) I calmly discuss the pros and cons with the variegated ivy in the corner. I've always had a fondness for this particular plant—it's about five feet tall, and beautifully proportioned, apart from one stem that sticks out too much. All of the other plants are far too perfect. I call this plant Daphne, because I think Daphne is a good, solid, no-nonsense kind of name. But still a pretty name.

And do you know what? Talking it through with Daphne really seems to help. There is something rather comforting about talking to plants, even silk ones. But I still don't like the way the discussion is going, because, it has to be said, Daphne isn't exactly talkative. Two questions seem to keep cropping up.

Questions: *Why did he cheat on me? Why didn't I suspect?*

Of course, if you are the *Cheated On* (me), you will probably be the last person to suspect that object of your affections, the *Cheater* (Adam) is not, as you thought, acting weirdly because he's building up the nerve to ask you to marry him.

He's building up the courage to *leave* you.

He's got the *five-month itch.*

The signs have all been there. In retrospect, it's easy to spot them. Like the fact that for the last three weeks he's been late home too many times with the lame excuse, "Business dinner. You know what it's like in the cutthroat world of advertising."

Well, if I didn't before, I sure as hell do now.

Another sign—his total lack of interest in sex. Well, obviously, if he's off for a furtive weekend with Stella then he *is* interested in sex. Just not with me. I mean, the sex was great in the beginning. But I have to say it. Adam is no longer the Sixty Minute Man. More like the Six Minute Man. Or at least he used to be. Three weeks ago. When he was still having sex with me.

But let's face it, even mediocre, short-lived sex is better than no sex at all, isn't it?

Oh God, *I may never have sex again!*

But back to the main point, before the threatened panic attack can seize control and I crumble into a boneless heap, only to be discovered Monday morning by an unsuspecting, innocent cleaning lady.

Questions: *Why did he cheat on me? Why didn't I suspect?*
Answer: I don't bloody know!

I rummage in my purse for my cell phone and speed dial Rachel.

"Rachel," I croak down the telephone line. "It's me."

And after she wishes me a happy thirtieth birthday, and tells me that thirty is no age at all, that life begins at forty for women on account of reaching their sexual peak, I burst into tears and spill all.

Rachel is my best friend from high school—brilliant, beautiful, but *single*, on account of all men being seriously intimidated by her MENSA intellect. Rachel doesn't exactly hate men, she just thinks they're mainly idiots and uses them for sex.

"Emma, sweetie, the basic problem is not *you*. It's *Adam*. He's a bastard ionic bonder," she rants, and I wish I'd paid more attention to sophomore chemistry.

"He is your classic alkali metal," she tells me, and I sigh down the telephone line with confusion.

Rachel has an intellect the size of Texas and it's not always easy for us lesser mortals to follow her meaning.

"Look, sweetie, let me put it in simple terms."

*Thank God.* Simple works for me every time.

"Adam is an atom with an extra electron," she enunciates slowly, as if speaking to a three-year-old. "He bonded temporarily with another atom, i.e., *you*. He's given you his electron, i.e., *had sex with you*. And he's generally used you to enhance his own career by ruthlessly stealing all your great ideas and passing them off as his own. And now he's leaving fully charged, and he's found another atom to bond with."

At this point I hold the receiver a little way from my ear because Rachel is now ranting full steam ahead.

"Bastard! God, I knew I should have warned you about

him. I mean, he's successful, attractive, never been married. That's not normal for a thirty-six-year-old guy!" she says, and I hear the angry clank of test tubes from her laboratory.

I hope I haven't just ruined years of painstaking research in the quest for the cure to some terrible disease.

"So you don't think it has anything to do with my breasts, then?" I mumble, seeking reassurance.

Yes, I know this is pathetic. But I am worried that my lack of mammary glands might have something to do with Adam's defection (the older woman in question is, as I said, fully loaded). You see, Adam is a self-confessed "breast man" and has occasionally (at least once a week) urged me to take up my plastic-surgeon father's offer to get his partner to surgically enhance what Mother Nature failed to provide.

"For God's sake, Emma," Rachel lectures me. "That's a fucking pathetic male-excuse crock. How many times have we gone through this? A mature, mutually fulfilling relationship has nothing to do with breast size."

More angry clanking of test tubes down the phone line.

I love Rachel. She's a lot like my mother with all her radical feminist theories. But sometimes you need a bit of sympathy, and not a scientific dissertation on why your boyfriend was wrong for you from the start, and how immature it is to obsess over your lack of cup size.

"What you need," Rachel tells me firmly, "is a covalent bonder."

A what?

"You *must* remember high school chemistry."

Must I?

"Er . . ." I squint at the window as I grope for the answer. Rachel forgets that she was in advanced-placement science and I wasn't. I struggled in the regular class. And I'm thinking, I'm trying hard to remember . . .

Nope. Too busy fantasizing about Chris Stevenson and Jon Bon Jovi in high school.

"Covalent bonding is when two atoms, i.e., a man and a

woman, bond and share electrons, thereby filling each other's outer electron fields and stabilizing each other. Look at David and Sylvester or Katy and Tom—the perfect covalently bonded relationships."

This doesn't cheer me up and I miserably wonder if all male covalent bonders of my acquaintance are either gay or married.

"Yes, but what should I do? Everyone knows I didn't get the promotion. And I can't face Adam and Stella. I feel like such an idiot . . ." I wail. Someone fix my life. Fix it quick!

"This is what you're going to do," Rachel tells me firmly.

Good. A clear voice of reason amidst chaos.

"Wipe all your files off your computer—no reason why Bastard Adam should steal any more of your fabulous ideas."

"Good, this is good," I say.

"Then shred his office diary, push a paper clip into his disk drive, and reformat his hard disk. For God's sake, you've already devoted three years to that testosterone-biased company. Call it quits and leave."

This is tempting. If I walk out, I won't have to face any of the people here (or Adam and Stella) again. But if I do that, they definitely won't give me a good reference (plus the thought of jail time is not tempting). And I can't just walk out of a job, not with the current economic climate. And if I don't have a job, I won't be able to make rent and . . .

*Oh, God, I've just realized that I'm homeless!*

At thirty years of age I've just become a street person! I *can't* move back to Julia's in London, or in with Dad and Peri and the twins . . .

As I said, Rachel is great but her advice is usually extreme.

I hang up on Rachel after she forces me to promise to meet her at Chez Nous in an hour. She's calling ahead to tell Sylvester and David my news, so I am spared the misery of having to repeat my tale of abject rejection and betrayal a million times. I don't really want to go out and party, because I have nothing to celebrate, but I know she won't take no for an answer. Besides, it will be good to get support and sympathy from people who really love me.

I dial Tish and repeat my tale of woe to her.

"Oh, Emma, that's terrible," she sniffles down the telephone line, already in floods of tears on my behalf.

Then she says something really un-Tish-like.

"I just *knew it.* I should have warned you about his shifty eyes—you can never trust a man who doesn't look you squarely in the eye without admiring his own reflection in them."

Now she does have a point, because Adam can be rather vain, but for Tish this is a radical statement. She's one of the nicest, sweetest people ever to grace the face of the planet with her presence, and for her to say Adam has shifty eyes is tantamount to the Pope announcing that he's gay and is leaving the Vatican to start a new life as a drag queen.

"Oh, sweetie." She continues to sniffle and I wonder who is supposed to be comforting who? She's now sobbing and I spend five minutes reassuring her that I'm not about to slit my wrists with the letter opener or join a nunnery. And then I tell her I'm fine, I'm meeting Rachel at Chez Nous earlier than planned. On account of no engagement dinner.

"Well, I'll come too. It's not like I have anything better to do. Rufus still doesn't know I exist." She sighs, and I sigh with her.

"But we did kind of have a breakthrough today," she tells me, brightening. "When he said, 'The usual?', I said, 'No, Rufus, today I'd like the whole-wheat muffin with cinnamon and raisins.' And then he actually *looked* at me. So that's a good thing. I mean, at least he's paying attention to me now and won't assume that I'll just have the banana-granola muffin every day."

At this point I am rolling my eyes and wondering how many varieties of muffin Tish and Rufus will get through before moving on to the different flavors of decaffeinated coffee.

"Well, it's certainly a move in the right direction," I tell her, not wanting to sound pessimistic about her chances of getting an actual date with Rufus this side of the next century. And then I remember that, unlike my cheating-rat *ex*-boyfriend, Rufus is coming to my ex-engagement-birthday un-party. Maybe I can give them both a push in the right direction. After all, just because I'm back on the spinsterhood shelf, there's no reason why I can't lend a helping hand to my best friend. Oh God, back on the spinsterhood shelf . . . how retread that sounds.

"Oh Emma, I'm being selfish. After all you've been through today, sweetie."

And then Tish gives me her opinion about my job options.

"Well, I agree you should wait until you get another job before you walk out. Can't you get a transfer to another department?"

This is an excellent idea.

And Tish tells me what to do about being homeless.

"Ditch Adam and move back in with me. It'll be like old times. It'll be fun."

Only problem is that when I moved out of our rented apartment, Tish bought a one-bedroom shoebox in Hoboken just around the corner from Rufus's deli. (This was no accident—she scoured the real estate agencies for two years before she found this one.) And although I'm small and don't take up much room, there isn't enough space in her shoebox to swing the proverbial cat.

Right. One thing at a time. One problem at the time. The first problem is how I get out of this powder room and out of the building?

After another chat with Daphne-the-ivy, I feel a bit better. I wash my face and carefully reapply my makeup, and you know, I don't look too bad. And I know what I'm going to do.

1. Swiftly sneak back to my cubicle and copy all my idea files to diskette before deleting them from the hard drive.

2. Ditto with hard copy—remove all personal papers relating to work ideas. As it happens, I have a fabulous idea for

Stella Burgoyne's company but don't see why she should get this, as well as getting my man. I hope her toilet-paper sales slump!

3. Slip up the back stairs (four flights, but don't want to ride the elevator in case I'm presented with more pity smiles and comments) to Human Resources before Tracey leaves for the weekend. Find out if there are any other secretarial jobs vacant within the company. Or resign.

4. Go to Chez Nous and meet my lovely, supportive friends who will pour Australian Shiraz down my throat in medicinally large quantities, and generally staunch the blood flowing from my wounds.

................

**4:55 P.M.**

Point one of my plan works perfectly. As it is Friday afternoon, most employees have slunk off early to enjoy the weekend with significant others and/or family, reminding me that as of now, I am yet again single and have no one to wake up with.

When I make it up the stairs to Human Resources, thankfully without seeing another soul, I am disappointed that Tracey has also gone for the weekend. And I remember that she and Dwayne, her fiancé, spend most of their summer weekends down at the shore, and I feel like an utter, abject failure. A retread.

This is a major blow, because (yes, I know this is unrealistic) I was hoping to arrange a quick transfer before Monday. At all costs I want to avoid sniggers and sly glances as people discuss my disappointment. But as they don't know about Adam and me, then hopefully I will be spared that particular humiliation. Can you imagine what it would be like— everyone pitying me because my boyfriend has left me for an older woman? I mean, I always thought men left their partners for *younger* women.

I am just about to slip furtively back down the stairs (this time I have eight flights to the first floor—at least it will help in building leg muscle), when Jacintha Bridges (Director of Human Resources) steps out of her office, the lovely diamond engagement ring on her finger glittering ominously.

"Emma," she says, smiling pleasantly. "I thought I might see you today."

Did she? I've always wondered if she's psychic.

"I, er, just came to ask Tracey something," I mumble, desperate to escape any kind of confrontation. "I'll come back Monday. Have a nice weekend."

"Do you have a minute? I'd like to speak with you."

Oh, God, why did I come up here? Jacintha, a very astute woman, is bound to guess about me and Adam!

..................

**5:45 P.M.**

Actually, Jacintha is very, very nice. It went well, I think. I only nearly burst into tears once. But I managed not to blurt out the whole sorry tale of Adam and me to her.

Apparently, there's a vacancy coming up in Human Resources next week due to maternity leave. I really think I can make Human Resources my thing, I really do . . .

It seems that Angie of the Cruella disposition has been waiting for a secretarial job to come up in Advertising for months—she wants to move up from reception. So she's the obvious candidate to replace me as Adam's secretary.

This is a *great* idea.

In fact, I'm already feeling a bit better.

Two days of Angie and Adam will be on his knees!

*A much better plan for revenge!* (And it obviously won't include me serving jail time.)

## 5

...........................................................................................

## Un-Party Time

### TO DO

1. Say "no" when am next offered worm-infested drink.

2. Remember to unplug telephone when am expecting to have crashing hangover next morning (caused not by excess wine, but by worm-infested drinks—see [1]).

3. Do not whine incessantly to my friends about traitorous boyfriend or lack of boobs. Instead, shall be wise-woman (as am now sad spinster again) counselor and selflessly help friends with *their* problems.

**8 P.M.**

Lovely, fabulous party. Lovely, caring friends. Delicious miniature *saumon en croûte* pastries (of which I have consumed more than my fair share) and shrimp in lemon batter, lots of champagne and Shiraz (of which I am valiantly striving to drink my fair share).

The only thing that has caused a blot on my landscape (obviously, apart from the whole Adam/Stella/nonpromotion blots on my landscape) is the cake. A traditional English fruitcake, made with all organic ingredients, specially baked by Rufus four months ago, at David and Sylvester's request (to allow it the appropriate time to mature in a sealed container).

During this four-month time period (quickly counting backwards in time, Rufus baked this cake a month before I took the plunge and moved in with Bastard Adam, but I push this thought ruthlessly aside), Rufus has carefully nurtured this cake. Every two weeks he has removed it from its sealed container and layer of aluminum foil, and he has meticulously poked holes in the top and spooned in brandy. How lovely of Rufus to do this for me, especially since my cheating, bastard boyfriend can't even remember it's my birthday.

Although this cake is charmingly decorated with lemon and white frosting, tiny yellow rosebuds and silver bells, it is fairly obvious that a last-minute repair job has taken place.

On the cake are the words, CONGRATULATIONS TO EMMA.

And I *know* instinctively that it used to say, CONGRATULATIONS TO EMMA AND ADAM. Because everyone thought they'd be celebrating my birthday *and* my engagement.

Not that Rufus didn't do a grand job of changing the lettering and rearranging the "Emma" so that it covered where "Emma and Adam" used to be, because he *did*. Do a grand job. You'd never notice the letters had been anywhere else but where they are now. But it's usual to say "Happy Birthday" rather than "Congratulations" on a birthday cake, isn't it? "Congratulations" is what people say when one gets engaged to be married. Or gives birth. Or gets promoted . . .

And, of course, none of those options now seem to feature in my future.

As I slice into the cake, amidst cheers of encouragement, I feel the tears building up behind my nose. Am I really so unlovable? Am I really so boring that Adam couldn't stay faithful to me after only *five months?*

"Don't even think about it," Rachel hisses quietly in my ear as I pass her a piece of cake. "He's not worth the salt of even one of your tears. So eat some damn cake, and think positive thoughts."

And then she thrusts a piece of the rich, moist cake into my mouth, and pours me another glass of wine. I feel instantly better. Much better.

Kind David and sweet Sylvester, I think, as I glance around the bistro-style restaurant. All lovely silver and pink balloons everywhere and a big banner saying BIRTHDAY GIRL.

And instead of subjecting me to the indignity of weeping my heart out and obsessing madly to a room full of people I don't know all that well (most of them, it has to be said, are David and Sylvester's friends—their parties are legendary), David spent an hour calling around to tell people the party was canceled.

Instead, this is an intimate gathering of my nearest and dearest. The people who love me and don't mind if I walk around pulling at my hair and wailing very loudly about sackcloth and ashes, and that the end is near, and blathering on about how much I love Adam . . . and how much I *detest* Adam . . .

When my whining self-pity graduated to shaving my head and moving to Thailand to become a Buddhist monk (I read somewhere that the first female monk was ordained there quite recently), they decided it was time to distract me from my grief with birthday gifts.

And this is what my lovely friends got me.

1. Tish. Three-month subscription to her gym. "You're always obsessing about your lack of muscle definition," she tells me. "This will help. We can go together, you, me and Rachel. It's Pilates, yoga, and kick-boxing—you'll love it." It's a great gift. The only problem is that the gym is in Hoboken, which means it's only convenient if I actually *live* in Hoboken. Which I don't—I live in Manhattan. But, of course, that may change in view of Bastard Adam, as I can't afford Manhattan rental prices. Unless some lovely godmother/real-estate agent appears in a poof of fairy dust and says those magic words—*rent controlled*. Still, this gift is a lovely thought. Very thoughtful person, Tish.

2. David and Sylvester. A three-month supply of a natural product that promises to enhance and expand my bust. "Darling, our friend Gloria swears by it," says David. *"Complètement, chérie."* Sylvester nods in agreement. "She went from a thirty-six B to a thirty-six C." But how long will I need to take this? Will it be every day for the rest of my life, like Rogaine? (Although, obviously, not hair-inducing but breast-inducing.) Apart from which, Gloria started out life as Danny, so I'm not sure about this. But again, very thoughtful. Do I really obsess all the time to all of my friends about my skinniness and lack of boobs?

3. Katy and Tom (only happily married straight couple of my acquaintance). A three-month supply of a milkshake-type body enhancer. To help me put on weight and build muscle. A good thought, but I don't want to resemble an eighties-style Iron Curtain female athlete. I make a mental note never to mention boobs or muscles to any of my friends ever again.

4. Rufus. An organic cookbook. Very nice. (Although he's not my closest, most personal friend, I did spend nearly three years having breakfast in his deli with Tish—so I suppose he qualifies as nearly being a close, personal friend. And he did make my cake, lovely man.) This is an especially nice gift, because Rufus wrote this book himself. Can you imagine it? I can now add "famous author-chef" to my list of close personal friends. And none of us knew about his achievement until tonight. A dark horse, Rufus. Much more to him than meets the eye.

5. Rachel. A gift voucher for Donna Karan. (At this moment I love Rachel the most out of all my dear friends—the voice of realism amidst body enhancing chaos, because everyone knows that really good clothes can cover a multitude of sins.) "Body-enhancing shakes," she tells me, with a dangerous glint in her eye. "Breast-enhancing pills." She shakes her head in disgust. "You don't need to

do this, Emma, because you will be pandering to society's stereotypical values that a woman should look a certain way in order to get a man."

"I don't want to do this," I say a little while later to my lovely friends, collectively seated around the table. They collectively protest, and I feel like a wimp.

"Don't be a girly wimp," Katy says, offering me the salt. "Show us what you're made of."

I take it and gingerly pour some onto my hand.

"I don't like the idea of worms in drinks," I moan. "It's unnatural." It surprises me that no one else seems to mind, but apparently it wouldn't be real tequila without the worm.

"Come on," Rachel urges me. "Live for once."

She's right. Although this—from a woman who lives with three cats and maniacally detoxifies her apartment at least twice a day—is saying something. Still, if Rachel doesn't mind drinks with worms in them—if she hasn't thought about where, exactly, the worm might have gone to the bathroom for the last time in its life—then neither will I. Or is it already dead when it gets put in there? Yuck. Neither option holds any appeal.

Time to try something new.

So I lick my salt, throw back the tequila in one swallow and gulp madly at the lime.

.................

**11 P.M.**

"Lovely party," I say to David, kissing him sloppily on the cheek. "You and Sylvester are the best friends in the world. Apart from Tish. And Rachel. And Katy and Tom. And Rufus."

But through my drink-hazed brain I remember that Adam isn't here.

"Wish Adam was here," I wail, getting ready for another major blubber. "I bet they skipped dinner. I bet they called room service instead, so they didn't have to get dressed, because they've spent the whole evening having hot, screaming sex. And right at this moment they're getting ready to have even more hot, screaming sex in some luxury hotel room . . . And you know what?" I slur rhetorically, not really waiting for anyone to respond. "Bastard Adam never took *me* to the bloody Bahamas."

Our sex has not been hot and screaming just recently, either, but I don't mention this.

"Darling girl, you must stop torturing yourself. You'll only make yourself feel worse." David pats my hand.

"But it must be something I did wrong," I wail. "I mean, what has Stella got that I haven't? Apart from the boobs, and money . . ."

"Zere's nothing wrong wiz you, *chérie,*" Sylvester says. "If I were straight, I'd fuck you in an instant."

"That's the nicest thing anyone's ever said to me," I sniffle, wondering if only gay men find me remotely attractive.

"Although it has to be said, Adam is very attractive in a macho kind of way." David sighs dreamily.

Now if my significant other were to say that about another woman while I was there, I'd probably have a major anxiety attack that he preferred the other woman to me. I wonder why David is doing this? He and Sylvester are perfect together. Doesn't he realize how lucky he is?

Then David catches Sylvester's glowering expression.

"But only if you go for that sort of thing. Which I don't, of course. You're much better-looking, Sylvester. Adam's a bastard ionic bonder."

He's obviously been talking to Rachel.

I drift across the room in search of another drink, leaving David and Sylvester to argue about Adam's masculine charms, and by now I am feeling quite warm and fuzzy. I know it is the effect of all the food and alcohol I have consumed, and I search for a nice, quiet place to have a little sit-down by myself.

"Emma." Tish grabs me before I can reach the sofa in the corner. "Why didn't you warn me Rufus would be here? If I'd known, I'd have worn something nicer. I should have gone home straight from work and changed," she frets, twirling a strand of hair compulsively around her finger.

"You look lovely," I tell her.

And she does. The blue silk dress hugs her curves and brings out the glossy brown of her hair. Wish I had those curves and that glossy brown hair.

"He's barely looked at me all night."

"Yes," I explain to her patiently. "But you never get near enough for him to get a really good look at you, and he's nearsighted."

"Is he?"

She thinks about this for a moment.

"So how come you know this and I don't? How come he makes you birthday cakes, and gives you personally signed cookbooks? How come he's cozying up in the corner with Rachel instead of me?"

She's right. I had noticed, actually, that Rachel and Rufus are getting on like a house on fire. They are very close, poring over the recipes in Rufus's book. Rachel laughs, and Rufus smiles at her. And although Rachel is undoubtedly the Brain of Biochemistry, she also qualifies in the Miss USA category. Tall, with long blonde hair, svelte and sexy. How can Rufus resist such temptation?

Oh God, Rachel *cannot do this* to Tish. Rachel is one of the most decent people I know. She has *Principles*.

"Go over there and find out what they're talking about," Tish orders me, giving me a push toward them.

"This is silly." I gently disengage my arm. "Why don't you just go across and talk to him?"

"But what would I talk *about*?"

"Have another glass of wine, then you won't care."

"Look. Rachel's gone to the bathroom. Go and talk to him for me."

"But *I* don't want to date him," I explain. "Just go over there and ask him about his book. That should get him talking."

She thinks about this for a moment, then gulps down half a glass of Chardonnay.

"Okay, I will."

Atta girl!

"But only if you come with me. *Pleeeese*, Emma?"

Greater love hath no woman than me for my friends.

So I *do* go with her. And, after I get Rufus chatting about organic muffins, and after I tell him about Tish's latest interior design conquest, they start to actually exchange words with each other. I think Rufus has drunk quite a lot of Guinness, so he's more forthcoming than usual. And then I see Rachel coming back from the bathroom so I leave them to it, to head her off at the pass.

"Thank fuck for that," Rachel tells me as she glances across at Rufus and Tish. "I've just spent the last hour bored to death, listening to Rufus blathering on about Tish and his recipes. But mainly about Tish. I thought she'd never take the hint and come over. The things one does for friendship."

I sigh with relief. Rachel is not a boyfriend-stealing bitch like Stella Burgoyne after all.

I love my friends. They're so nice.

And then Rachel touches my arm and leans toward me, genuine concern written on her face.

"So how are *you* doing, kiddo?"

And *ka-bam*, I remember Adam. In the midst of Tish's Rufus crisis, I'd kind of forgotten about him. Kind of. And Rachel realizes her mistake for reminding me, and tells me again what a worthless shit Adam is, and then promptly changes the subject to the pros and cons of genetic screening. I relax with this. Even though I don't understand much of what she says, Rachel's uncharacteristic display of concern was almost my undoing again.

Not that Rachel isn't kind, because she is. But her variety of sympathy is more the "pick yourself up, dust yourself off" variety, rather than the "poor old you" variety.

"Emma, Rachel, you *must* both come over tomorrow night," Katy announces as she sails full steam toward us, and I cringe, because Katy can be rather overenthusiastic in her quest to fit in with the Pre-Preschool PTA mothers (or PPPTA for short). It's not that she's pushy, she just tries really hard.

"Marion and the girls are all coming over for the evening. I'm doing snacks and margaritas. It'll be fun."

I've just changed my mind about Rachel. She is *so* no longer my favorite best friend because she has slipped quietly away with some lame excuse or other about getting a drink, and has left me to Katy's tender but insistent mercies.

Now Katy is lovely, but Marion Lacy (chairperson of the PPPTA) is a *huge* pain in the butt. And at the moment, Katy is trying to prove herself a caring, interested parent. Marion (and I know this because I've met her twice) believes herself to be the world authority on what a caring, interested parent should be, so when she says "jump," poor Katy becomes an Olympic-style hurdle jumper.

"We're forming a group," Katy tells me.

Not another one. Oh God. I remember that last time she persuaded me to join one of her protest groups. It was Parents Against Drunk Drivers, or PADD for short. I spent one very unmemorable evening with Katy and Marion, driving up and down the New Jersey Turnpike between the Lincoln Tunnel and Newark Airport, carefully scanning the lanes for erratic driving.

Not that scanning roadways for drunk drivers isn't worthwhile, because obviously it is. But that's why we have the state police. And anyway, I think Katy's main reason for wanting *me* there was so that Marion had someone else to intimidate.

"We're calling ourselves Mothers Against Sexual SPAM. MASS for short. What do you think?"

"Er, very catchy. What is it for?"

As soon as I ask the question I regret it. I do not want to spend any more time in Marion's company and if I show interest, it will be hard to say no to Katy.

"Well, it's basically mothers against sexual SPAM on the Internet."

I feel very stupid because I think that SPAM is chopped meat that comes in a can. But sexual SPAM? My mind boggles at the thought, and I don't want to display my complete ignorance by asking.

"You wouldn't believe the trash mail that Alex gets in his e-mail. 'Add extra inches to your penis,' 'Visit this site for sexy young girls.' We are talking about kids being corrupted by stupid, mindless idiots. I mean, my kid's only two. He doesn't need the exposure to that kind of trash."

"Yes, but he doesn't, you know, technically need to have his own e-mail account at two years of age, does he?" I point out.

Let's face it, the kid can't read yet. But I don't say this, obviously.

Alex is a great kid. Unlike Jack Junior and Joe Junior, my half brothers, he restores my faith in reproduction. If I could have a kid (which now looks uncertain due to my lack of fiancé), I'd want him or her to be exactly like Alex. Unfortunately, Katy—although a completely great mother—has him enrolled in all kinds of classes that help his personal development. Because Marion and all the other mothers told her to. Actually, they didn't *tell* her to at all, just sort of implied it . . . that PPPTA crowd can be pretty intimidating. *I* would not want to cross them.

"I know," Katy sighs. "But Emma, you wouldn't believe how important it is for preschoolers to get to grips with modern technology. All the other preschoolers have their own computers. Marion says that if we don't give them the basic skills they need for school, they're behind before they can get ahead."

We both sigh. Me, because Katy is so nice, and trying so hard to fit in with the other mothers. I tend to forget, sometimes, that most of her friends (us) are single and childless.

"Hey." Tom places an affectionate arm around Katy's waist and kisses her on the cheek.

"You girls having fun? Is Katy boring you with her MADD mothers, Emma?"

"Er, no," I say, not wanting to be the cause of marital disharmony. "It's very interesting."

"It's MASS mothers, and you know it. Don't be so dismissive, Tom." Katy smiles and waves a warning finger at him. "Not if you want to get laid tonight."

"My lips are sealed." He smiles back at her. "Come on, woman, take me home. We told the babysitter we'd be home by midnight."

And I am envious. They are so obviously in love. They have been married forever, and yet he still looks at her as if the sun rises and shines in her face.

And suddenly I feel so alone. And tired. I want to go home.

Wherever that may be.

................

**Saturday morning, 6 A.M.**

Mick Jagger is jumping-jack-flashing around my poor, demented brain, and I realize that I forgot to switch off the radio alarm before I crashed out last night. I love Mick and the boys. But not when I have such a monumentally killer hangover.

It is painful to move, but I finally manage to reach the radio and flip the switch, then I gulp some of the water I remembered to leave by the bed last night. I sink gratefully back into my pillow.

**7 A.M.**

Who the hell telephones anyone at this ungodly hour of the morning? I try to ignore its persistent ringing, and after four rings, it switches to voicemail. But then it rings again, and then again, and I know that I have to answer it to get any peace and quiet whatsoever, because whoever is calling me *knows that I am here.*

"Hey, it's me."

Tish. She is happy and perky. Why isn't she in bed with a hangover, too?

"Get yourself out of bed, sleepyhead. You promised to go to the gym with me this morning. And you'll never guess what!"

"No, I won't," I croak. "And I don't want to go to the gym. I want to die."

"Rufus asked me on a date."

"That's fabulous," I tell her, with more enthusiasm than I feel, because it *is* fabulous and she's wanted this for so long. "When is the happy occasion?"

"Well, that's the problem. We didn't get as far as fixing a specific time or day . . ."

Typical. At this rate they'll be collecting their pensions before they make it to the bedroom, and by then they'll have forgotten what sex is.

"So we have to go to the deli for breakfast after the gym. I said I'd call in so we could, you know—"

"Can't you go by yourself?"

Yes, I am callous and uncaring.

"Pleeeese, Emma. Please come with me. It'll take your mind off Adam."

Up until this moment I had forgotten all about him.

. . . . . . . . . . . . . . . .

**11 A.M.**

I have spent a painful hour contorting my body into strange, apparently body-lengthening postures. I have been a Mermaid, a Dancer, and a Proud Warrior. But the hangover is no longer torturing me, having been frightened away by the flow of endorphins and several bottles of water.

So by the time Tish, Rachel, and I arrive at Rufus's deli, I feel moderately human and in need of sustenance.

But disaster strikes. Rufus is not there. Rufus has taken the day off.

"But why?" poor Tish asks Rufus's assistant, who has no idea, because Rufus isn't the most talkative of people. "He never mentioned a day off last night when he kissed me good-night."

"He kissed you?" This is amazing. This is a major break-through after three years of barely speaking to each other.

"Did it involve tongues?"

Trust Rachel to ask that particular question.

"No. Only a peck on the cheek." Tish looks down at her muffin. "That's it. I give up. The man obviously doesn't want to date me, and has taken the day off to *avoid me.*"

We munch disconsolately at our banana-granola muffins, and after much sighing on Tish's part, and much head shak-ing on my part, Rachel creates a whole new category of Men Who Cannot Commit.

"He's your classic noble gas," Rachel tells us, nodding knowingly.

And then, when we both gaze at her in complete incom-prehension, she adds an explanation.

"His electron field is totally full, so he's completely stable and doesn't need to bond at all."

This does not cheer up poor Tish. This does not make me feel good about life in general.

Are there no decent straight men left in the world?

# 6

## The Worm Turns

### TO DO

1. ~~Get sofa and rug dry cleaned~~. Why bother?
2. ~~Pack worldly possessions~~. Go shopping.
3. ~~Clean apartment in advance of moving out~~. After all, a few dirty dishes, crumbs on the floor, and wine stains will only add character. Plus, this will irritate Adam, which is good. (Also, am not intending to move out yet . . .)

**Sunday, 7 A.M.**

I have just dragged myself out of bed and poured half a pot of coffee down my throat in an attempt to wake up. Tish and Rachel are convinced that if left home alone today, I will do myself some serious damage because of being seriously depressed about the whole Adam/Stella affair and nonpromotion disaster. I can't imagine why they think I'll hurt myself, because I am completely allergic to pain in any shape or form. The worst I could do to Adam would be to upset his cream décor—although I *have* had dark thoughts about repainting the apartment black and red in his absence. (Obviously symbolic—black for the death of love and red for my bleeding heart . . . and revenge.)

Rachel and I are *equally* convinced that Tish will do something radically self-destructive because of Rufus's apparent change of heart re: their nondate and his nonappearance at the deli yesterday. Although Tish is gentle and sweet, she is half Italian, and you just never know when the hot, Latin-blooded side of her genetic makeup might rear its head.

Tish and I are certain that Rachel will commit murder, thereby destroying her chances of ever receiving the Nobel Prize for her contribution to science. Which would be tragic.

Hugh Peters, the super-brain, top scientist who joined Rachel's research team a month ago (and is, in effect, her boss), is the new bane of her existence. This is obviously because he's cleverer than she is but we don't tell her this. And because she can't bully him into submission, as she does with all her other work colleagues, but we don't tell her *this,* either. She cannot say his name without the accompaniment of the most foul curse words you can imagine. I wonder if someone ought to warn Hugh Peters about Rachel's black belt?

Because of this shared concern over our well-being (we are lovely, worthwhile people), we agreed, last night, after takeout Chinese and many glasses of Adam's Special Reserve wine, to meet at the gym at nine this morning.

Speaking of Adam's Special Reserve wine . . . his sofa is a complete mess. I think Rachel did it accidentally on purpose, mid-"fucking bastard" rant, to punish Adam. I got a bit carried away and "accidentally" spilled some on the cream rug, too. At least it adds a bit of lived-in color to this antiseptic place. Serves him right, ionic bonding bastard!

Anyway. Meeting at the gym at nine A.M. on Sunday morning is equally as bad as meeting at the gym at nine A.M. on Saturday morning, but we have agreed to do this because we are Supporting Each Other in Our Despair. Plus, we do not have significant others to spend our weekends with. And this fact does not make us sad and unlovable, oh no.

This makes us choosy.

We do not have mates because we *choose* not to select one from the poor array of single males we have so far encountered in this city.

Yoga will be followed by breakfast at the really great Spanish café on Washington, because Tish has forbidden us to ever darken Rufus's deli door again. I wonder, fleetingly, if Rufus's business account will swing violently into the red because of our boycott. I foresee a massive downward surge in muffin sales.

After delicious cake therapy, we are heading off for some retail therapy.

We are going *outletting*.

*To outlet:* a new verb we created. Here is an example of how it might be used: Today, I plan to go outletting with my good friends Tish and Rachel. To the designer outlets.

This may seem frivolous in view of everything that has happened over the last few days. My time *might* be better spent starting the hunt for a new apartment. Or at least packing my things and moving in with Tish later today, as planned. Maybe I *should* scour *The New York Times* Sunday edition for possible career opportunities.

But, you see, apart from the Donna Karan gift voucher burning a hole in my purse (thank you, Rachel), I have (with Rachel's ranting encouragement last night) gone past the "poor me, why me" stage of rejection and have moved on to anger and resentment. The idea of making life difficult for Adam is very appealing. This is my plan:

1. Do not move out of his apartment just yet. Why should I cleanly remove all traces of myself before his return from the Bahamas with man-stealing bitch Stella?

2. Do not leave Cougan & Cray. Would be completely bad career move at this time and my daily presence will serve to remind Adam how badly he has treated me. (Although I will go and see Jacintha Bridges re: Human Resources job tomorrow—don't want to actually work *with* Adam.)

Why should *his* life continue without even a slight hiccup after the way he's behaved?

Another reason I am nurturing dark thoughts about how to complicate Adam's life and generally be a pain in his side is because Adam just called me. From the Bahamas.

The phone rings just as I am about to leave the apartment to head for the Fourteenth Street PATH station. And I'm not going to bother picking up because I assume it will be either Katy, calling to find out why we didn't attend her Mothers Against Sexy (or was it Sexual?) SPAM meeting last night (feel a bit guilty for not turning up to protect her from Marion bloody Lacy but don't want to make up pathetic, unbelievable excuses to her at this time of the morning), or some bloody bane-of-the-weekend telemarketer.

I *hate* it when someone tries to sell me something that I really don't want or need, and I have such a hard time telling them no because they are so persistent and aggressive. Plus, I always end up feeling sorry for them because it must be a really shit job. Can you imagine sitting there, day in and day out, calling people all across the country and knowing that the best you can expect is verbal abuse?

This is exactly why I have Caller ID and voicemail. To shield me from the bastard pushy person on the other end, determined to extract cash from me. But I am so pissed to get an "out of area" call at eight on Sunday morning that I pick up, determined to tell "Hello, this is Chuck, how are you today?" to stick his head where the sun don't shine.

"Hello," I bark, ready to vent my spleen on the doomed, hapless Chuck who is, poor soul, only doing his job.

"Emmeline? Is that you?"

Oh, God. It's Adam. Despite harboring dark, vengeful thoughts about him, I am unable to stop the pathetic pitty-pat of my heart at the sound of his beloved voice. And then reality reasserts itself. This is the same lying, cheating, ionic-bonding Adam who has just wrecked my life.

"Yes," I say, curtly, as images of Adam and Stella frolicking wantonly on a Bahamian beach flash in front of me.

"Thank God. For a moment there I thought it was your dreadful friend, Rachel."

Now, insulting my best friend is not a good way to start a telephone conversation after shafting me both at work and at home, and as you might imagine, my temper (which has already been stoked very nicely by Rachel the night before) fires up.

"Just called to see how your weekend's going," he tells me cheerfully. "Did you have a good time on Friday night?"

Did I have a *good time* on Friday night? What kind of a weekend am I *having?* How *dare* he sound so . . . so cheerful! He casually ruins my life and my birthday, and then has the audacity to call me and ask if I've had a *good time.* I don't believe this!

And then I *know* how I am going to handle this conversation.

"I'm having a *totally fab* weekend," I lie. "The apartment looks *completely great.* You're going to *love* the new black and red décor."

"What?"

I can't help a smug smile as I imagine the shock-horror of his face. Outraged Adam. Y-e-s!

"Tell me this is a joke."

He really does sound upset. This is *great.*

"You won't recognize the old place. It's amazing how quickly you can transform a room with a coat of paint," I breeze at him. And then, before he can get a word in edgewise, "How is *your* weekend, Adam? Stella tells me that the Bahamas are lovely at any time of year."

There is a momentary pause, but only a very slight one before Adam pushes manfully on.

"Darling, it's pretty much as I told you. Boring work, lots of meetings, not much time to enjoy the surroundings. We might as well be back in Manhattan."

How can he still call me darling? Has he no principles?

"Well," I say, now huffy with indignation and resentment.

"I imagine that I'd rather be at a *business weekend* in the Bahamas than forcing my body into strange yoga positions. Did I tell you I've taken up yoga? It's very *enlightening.*"

"About the apartment. What exactly have you done to—"

"Talking about enlightenment," I interrupt, smug that he's now really worried about what I've done or not done to his décor. "There are some things that you need to enlighten *me* about."

"I—yes, you're right." He sighs. "Look, I was going to tell you before I left for this trip but there just wasn't time. It never seemed to be the right occasion. But you deserve to hear this from me—"

"Actually, I don't have time right now. I've got to go be a Proud Warrior and a Mermaid," I say. I am not going to be dismissed on the telephone as if I am some insignificant amoeba. I deserve more than that. Face to face, at the very least.

"A proud what? Emma, did you say mermaid? Have you lost your senses?"

"Actually, nothing could be further from the truth. You could say I've *come* to my senses. What time will you be back tomorrow?"

"Five in the afternoon. What does that have to do with—"

"I'll book a table at La Trattoria for six," I tell him firmly. "Then we can have a good long chat about the Bahamas and why I didn't get that promotion. And other things."

"I told you why you didn't get the job." He sighs, and I imagine him pushing his blond hair off his forehead. "It had nothing to do with your ideas. You're very talented, you have some great ideas. It was more to do with experience and outlook."

"I *am* experienced, and I have a very cheerful outlook. *Usually.*"

"But—"

"Look, I'll see you tomorrow," I say, borrowing my mother's Mrs. Thatcher no-nonsense tone. "Oh," I add as a parting shot. "And I'm sure the red wine stains will come out of the sofa and the rug." Click. I hang up and punch air.

This is great!


I decide to wait until we are at the Spanish café until I broach the subject of torturing Adam with Rachel and Tish.

We are sitting outside, eating delicious strawberry tartlets. It is very hot out here. It is actually in the high eighties, but feels like the high nineties on account of the late June humidity. And the reason we are out here in the sauna, instead of enjoying the lovely, cool, air-conditioned interior, is because this café is almost exactly opposite Rufus's deli.

"There's no point boycotting his deli if he doesn't realize what we're doing," Tish tells us. "I want him to see what he's missing."

She certainly looks great enough to miss in the skimpy summer dress. The top has tiny spaghetti straps and clings lovingly to her ample bosom, and I am jealous as hell. The flirty skirt skims the top of her brown knees. It is also very red. This is a very un-Tish-style dress and it is blatantly sexy—so blatantly sexy it may as well be emblazoned with the words FUCK ME NOW, but my God, does she look good. She is also the only one of us not sweating profusely, and I wonder if this is due to a secret formula body lotion that the Italians have not shared with the rest of us.

"Oh, there he is," she says, and I glance over my shoulder to look.

"Don't look." She kicks me under the table. "I don't want him to think I'm sitting here on purpose like some sad, unattractive stalker who can't get a date."

"I can't believe you're doing this," Rachel tells her. "I can't believe *I'm* doing this. Jesus, I'm risking skin cancer for the sake of your fuck." Rachel slides her chair sideways to get a good position under the shade of the canopy. "Can't you just forget about Rufus and move on to a more

receptive guy? That waiter who served us was very interested in you."

"It's not about a fuck," Tish says, and I gasp.

Tish *never* says *fuck*. She is the most clean-mouthed of all
my friends, on account of her strict Catholic upbringing with
Saturday confessions and Sunday mass.

"You *never* say fuck," I accuse her. "The Pope will have a
stroke."

"Yes. Well, to paraphrase the great Bob Dylan, times are
changing. I'm changing. I want Rufus to see what he's
missed. Fuck, fuck, *fuck*. God, that feels good." And then she
begins to laugh, hysterically, tossing her glossy brown hair
over her shoulder.

Have I just missed something? Okay, Tish saying *fuck* is
unusual, but it's not that funny. I glance across at Rachel,
who scowls.

"Hahaha." Tish leans back languorously in her chair to
show her breasts to their full advantage. And then she
swings one knee sexily over the other. Her red strappy shoes
are divine.

"That was just too fucking *funny*." She giggles, then leans
across and playfully taps my arm. "Hahaha, can't you just go
along with me and laugh? Pretend I just told you something
totally hilarious—Rufus is watching."

*Aha.* Now we get it. I self-consciously join in. But Rachel
doesn't.

"This is just too fucking *degrading*," Rachel announces,
and gets to her feet, nearly collapsing her chair. "Why don't
you just point your fanny in the direction of Rufus's deli,
then open your legs really wide. Even *he* should get *that* message."

Tish, crestfallen, stops laughing mid-haha.

"Hey, that was a bit . . . unfair," I say, before I can stop
myself.

Because I have said this, because I never contradict her,
Rachel scowls and I cringe as I wait for the next lash of her

tongue. I can almost see the cogs clicking behind her eyes as I wait for the diatribe that is sure to come.

But I know that I am right, because it *was* unkind. Tish doesn't deserve it. And although Rachel is one tough cookie, she is not usually a bitch. At least, not to us. And then something very strange occurs. Just as she opens her mouth to shrivel me with acerbic words, she does a complete about-face.

"You're right. I'm sorry, honey," Rachel says, as she places a placatory hand on Tish's shoulder.

*Well, knock me down with a feather.*

"Forgive me for being an unfeeling, hardhearted, callous bitch. You laugh and flirt all you want. Rufus is a dickhead for not dragging you immediately up to his apartment to fuck the living daylights out of you."

And as Tish and I stare at her, our mouths appropriately open in fly-catching mode, she smiles sweetly. "Anyone for more fucking cake?"

"What was all that about?" I ask Tish, once I'm sure Rachel is inside the café (and out of earshot). "She never puts herself down like that. It's rare enough to hear her apologize."

"It's that guy at work," Tish tells me. "He had the nerve to question her army-style running of the project when she laid into a junior technician for adding the wrong amino acid to—well, I can't remember what the amino acid was added to. But Rachel was very upset about it. Apparently it ruined a month of careful work. So you can understand why she was pissed."

We both ponder this in silence, because we don't get what it is that Rachel actually does. Whenever we ask, she pats the side of her nose with her finger because it's top secret. Our theory is that she's working for the government on a new cure to a dreadful disease. Or that she's trying to clone a friend sheep for Dolly.

"You know, maybe she does go a little over the top," Tish

adds, with a giggle, and I giggle, too, because I would not like to be at the receiving end of Rachel's sharp tongue.

"Oh, God. You can just imagine it, can't you?" I say, feeling sympathy for the poor technician. Much as I love Rachel, I would not work for her if you bribed me with a million dollars.

"Anyway," Tish says. "Apparently Hugh walked in just as she was yelling at the technician. So he pulls her into his office and calls her, and I quote, 'an unfeeling, hardhearted, callous bitch.' She's really taken it to heart."

"My God. That's awful. Rachel's a perfectionist, but she doesn't deserve that kind of language."

"Ah, yes, but it turns out that she insulted him first."

"Tell me more." I lean closer to Tish, intrigued by the thought of someone having the nerve to shout at Rachel.

"Okay. But promise you won't say anything about it to her?"

"Absolutely. Give it up."

"All right." Tish leans even closer and whispers to me. "He only called her that after she called him a motherfucking, interfering, misogynist bastard who couldn't tell a double helix from his ass."

"Oh, my. If only I'd been a fly on *that* wall. But why didn't she tell *me?*" I ask, feeling left out, because I have known Rachel for much longer than Tish has.

"It happened Friday. She didn't want to tell you after the terrible day you had."

Am I really that unapproachable and self-centered? I make a mental note to stop whining on and on about my own problems all the time, and to pay more attention to my friends. Wonder when I should broach the subject of me not moving out of Adam's apartment?

"Besides." Tish grins. "I think that Hugh guy is just what she needs. It's good to have at least one person who doesn't agree with you all of the time."

"Have you ever seen him?"

"No. But Rachel says he's a baboon, so I guess he's ugly and hairy. Just serve her right if she fell madly in love with him. I'd like to see her in love, just once."

"Yeah." I grin, mentally picturing Rachel at an altar, in a white billowing frock, being offered a banana.

Rachel, as far as we are aware, has never actually been in love. In high school, she didn't date at all on account of all the boys in her peer group being maniacally scared of her IQ. But that doesn't mean anything, because I didn't date either, until I started college.

But during her college years (Harvard, of course) she approached sex as she does everything else. She decided it was time to see what all the fuss was about, and proceeded to treat it like a scientific experiment. She does like sex, as we know, because she is not short of willing men to help her out in this department, but she never really dates the same guy for more than a couple of weeks. I don't think she's a nymphomaniac or anti-men. I think she just gets bored with them really quickly.

"Here were are, my friends." Rachel breezes through the door, followed by the attractive, dark-haired waiter.

"Thank you so much," Tish tells him, as he places our cakes on the table, and she flashes him such a come-on smile, that he nearly falls on the floor at her feet.

"See." Rachel nods encouragingly after the hot waiter. "He'd fuck you like a shot. Now let's recap the plan."

There's nothing Rachel loves more than a good list. Today's list plots out what we are going to do, and when we are going to do it.

"When we've finished up here, we'll head straight to the outlets. That should give us a clear three-hour outletting gap, then back here to Chez Nous for an early dinner with the boys. Then back to Bastard Ionic Bonder Adam's place to pack your stuff and move you to Tish's place."

Perhaps now would be a good time to mention the new plan.

"Actually, I'm not moving out just yet," I tell them, as I concentrate all my attention on my plate.

"I mean, why should I rush? After all, he asked me to move in. Which is exactly why I don't have my own apartment anymore. Why should the bastard get rid of me so easily? He deserves to suffer," I add, warming to my theme.

"Good for you," Rachel tells me. "Get the fucking locks changed, that will really piss him off. You could hold a decorating party. We could all come over and help paint it some really disgusting color."

I knew Rachel would approve!

"Emma, are you sure about this?" Tish asks, her brow furrowed with concern. "Sweetie, wouldn't it be better just to make a clean break and move out? You've already been hurt—why risk more?"

"Because he's a fucking ionic bonder who deserves to suffer," Rachel rants. "You go, girl."

"Well, if you think it's the right thing to do . . ." Tish trails off, and I wonder if she has a point. Do I really want to stay there with all the memories of happier times?

As we leave the café, I feel more depressed than vengeful.

Glancing across the road, I see Rufus watching Tish walk down the street. And I don't know if it's just the sunlight blinding me, even through my sunshades, but his expression freezes me in my tracks. Every nerve end of his body is filled with longing.

And I wonder if Adam ever looked at *me* like that?


Sunday supper at Chez Nous reminds me of old times with good friends. After two glasses of Chardonnay to go with the delicious *coq au vin,* followed by *crème brûlée* and a large snifter of Chivas Regal, I'm feeling very mellow as I glance around the table.

Sunday evenings are always quiet, so when David and Sylvester first opened Chez Nous, we made a point of eating here to boost Sunday sales. That was two years ago, and we're still eating here. And Sunday evenings are still quiet. Apart from the older couple and the two yuppie types, we have the place to ourselves.

Tish, Rachel, Katy, Tom, Sylvester, and David (although Sylvester and David have been taking it in turns to spend time in the kitchen to cook and serve the delicious food). And little Alex, of course, peacefully asleep on the couch in the corner, despite the noise of our chatter and laughter. When he was a baby, Katy and Tom made a point of placing his bassinet close to the television so he'd be able to sleep through anything.

It certainly worked, and when I have my babies, I will do this too. Except not with television, but with music. Led Zeppelin, obviously. Which will not only teach them to sleep despite the noise, but will also give them excellent taste in music. Yes, I will definitely do this with *my* babies. I fondly imagine Adam and me standing over the bassinet, gazing lovingly at the blonde cherub sleeping soundly to the strains of "Stairway to Heaven" . . . Oh. Except I won't be having Adam's babies . . .

I wonder what they're doing now . . . I feel the buildup of tears behind my eyes as my imagination conjures up images of Adam and Stella feeding each other lobster on a candlelit terrace, Adam and Stella strolling hand in hand on a lovely, romantic Bahamian beach, the waves lapping at their ankles . . . Adam, hopping around in horrendously complete agony after being stung by a jellyfish . . .

You know, now I come to think of it, since moving in with Adam I've only been back once for Sunday supper. And that was the time I brought him with me to meet everyone, which wasn't exactly a success. Why didn't I realize then that our relationship was doomed? Was I blind?

If I ever get involved with any man, ever again, I will *never* give up my Sunday evenings with friends.

"I think that's disgusting." Rachel pounds the table with her fist.

"Marion read a report about it," Katy says. "You just don't know what a problem this has become."

"Marion Lacy, oh font of all knowledge," Tom says, rolling his eyes. "At least Alex's e-mail problem is fixed. I've changed the settings and they only allow him to receive mail from a designated list. He won't be getting any more junk mail."

"You're my hero." Katy smiles and touches his arm. "I told the other mothers that I'd show them how to do it too. But Marion says we shouldn't have to—"

"You know, it wouldn't be so bad if you could tell these bastards to remove you from their goddamned mail list," Rachel interrupts her, warming up for a bit of a rant.

I think that Hugh person at work has really got to her. I also think that the older couple in the corner seem a little apprehensive. But Rachel *is* speaking rather loudly.

"I mean, these . . . these bastard e-mails *always* come with the option to *remove* your name from their disgusting e-mail list, but it doesn't goddamned work."

"I know." David nods in agreement. "You hit 'reply' and send them an e-mail with 'remove' in the title, and then they're supposed to remove you from the list."

"Yes, but that's the bastard thing about it," Rachel says, taking a large gulp of her brandy. "You do it, just so they know that you don't want any more of their goddamned filth. And then what happens, huh? What happens then?"

She glances around at us, but before anyone can offer a reply, she continues in full rant mode.

"I'll *tell* you what happens. The goddamned e-mail gets returned to you as *undeliverable,* and they carry on sending their dirty, filthy e-mails without a care in the world. I mean, what are things coming to?"

"But who *owns* ze Internet? Where *is* ze World Wide Web?" Sylvester's question is a good one. One to which no one seems to know the answer, and for a moment there is silence as we look around at each other.

"Well anyway," Katy tells us, looking down nervously at her hands. "Marion's arranged a march for next Thursday."

"Independence Day?" I ask. "Isn't there a parade?"

"Yes, of course. We're marching *after* the parade."

"Count me in," Rachel says, unsurprisingly.

"But your parents are coming over," says Tom. "Tell me you didn't agree."

"Well . . ." Katy picks up a spoon and fiddles with it, and I get a very uneasy feeling.

"You did, didn't you? Katy, you have *got* to put your foot down with this woman. She does not *own* you. You do not have to do everything she suggests." Tom runs a hand through his hair, and I notice how tired he looks.

Embarrassing silence falls on the room. I wonder if they're having problems. I hope not. But it's not really like Tom to get upset like this. Katy's only trying to do the right thing.

"Emma, sweetie." David breaks the deadlock as he pours more brandy. "How *are* you?"

"I'm okay," I say brightly as all attention is focused on me. A little too brightly. I take a gulp of my brandy to stop myself from melting into a little puddle of self-pity.

"It's just like old times again, isn't it?" Katy says. "You and Tish sharing again. It's great to have you back, Emma."

I wonder if now would be a good time to tell them . . .

"There's been a change of plan," Rachel announces to the table. "Emma's not moving out of Adam's place. And I think it's a great idea. Make the bastard suffer, that's what I say." I jump as she pounds on the table again. "He deserves inconvenience after what he's done to Emma."

"Are you sure you want to do this?" Tom asks.

"Of course she is sure," Sylvester says. "Zat Adam, pah. You must stay zere until ze cops come wiz ze eviction notice, is what I say."

Well, I hadn't exactly intended to let things get as far as court appearances and eviction notices . . .

And before I can stop it, I picture myself boarded up in

Adam's apartment as the police lay siege outside. I'm lounging weakly on the sofa and I don't even have the strength to operate the TV remote control. The food is long finished, there's no electricity, no water, and I have been forced to eat toothpaste to survive . . .

"I think you should make a clean break of it," Tom tells me quietly. "Don't let him hurt you anymore than he already has."

"Hey," I say, and glance across the table at Katy, who is chatting animatedly to Rachel and Tish. "You guys are okay, aren't you? I mean, this PPPTA thing. It's just Katy's way of trying to fit in. She really loves you, and you really love her, don't you?"

"Of course I love her. But you know, I'm just so tired of coming home every day and finding the house overrun with Marion Lacy and the PADD or MASS mothers. Katy doesn't have to do all this stuff to prove what a great mom she is—all you have to do is look at her with Alex. With all the trouble at work, sometimes I just want to come home and veg out in front of the television. It's tiring, constantly trying to save the world. And it's wearing her out. She needs to take it easier. She needs to stop beating herself up over this stuff."

"Your job isn't in any danger, is it?" I ask, because Tom works for a major financial institution on Wall Street and things are not exactly rosy at the moment.

"I don't know, Emma," he says, and I notice, again, how tired he looks. "More redundancies are due. I don't think I'm in the firing line but we'll have to wait and see."

"Oh, God, Tom, I'm so sorry. Does Katy know?"

"No. Not yet. She has enough to worry about these days," he says, morosely gazing into his brandy.

"You should tell her."

"I don't know. She's so stressed out with the bitch woman Marion. I think she's maybe suffering from postpartum depression, too. Do you think you could talk to her?"

He's so lovely to worry so much about Katy. And she's so lovely to try so hard to be the perfect mom.

"But . . . but wouldn't it be better from you?" Much as I appreciate his faith in my mediating skills, I do think that *he* should be the one to talk to Katy.

"It would be better coming from another woman," Tom says firmly. "Thanks for doing this, Emma."

I'm flattered that he's so certain I can help. Now that I'm a lonely spinster again, I *should* try to help others more . . .

"I zink it is good zat you make Adam suffer," Sylvester hisses in my ear. And then he adds, darkly, "I zink zat David is having an affair."

Oh, God.

"No. Not David," I tell him. "You must be wrong."

"But he is so secretive. I try to talk to him, but you know, if I'm wrong, always he will remember and zink zat I don't trust him. *Mon Dieu,* then he get sick of me and leave me."

Sylvester lowers his head to the table and I pat his shoulder. David, who is chatting to the yuppie couple in the corner (the guy is very attractive), is happily oblivious.

"But why do you think he's seeing someone else?"

"He sneaks off in ze afternoon sometimes and never tells me where he goes."

"Have you tried asking him? Subtly, of course."

"No," he wails. "If he wants me to know, he tell me, *n'est-ce pas?* Obviously he is hiding something. Emma, can you speak wiz him? You are a good person, you will do zis, *oui?*"

"I . . ." I don't know what to say.

Sylvester is obviously wrong, because I'm sure David would never do anything to hurt him. He can be such a drama queen.

"You are *ma belle diplomate,*" he tells me, planting a kiss on both my cheeks. "I know I can rely on you."

What can I say to that? Despite not wanting to get involved, I am flattered that my friends are able to come to me with their innermost problems. Immediately, I fall into daydream mode, reinventing myself as a wise counselor for friends' personal problems.

# 7

......................................................................................

## Wild Salmon

### TO DO

1. Pack.

2. Leave.

3. Call lawyer to check likely jail time I'd serve for wanton destruction of Adam's apartment.


**8:30 P.M.**

Monday. The telephone rings and I lunge for it. "Out of area." Excellent.

"Hello," I say, with such sparky merriment that cheerleaders across the nation would envy me.

"Good evening. Am I speaking with Emmeline Taylor?"

"Indeed you are," I say cheerfully, as I hike up *Led Zeppelin II* to full blast. I have the telephone positioned right next to the music center, and I hold the receiver down to the speaker before putting it back to my ear.

"Sorry," I yell. "Can't hear you. Nope, no good, can't hear a word." And I crash down the receiver.


**8:50 P.M.**

Telephone rings again. "Out of area."

*Yes!*

"Yes," I say.

"May I please speak with Emmeline?"

"Do I know you?"

"No, ma'am, this is Chuck. How are you this evening?"

I do not believe this.

"Actually, Chuck, I'm really terrible this evening. I just had an expensive nondinner with my cheating boyfriend so that he could tell me he's leaving me for another woman. And that they're engaged! So I have to find somewhere to live, and I have to find a new job, on account of this being his apartment, and did I mention he's my boss? Yes, I know it's a cliché, Chuck. So I'm having a really shit day. And Chuck, this may come as a surprise but I'm not exactly in the mood to chat. Did you get all that?"

This guy is slick. With barely a pause in the conversation he beams his little ray of sunshine right down the telephone line at my undeserving self.

"I'm sorry to trouble you, ma'am. Thank you for your time. May I just say that I love your accent? You have a great evening, now."

God. I am such a bitch.

Easily amused, I am spending my evening taking revenge for Adam's betrayal by inventing new ways to torture telemarketers. This is not kind, and I am now starting to feel extremely guilty. I imagine that Chuck is a very nice medical student, working the telephone to earn extra cash to put himself through medical school.

As you may have guessed, my earlier dinner with Adam was awful . . .

## Monday evening, 6 P.M.

I am strong. I am empowered (ohm). Yes I am. I am *so* not a girly wimp (ohm). I am so going to kick Adam's ass, yes I am.

Actually, I don't feel strong or empowered at all. But at

least I look good. Yesterday's outletting trip yielded a pastel, flirty skirt and a baby blue top. Pastels are the new black this year, apparently. And the baby blue top, so Rachel and Tish tell me, brings out the creamy bloom in my cheeks (okay, so the bloom in my cheeks is the result of clever makeup) and enhances the baby blue of my eyes (dark shadows under eyes cleverly hidden by concealer).

After all, one should always look as good as possible when being dumped by one's boyfriend, and under different circumstances, this would be a great look for me.

"Emma, *carissima,* my poor darling." Luigi—otherwise known as Steve from Brooklyn but he thinks Luigi fits better with the rustic Italian ambiance of his restaurant—takes my hands and kisses my cheeks. "Sylvester called me and told me all about it," he tells me, shaking his head. "I have the perfect table for you."

Everyone knowing your business is one of the downsides of Sylvester and David knowing every gay (and straight) restaurateur in Greenwich Village. I make a mental note to have a word with Sylvester about this.

As Luigi leads me to a secluded corner, my empowerment shrivels just a bit more at the thought of the forthcoming confrontation with Adam.

The table is very private, because apart from being at the far corner of the restaurant, Luigi has artfully arranged very large potted plants all around the area. This is a very sweet thought.

"Mario is your waiter for tonight," Luigi says. "He knows all about Bastard Ionic Bonder Adam, so he'll be watching out for you in case of trouble."

Rachel's theory about men seems to be catching on.

"Emma." Mario beams at me. "No worries. One false move from him and I'll beat him to a pulp."

Adam, as you may have gathered, is not the most popular of people on account of being rather condescending to the wait staff. Plus, he does not tip generously.

"Thank you, Mario, but I can handle it," I tell them both with more courage than I feel. "Just don't use the best china in case I get the urge to throw something. Hahahaha."

"*Brava.*" Luigi nods approvingly as Mario places a basket of bread and a bowl of olive oil on the table. "Here, eat something. You need to keep up your strength."

"Compliments of the house." Giorgio, the wine waiter, flourishes a bottle of very expensive wine and pours me a glass. "For stamina and courage."

Does everyone in this place know about Adam? I really must speak to Sylvester and David about this . . .

But anyway, back to Adam. He's late. And that's odd, because he hates lateness. God, you should have seen the way he behaved last month when I was a bit late meeting him at the theater. We went to see *Rent*—free tickets from a happy client. Perfect Pantyhose, I think. Anyway, he hated the show, but I *loved* it. Also, I think the theater wasn't posh enough for him, on account of not actually being on Broadway but on a side street. Plus, it was full of tourists. Adam is not keen on tourists. (Now I think about it, Adam isn't very keen on many people.)

He was so red-faced by the time I *did* arrive I thought he was going to explode. In fact, he was so pissed he barely spoke two words to me the whole evening. I was only *ten* minutes late, on account of having to stop at an ATM machine to get some extra cash. You see, I needed the money to pay for the expensive supper we'd planned for later. But my credit card was maxed out so I couldn't use that, obviously, so I had to have the extra cash.

Adam totally believes in equal rights, so equal shares of the check. Which, now I come to think of it, is very mean when one of us makes six figures (plus lovely bonuses) and the other makes just over thirty thousand. . . . I thought that was fair, at first, on account of not having to pay rent. At least now I'll save a fortune on expensive dinners . . .

Oh, why didn't I see him for what he was? A mean, hard-to-please ionic bonder . . .

I went to see Jacintha Bridges in Human Resources this morning. Obviously, I can't continue working with Adam. So I'm working for Jacintha starting next Monday. I didn't mention Adam's name at all, and neither did she. She's very diplomatic, as well as psychic. Yes, I think I can make human resources my thing, rather than advertising.

Angie (Cruella) was very nice to me today, now that she's getting my job. I showed her what to do, and told her about Adam's likes and dislikes re: coffee and sandwiches. She laughed and raised her Cruella eyebrows, as if to say, "You gotta be joking." I feel, somehow, that she won't be the fetch-coffee-go-get-lunch type of secretary.

### 6:15 P.M.

No sign of Adam. Oh, God. Not only is he cheating on me, he's standing me up for my own break-up scene!

"Drink more of the wine," says Luigi from behind a potted plant. "Build up your courage."

### 6:25 P.M.

Every time I take a sip of wine, either Mario, Luigi, or Giorgio fills my glass to the brim. It's nice that they're so concerned about me, but I don't really want them hiding in the potted plants all evening.

"He's here," Mario hisses at me.

Oh, God.

"Oh, good," I say, as my stomach lurches with nerves.

"Don't forget," Giorgio says. "One false move and we'll surround him."

What do they imagine Adam will do to me? Or maybe they're more concerned about what I will do to him . . .

Oh. Here he is.

My courage falters badly at the sight of him. Gorgeous and tanned, he's wearing his deep blue cotton shirt and stone chino pants. I'd forgotten just how handsome he actually is . . . How can he wear my *favorite* outfit? I bet he did it on purpose, you know, just to add agony to insult.

"Adam," I say evenly, as I take another sip of wine.

"Hello, Emma." He smiles a little uncertainly at me as he waits for Mario to pull back his chair. But Mario has receded to a place behind the large palm, because as I spot him peeking between the leaves he flashes me a thumbs-up. Adam will just have to learn how to sit down without assistance, I think, biting back the urge to giggle hysterically.

"I see you've already ordered a bottle of red." Adam inspects the label and I want to tell him to forget about the bloody wine. "Hmm—good vintage. But I think I'll have white—I'm in a fish kind of mood. Waiter." Adam snaps his fingers very rudely. "Bring me the wine list."

He's in a *fish* kind of *mood?* How can he be hungry at a time like this?

"You look . . . great." Adam flashes his perfect teeth at me.

"Well, what did you expect?" I ask. "Sackcloth and ashes?"

But my comment falls on deaf ears as Giorgio brings the wine. Adam tastes the Chablis, scowls, and sends it back, which is another annoying habit of his. There is probably nothing wrong with the wine.

"Let's not bother with the first course," Adam tells me. "Let's head straight for the main course. I'll have the wild salmon."

I know that I've hardly uttered a word so far. Where do I begin? How can he even think about food? So I order the same, even though I'm not sure what the difference is between normal salmon and wild salmon. Probably the wildly inflated price we (Adam) will be paying for it.

Luigi winks at me from across the restaurant and I take a deep breath. The sooner this is over the better.

"So, Adam, don't you have something to tell me about Stella?" There. I said it.

"I was going to wait until we'd eaten," he begins, pausing to reach over the table and squeeze my hand.

I flinch and pull away. But he hardly seems to notice.

"It's such a relief to have it in the open. I hated sneaking around behind your back. Stella told me to tell you, but I really didn't want to hurt you."

"Good old Stella," I say. "How thoughtful of her."

"Yes, she is a very thoughtful person," Adam tells me earnestly, and I want to cry. He is so engrossed in Stella that my sarcasm is lost on him.

"The thing is . . . I can't tell you what a tower of support you've been for me. Over the past few months you've helped me get over Sabrina's rejection. You've been so sweet and kind. My recovery is all due to you, Emmeline. I really appreciate your friendship and encouragement. You've made me see that it is possible to love again . . ."

Oh God, this is more than I can take. Come on, Adam, spit it out.

"I never meant to fall for Stella. I suppose because we've been working together so closely, it just sort of crept up and swept me away before I knew what was happening. I just can't *believe* she feels exactly the same way about me."

And because I am so totally shocked that I am sitting here with my tongue glued to the top of my mouth, Adam takes this as a sign of encouragement and continues to wax lyrical about the joy of his new love.

"Stella could have been designed for me. She seems to know exactly what I'm thinking before I think it. Do you know what I mean?"

I cannot believe this.

"But . . . but . . . Why didn't you *tell* me all of this *before*? We *live* together." I finally find my voice. "How can you propose to another woman when I'm still sharing your bed? That's . . . that's despicable."

"Emmeline, you're a really sweet girl." He sighs.

And then I wait for the *but*.

"Really sweet," he reasons with me. "But let's face it, we both knew that what we've shared isn't love."

"*I* didn't know that."

"More a question of mutual need at a certain point in our lives," he continues, as if I haven't said a word. "And I'm sure you'll meet the right guy for you, just as I've met the right girl for me."

At this point, our wild salmon arrives. And instead of thinking of all the clever, biting things I should say to Adam, I find myself wondering about it. It is delicately broiled, and beautifully garnished with lemon wedges and parsley sprigs, and I wonder how wild a life it led before it found itself on my plate.

I imagine a heavily tattooed salmon dude, complete in red bandanna, swimming upstream with his wildly partying friends. They all have cigarettes hanging out of their mouths, and are swigging back neat whiskey as if it were soda. I wonder if the trout ever complain about the noise these party salmon make? I imagine that Harry would be a good name for this salmon, and now that I've given him a name, I cannot possibly eat him. It would be like cannibalism.

"Of course, you must take as much time as you need to move out of my apartment." Adam pauses to fork salmon into his mouth, and I just don't get how unbelievably cool and callous he can be.

"I'll be staying with Stella in Trump Tower for now, but we don't really want to live together until after we're married. She's very old-fashioned about that."

*Oh, if only I had been as old-fashioned as dear old Stella,* I think nastily. I should never have moved in with him. He thinks I'm *easy!*

"I'm not sure if we'll keep my apartment or not. We don't really need two apartments in New York City. Although Stella did suggest that we rent my place—real estate prices are going up all the time, and it's in a great location."

Adam has totally forgotten that I am here, so wrapped up is he in his Stella fantasy.

And then comes the final blow.

"As a sign of our friendship, I brought you this," he tells me, pulling a small, ring-sized box from his pocket and placing it on the table. Obviously, it is not a Tiffany's box because that one was for Stella, not me.

I feel sick. I have to leave now, before I cry or puke all over Harry-the-salmon. And then I know what I'm going to do.

I stand up, inadvertently sending my chair crashing backward, and the whole restaurant pauses mid-conversation to try and peer through the potted plants. Mario and Giorgio are not even pretending to hide now. They have brazenly listened to every word Adam has said and look like they might commit violence.

"Adam, you are a bastard," I tell him. "You sit here calmly telling *me,* your live-in girlfriend, that you've fallen in love with someone else. You've actually *proposed* to the other woman, but you didn't want tell me sooner because you didn't want to *hurt* me? And now you're trying to placate me with some *stupid friendship gift?* What a terrible trick that is."

"Now, Emma—"

"Don't you dare 'Now Emma' me, you bastard ionic bonder. Let's see how you like this trick."

Before I can think about it I grasp the edge of the crisp white tablecloth, and yank it. The old pull-out-tablecloth-from-under-crockery trick. The entire contents of our table fall into Adam's lap, and crash to the floor in a mess of broken crockery, smashed glasses, and food.

"Oops," I say, into the complete silence of the restaurant. "That trick didn't work either."

Luigi begins the clapping. Then Mario and Giorgio join in. And then the diners add their support, and the crescendo builds.

To the cries of *"Brava"* I swirl on my heel and head toward the restaurant door.

*"Brava."* Luigi kisses my cheek. *"Brava."*

"Sorry about the crockery," I tell him. "Just send me the bill."

"Are you joking? It was worth it just to see Adam's face. And besides, I used the second-best china."

.................

**10:30 P.M.**

"What a *bastard*," Tish tells me for the hundredth time as we take a last look around Adam's apartment for anything I've missed.

As soon as I called to tell her my tale of woe—between heartbroken sobs—after poor, hapless, possible-medical-student Chuck I couldn't even be bothered to torture any more telemarketers—she immediately called a cab and came straight over. And she is angry. More than angry, she is completely furious with Adam, which at this point is much better than sad and depressed because she is not crying. If she were to cry, I would cry, too, and I've pretty well cried myself out over the past few hours.

But not once has she said "I told you so."

My eyelids are so puffy and red that my eyes have been reduced to bloodshot slits. And my head aches. This really is not a good look for me. But it *is* appropriate. I look *exactly* like a woman who has just been right royally shafted by her significant other.

"I just can't *believe* it," Tish tuts, "I mean, what a complete and utter *bastard. Scumbag.* Ionic bonder fucking *bastard.*"

"You're getting very good at cursing," I say, as I stuff the last of my CDs into a tote bag.

"Yeah, I've been driven to it by the idiot, bastard men in this godforsaken place. It's therapeutic. And cheaper than a shrink. God, this place is still too clean. I want to dirty it. We should throw a leaving party and invite everyone we know. What do you say?"

"Tempting. But you know what I want to do? I want to follow through on my threat to redecorate it with really disgusting colors and trashy furniture. He'd really hate that."

I look around at all the creams and whites and shiver. It really is cold and hard, just like Adam's heart. I shiver again and rub my arms. If I'm honest, it never really has felt like home because everything in here is Adam's.

"I saw this show about avenging ex-girlfriends and wives," Tish says. "It was really good. There was one woman—really pretty fortysomething—and her husband of twenty years ran off with his bimbo secretary. I mean, how clichéd is *that?*" Tish stops midrant and puts her arms around me. "Oh, I'm sorry, honey. I don't mean *you're* a cliché."

But I am. I am a cliché in reverse.

*My boss has left me for an older wife.*

"Anyway, her husband tried to hide bank accounts, stocks and bonds—any material assets so he could screw every last penny out of the divorce. So you know what she did? She waited till her husband and his slut were out and broke into his apartment. Then she cut all his expensive suits to shreds. She was *so* cool—she splashed his Mercedes with paint. And then she smashed his expensive wine collection—you know, it was worth hundreds of dollars. Man, was he *pissed.* It was *great!*"

"How much jail time did she serve?" I ask, as I nervously imagine Tish running amok with Adam's wardrobe and a pair of scissors.

"Oh, hardly any at all. She pleaded diminished responsibility. Six months, maybe. But it was worth it, don't you think?"

I am too sad to think about revenge. Too disillusioned to care about getting even.

"What I really want to do is just leave and never come back," I say sadly. "I think I have everything."

All of my belongings are packed into my yellow Volkswagen Beetle, which is illegally parked on the street below. It is stuffed to the rafters with my clothes and shoes, my toiletries and knickknacks. Not much to show, really, for thirty years on the planet.

It's completely impractical, having a car in the city. And outrageously expensive. But I love this car—I'm so glad that I didn't give it up when I moved in with Adam. At least I won't have to pay exorbitant Manhattan garage fees anymore.

"No, I *know* we've forgotten *something*." Tish marches into the kitchen so I follow her.

"But none of the kitchen stuff is mine."

"Adam owes you," she says, checking out the wine rack. "These should do it."

Oh, God. The thing with Rufus has sent her over the edge. She's going to smash his wine collection.

"Listen, Tish, let's not do anything too hasty here," I tell her.

She pulls out six bottles of his most expensive wine and I cringe.

"Oh, we're not going to smash them," she tells me with a sly grin. "We're going to drink them. Call it therapy."

# 8

...........................................................................

## Picture Perfect . . .

### TO DO

1. ~~Sell all worldly possessions~~. Donate all worldly possessions to charity.

2. Emigrate to Thailand (no one there has ever heard of me
or Adam).

3. Shave head. Wear only sackcloth. Become world's second
female Buddhist monk, thereby removing need to concern myself with worldly trivialities. Will only be concerned about immortal soul and doing good deeds. Plus,
will no longer need a boyfriend or worry about shallow issues such as small breasts.

Total Humiliation.
*Complete, utter, total, abject humiliation.*
I will *never* be able to hold my head up high, ever again. Instead, I will bow my head in shame and despair. Everyone I
know will learn of my demise over the next twenty-four hours.
There it is, in black and white, for the whole world to see.
The news of Adam and Stella's engagement is in today's
newspaper. Along with a very flattering photograph of the
happy couple.
The photograph was taken *last night* at some posh charity
event. I mean, I just can't believe it!

Last night! Merely *hours* after he dumped *me*. I mean, I know that I have to tell the rest of my friends and family about Adam's defection at some point (if, in fact, David and Sylvester haven't done this already), but I was rather hoping for a few days' grace before I have to face them.

My *God,* but the man is a fast mover. No wonder he only wanted to eat the main course at dinner with me. Was he working from a timed agenda, or what? I can just imagine how he planned it out.

1. 5:00 P.M. Arrive at JFK from romantic, sea-and-sand, sex-filled weekend with new (extremely rich) fiancée who is sporting my twenty-five-thousand-dollar engagement ring (an investment for the future).

2. 6:25 P.M. Meet old live-in girlfriend and dump her (being sure to wear the outfit she most likes just to rub salt in the wound). Tell her to vacate my apartment, because I am a callous bastard. And don't worry too much because she is a poor and lowly worker, and cannot benefit my career or my fortune. But don't forget to thank her for the therapy, because she is a good secretary, and may be useful.

3. 6:40 P.M. After crushed ex-girlfriend leaves (after causing totally uncalled-for scene with wild salmon), hastily exit hostile restaurant without getting knees smashed by violent-looking waiters (good help is so hard to find these days), grab cab uptown to Trump Tower. (Do not leave tip. After all, dinner was ruined and therefore I should not even have to pay the check in first place, because I am a mean bastard.)

4. 8:00 P.M. Arrive at charity event with Stella, after having slipped into elegant tuxedo, because I am a smooth bastard.

All the while he was with me, he must have been *counting the seconds* till he could escape back to *Stella.* All the while he was explaining his new love to me, he was watching the clock!

But they do look lovely together. It's not fair! Adam, all tall and handsome in the black tux. And Stella, tall and dark-haired, with her C cups lovingly encased in a glamorous Oscar de la Renta evening dress that I saw in *Vogue,* and covet wildly. She may be forty-five, but even *I* have to admit that she is truly stunning. After torturing myself with the happy smiles on their faces, I scan the article below.

### A Marriage of Public Convenience?

Stella Burgoyne, CEO of Burgoyne's Fine Papers, arrives with her new fiancé, Adam Blakestock. Previously a wunderkind at Sezuma Advertising, Mr. Blakestock is now the wunderkind Director of Advertising at Cougan & Cray.

When spotted earlier at JFK wearing a delicious Tiffany's engagement ring, Ms. Burgoyne confirmed that Mr. Blakestock had popped the question during their romantic weekend at the Bahamas holiday home of William Cougan, CEO of Cougan & Cray.

The couple met when Ms. Burgoyne approached Cougan & Cray after their wonderful success stories with Perfect Pantyhose and Kitty Crunch.

"I'm looking for a whole new concept in toilet paper," Ms. Burgoyne told reporters. "I think Cougan & Cray have the right blend of artistic foresight for my company."

The couple plan to marry in late October, but would not reveal details.

The *bastard.*

I wonder if he kept me in reserve, just in case she refused. And now, after this (and table-contents-in-lap trick) I have to go to work and face him.

I feel fresh tears springing to my eyes, but I ruthlessly

squash them. I will not cry on a packed PATH train as it speeds under the Hudson River and into Manhattan.

But why am I going to work today? Why am I torturing myself this way? Why didn't I just stay in Tish's sofabed and call in sick? Because Tish *made* me.

"Come on, Emma, you have to get out of bed and go to work. You have to show Bastard Ionic Bonder Adam that you don't care."

"But I do," I wail, clutching the pillow to my face.

"Out," Tish tells me, pulling at the comforter. "You *are* going to work. Don't you see what he'll think if you play hooky? He'll think you're heartbroken and that you can't face him."

"He'd be right. I feel terrible. I want to die."

"No you don't. You are a strong, beautiful, intelligent woman and you will *bounce back to love another day.*"

"Have you been reading those pathetic self-help books again?" I grumble. "You sound like a quote. And anyway, if we're such strong, beautiful, intelligent women, why are you still avoiding Rufus? How come *you* get to hide from *him* and you won't let *me* hide from *Adam?*"

"It's different with me and Rufus," she says, but still has the grace to blush. "We were never an item. And now that I can see he's never going to ask me out, I have *put him behind me* and *moved on.*"

"You sound like you're speaking in italics. You've definitely been reading self-help books."

"Okay, so maybe I have. Just one—*Your Ex: How to Behave in His Presence*—and it really, you know, really *speaks* to me. Emma, you have to face your fears before you can have closure and move on. It's the only way."

"Oh, so we're not boycotting the deli anymore, then?"

"Of course we are."

"But that's not fair. If I have to face my fears, you have to face yours, too."

"No one ever said life was fair," she says, smoothly changing the subject. "I think you should wear the white Donna Karan silk dress with the matching jacket. Cool, crisp, elegant."

She riffles through my clothes, which are neatly hung on the portable clothes rail in the corner of her living room, and I know that she is right. Much as I want to pretend that I have vanished off the face of the planet, I do have my pride.

"Go get in the shower and I'll do your makeup. Your eyes still look terrible, but we can fix that."

When the PATH train stops at 23rd Street, I leave my newspaper on the seat and scramble off before the doors close.

Thank God I only have to put up with Adam for another few days before heading off to Human Resources.

It is only 10 A.M. and I am already having the most shit day imaginable. Adam is not happy about Cruella replacing me as his secretary, as I found out when I arrived at work (ten minutes late but I couldn't rustle up the emotion to worry about it). Angie is sitting at her usual place at reception. She glares at me without even bothering to disguise her hostility, and I wonder what happened to the temp who's been booked to be her temporary replacement. Angie's scowl is so ferocious, I don't ask.

"I'd like to see you in my office right now," Adam tells me from his office door as soon as I reach my cubicle, and I get the impression that he has been hovering there waiting for me to arrive.

So I follow, my heart leaping with angst as I wonder if he's going to fire me. He's probably going to ask me for half of last night's dinner check. Or to demand that I pay for his clothes to be cleaned.

"Right," he says from behind his desk. "Please explain why Angie was sitting at your computer when I arrived this morning."

"She's my replacement," I tell him. "I'm switching departments."

"But *I* wasn't consulted about this. Who agreed to this?"

I thought he'd be happy about this, given the circumstances. Apparently not, but I can't imagine why.

"I decided it was time to take a sideways transfer, since I'm obviously not making any progress in this department," I tell him, pleased that my voice sounds firm and completely unapologetic. "I went to see Jacintha Bridges last Friday. I'm moving to Human Resources at the end of the week, so I'll have plenty of time to train Angie before I go. I'm sure she'll work out very well for you. She has a world-class typing speed."

"I can't believe you did this behind my back. Emmeline, this is so petty," he says.

Me? Petty? A case of the pot calling the kettle.

"Just because we're not personally involved with each other anymore doesn't mean that we can't act like mature, intelligent adults at work. We're a good team. You know that." He pauses to flash me his best charming smile, but all I feel is ice around my heart.

And I don't get it.

Why on earth would he want me to stay here working for him? Does he want me to stay because he's pissed I went behind his back, or does he want me to come up with more great ideas so he can steal them? Possibly both.

"And I'm sure that if you stick with this department, and concentrate on helping with some high-profile accounts, you'll get your promotion. You'd be wasted in Human Resources."

This is rich, coming from him. I feel the bile rising in my throat.

"Adam, I know you didn't recommend me for promotion," I tell him.

"That's a lie," he lies, and I can't help but admire his expression of outraged indignance.

"But I saw your memo to William Cougan," I tell him.

"You forgot to close your personal e-mail before you took off for your romantic weekend. You should be more careful. You never know who might walk into your office when you're not around."

"Okay," he tells me, segueing smoothly into a different counterargument with barely a pause. "I admit it. I don't feel you're ready for your own accounts yet, but just wait six months and gain more experience—"

"And frankly, I've lost interest in advertising," I interrupt before he can spin me the line. "I feel that human resources would be a good challenge for me."

"I've spoken to Jacintha," Adam tells me bluntly. "You're staying right where you are."

Bastard.

He already knew about my transfer but wanted to put me on the spot and explain myself to him. Was he always like this?

"Maybe I should take this to Mr. Cougan," I say, with false bravado. I do not want to tell William Cougan that I've been sleeping with Adam—the fewer people who know, the better.

"William," Adam says, placing emphasis on the fact that they're on a first-name basis, "is already aware of the situation between us, and he doesn't see a problem with our continuing to work together."

Oh, God. I will never be able to look William Cougan in the face again.

"So you see, the matter is closed. You're staying exactly where you are."

I stand to leave because I can't think of a damned thing to say. Adam has burned my bridges. The only way I can escape this is to leave the company. I am tempted to quit right this moment, but I'm not sure when I'd be able to get another job and I certainly won't get a good reference from Cougan & Cray if I just desert them.

"Emmeline," he says, as I reach for the door handle. "Look." He runs a hand through his hair and I feel a pang of longing because he is so handsome. I *know* he's a bastard, but I can't help myself.

"I'm not doing this to make life difficult for you, you know," he says, more gently. "I'm thinking of you and your future. I'd hate to see such talent wasted because things didn't work out between us personally."

"Maybe you should have made it clear from the start that you just wanted to fuck me to get over Sabrina."

I didn't mean to let that slip out, but right now I figure that I am entitled to be marginally bitter.

"This is business, Emmeline," he says, and then, "By the way, I do hope that you'll be picking up the check for last night's debacle."

"If you have the money to buy expensive Tiffany's engagement rings, you can afford to pay for last night," I tell him.

His eyes narrow as he considers my words, then he glances at his computer screen and he knows that I know about the huge bonuses he received.

I do not say another word.

I just leave the office with visions of smashed wine bottles and slashed suits dancing before my eyes.

................

**10:10 A.M.**

I pick up my ringing telephone.

"*Chérie*, we just saw ze newspaper," Sylvester says. "I know you can't talk, just say yes or no."

"Okay."

"Are you all right?"

"Yes."

"Luigi told me about your performance last night. *Merveilleuse.*"

I'm surprised there isn't a photo of Adam and me in

today's paper after our scene in La Trattoria last night, given the fact that the whole of Greenwich Village knew about it in advance.

"Shall we come and meet you for lunch?"

"No," I say. I *am* okay, because I am fueled by my anger with Adam. But if I meet Sylvester and David for lunch I will collapse in a fit of self-pity because of their kindness and concern. It's lovely of them to consider deserting Chez Nous at lunchtime just for me.

"We understand." And then, *"Non,"* Sylvester says to David, "she doesn't want to. Okay. David says to come here straight after work. We're zinking about you, *chérie.*"

Oh God, what lovely friends I have.

**10:15 A.M.**

Phone rings again.

"It's me." Katy. "I just saw today's paper. Is it true?"

"Yes."

"Oh, you poor, *poor* girl. What a cheap bastard, leading you on like that. It's positively *disgusting,* the way he's used you and all the time he was cheating on you with that woman—"

Katy is so upset on my behalf. I appreciate her concern, but if she continues I *will* cry.

"—it's outrageous! Rachel told me all about him stealing ideas from you. You should sue him for professional misconduct, and for leading you on by dangling the matrimony carrot in front of you. Sylvester and David told me about your dinner with Adam last night—my God, what an exit."

"Yes," I say, as William Cougan approaches my cubicle.

Oh God, now he will catch me in the middle of a personal conversation when I am supposed to be working. He does not approve of personal calls at work, and I do not want him to think worse of me than he already does.

"I'll certainly tell Mr. Blakestock you called, ma'am," I tell Katy, hoping she'll get the hint.

"Oh, you can't talk?"

"That's right."

"Oh, you poor, *poor* girl. You can't talk because you're at work, and if you talk about it you'll cry. I understand. I really do. You know, I saw a show about girlfriends and ex-wives whose partners had cheated on them, and what they did to get revenge—"

"Yes, ma'am," I tell her. Am I the only person who didn't see this show? "Thank you again, ma'am," I tell her, because William Cougan is now right in front of me.

"Can I help you, Mr. Cougan?" I ask with a false smile, as I put down the receiver.

"Everything all right, Emma?"

"Yes, sir." This is so embarrassing. "Did you want to speak to Mr. Blakestock?" God, I hope he hasn't come here to speak to *me*.

"Yes, I can see he's free. No need to see me into his office. Emma?"

"Sir?" Oh, no. *Here it comes.*

"Keep up the good work."

"Of course."

Whew.

**10:40 A.M.**

My phone rings again. Thank goodness William Cougan has gone.

"Emma, it's me." It's Rachel. I'm surprised she didn't call earlier because she eats the paper from cover to cover by the end of her morning coffee break. I'm also a little apprehensive, because I didn't call her last night when I called Tish. I just couldn't face her telling me that she knew all along what a jerk Adam is, and how right she is.

"I know you can't talk," she says. "Hang up and call me

from the restroom on your cell phone. Call me on my cell phone, not my office phone. Can you get away?"

"Yes."

Five minutes later, after checking that the restroom is empty, I speed dial Rachel.

"Christ," she says. "That man is a fucking idiot! A complete, utter, bastard, *fucking idiot!*"

It's nice that she feels so strongly on my behalf.

"You would not believe the crappy day I'm having," she says.

Her and me both.

"Do you know what he did? Do you know?" she rants, and I realize that we are not talking about Adam, but about Hugh.

"What did he do, sweetie?" I ask, pleased to be cast yet again in the role of wise confidante counselor friend. But I am a bit surprised, because I expected her opening gambit to be something along the lines of "I told you it would all end in tears but would you listen to me?"

"Bastard. *Fucking bastard!*"

She is so upset she can hardly speak. This must be really bad.

"Sweetie, take deep breaths and then tell me what's wrong," I tell her.

"After he cross-examines me about the list of supplies I've specified for the project—my God, what a cheap bastard—he tells me he wants me to *compromise* and order *cheaper, generic* materials. How cheapskate is that? So when I tell him *exactly* what I think of his despicable, stingy cutbacks, he asks me on a *date,*" she says, before dissolving into a longer string of curses. "Can you believe it? He actually asks me out to *dinner.*"

Oh. I don't know just what it was I expected, but it wasn't this. Hugh must be either very brave or exceptionally stupid. But how nice is that? Because it *is* nice, isn't it, when someone likes you enough to ask you for a date? But the way Rachel said it, you'd think Hugh had asked her to dance naked in a pit of scorpions. I mean, *really . . .*

"What a *bastard*. He actually asked you on a *date?*" I say, and she is so mad that she doesn't hear the irony in my question. "So what did you say?"

"I couldn't think of anything *to* say."

I can't believe it. Rachel may be many things, but *speechless* is not a word that comes to mind when I think of her.

"So I just walked out of his office and now I'm in the friggin' restroom."

Well, that makes two of us.

"I mean, it's so fucking *ridiculous!* What do you think he wants? He must have an ulterior motive. Maybe he wants to lull me into a false sense of security, then trounce me with some bad news. Maybe my project's been canceled. Maybe I've been replaced by some stupid putz who doesn't argue back."

"And maybe, just maybe he wants to eat dinner with you," I point out. "Maybe he feels you got off to a bad start and wants to get to know you—you know—to oil the wheels of your professional relationship."

I am just about to congratulate myself on my sensitive handling of the situation when Rachel decides to take my advice the wrong way.

"So are you saying that he's not asking me out as a woman? Do you mean that he can't *possibly* find me *attractive* and want dinner with me for the *sheer pleasure* of my *company?*"

"No, you weren't listening to me. Don't put words in my mouth. Rachel, will you stop obsessing. I never *said* that. I'm sure he finds you completely fuckable."

"Oh, so I'm obsessing now, am I?"

"Just a little, yes."

"So it's not like you obsess about Adam all the time? God, you'd think he was the second coming the way you talk."

"I do *not*." Do I?

"You do so. Anyway, what if I *do* decide to have dinner with Hugh?"

"You are not serious."

"Well, I'm thinking about it . . ."

"But you hate him. You can't *stand* him. He's a baboon."

"Well, y-e-s . . ."

"And when I first started dating Adam, you told me not to date my boss because that's the oldest cliché in the world, and that he'd screw me in more ways than just in the bedroom, didn't you?"

"Well, y-e-s. I suppose I did. But this is different."

"How different?" I bristle.

I just can't *wait* to hear this one.

"Well, I'm not his *secretary*. We're both professionals, with doctorates. And he isn't exactly my boss—more the project administrator. So you see, it's completely different."

I'm *so* not in the mood to take double-standard-type crap today, and I find myself getting even more angry with her for her hypocrisy.

"Oh, so just because I'm a mere *secretary,* and you're some high-up *doctor of science,* it makes it okay?"

"Well, yes. Yes I do mean that, now you ask. Because, as I said, Hugh is not the boss of *me.*"

This is so unfair. I know that it is anger transference, because Adam is the bad guy, but Rachel can be totally obnoxious at times.

"I think I *will* have dinner with him. Yes, I definitely will. Just to see what he wants. So how did the revenge dinner go with the Adam last night?"

Her tone is more than just a little sarcastic and I bristle before answering. She obviously hasn't heard the details from Sylvester or David, which is strange.

"For your information, I was marvelous last night. I told him what for, tipped the food into his lap, then marched out. Then I moved out of his apartment."

"Oh. So that was last night?"

"Yes."

"What happened to the 'he deserves to suffer, I'm not

moving out of his apartment under any circumstances' speech you gave us on Sunday?"

"I changed my mind. Tish came and helped me pack my stuff."

"Oh."

Then there is silence at the end of the line.

"Are you still there?"

"Yes, I friggin' well am here. I just can't believe you'd do this to me, Emma."

"What?"

"We've been friends for years longer, but you called her and not me. I suppose I'm the last to find out."

"I would have called you, but I was in such a state—"

"Sure. I understand. You couldn't even be bothered to pick up the telephone to tell your oldest friend."

She is furious, and I am not going to back down because she is being completely unreasonable.

"Well, you've got to admit that you're not exactly the most sympathetic of people, are you? I couldn't face any 'I told you sos' last night. I was going to call you later—"

"Oh, so I'm a cold, unfeeling bitch, am I?"

"I didn't say that. But you could make an effort to be more understanding. We're not all as perfect as you."

"I'm hanging up now. See you."

I stare at the cell phone and curse at myself. I think I've just lost my oldest, best friend.

I burst into tears and comfort myself by having a chat with Daphne the silk ivy.


My day does not get appreciably better.

When I go to the coffee cubicle to get a caffeine fix, I over-hear one of the twentysomething secretaries twittering brain-lessly to another twentysomething secretary.

"No. That's completely, like, outrageous. How did you, like, find out?"

"Tracey in Human Resources told me."

"My God, like, how embarrassing is that?"

"If that happened to me I could never come back to work again. You gotta give it to her, she's got some balls."

And when they see me, they stop talking so I know that it is about me and Adam. I wonder how Tracey found out about this, but then I wonder how she finds out about anything. So now my humiliation is complete, because the people at work know I have slept with the boss. This does not make me feel good, but I smile frigidly at the gossips, and help myself to some coffee.

"How are you?" Barbie, Zoe, or Christie asks me.

"You're so brave," says the other Barbie, Zoe, or Christie.

I escape back to my cubicle to sulk. Only an hour to go, then I can leave. I hate Bastard Ionic Bonder Adam for doing this to me.

**4:30 P.M.**

I am extremely petty, yes I am.

But it feels *great!*

You see, Stella called about five minutes ago, and although she is the least likely person on the face of the planet with whom I want to hold a conversation, on account of her getting my engagement ring, this is what happened.

"Emily, it's Stella Burgoyne. How *are* you, dear?"

Bitch. She *still* can't get my name right.

"Stella, I'm great," I tell her with false enthusiasm. "Such lovely news—the engagement. Congratu-*lay*-shens."

"Thank you *so* much," she says. "Adam is such a dear man—what a beautiful, beautiful ring."

*Don't go on about it,* I think, but obviously do not say.

"How can I help you?" I say instead.

"Is he there?"

"Well, actually, he's—" talking to William Cougan. But before I can say this, she rudely interrupts.

"Put him on, will you, dear? It's urgent. So many details to work through for the wedding, you know."

And then I know what I'm going to do. Call me spiteful, if you like, but surely I deserve a little bit of revenge?

"Of course," I tell her. "Just hold the line a moment."

Now I could just use the telephone to tell Adam that Stella is on the line, but I don't. Adam is deep in conversation with William Cougan as I knock and walk straight in.

"So sorry to disturb you," I say to Adam. "Miss Burgoyne is on the line and insists that she speak to you about the wedding."

"Tell her I'll call her back."

"I'm sorry, Mr. Blakestock, but she's really insistent."

Adam glares at me, and if looks could kill then I'd be fried to a crisp.

"Put her through."

*Y-e-s!*

Before I leave for the day, I take Adam the spreadsheets I have prepared for him, plus my leave sheet.

"Here are the projected costs for the McAdams account," I tell him. "I need some time off," I add. "To hunt for an apartment."

"I need you here next week. I expect you to help Lou Russo to find his feet."

Lou bloody Russo. Lou friggin' Russo . . .

"Tomorrow and Friday," I tell him. "Everything's up to date. Angie can cover any typing you need between now and next week."

"She knows where all your files are?" Adam asks, his face brightening. "And your computer files?"

"Yes," I say, and I mentally thank Rachel for telling me to remove my personal files from the computer. If Adam thinks he's going to find any more great ideas to steal, he's got another think coming. And then I remember that I've fallen out with Rachel.

"Okay." Adam signs my leave sheet. "And Emma?"

I notice that he hasn't called me Emmeline.

"Yes?"

"Don't embarrass me in front of William again."

"Adam," I say, dropping his apartment keys on his desk, "I don't know what you mean."

# 9

## Serially Single

### TO DO

1. ~~Buy more goats!~~ Buy an ass and have it delivered to Adam. Because he *is* one.

"Here, hon, drink this." David hands me a large glass of Cabernet Sauvignon. "And I guarantee you'll feel better. Got more customers coming in—back in a minute."

Sylvester is overseeing the preparation of something complicated which involves shiitake mushrooms and double cream. It also involves quite a lot of cursing. The kitchen is steaming with his bad language, the July heat (no air conditioning), and cooking, as he and his sous-chefs prepare the evening menu.

Beneath the silk of my dress, rivulets of perspiration are trickling down my spine. I feel crumpled, and hot, and miserable.

"*Non, crétin,*" Sylvester says, which means something very rude in French, I think. "*Non, non, non!* Not like zat. Like zis." He wrestles the wooden spoon from the poor chef. "You don't want to curdle the cream. You see? Now you do it."

"Sylvester, I need two orders of spinach soufflé for table two," David calls from the door, then heads back to the restaurant.

"*Chérie,* I'm so sorry." Sylvester sits down next to me at

the large wooden table. "We have the early dinner crowd to feed, what can I say?"

"It's fine, don't worry," I say, taking a large swallow of the excellent wine.

"Oh, but you are so brave to go into work and face zat pig. I couldn't believe it when I saw his picture in ze paper—I mean, *quel bâtard!* So brave . . ." He shakes his head at me. "Was it really terrible?"

"Worse than that," I say, and I glumly give him the recap of my day, but don't tell him about falling out with Rachel.

I'm feeling very bad about Rachel. I should have been more understanding. But I do think that she was out of order for speaking to me the way she did. This time she's gone too far and I am not making the first move.

"Zat was very naughty, putting ze call from *la femme terrible* through to him while he is speaking wiz his boss. Naughty for *you*, Emma, because you are too sweet. If it were me, I would make him suffer like you wouldn't *believe!* I would cut up his designer suits and splash paint on his car . . . But he doesn't have a car, *n'est-ce pas? Non.* Then I would splash paint on the walls of his antiseptic apartment—"

"And smash his wine collection." I prompt him, because, of course, I've heard this before. I really am the only person who didn't see that show. I wonder if it will be rerun soon.

"*Sacré bleu,* not ze wine," Sylvester tells me, shocked at the mere thought. "Zat would be sacrilege, to destroy such—such gastronomic *art!* No, I wouldn't smash ze wine. I would *drink* it," he says, as he takes a large gulp of *my* wine.

"Don't worry. Tish stole six bottles of his best stuff."

"*Très bien!* She should have stolen *all of it.* Here, drink." Sylvester refills my glass, then leans closer to me in a very conspiratorial manner. "He did it again today. David. He disappeared for *two hours* after we'd finished ze lunchtime rush. What am I supposed to zink? Pierre," he yells across the kitchen. "*Beat* ze eggs. Beat zem like you mean it. You are *not* afraid of zem. Zey are just *eggs.*" He shakes his head with a mournful sigh. "I can't turn my head for a moment—you see what I have to put up with?"

"Yes. About David," I remind him. "Did he say where he was going?"

"Would I be worried if he had? No, I'm sure he's seeing someone else. I'm getting too old and he's found a younger chicken."

Frankly, the idea that David has found someone else is ridiculous. Sylvester, a well-preserved thirty-nine, is a complete Adonis. He is also a lovely human being, despite his volatile Gallic temper. David is thirty-two, and although I love him dearly, I would not describe him as gorgeous. He's attractive in a small, dark, skinny way.

"You must speak wiz him for me, Emma." Sylvester grabs my arm.

"And say what? I can't blurt it out, can I? 'David, are you having an affair?' just isn't subtle."

"You will zink of somezing," Sylvester tells me with complete confidence, and I feel my heart sink. I can't even manage my own relationship. I am the last person in the world to help save someone else's.

"Sylvester, *darling,* what are you doing? Table two are still waiting for their *hors d'oeuvres,*" David says. "Come on, dear, chop chop."

"*Zut alors,* the spinach soufflés."

"I don't know what's got into him," David tells me as he sits down and takes a gulp of my wine. At this rate, I will be lucky to get another sip of it.

"I think he's worried about his birthday," David says. "He's paranoid he's getting old, poor dear. He's started using wrinkle cream. Oh God, that's the doorbell. I gotta go, honey. Sorry about this. Stay for dinner and we'll talk later?"

"No, it's fine," I tell his disappearing back. "I have stuff to do."

I am so very hot. The heat of the kitchen, combined with an empty stomach and the small amount of wine that has actually made it past my lips, does not agree with me. I really just want to go back to Tish's apartment and lie down for a while in the blissful cool of the air conditioning before I have to torture myself with phone calls to my family to tell them about Adam. I don't really want to face this yet, but if they call me at Adam's apartment and don't get an answer, they'll worry . . . Even worse, Adam himself might pick up the telephone.

As I leave, Sylvester thrusts a package into my hands.

"You must eat," he tells me, kissing me on both cheeks. "You are too *maigre*. I worry about you, you know?"

Yes, I know I'm too thin. Too thin, too small, too flat chested, too nice . . .

*Too hot and sticky.*

When I let myself into Tish's apartment, she is in the bedroom getting changed, so I slink into the bathroom and slip out of the Donna Karan dress. It's a lovely dress, and holds up well in the heat of the city. This dress is usually a very good look for me, but after a day of stress and upset, my complexion is pale and wan, and I look like a ghost. It seems all my wishes for wrinkles are coming true, because I have bags under my eyes. Now that I am yet again single, with no career prospects, I should take more care of my skin. Maybe I'll get some wrinkle cream.

After my shower, I feel marginally better as I slip into my ratty old comfort-bathrobe. The cream silk reminds me too much of Adam and I have consigned it to the trash.

"Darling," Tish says. "How did it go? I nearly called you to give you some moral support after I saw that appalling picture in the paper. But I thought that might make you feel worse." She shakes her head. "I just can't believe how callous he's been. Still, I think he's only marrying Stella for her money—she's worth millions in toilet paper and tissues."

So I repeat my day of woe to Tish. I'm getting good at this now and give her the abridged version. Of course, minus the fight with Rachel.

"I hope they're really miserable together," Tish tells me. "I hope her breasts droop and her face sags, and she gets cellulite round her thighs. God, am I a bitch or what?"

"I appreciate the support, honey. Personally, I hope she leaves Adam for a twenty-year-old god so he knows how it feels to be a retread. Anyway, you're looking particularly lovely tonight," I tell her, because I don't want to talk about Adam anymore. Plus, she really does look lovely.

The black cropped bodice and hip-hugging black pants (Calvin Klein, courtesy of Sunday's outletting trip) are ultra chic but casual. She's fresh as a daisy and sparkling with enthusiasm.

"I've got a date," she says. "You don't mind, do you? But if you need me here, I can cancel. It's nothing serious."

How nice is that? And how quickly she's got over Rufus, but (obviously) I don't say so.

"No, no. I'll be okay," I say, and mean it. It will be a relief to have the place to myself for a few hours. I can have a good old wallow in self-pity, cry my eyes out (yet again), put Led Zepp on the CD player (but not as loud as I'd like on account of the neighbors), and spend hours playing air guitar with Jimmy. Because I am a very sad person with no life.

"I've got to phone round the family and give them the bad news." I sigh, because I know I cannot put it off. "Peri will be crushed that she doesn't have a wedding to plan and Julia will remind me how great it is to be single. No doubt—*no doubt,* she'll quote famous feminists at me."

"You sure? How about Rachel? Why don't you give her a call and see if she wants to come over?"

"No, I need to be alone for a bit," I say, then quickly change the subject. "So who's the hot date?"

"This guy, John. Remember I redid his office on Hudson Street a few months ago?"

I do remember, because he comes into her store all the time to buy things he doesn't need, just so that he can talk to Tish. He is not the only one. Anyway, John is thirtysomething, fit, balding, still lives with his mother, and is homely in appearance. A nice guy, and looks aren't everything, are they? But I just don't *see* him with Tish.

"He's always coming into the store to buy *objets* and paintings for his house. Today, after he bought a lovely Chinese wood cut for his living room, we got to chatting. And he just kind of asked if I wanted to have dinner. And I know he's no oil painting, but looks aren't everything. And he's *so* sweet to his mother. So I said yes."

"Where's he taking you?" Home to meet Mom? But I don't (obviously) say this.

"Tonight is strictly casual—you know, no big deal. Just as friends. We're meeting in O'Malley's for a drink, then pizza at La Luna."

O'Malley's just happens to be Rufus's local bar, and he can be found in there most evenings playing pool with his buddies. But I don't mention this, either, and neither does Tish. Now I understand the sparkle in her eyes.

"Okay, babe," I tell her. "Go have fun."

I hope Rufus is ready for this.

Before I make any calls, I decide to eat. I'm not hungry, but I already resemble a scarecrow and I cannot afford to lose any weight, so I investigate the package that Sylvester gave me.

Homemade ciabatta bread, stuffed with Sylvester's special preparation of onions, garlic, sun-dried tomatoes, *herbes de Provençe* and Stilton cheese. This is my favorite thing in the whole world and I am touched that Sylvester has made this especially for me. Hmm . . . heavenly, especially with a glass of Adam's Special Reserve.

I now feel strong enough to make the phone calls. I call Julia first, because of the five-hour time difference.

"Emmeline, I was just thinking about you, darling. We had a simply splendid weekend with the Smythe-Joneses. Very picturesque. Anyway, you'll never believe it—I got arrested for indecent exposure, it was so exciting . . ."

I hardly dare ask but she'll tell me anyway.

"Bloody Lord Farleigh-Coombs and his hunt! We blockaded his route on Sunday, to stop the wanton, cruel killing of those poor little innocent foxes. When he tried to get us to move, I asked him how he'd feel, being ripped to shreds by a pack of ravaging hounds? How would he feel, minus his skin? He made some big pathetic excuse about how humane it is, and how foxes are a nuisance, and had I ever seen a chicken coop after the foxes had been at it? So I told him, 'That's all very well, but does the killing of foxes really require a troop of fat old men on horses wearing silly outfits, generally enjoying the barbaric plight of small mammals?' To emphasize my point, I stripped off my clothes. The BBC came, so it was on television. It caused quite a stir."

"I can imagine. But won't you be disbarred or something if the Law Society gets wind of it?"

What I *can't* imagine is how she ever came to marry my father, even if it was extremely short-lived. She went to Harvard as a postgraduate law student—some sort of exchange trip. Anyway, she met my dad, a handsome medical student. They fell in love, got married, and three months later the honeymoon was well and truly over when she realized he was serious about specializing in plastic surgery. Which, of course, she considers abhorrent and pandering to society's superficial standards. Shortly after her return to England, she found out she was pregnant with me.

When I'm asked what is it that my parents do, people are usually shocked when I tell them that my father is one of the top plastic surgeons in the tristate area, and that my mother is a top London barrister, specializing in battered wives, cruelty to animals, and asylum seekers. She's also sued the occasional plastic surgeon on behalf of disfigured clients.

One thing about Julia that I really, really admire is that she never takes a client unless she knows that they are innocent—

a luxury she can well afford, because she has a trust fund so doesn't have to worry about her income. The trust fund is not huge, but enough to keep the rambling house in Holland Park from crumbling to dust. Plus, of course, she gets her rosebushes trimmed for free. George, Julia's boyfriend, is also fairly handy with repairs . . .

"Of course, I didn't get charged," Julia tells me indignantly. "Marjorie Smythe-Jones is very friendly with the local chief of police, so it was all very amicable, really. Lovely man, Chief Inspector Wallis. Anyway, enough of that. How was *your* weekend?"

"It was completely awful," I tell her. "Adam dumped me and got engaged to another woman."

"Darling, that's terrible. But *do* remember what Lady Astor said. 'I married beneath me. All women do.' Typical man. Bastard typical man. You just can't trust any of them for more than five minutes at a time."

I hear the rumble of a deep voice in the background.

"No, George, not you. *Do* stop eavesdropping."

George started out as Julia's gardener, seven years ago, and by the time he'd finished landscaping the garden he'd moved into her basement apartment. He still pretends to live in the basement, but I know for a fact that he hasn't slept down there for years.

"George sends his love," Julia says. And then, "So I suppose she's younger than you, this new fiancée? I bet she's some young, twenty-year-old cheerleader."

"Actually, she's fifteen years older than me."

"Oh."

This is a bit of a sore point for Julia, because George is ten years her junior and I think she worries about it sometimes.

"Not that there's anything wrong with older women," I tell her. "It's just that Adam didn't finish with me before he proposed to her. He was stringing me along until something better came along . . ." I feel myself sinking back into self-pity.

"Now come on, Emmeline, self-pity is so self-destructive,

and also shows lack of moral fiber," she tells me in her no-nonsense voice. "At least you didn't marry him, then discover he was having affairs. You should thank your lucky stars you had such a close escape."

So much for motherly concern. I don't feel lucky, but know that this is just Julia's way.

"So tell me, did you get the information from the relief angency about your herd of goats?"

"No," I tell her glumly. "My mail's being redirected to Tish's apartment and it hasn't found me yet."

"Well, cheer up, darling."

"I will. Julia?"

"Yes?"

"I love you."

"I know that, dear. Me too."

I sigh, and dial Peri and Dad's number.

"Hi, Dad."

"Hey, how's my little girl? Can't wait to see you on Thursday. You are coming, aren't you? Peri and the boys are really excited—they're out at some party at the moment so I've got the house to myself for a change. My God, you wouldn't believe how tiring those boys are. So how's that handsome boyfriend of yours? He popped the question yet?"

"Actually, Dad, that's why I wanted to speak to you. We've split up and I've moved in with Tish. I just wanted to give you my new address and telephone number."

I figure that the less information I reveal, the better. Let them think it was a mutual decision, so they won't be sorry for the poor dumpee, me.

"Oh. Bad luck, honey. But these things happen. Plenty more fish out there waiting to be caught. Especially by a little cutie pie like you."

Ahh. My dad can be so lovely.

"Yeah, Dad. Thanks. Have you got a pen and paper?"

After he writes down my number, he comes up with a bright idea. This is not a new idea. It is the same one he came up with last Christmas, and last Thanksgiving, but I do not tell him this.

"Say, have you met Norbert Boyle, my junior partner?"

"Yes," I sigh, knowing what's coming next.

"He's still single. Very eligible young man—well established, own home, nice income. He'd make a great catch for some lucky girl. I can't understand why he's still alone."

Oh, I do. I do not want to be the lucky girl who snags him. Norbert is completely obnoxious, and I perfectly understand why he's still single.

"I'm not looking for anyone else just yet. But thanks, Dad," I add, because I know he has my best interests at heart.

"So we'll see you on Thursday."

"You bet." I'm actually looking forward to seeing them now, because a girl needs her family around her at times like this. I'm even having warm thoughts about Joe Junior and Jack Junior . . .

"Shall I get Peri to give you a call? You need to have a womanly chat with her?"

"Er, no. Really. I feel fine. Tell her I'll see her Thursday. Bye, Dad." Much as I love Peri, now is not the time to "share" with her.

................

**Wednesday, 7:45 A.M.**

Tish has gone to meet Rachel at the gym. I, of course, cannot go with them on account of Rachel's bitchy comments to me yesterday. But I do not tell Tish this. Instead, I plead a headache.

But I don't have a headache. In fact, I feel quite good today. Very cheerful, in fact. You see, fifteen minutes ago Adam called me and he really made my day.

This is what happened.

"Hello," I say, ready for another bout of telemarketer torture. These people really are outrageous—calling a person at 7:30 in the morning before they head off to work.

"First my sofa and rug, and now this. It's just so childish," Adam says. He sounds very angry. "I can't believe you'd do this. What the hell were you thinking? Today I'll torture Adam with a herd of goats?"

"Calm down," I tell him, "Don't overreact." Oh dear . . .

"Don't overreact?" He splutters. "How would you feel if some guys turned up at your apartment with a herd of goats? Oh, you're such a flake you'd probably keep the damned goats and let them eat the rugs and the drapes."

And I know instantly what has happened. Julia's birthday gift has been delivered to Adam in Manhattan, instead of the Msoze family, in Uganda.

*This is great. This is amazing.*

Though not, obviously, for the goats. Or the Msoze family.

"I want them removed from my property this instant or I'll, I'll . . . I'll sue you."

"Get a grip," I say, and I can't help laughing.

"This is not funny."

Oh, yes it is. Am I really a flake?

"Emma? When you've finished laughing, perhaps you'd better speak with the delivery guy?"

"Why should I? I didn't order any damned goats." I hear them bleating in the background. "For all I care they can live with you and Stella in Trump Tower."

Revenge is sweet!

"Good-bye, Adam," I say, and hang up the telephone.

When he calls back, which I know he will, I pick up because I am very sorry for the goats.

"What do you want?"

"The goats are addressed to you. At this apartment. The delivery guy won't take them away until you speak to him."

"So what do you want *me* to do?" I will not make this easy for him. He doesn't deserve it.

"I want you to tell the delivery guy to take them away."

"And?"

"And what?"

"What's the magic word?"

Adam sighs, but then complies. This is even more fun than a telemarketer.

"Please," he says.

"Sure. I think I know what's happened. Put the guy on the phone."

Muffled voices and bleating goats as Adam passes over the telephone.

"Yeah?"

"Hi, this is Emma Taylor. I understand you have a delivery of goats for me?"

"That's right, ma'am."

"What's your name?"

"Gus, ma'am."

"Well, Gus, let's see if we can sort this out. These goats were ordered by my mother, but they were supposed to go to Uganda. From me. For my birthday. To the Msoze family."

"Your mother buys goats for someone else for *your* birthday?"

"Yes—she's a very unusual person. The thing is, Gus, the goats won't be happy in Manhattan. You got the paperwork on you?"

"Sure."

Seconds later, after much rustling of paper (and more bleating of goats), Gus comes back on the line.

"Looks like a clerical error from the administration office. They put the wrong delivery address on this. You were just supposed to get the receipt."

"Oh, good. So you'll take the goats away, then, and make sure they get on their way to Africa?"

"I don't know about that. This guy here, he ain't exactly been polite about the whole thing. Me and the boys carried these crates up to his apartment, too. . . ."

Aha. I completely understand what this is about, now.

"I understand," I tell Gus. "How about Mr. Blakestock gives you a hundred dollars for your trouble, and you take the goats away?"

"Sure. Sounds good to me."

"Great." Although I don't want Adam to get off the hook so lightly, the goats deserve better. "Put him on, will you, so I can explain our agreement."

"Well?" Adam growls.

"All fixed," I say. "They had the wrong delivery address, that's all. Now if you'll just give them a hundred dollars for their trouble—"

"What? Are you out of your mind?"

"Okay, bye, Adam. Enjoy the goats."

"No, wait." And then, "Okay. I'll do it."

"Good. Have a nice day now," I tell him and hang up.

Y-e-s!

## 10

........................................................

# Independence Day

### TO DO

1. Drink many worm-infested drinks before next visit to family, because hangover will be so bad, won't remember visit to family.

2. Drink many worm-infested drinks before next show Jack my breasts. Hangover will be so excruciating, won't remember Jack seeing my breasts.

3. Think of really convincing line to explain single status. I am single because: (a)?, (b),? (c)? *Why* am I single again? What's *wrong* with me?

I am strong.
I am, as the song says, invincible.
Because *I am Woman*.
For my journey into the deepest, darkest depths of New Jersey to spend the day with Dad, Peri, and the terrible twins, I have chosen only music with a positive message. Last night, while Tish had her second date with John (just like the previous evening, she met him in O'Malley's—I hope he develops a taste for Guinness), I spent two hours carefully taping each track. On this occasion, I have forgone my gods of rock, Led Zeppelin (although I do have *Houses of the Holy* for

the return journey tomorrow morning), and am listening only to strong, invincible women.

As I listen to Aretha Franklin singing about respect, I sing loudly along with her. And I actually feel quite good. Not exactly happy, but not totally in the pit of despair, either.

As Rachel says, there's nothing wrong with being a single woman of independent means. Well, at least Rachel used to say this, when we were friends. The thought of Rachel casts a dark cloud over my day. I've been thinking about our argument, and she *did* have a point. I will call her tomorrow and eat some humble pie, because we have, after all, been friends for sixteen years and you don't throw away that kind of friendship for a few ill-chosen words.

But anyway, this is the twenty-first century, and just because I'm thirty and don't have a boyfriend or husband, this does not mean that there is something wrong with me, no. It means that I can't find a man worth giving up my freedom for. This is, after all, the day for being independent (although I'm always a bit confused whether or not to celebrate—being half American and half English can be a problem on days like this).

Yes, an independent woman. That's exactly it.

And that is what I'm going to say to explain Adam's nonappearance with me.

"We split up because I am an independent woman," I say aloud.

This doesn't sound convincing.

I'll have to think of something else. I ruthlessly push aside thoughts of Adam and concentrate on my new swimsuit, which is safely tucked in my overnight bag.

It's black, with high-cut legs, and is artfully padded around the breast area. Not *too* padded so that I look *too* different, you understand, because that would be tantamount to admitting defeat and saying to the world, "hey, I know my boobs are too small," but just enough to squeeze together what I have got, and push it up into amazing cleavage.

Amazingly *small* cleavage, but cleavage nonetheless.

It cost an absolute arm and leg, but David assured me it was worth every penny. Actually, it didn't cost an arm and a leg because I bought it from an up-and-coming new designer. That's one of the benefits of having gay men friends. They always know where to go shopping for whatever it is you happen to want. And David's friend Simon is so up-and-coming that no one has actually heard of him yet, but boy does he know how to dress women! And which is why he gave me a great deal. Plus he actually raved about my smallness, and how great I'd be as a mannequin.

Can you imagine it? Me, the next supermodel. Naomi, Chandra, and Kate will be my new best friends. Jean-Paul Gaultier will design lovely bustiers for me à la Madonna, and pop stars will want to date me!

Armed with this daydream, plus riding in my lovely daffodil yellow Beetle always makes me feel good, I happily while away the journey imagining exotic locations, and men with bulging biceps drooling over me. When I'm in London, Guy Ritchie and Madonna will invite me to dinner, along with Sting and Trudie Styler . . .

Didn't quite manage to ask David if he was having an affair, though . . . It's not something that comes up easily in conversation. I will have to figure out a way to broach the subject. But if he is having an affair, it's definitely not with his designer friend Simon, so that's good, isn't it?

My newfound bravado deserts me as I pull up the drive in front of Dad and Peri's ranch house. I thought this was going to be family only, but there are several extra cars parked on the drive (all of them Mercedes or BMWs).

I nearly turn my car around and head back down the drive when the front door opens and out trots Peri, resplendent in a pink and yellow flowered bikini and matching sarong.

"Darling, you're here," she tells me as she squashes me in a huge bear hug, before taking my face in her hands. "I'm just so *pleased* to *see* you." She plants kisses all over my face as if I am her favorite teddy bear. Peri is the human equivalent of a Labrador puppy—enthusiastic, overenergetic, but basically loving and friendly.

"Daddy was starting to worry you'd had an accident—you know, because of being depressed about Adam and not paying attention to the Jersey drivers. Oh, you poor darling," she says, pulling me back against her bosom. "Daddy told me about Adam. You poor, *poor* girl. He'll come around, you'll see. He'll be back begging you to marry him by the end of the month."

Peri, ever the optimist. Fat chance of that. No one will ever want to marry me.

"Come on." She grabs my arm and leads me into the house. "I know what'll cheer you up. Norbert's here and he can't *wait* to see you again."

But I don't like Norbert, I don't say, because he is a pompous, sexist ass who talks continually about his money, his belongings, his past girlfriends, and his prowess in the bedroom. God knows why Peri likes him!

"He's still single. You know, I don't *get* it. He's rich, attractive, successful . . . and he's really fond of you, you know. Come on." She pauses momentarily to draw breath. "Let's get you into your birthday bikini, then you can join the party. It's just the usual crowd, including Uncle Derek, Norbert, Gracie and Lou, oh, and you'll never believe it. Uncle Derek's got a new girlfriend—Kaylie—she seems like a nice person and he did do a great job on her implants, but he's still stressed out from the divorce . . ."

"Actually, I have a new—" swimsuit. I nearly manage to say it, but before I do, Peri foils me.

"Darling, go on up and change—I've left your new bikini in your old room. As soon as I saw it I thought of you, you are just going to *love* it. It's so *cute.*"

Peri is lovely, but fashion is not her forte. I anxiously eye her pink and yellow flowers.

"Go on, up you go," she urges me. "The boys are dying to see you in it. They helped me choose it."

"Oh, I can't wait to see them, either," I lie, trying to imagine what this bikini is like, having been chosen by three-year-old demons who take great delight in tormenting me.

*What a horrible person I am.*

Not only do I *not* want to see the boys, I *don't* want to wear Peri's bikini. What sort of mean, selfish person am I? If I don't wear the bikini that Peri has especially chosen for me, I will hurt her feelings. Would it kill me to make Peri happy? Besides, all Peri and Dad's friends won't care how I look, will they?

This thought holds me until I put it on.

It is truly ghastly.

The lime green, itsy-bitsy bikini leeches the color from my skin. It has a halter-neck top, with two tiny triangles of fabric that literally leave nothing to the imagination and show off my small, but at least firm, breasts. I nastily hope that all of the other women are at least forty, with drooping boobs, and will be jealous of my neat little perky 32AAs.

But how likely is that? Most of Dad and Peri's friends are plastic surgeons and their wives have absolutely no reason to have droopy breasts or flabby thighs.

I glare at myself in the full-length mirror, and anxiously fiddle with my pixie-short blonde hair. It is the only thing about me that looks well nourished (thanks to Sylvester's hairdresser friend, Jason, who introduced me to this new, super tea-tree conditioner for fine hair).

Maybe if I tie my sarong around my boobs and don't get into the pool, I'll be able to get away with it.

"Emma, what are you doing up there?" Peri calls to me, and I realize that I have been up here for at least twenty minutes.

"Come on, darling, everyone's dying to say hello to you."

Oh, God, the sarong (black, to match my lovely new swimsuit) looks like a tent. It was supposed to be tied around my hips, to make them look a little wider. Instead, I tie the knot just above my breasts, which gives me the appearance of having *one boob right in the middle of my chest.*

But it *is* an improvement on the lime green, so I sigh and leave the room after slyly hiding my purse and my car keys under the loose floorboard that hopefully the twins haven't discovered yet. I used to hide all my private things in here during high school, when I lived with Dad.

As I step self-consciously onto the terrace, Peri shrieks in delight.

"Look, everyone, here's Emma."

I feel like a freak exhibit in the zoo as all eyes turn towards me.

"Darling." Dad kisses me. "Sorry about . . . er . . . your guy. Very sad. You all right?"

"Yeah. You know."

He pats my shoulder without saying a word. He's not the most vocal of people when it comes to affairs of the heart, so the pat is worth a thousand words and I appreciate it. I appreciate his next words even more.

"Can I get you a drink?"

"Yes—something deadly would be nice."

"Something with vodka." He winks at me, then turns back. "Oh, Norbert's here."

"Oh, good." *Oh God.*

"Emma." Uncle Derek, pink as a lobster, his stomach hanging unflatteringly over his swimsuit, plants a kiss on my cheek. "Heard about your disappointment with Adam," he addresses my breasts. "Single again! I dunno what it is with modern women, you just can't seem to stick with one guy."

"Ha ha." I feebly attempt a laugh, to avoid conversation. I don't want to mention his three ex-wives, because this would be mean of me.

"You really should give more thought to getting implants. Men like a woman with curves."

And women like a man who is not desperately in need of liposuction and hair implants, but I do not say that, either.

"Emma." Gracie air-kisses me. She is Peri's best friend. Although a bit of a ditz (in a very nice way) she has the uncanny ability to memorize complete trivia and regurgitate it at inappropriate moments.

"So sorry to hear about you and Adam. We never did get to meet him, did we? Well . . . Norbert's here."

"Yes, so I hear." I force myself to smile. I do not understand why everyone seems so determined to throw Norbert at me.

"Oh, you'll never believe what Gracie saw in the newspaper on Tuesday," Peri tells me. "It's such a coincidence."

Oh God.

"Yeah," Gracie says. "There was a photo of that rich woman toilet-paper magnate—you know the one I mean? Oh. What's her name, Peri?"

"Can't remember. Sheila or Susan something."

Stella *bitch-man-stealing* Burgoyne. But I don't say this.

"Whatever, but she has great taste in clothes. She was wearing this really great Oscar de la Renta dress. Did you see it in *Vogue*, Peri? Completely fabulous."

I plaster the smile more firmly to my face because I know what's coming next.

"Well anyway, she's worth a *fortune* and she's just got herself engaged to this younger guy."

"Gigolo," Peri announces, wrinkling her nose. "He's, like, ten years younger than her—he *must* be marrying her for her money."

Peri tends to forget that she is sixteen years younger than my dad.

"But you'll never guess," Peri says. "He's called Adam Blakestock, too. What a *coincidence*. I mean, like, I'd never have remembered that your Adam was called Blakestock if Gracie hadn't reminded me." Peri laughs, and I feel the color drain from my face.

"Obviously not *your* Adam Blakestock, but don't you, like, think it's a strange coincidence that there are two guys with the same name living in Manhattan?"

"How *weird* is that?" Gracie giggles.

"Oh, we shouldn't have mentioned his name. See what we've done, Gracie? We've reminded her about her breakup with *her* Adam Blakestock."

"No, it's okay. Really . . ."

"Oh." Gracie puts a hand to her mouth. "I'm *so sorry,* Emma, Lou's always telling me to think before I open my great big mouth. I'll, er, just go see if he needs help with the barbecue."

Peri drags me around to say hi to everyone, and I narrowly avoid getting stuck with Norbert. For the moment, he has a captive audience by the name of Kaylie, Uncle Derek's date. He's amazing her with trivial details about his five trillion million–dollar sports car. Fascinatingly enough, his new car has fifty cup holders. *Imagine that!*

And just when I think I can escape Peri and find a quiet corner, preferably with a large, extremely alcoholic drink, she calls out to Joe Junior and Jack Junior, who are splashing around in the pool.

*With Jack Senior.*

Jack Senior, or just plain Jack, is Peri's younger brother. And let me make something very clear.

*We do not like each other.*

This is because of what happened at Dad and Peri's wedding, nine years ago, when I was a sophisticated graduate of twenty-one and Jack was a varsity jock—a mere boy of nineteen.

"I told you we had a special guest," Peri tells me. She fondly imagines that because Jack and I are related by marriage, we must be the greatest of friends.

"Emma," the terrible twins cry my name in unison, and it sounds more like a threat than a greeting. Within seconds, they are out of the pool and attached to my legs like leeches as they tug at the sarong. The sarong duly complies and slithers down to reveal the lime green bikini.

I think I hear titters of amusement from the gathered party as the twins run off, firmly clutching my sarong.

"Now boys, be nice to Emma." Peri descends after her flock, leaving me to Jack's tender mercies.

"Jack," I say, blushing at my vile green, near-nakedness. "What are you doing here?" I ask, and I know that my voice sounds harsh and unfriendly. "I thought you were in Helsinki. Or Honolulu." At least, somewhere beginning with H. I should remember because Peri keeps me up to date on Jack's life. But I usually stop listening when she starts, because I really *don't* want to hear about his *amazing career*, the latest architectural *award* he's picked up or which *girlfriend* he's currently dating. Jack dates a lot.

"Nice to see you too, Emma. Hong Kong," Jack tells me.

He looks fabulous, damn him. He's obviously been working out.

"Fabulous bikini," he lies, giving me the once up and down. "You haven't changed an inch."

I know that he is referring to my bust size, and I blush even more brightly. This is not kind, so I respond in a similar way.

"How's the knee, James?" I ask, smiling sweetly.

You see, his real name is James. James Brown. His parents had a strange sense of humor, as well as a deep, abiding love for the music of Mr. Brown. And, like his namesake, Jack has problems with his knees. One knee, actually. Not from falling to them on stage, but he tore a ligament during a Varsity football game. It was the end of his football career. Which was a tragedy, apparently, because according to Peri he showed great promise.

"I haven't had any complaints about my passes." He smiles, smugly.

What a slut he is.

"Well . . . *interesting* to see you again," I say, choosing my adjective with care.

"Sure. Maybe we'll bump into each other in another couple of years if we're unlucky."

"Not if I see you first, hahaha. Just my little joke."

"Yeah, you said it. Oh, heard you got dumped. Sorry. Happens to us all."

I scowl at his disappearing (but amazingly muscular) back, and head off in search of a large towel and the liquid refreshment Dad has promised me.

You see, I once nearly made the mistake of sleeping with Jack. Nine years ago at Dad and Peri's wedding. Thank God, I didn't, but I would have if I hadn't overheard him bragging to his friend Chip.

This is what happened.

I was twenty-one. I'd drunk too much champagne, because I was just legally old enough to consume alcohol so I made the most of the occasion. Jack and his college pal Chip (completely sober or so I thought, on account of being nineteen) spent the whole of the reception flirting with me, dancing with me and generally making me feel that I was the most beautiful girl in the world. It was so—so wonderful, that two attractive young men should compete for me.

And I, in my drunken haze, lapped it all up. Although the fuchsia bridesmaid dress (carefully but inappropriately chosen by Peri) was terrible, after a couple of glasses of champagne I truly considered myself on a par with Grace Kelly.

I was *beautiful.*

I was *desirable.*

Handsome young men were flirting with me! And I was having the time of my *life!*

Plus, I really went for Jack in a big way. Tall, lean, dark-haired, with the most amazing chocolate brown eyes and a kind smile. Chip was okay, if you go for the "I'm God's gift to women" type, but basically an overbred idiot with an eye for anything in a skirt.

After a trip to the restroom to freshen up (and to brush my teeth in case of kissing opportunities), I decide to cool off on the hotel patio, and this is when I see Jack and Chip. They are smoking cigarettes and drinking underage beer, and I am just about to go and join them when something stops me.

They are laughing and talking. About me.

This is what they say.

Chip: "The titless blonde's really up for it. Christ, you'd think she'd get implants or something. Can you believe her father's a plastic surgeon?"

Jack: "Yeah, I know what you mean."

Chip: "Well she's not my usual type, my friend, but beggars can't be chosers."

Jack: "Yeah." Followed by laughter.

Chip: "But she's the only vaguely decent chick at this wedding—the only *single* chick at this wedding. You got a coin? We'll toss for her."

I don't stay to listen to any more. Suddenly, I am completely sober, and flee back to the restroom. The full-length mirror, which only minutes before told me I was beautiful and desirable à la Grace Kelly, is now harsh and unforgiving in the glare of the light.

I curse myself for being an idiot. If I were a lesbian, I would not fancy myself in this dress. So after I have a bit of a cry, I carefully reapply my makeup, and smooth wisps of hair that have escaped the elaborate French chignon. Much as I would like to run and hide, I know that Peri and Dad will miss me so I make my way back to the reception. Plus, now that I have finished crying, I am getting angry and feel a strong compulsion to get even with these two brash young guys who think they're so irresistible. And as I take my seat at the head table, Jack wastes no time in joining me. Obviously, he won the toss.

Jack: "You want to dance or something?"

Me: "No, thank you." In my most frigid tone of voice.

Jack: "Come on, it'll be fun." He tugs at my hand.

Now the alcohol has made me brave, so instead of just refusing and forgetting all about some brainless comments made by a couple of idiot jocks, I am now extremely angry.

Me: "I may be titless, but I'm not desperate. Go away, little boy."

So you see, our relationship did not get off to a good start, and since that day I make a point of avoiding him if at all possible. Nine years is a long time to hold a grudge, and you might think that I'd forgive and forget, but I can't. Especially now, after Adam's betrayal . . .

On the occasions we *do* meet, we're not exactly hostile to each other. We just trade the occasional insult and part company.

Two large Bloody Marys later, I am feeling much better. Peri has been momentarily distracted by the twins. I think they did something vile to the salad dressing, so I will remember to avoid it. I have settled myself on a lounger at the far side of the pool. The umbrella is nicely positioned to avoid any chance of the sun touching my skin, and I have a lovely beach towel wrapped around the hated lime green concoction. All in all, I am quite happy with my solitude and could easily have a little doze . . .

Five minutes later my eyes jerk open as droplets of water trickle over my legs.

"Norbert," I say.

"Emma. Good to see you. I've just been for a swim."

I know this because (and this is a really *big* clue) he is dripping wet.

"That's nice."

"Yeah. Your parents have a great pool. Did I tell you about the pool I'm having built? Well, it's kinda like this one, except bigger."

"Oh." Everything about Norbert has to be bigger and better. I think he has a bad case of penis envy. I am the first to say that size does not matter, but I can think of no other reason for the sizeist chip on Norbert's shoulder.

"Yeah. So, I hear you got ditched by your boyfriend."

"It was a mutual decision," I tell him. "We split up because I am an independent woman." This line still does not sound convincing. I must work on it.

"Oh. Right. So you're unattached then? Because I'm between regular girlfriends at the moment."

"That's unbelievable," I tell him, willing him to go away and leave me in peace.

"Yeah, I know. I'm just, you know, dating lots of different girls right now. So if you want to have dinner sometime, I can check my datebook to see when I'm free."

"It's very nice of you to ask, but I'm not really ready to start dating again just yet."

"Oh, sure. I understand. But maybe after a couple of weeks, when you've got over the split with your boyfriend—"

"I'll keep you in mind."

"So, you'd better give me your telephone number. So's I can call you."

How did this guy make it through medical school? He must be hiding his intelligence quota under the proverbial bushel.

"I'm staying with a friend and I just can't remember the number off the top of my head," I lie.

"Oh. Well, I'll give you my card later so you can give me a call."

"Sure."

Never in a million years will I go out with Norbert. Why does he automatically assume that all girls are attracted to him? I mean, he's not bad looking, or anything. His double chin is very sweet, really. And he does have all his own teeth. And I'm sure some girls find hairy backs a real turn-on . . .

And just when I think my brief encounter with Norbert is over, he makes himself comfortable on an adjacent lounger.

"That Kaylie is a real cool chick," Norbert tells me. "I don't like to poach on Derek's territory, you know, but she was really fascinated by my new car. Did I tell you about my new car?"

"Yes, Norbert. At Easter." At great length.

"Oh, right. You know, Derek did a great job on her implants, don't you think? That's how he met her. She'd just got her divorce, and decided to get surgery to celebrate. They didn't start dating until after she stopped being his patient, because that would be unethical, see. But that's a really romantic way to meet, don't you think?"

"Yes." On the romance stakes front, it's right up there with "How about a fuck?" But I don't say this. I don't want to encourage Norbert to talk to me for any longer than necessary.

"You know something, Emma?"

"No." But I'm sure you're going to tell me, I think, as I see Jack heading back this way. Oh goody, another obnoxious male to torture me. What do I need to do? Hold up a sign that says "I want to be alone"?

"I don't get it," Norbert drones on.

Jack is getting closer.

"What's that, Norbert?" My, Jack *does* look good. Shame about his jock personality and tendency for serial monogamy.

"Hi guys, mind if I join you?" Jack asks, which is rhetorical because he immediately claims a lounger.

"Sure, big fella," Norbert says. "I was just saying to Emma that I don't get it. I mean, you're a great-looking chick and all, Emma, but why don't you get breast implants?"

See what I mean about Norbert's penis-envy, sizeist issue? I feel my face getting hotter. Jack, obviously, is enjoying this enormously and is grinning from ear to ear.

*Shut up, Norbert,* I pray, but of course he doesn't.

"I know your dad can't do them for you, because he's your dad. But Derek is truly a master surgeon. I mean, you can't tell Kaylie's are false, can you, Jack?"

"No. They look very real. And very large."

"Oh, I get it," Norbert says. "Derek's kind of like family, isn't he? Well, if you're uncomfortable with Derek, I could do them for you. I'd be happy to do them."

"Yes, thank you, Norbert," I tell him, my face flaming as I jump to my feet. Norbert has larger breasts than me.

Oh, the injustice of it all.

"I'll certainly think about what you said," I say. "Well, you guys have a nice bond. I'm off for a swim."

As I approach the pool, I drop the towel at the very last possibly moment and dive cleanly into the water. After a few laps, I feel better, and then the twins decide to join me. As I reach the shallow end, they jump in and ambush me. Jack Junior is on my back, and Joe Junior is clinging to my midriff.

"Oh, how sweet," Peri calls from the side. "The boys want to play with their sister. Don't get too rough now, boys. Emma's not used to it."

"Giddy up, horsey," cries Jack Junior.

"Me want a turn," cries Joe Junior, elbowing at his twin.

And as they are fighting over whose turn it is to drown me, large hands extricate them from my person. It is Jack.

"Come on, guys, give Emma a break."

"We wanna play," says Jack Junior.

"Yeah. My turn," says Joe Junior, grabbing me in a chokehold.

"Let go, brats."

"No!" they cry in unison, and I think that I am doomed.

"Remember that talk we had last night, boys? You know what happens to naughty little brats who are mean to people?"

Oddly, this works, and the twins release me. I wonder how Jack did that? I make a mental note to ask him. But before the boys change their minds and decide that I am fair game, I make my escape back to the deep end.

Jack is already there and on the side of the pool waiting for me. He offers me a hand and hauls me up out of the water, and I wonder why he is being so helpful. But I am thankful that Norbert, distracted by the possibility of food, has deserted my table.

And it is just then that I realize that I am no longer wearing the hated vile green bikini top and that Jack has a wonderful view of my 32AA's.

"You lost this." He grins, as he holds out the scrap of lime-green. And he is having a really, *really* good look at my boobs.

I cover my breasts with one arm, and grab the hated bikini top with the other.

"Here." Jack hands me my towel and I scowl because I am totally embarrassed and don't know what to do.

"I don't think anyone else saw you." Jack gives me a lazy smile, and I want to punch him because I know that he will make a nasty comment.

"Don't you dare," I warn him. "If anyone else says a word about my boobs, or lack of them, or implants, I will punch them in the nose."

"Hey." Jack grins holding up both hands. "Would I?"

Yes, he bloody well would.

"You know what I think?"

"Do I want to hear this?"

"More than a mouthful's a waste. Nice boobs. Don't change them an inch."

As he saunters back around to the other side of the pool he is whistling cheerfully, and I want the ground to open up and swallow me.

*Jack Brown has seen my breasts.*

And, oddly, he seems to like them.

# 11

# All By Myself

## TO DO

1. Sneak out of house before Jack gets up. Can't face him after breast-revealing episode.

2. Buy Peri something really, really embarrassing for her birthday and present to her in front of all her friends for maximum squirm value!

3. Study *How to Rekindle Your Sex Life* in detail and at great length. Will then be complete sexpert and maybe men (but not Norbert) will want to date me!

**Friday, 5:30 A.M.**

I'm awake, so I might as well go back to Hoboken because I don't want to get caught in the commuter traffic heading for the Lincoln Tunnel. Plus, after the breast-exposing incident yesterday, I would rather avoid Jack if I can.

*I cannot believe he saw my breasts.*

**5:45 A.M.**

"Emma, darling, you're up early," Peri bubbles at me as she grinds coffee beans.

How can anyone be this cheerful so early in the day?

"I had a feeling you wanted to get up and go, so I thought I'd catch you before you left. We can have a little girlie chat. We didn't really get the chance yesterday, with everyone here, and the boys are such a handful. Coffee?"

"Great." The coffee would be very good, indeed. But the girlie chat?

*Nonono.*

I brace myself and sit at the kitchen table.

"Oh, I also wanted to give you your birthday gifts," she tells me, placing two gaily wrapped parcels in front of me. "I didn't want to, like, give them to you in front of everyone and the boys," she says, "because they're a little bit, like, *naughty.* I bought them before you and Adam split, but I'm sure they'll come in useful in the future."

God, I can hardly wait to open the packages, I think, dreading it. What on earth could she have bought me?

"Morning, Jack, did you sleep well?" Peri smiles over my shoulder and I blink with dread.

Doesn't anyone around this place ever sleep late?

"Like a log. Morning, ladies."

Jack, resplendent in his boxer shorts, is sporting "I just got up" hair, which is standing on end, but still manages to look sexy. How can he look that way without any work?

"Come on, Emma, open your gifts."

"Maybe I'll save them till later . . ." I hedge.

"Don't mind Jack, he's, like, family. You don't have to be embarrassed in front of Jack, does she, Jack?"

"Nope. Emma and me go back a long way." He winks at me. "We have no secrets."

And I look down at the gifts because I am blushing. I open the book-shaped parcel, first, because I figure this can't be that embarrassing.

But I am wrong.

It is *How to Rekindle Your Sex Life,* and assures me that my man will never stray if I try the techniques mentioned within its pages.

The second gift is a vibrator.

"I'll look at it later," I say, pushing the box to one side with just a hint of the desperation that I feel.

"Come on, don't be a killjoy." Jack grins. "This I want to see."

"Don't be embarrassed, Emma, we're all adults here," Peri tells me, and I don't tell her that Jack is excluded from that statement.

The vibrator is *enormous*.

It is also very pink, and is ridged down each side to afford maximum feminine pleasure, so the packaging assures me. It is complete with plastic balls and a mop of pink fuzz.

It's completely awful.

"Oh," Peri squeals like a teenager, "I just couldn't resist it. Gracie had a sex party last month and I just had to get it. It's such a hoot, don't you think?"

"Yeah," I mumble, avoiding eye contact with Jack.

"Here." Peri grabs the pink appliance. "Let me show you how it works." She fumbles with it for a moment, delaying my agony.

"Actually, I think I can figure that out for myself," I tell her. "Later." Much later.

Oh, God, now they think I'll be giving it a test run tonight.

"Can I watch?" Jack asks, giving me a leer as he pulls it away from Peri. He switches it on and it . . . well . . . it *vibrates*.

Rather alarmingly. And loudly.

In and out it moves, squishing the plastic ridges like a concertina before expanding outwards again. And even if I am desperate, on account of never getting any actual sex, I could never use this vibrator because *everyone within a five-mile radius will know what I am doing*.

They will *know* that I am a sad, hopeless woman who cannot get a boyfriend and that I have resorted to having sex with a very loud mechanical device.

"Switch it off, Jack, you'll wake up the boys," Peri tells him. "This is, like, not appropriate for them at all. I'd better just go check on them."

*It is too dreadful for words.*

"This is *great*," Jack tells me, handing me back my ten-inch vibrating bundle of joy, and I push the hateful thing back into its box. "I wonder what Norbert would make of it?"

"Not that he'll ever get the chance to see it," I tell Jack, then giggle as a naughty thought occurs to me. "But if he did, I'm sure he'd be very jealous. Every time he suggests implants to me, I shall recommend to him at every opportunity to get a penis extension. In fact, I will buy one of these for Christmas for every male of my acquaintance who has ever said the words *breast implants* to me. Just to make them feel inadequate and small." And then I remember that this is Jack I'm speaking to and that he has actually *seen* my breasts, so I shut up.

"Emma . . ." he begins, pushing a hand through his sticking up hair, and whatever it is he intends to say (and I'm sure it is something really embarrassing) is thankfully lost, because Peri bustles back into the kitchen and pours the coffee.

"You know, Emma, I completely swear by that book. I can't tell you what it's done for our marriage."

Oh, *please* don't, I think. I really don't need to know about my dad's sex life.

"I bought it for Jack, too, after he got engaged . . . Oh, sorry, Jack, didn't mean to, like, bring back sad memories."

Jack was *engaged?*

"You were engaged?" I ask, stunned by this new insight into his previously serially monogamous existence.

"Briefly," he says. "It didn't work out. No big deal."

"Oh." I am dying to know what happened, but obviously I cannot ask him. I feel a bit sorry for him, actually, because just for a moment there he looked very sad. Maybe I can pump Peri at a future opportunity.

"So." Peri sits herself down opposite me. "What are you going to do about an apartment?"

"Well, start looking, I suppose," I say.

This is not a chore I relish because I have a sneaky suspicion that all of the apartments I like, in all of the areas that I favor, will be way too high for my modest salary.

"I can stay with Tish for as long as I need to," I say. "But her apartment's so tiny, I don't think it can be for long . . . We get along great, but I'm sleeping on her sofa and my clothes take up most of her living room, so it's not ideal."

"That's what I thought!" Peri says, with great joy. "You see, I've been giving it a lot of thought. And I've come up with the perfect solution."

I do not want to live with Dad and Peri and the twins. It is too horrible to contemplate.

"You can live with Jack!" Peri claps her hands as if she's just announced we've won the lottery.

"What?" I say.

"What?" Jack is equally stunned.

"Yeah, I was talking to Daddy about it last night, and we think it's perfect."

"I really don't think—" I say, but Peri is steaming full-speed ahead.

"Jack has this great brownstone house at the top end of Hoboken, you know, one of those tree-lined roads up by the college? And it has so many bedrooms, and you're so tiny and you don't take up much space. So what do you think, guys?"

"Don't you have it rented out to a bunch of students?" I ask him.

"No, silly, he didn't renew the lease when he decided to come back home from Hong Kong."

"Oh, you're back here in the States permanently? In Hoboken?"

"Yeah."

"How . . . nice," I lie.

"Isn't it great?" Peri bubbles.

"The house needs a lot of work," Jack begins. "Lots of floors to be restored, lots of painting to be done—"

"Emma won't mind, will you, Emma? Anyway, you can't

paint all the rooms at once. You can move around as you need to. It's not like you don't have the space. And you can charge Emma a reduced rent, so the disruption wouldn't be a problem for her, would it, Emma? You should, like, charge her a reduced rent, anyway, because family should help each other, shouldn't they? We think five hundred dollars a month would be, like, fair. And Jack, I *do* hate to think of you rambling around alone in that huge house."

"Er . . ." Jack scratches his head and I know that he feels pressured.

He is not alone.

But five hundred dollars a month is really, really cheap. Maybe I should think about it . . . Maybe I need my head examined for even considering moving in with him. No, this is definitely not a good plan. But I think I'll let him suffer for a couple of seconds longer before I refuse, because it's nice to have the boot on the other foot for a change.

Plus, I know he feels beholden to my father. You see, Dad lent him rather a lot of money a few years ago for the down payment on the house. At that time, Hoboken was just about to become up-and-coming, so he got the house for a really good price. It must be worth a fortune, now that Hoboken is awash with the Manhattan overflow, and Jack knows it's all due to Dad. Therefore he feels *guilty* saying no to me.

I feel guilty for pressuring *him*.

"It's okay, Jack, I'm sure I'll find something."

"No, it's fine, really," he says, but his sincerity is questionable.

"Of *course* it's fine," Peri says. "It's the perfect solution. And besides, Emma's family. It's not like you'd be living together, like really living together."

"Well, we'll see," I say, looking down at my new book. It has the most amazing pictures on the front . . .

"Oh, Jack, go get ready. Come on, hurry up," Peri tells him. "You haven't got all day."

"You going somewhere?" I ask Peri.

"No, silly, but you're driving back to Hoboken, aren't you? Jack hasn't got a car yet so he may as well travel with you. It'll be nice to have company for the journey, won't it? And it'll save Daddy or me having to drive him later."

"Oh, fabulous," I say.

. . . . . . . . . . . . . . . .

**2 P.M.**

Tish's apartment really is too small. Her living room, already fairly cramped, resembles my life.

Messy and overcrowded with baggage.

I am depressed.

You see, the boys found my secret loose floorboard hideaway, and my car keys were once again fair game. No amount of coercing by Peri could persuade them to reveal the location of the keys. But this is not why I am depressed, because, for once, I am happy with the charming antics of my demon half brothers. You see, it meant that I couldn't drive my car back to Hoboken. Which is great, because I could do with leaving it at Peri and Dad's house for a while. It is always so hard to find parking spaces in Hoboken, and the multistory car lots are horrendously expensive, so this will save me money. Which is good.

The other obvious benefit of having no car keys is that I couldn't drive Jack back with me, which means I did not have to suffer an hour of his company in a confined space.

No, the real reason I am depressed is because Jack *was so glad that he didn't have to drive with me.*

He was positively *euphoric* when I announced that the twins had, in all probability, fed my keys to the garbage disposal again. He smiled. He actually *smiled.* Because, obviously, he can think of nothing worse than having to sit in a car with me. *He cannot bear to spend more than a few minutes in my company.*

Obviously, I do not have any warm feelings for Jack. And I would have to be really desperate to date him, and he is a serial dater without a conscience. But it hurts that I am so unattractive to men in general.

I couldn't face the torment of a ride back to Hoboken with Peri and the twins, so instead, I have spent the past four hours missing buses and getting on express trains instead of local trains, and ending up in places I definitely don't want to be.

I am going to the gym to get rid of my post-traveling commuter rage.


A lonely Friday evening looms ahead of me and I feel like a freak. Only a week since my thirtieth birthday, and it's already a bad year for me. I am drinking my second glass of Adam's delicious wine and eating instant cup of noodles (just add boiling water, hey presto, dinner), because I can't conjure up the enthusiasm to either (a) cook something, or (b) pick up the telephone and order something. Plus, I need to save all the money I can for a rental deposit.

The wine makes me think of Adam, and I can't help but torture myself with thoughts of him and Stella having wild sex and laughing about me. I can't believe he'd be this cruel. I can't believe how much I miss him, despite his being a bastard ionic bonder. I'm lonely, and I want a friendly shoulder to cry on.

Sylvester and David are a no because it's their most hectic night of the week, so they're too busy to listen to my "poor me, why me" ramblings. I *could* go round and see Katy and Tom, but they need some space. Some alone time, without me (or Marion Lacy) playing third wheel. Apparently, when Katy tried to sneak home early after the MASS mothers march yesterday, Marion Lacy (and some of the mothers) followed Katy home and invited themselves to her barbecue. Something has to be done about that woman!

Tish is out with John again (via O'Malley's, of course). That's three times in four days. At this rate, Tish will reach her sex limit by tomorrow night. She firmly believes that after four dates, you should sleep with a guy just so that you can check out if you're sexually compatible, and thus avoid the need to waste time and money on more dates if the sex is crap.

Oh God, what on earth will I do if she wants to bring him back here to have sex? They can't go back to his place, on account of his mother. And the walls between her bedroom and the living room are so thin. I just can't lie here and listen to them cavorting in the bedroom. Maybe the noise from my new vibrator will drown them out . . .

I could call Rachel . . . I *should* call Rachel. I really *miss* her . . .

I decide to watch a video and have some more wine to build up my courage. I decide on *A Knight's Tale*, because although Heath Ledger is (but only marginally) too young for me, he is certainly easy on the eye. Plus, the actor who plays the Prince of Wales is lovely, so I keep winding forward to the bit in the film where he makes Heath a real knight, and then to the end where he kisses his pretend actress wife. Then back to the bits where the Geoffry Chaucer character is naked, because I like him, too . . . Plus, this might be the only chance I will get to see a naked man ever again . . .

I am just about to have a good cry because Heath Ledger has been reunited with his poor, blind father, whom he hasn't seen in twelve years, when the doorbell rings.

It's Rachel.

"Hi," she says, rather coolly. "I brought you this."

It is a large ferny type of plant. I am not good with houseplants because I overobsess that they will die on me. So then I overfeed them, overwater them, and then they do, in fact, die, despite the fact that I try to place them in appropriate places, according to the houseplant book.

But it is a kind thought, and Rachel never buys flowers,

because (a) they are expensive, (b) a waste of good money, (c) they die, and (d) they look better growing in fields and gardens, where they belong.

"Thanks," I say, awkwardly, because I know that the plant is as close to an apology as I'm going to get from Rachel.

"Do you want to come in?" I ask. "I'm just drinking the expensive wine Tish stole from Adam's apartment . . ." I really want to be friends with her again. I hate confrontations.

"Sure. What else do I have to do on a Friday night? It's not like I have a hot date or anything," Rachel says as she climbs the stairs.

Thank God I am not alone in my Friday-night misery. And she can't be too pissed with me if she's bringing me gifts and saying yes to wine. I wonder why she's dateless? She's never dateless.

This fern is really huge. Close to tree size, in fact. Where the hell will I put it? There's barely enough room in Tish's living room for me.

Oh God, plants don't photosynthesize very much at night, do they? I think they absorb oxygen when it's dark, so this one probably absorbs quite a lot. Will it absorb my oxygen share overnight and asphyxiate me? I can just see the headlines now: GIRL SUFFOCATED BY KILLER PLANT. And I envisage a John Wyndham–style Triffid slithering along the floor to the sofa bed and eating me as I lay asleep and unsuspecting . . .

*Get a grip,* I tell myself, as I drag it up the stairs. *It's just a plant . . .*

"God, this stuff is disgusting," Rachel says through a mouthful of my noodles. "How can you eat it?"

"Hey, get your own disgusting stuff," I say, grabbing back my dinner.

"Emma, you need to eat proper food. Just because Bastard Ionic Bonder Adam is stupid, and does not know a good woman when he gets one, it's no excuse to let yourself go.

You need sustenance," Rachel says, then disappears into the kitchen to get some wine.

Thank God. Rachel is back in normal bossy mode as if our Tuesday argument never happened. I feel quite teary with emotion.

"We're ordering pizza—with extra cheese, because you need protein and calcium. What video are you watching? Oh, *A Knight's Tale*—I suppose I could sit through that again," she says, but I know for a fact that she, too, thinks that Heath Ledger is hot.

"Hey," Tish says from the doorway. "What are you doing, guys? Can I do it, too? My God, that's a big plant."

"I thought you had a date," I tell her.

"I broke up with John. He just wasn't right for me."

"I am not going to say 'I told you so,' " Rachel says, looking first to Tish and then to me in a very pointed way. And then, "What pizza do you want?"

"What was wrong with him?" I ask, because I don't understand why she dated him in the first place.

"Nothing. He's a nice guy. But I just felt things were moving too fast."

"You've only been dating for a few days."

"Yeah, but he wants to take me home to meet his mother."

"That's fast. It usually takes at least a year and a shotgun to get a guy to take you home to meet his folks," Rachel says.

"How can I meet his mother? We haven't even had sex yet. And he didn't want to stay in O'Malley's the whole night again."

"Oh. That explains it," Rachel says.

As we are eating our double-cheese, double-pepperoni pizza, and as Heath Ledger is about to de-horse the bad guy, win the tournament, and kiss the girl, Rachel suddenly announces that she has a date with her boss.

"I've got a date with Hugh on Monday night."

*Come again?*

I don't say a word, because I don't want to put my foot in

it again now that we are friends. But I just don't believe she's serious after all she's said to me about dating my *boss*.

"Monday night is good," Tish says, nodding with approval. "A Monday-night date tells him that you are just so busy and inundated with other men that you can only fit him in on the most nondate night of the week."

"Exactly." Rachel nods her head vigorously. "And it's not like a real date, or anything. God forbid I should date my *boss*." She rolls her eyes at me. "You're right about that, Emma, although you could have been a little kinder about the way you said it." She sniffs and I decide it's time to go for World Peace. At least, peace in my own little world.

"I know. I'm sorry. I was out of order, but then I *do* know what I'm talking about. It's not every day your boss/live-in lover gets engaged before he ditches you," I say. My eyes fill with Adam tears again and Tish hands me a tissue.

"I was a little hasty about the Adam situation," Rachel says. "I didn't see the picture in the paper until after I'd spoken to you, honey. What a complete and utter *ionic bonder bastard*. He couldn't even wait for you to vacate his bed before asking another woman to marry him. . . ."

And she's off in full Rachel rant mode as she lists his varying faults, cunningly moving the conversation away from her forthcoming date with Hugh.

By this time we have all drunk a little too much of Adam's wine.

"I think we should act like guys," Tish says. "They don't worry about meeting and only dating Miss Right. They play the field without getting emotionally involved, and I think we should do the same. Instead of obsessing over finding Mr. Right, we should polydate."

"I may be desperate," I tell her, "but I have no intention of dating parrots, or any other kind of bird, for that matter."

This is a bad joke and they both scowl at me before Tish continues.

"I mean we should date more than one guy at the same

time. You know, a different guy for each night of the dating week. Anyway, I've already accepted two dates for next week. Wednesday is Greg and Thursday is Julio."

"Julio the hot waiter from the Spanish café?" Rachel raises an eyebrow and I can see she is impressed. "Tell us more."

"I went in there earlier to get a sandwich and I just kind of asked him. Do you think that was too forward of me?" she asks, chewing on her bottom lip.

"No," I tell her, envying her for being so brave.

"No. You go, girl," Rachel says. "I've been telling you both for years to take the bull by the horns and get out there."

"I think we should make a pact," Tish says, her face lighting up with the beginnings of an idea. "Tomorrow night we should, you know, hit a singles bar or something and see how many men we can pick up."

"Count me in," Rachel says. "I need to meet some new men—I can't be bothered to date the ones I've already slept with. Too boring."

"Count me out," I tell them, gloomily. "I'm too depressed to date." And then I tell them all about Norbert and Jack, but omit the part where Jack sees my boobs.

"Honey, you should think about sharing his house," Tish tells me. "You can stay here for as long as you like, but—"

"This place is just too small for both of you," Rachel finishes. "Darling, five hundred bucks a month is a song for Hoboken. Besides, it's better to live with a man you don't like—it only complicates things if you sleep with your roommate."

"Sharing with Jack is not an option," I tell them. "Especially now he thinks I'm some sad spinster with a pink vibrator. There must be something somewhere I can afford."

"Pink vibrator?" Rachel raises an eyebrow. "Honey, rewind the conversation a few seconds. How did the words *vibrator* and *Jack* get to coexist in the same sentence?"

"Peri bought it for me," I tell them, and rummage in my tote bag to show them.

They are speechless. But I don't think it's with envy.

"I'm seriously thinking of giving up men forever," I tell them. "Because the vibrator may be loud, but it *is* ten inches long. And at least it won't make me sleep on the damp patch."

"Honey," Rachel tells me with a steely glint in her eye. "You won't be needing that. I've fixed you up with a fuck."

## 12

# The Three-Day Week?

## TO DO

1. Send Stella Burgoyne huge bouquet of flowers for stealing Adam away from me. Is the least I can do.

2. Never. Again. Go. On. Arranged-by-Rachel. Blind. Date.

3. Never. Again. Flirt. With. Norbert (but will forgive myself this once. Robert Plant is, after all, *Robert Plant)*.

*Monday, Bloody Monday.*
This is never a good day for me. The first day of the working week, it is hard to muster up enthusiasm for the rat race after a long weekend of freedom away from the sewers.

I personally feel that the weekend should be extended to three, possibly four days (but on full salary, obviously), thus creating job-share opportunities and thereby eliminating unemployment in one fell swoop. It would also increase shopping opportunities, thereby stimulating economic growth. This is a *great* idea, I don't know why no one's thought of this before—it would be a great vote winner! I should have been a politician! Maybe I could be the first female president . . .

Plus, of course, it would give one extra necessary time to recover from weekend overindulgence. Our weekly dinner at Chez Nous extended from Sunday night into the wee hours of Monday morning, along with the opening of more bottles of wine, and I could cheerfully have stayed in bed for an extra few hours this morning to nurse my hangover. Hmm . . . I wonder if the government *would* agree to a three-day week?

I must mention this to Katy—if Marion Lacy has another campaign to organize, maybe she'll leave Katy alone.

We could call it Workers in Favor of Shorter Working Weeks, or WIFOSWW for short. No, not catchy. Oh, I know. How about Salaried Help Overcomes Plutocratic Predilection to Influence Nation's Growth? Appropriately, SHOPPING for short. Hmm . . . maybe not. Although a catchy, memorable acronym, no one will remember what it actually stands for. I must check the dictionary for the exact meaning of *predilection* . . . I always associate it with prominent political or entertainment figures caught *in flagrante delicto,* pants around the ankles, handcuffed to the bedpost. In a very seedy hotel, of course, in the company of a secretary or a prostitute. *Senator X resigns after admitting predilection for kinky sex . . .*

I'm really worried about Katy and Tom, though. Last night they both seemed tired and distracted. I must think up a way to get rid of Marion.

Also, the situation between Sylvester and David is not resolved, despite my assurances, yet again, to Sylvester that David wouldn't hurt him for all the tea in China.

But anyway, Mondays are especially not good when you have to endure working with your very recent ex-lover. Plus the arrogant young upstart who got the job that should, by rights, have been *yours,* i.e. Lou Russo, starts work tomorrow.

I can hardly *wait.*

This morning, despite lack of sleep (and last night's excess of alcohol) and lack of time in Tish's bathroom on account of both of us needing to get in there at the same time, I am looking spectacularly lovely, even if I do say so myself. Maybe not *spectacularly* lovely. But I do look as good as I get.

I am wearing a pale pink, flirty, gauzy dress that I bought in a chain store last year for the bargain price of forty dollars. It is my feel-good dress, and hints at curves even though I don't have many. It is sleeveless, with a slash neckline, dipping into a slight V at the back. But not too sexy, obviously, because you should never look too sexy for work. But when faced with an ex, it is always imperative to look one's best to (a) show him what he is missing and make him miss you even more, and (b) that you are *so* over him.

Plus, I have a date tonight. With Helmut. I still think it's a bit early to start dating again, but Rachel got me Helmut to say sorry for our little fall out. According to Rachel he's tall, blond, gorgeous, and completely fuckable. He's also a scientist, so he's intelligent as well as gorgeous. But if he's so gorgeous, why hasn't someone else snapped him up? Why isn't Rachel sleeping with him? Hmm . . .

Anyway, just after I arrive at work Adam calls me into his office.

This is what happens.

Adam is seated once again behind his impressive desk. I am seated once again at the other side of the desk in the lower seat, so that I have to look up to him. He looks healthy and fit and relaxed, and I can't help but wonder how much sex he and Stella had this weekend. I also can't help but wonder if I am about to be raked over the coals for (a) ruining his sofa and rug with his good wine, (b) stealing his good wine, or (c) the goat incident. And if, indeed, I will be joining the ranks of the unemployed.

Instead of any of these nonattractive options, he does a complete about-face.

"Emmeline," he says, flashing me a "let's be reasonable" smile.

I don't smile back, because to tell the truth, I feel totally unreasonable at this point.

And he's calling me Emmeline again. Interesting. Maybe he and Stella had a fight. Maybe he *misses* me and wants me back . . .

No, I'm not being weak and pathetic. But it's always good to have the chance to reject someone after *they* dumped *you* and then realize what a good thing they had after all. Of course, if he really did want me back, I wouldn't have him.

Not in a *million*. Never.

"Did you have a good break? Family all okay?"

"Yes." Get to the bloody point, Adam.

"Good. Good. Well, I just wanted to clear the air between us, you know, to make sure there are no hard feelings."

I don't say a word. I have a lot of feelings, and hard is definitely one of them.

"I think that I might have appeared to be a tad insensitive last Monday at the restaurant."

A tad insensitive? A bull in a china shop has more delicacy. But obviously I don't say this as I wait for the point of the conversation.

"Well, I just wanted to say that I'm really sorry if I hurt you. And that I forgive you for the scene you caused in the restaurant. And for ruining the sofa and the rug."

Oh, God, this is awful. I've never received such a lacking-in-remorse apology before, and his pity is so condescending that I feel like shit. Hard feelings, inexplicably, make me think of the pink vibrator and before I realize what I am going to do, I mentally transfer it to Adam's head. *Voilà!* There he is.

A talking penis!

"I just hope that we can continue to work together in an adult, reasonable way," Penis Head says, and I smile.

As his mouth opens and closes, as he blathers on and on about something or other (can't remember—too busy trying not to laugh) I imagine the vibrator pumping up and down, up and down, climaxing in a spout of verbal semen . . .

"So what do you think?"

"Sorry?" What did he just say to me?

"Emmeline, what do you say we scrub the past and start anew with our professional relationship?"

And then he does the strangest thing.

"Emmeline, it's good to meet you," he says, and holds out his hand. "I'm sure we can work very well together."

The man is an idiot. *An idiot.* Was he always like this, or was I just so lust-crazed that I didn't notice?

And I know, in that instant, what a lucky escape I had. What was I thinking, imagining I could be happy with such a completely self-obsessed jerk?

Stella can have him!

................

## Monday evening

All I can say about Helmut is stinky plants and worms!

Actually, I have rather a lot more to say about Helmut than that, and as you may have already gathered, our evening together is not a success.

As organized by Rachel, I meet him in a rather charming restaurant in Little Italy. Helmut has already arrived. At first, as the waiter leads me to the table, and to Helmut, my first impression is, well, to be frank, I really *do* wonder why Rachel has set him up with *me* and is not sleeping with him *herself.* Blond, tanned, well-dressed . . . Okay, something is definitely wrong with this picture.

As he stands, I look up. And look up. And look up some more. Helmut must be at least *six feet seven inches* tall. I wonder what the Germans put in their water.

Okay, so he's a little tall for someone who is only four feet eleven, but I won't hold it against him, I think, as I crane my neck to smile up at him. I'm the last person to have sizeist issues.

He doesn't smile back.

"You are Emma," he says, holding out an incredibly large hand.

"Helmut?" I wince as he crushes my hand.

"Sit down," he tells (orders) me.

So I do. And then an awkward silence descends. And then the conversation really gets off (not) to a flying start.

"Rachel tells me you've broken up with your boyfriend, *ja?*"

"*Ja.* I mean, yes." I wonder what else Rachel told him. Come to think about it, she didn't really tell me much about Helmut.

"I just broke up with my girlfriend too."

Oh, so *that's* why he's so unsmily and quiet. I *must* give him a chance.

"I'm sorry."

"*Nein,* sorry is not necessary. I am bored with her, so this is a good thing. The sex was not so good. Shall we order food?"

Instant feelings of inadequacy re: my sexual performance. I have not yet read the book about sex that Peri bought me for my birthday and worry that Helmut will find me lacking.

*Hold on,* I tell myself. *Get a grip. This is a casual dinner. A first date. I have not committed myself to a wild night of complicated sex.* Food. Yes! That would be good. The quicker we eat, the quicker I can get out of here.

He orders spaghetti Bolognese. So I order spaghetti Bolognese, too, because this is a truly good way to put a man off you on a first date. Once he watches you slurp spaghetti, he'll never want to see you again. Plus, this morning the scales told me that I've dropped two pounds since my split with Adam and the half-starved skeletal look is not a good one for me.

I also order a large glass of wine, because I need alcohol to cocoon me. Helmut orders tequila. Worm-infested drinks are a sure sign of Bad Things to Come. And I should know this, but instead, I try to give Helmut a real chance, and not make snap decisions about him.

"So, Helmut," I say. "Tell me about yourself." Yes, I know this is a boring, clichéd thing to say, but at least it will pass the time more quickly. "Do you have any hobbies?"

"*Ja.* Many interests. In fact, a friend of mine is involved in a fascinating study. Very exciting—he thinks that they have discovered a new species of centipede in Central Park."

"Oh? So you like insects, then?" This, also, is not a good sign. More worms.

"A centipede is not an insect," Helmut lectures me. "They are chilopods."

"Sorry." I'm not really sorry at all.

"It's completely fascinating. To discover a completely new species. Think about it! It's thought that they came from East Asia in a tropical plant maybe a hundred years ago. They are small and yellow, with eighty-four legs and pincerlike jaws."

At this point our food arrives, and I think a swift change of subject is in order because I do not want to discuss worms or chilopods, or any other sort of wormlike creature while eating spaghetti.

And when the waiter brings the Parmesan cheese, I nod my head vigorously (good protein) and search my brain for something else we can talk about.

"Are you going on vacation?" I ask him brightly. This is inspired. This is definitely a safe subject.

"*Ja.* I went to England in May."

Silence descends again, so I try harder.

"And did you have fun?" I take a gulp of wine.

"It was highly interesting," Helmut tells me, slurping spaghetti in a very unattractive way. "I go to Kew Botanical Gardens to view the flowering of a very rare plant— *Amorphophallus titanum.*"

I didn't quite get the whole name, but the *phallus* part definitely registered. Must be my lack of sex.

"Does it look like a penis, then?" Oh, good question, Emmeline.

"*Ja.* A giant red phallus is a very good way to describe it. It's extremely difficult to propagate, but you know the most fascinating thing about it?"

"No." But I'm sure you're about to tell me.

"It blooms only very rarely, but when it does, it gives off a pungent smell. Like the smell of feces and the dead carcass of an animal. And it's so strong you can smell it a kilometer away."

"Fancy that!"

As Helmut goes on to tell me even more about his stinky plant, and as he shovels huge quantities of spaghetti into his mouth, I realize that I've lost my appetite.

Worms and stinky plants do not go well with spaghetti and stinky cheese.

After we've finished (and after Helmut has finished my food), we leave the restaurant and hail a cab.

Just before I climb in, Helmut turns to me.

"So now we have sex, *ja?* Your apartment or mine?"

I wonder what the German is for "not in this lifetime"?

..................

## Tuesday morning

"I hate him. I *bloody* hate him," I hiss down the phone to Tish.

Yet again I am in the restroom. I should just move my desk in here and be done, because I've spent more time in the restroom over the past few days than in my cubicle. Daphne-the-ivy has become my new best friend, and the other women on my floor suspect that I either have a strange bathroom fetish, or that I am the cleaning woman. Or possibly that I've become a lesbian because of my disillusionment with the male sex, and am trying to meet new potential partners.

"Calm down, sweetie," Tish says. "If you need a stronger curse, just say *fuck*. You'll feel better—it's so liberating, I promise. What *exactly* did fucking Adam say?"

"He's made me Lou Russo's fucking *nursemaid!* Talk about adding insult to injury. He's given Lou Russo *complete* power to order me about at will."

"Or maybe he's given you the hangman's noose."

"Come again?"

"He wasn't specific about what exactly you have to do to help Lou?"

"No."

"Well, don't you see? Give Lou enough rope and he'll hang himself. Be nice, be pleasant, but stick firmly to your job guidelines."

"You mean like don't work late, don't do any extras, just do my job?"

"Not exactly. Cause disruption. If Lou needs something, let it take precedence over Adam's work. That kind of thing."

Actually, she has a good point. I swing myself up onto the counter as Angie comes out of the cubicle.

"Hmm . . . You might be right," I say, chewing glumly on a fingernail. "I'll have to think about it."

"I'll think about it, too. I'm sure we can come up with something. Oh, gotta go—a divine man's just coming into the store. See you later."

As Angie washes and dries her hands, I chew on the fingernail more aggressively as I mentally chew on Tish's words.

"You should take your friend's advice," Angie says, catching my eye as she reapplies her lipstick.

I am so shocked that Cruella has spoken to me without prompting, I can only stare at her with open-mouthed surprise.

"You give 'em hell, do you hear?" she tells me as she pauses at the door. "We girls have to stick together."

Before I can absorb her words, my cell phone rings.

"I hate him. I *detest* the motherfucking bastard," Rachel hisses down the phone to me.

Her night was as bad as mine, it would seem. I think better not to mention Helmut to her right now, though.

"Oh. Would this be Hugh?"

She launches into a spleen-venting bout of cursing, and it's obvious that last night's date was not a success.

"What happened, sweetie?" I soothe her.

"I just don't get it. I mean I just don't fucking get it. I'm pretty, aren't I?"

"You're gorgeous, hon," I tell her, because she is. "Was last night that awful? Did you have a terrible time?"

"We had a—*quite* a nice time. He's not too bad away from work, which was a surprise. He was fairly charming and funny. So, we have dinner and he's making me laugh, and we're getting on like a house on fire, and he's sort of flirting with me. And I'm kind of flirting back. . . ."

"So what's the problem?" I prompt her.

"So how come he didn't so much as make a tiny pass at me?" Rachel switches back to rant mode. "I mean, the guy offers to drive me home. He insists on walking me to the front door, even after I've told him about my black belt and that muggers are not a problem. So I assume he wants to, you know, come in. For a nightcap. Followed by sex."

"But you don't want to have sex with him. Do you?"

"No, of course not, but a girl has her pride. It's always nice to be asked, just so you can say no. Anyway, Emma, you've made me lose my thread. Where was I?"

"Front door. Nightcap followed by sex."

"Yes. So we get to the door, he takes the key from me and opens it for me, and then—God, this is so humiliating."

And she's off again, cursing and generally suggesting Hugh should do physically impossible things to himself.

"Yes, but what did he actually do?" I ask, to get her back on track.

"He hands me back my keys, shakes my hand, and tells me what a *pleasant evening* he's had, and how he hopes we can *do it again* sometime. Hell, Emma, the man *shook my hand*. Not even a peck on the cheek."

"But that's . . ." *Unbelievable,* but I don't say that because it will only make matters worse. But it is unbelievable, because a guy would have to be dead a week not to hit on Rachel. Think about the most gorgeous woman you've ever seen, then double it. That's how stunning she is.

"That's . . . very civilized of him," I say, as I desperately grapple for the right words. "Think about it, Rachel. You two don't exactly get on that well. And you still have to work together, so maybe he's trying not to complicate things. Maybe last night was just a way to try to get to know you better, so the two of you can get along in the lab without throwing test tubes at each other. I mean, I'll bet leaving you last night was the hardest thing he ever had to do, I'll bet he took a cold shower as soon as he got home. But you've got to see it from his point of view." Whew.

"You know, maybe you've got a point. Maybe I should torture him a little."

I have visions of handcuffs and whips.

"Er, maybe not."

"Oh, I don't mean in a *bad* way," Rachel says, and she sounds very cheerful indeed. "I mean in a *sexy* way. You know, brushing against him, stuff like that. To make him suffer. By the time I've finished, he'll be *begging* me to let him fuck me. Thanks, Emma, you've been really helpful," she tells me, and hangs up.

*Oh God, I've created a monster.*

When I get back to my cubicle, Lou is waiting for me.

"Emma, can you get me some coffee?"

He has walked *all the way across the office,* away from the coffee cubicle, to stand and wait at my desk for me. His mission complete, he now strolls all the way back across the office to his desk.

I spend the rest of the afternoon plotting my strategy.

................

**Wednesday afternoon**

This morning, the scales told me that I have dropped another pound. So in desperation I tried one of the bodybuilder shakes that Katy and Tom so kindly bought me for my birthday. And you know what? It tasted like shit. But I drank it anyway, because it's also supposed to stimulate my appetite.

It's *definitely* working.

When Lou sent me to get him a doughnut for his morning snack, I walked the extra six blocks to the really nice pastry shop. The alternative shop, only a half block from the office, has awful cardboard-flavored doughnuts, so the extra five-and-a-half-block journey is definitely worth it. Besides, it's such a lovely July day, I really didn't mind the walk. And I got a doughnut for Adam and me, too.

Then, when Lou sent me to get him a lox and cream cheese bagel for lunch, I was hungry *again,* so I killed two birds with one stone and got one of those for me, too. Adam didn't want one—he had a lunch meeting. But I still (obviously) took my full-hour lunch break. I usually just eat at my desk, but today I am trying out my new work-to-the-rule-book campaign. I spent my time in the park enjoying the summer sun instead. I think it's going rather well.

"Emma, can you type this for me right away?"

"Sure, Lou." I smile, putting aside Adam's urgent cost report to type Lou's *really urgent* letter to Requisitions. He needs many things, including a new computer (this is fine, because the spare computer is about ten years old and its RAM isn't what it used to be), a new desk (I do not understand this, because my dearly departed ex-boss's old desk is lovely), and a multitude of other miscellaneous items. His letter of explanation *(I need a new trashcan because . . .)* is *terrible.* How Lou graduated from college I will never know (Daddy has friends in high places?), because the guy cannot string two sentences together. But I will faithfully type his report. I will not actually change it, I will only correct his (many) spelling mistakes.

"Emma, can you get me some coffee?"

"Sure, Lou," I say. "No trouble. Adam?" I pop my head around his office door for at least the tenth time today. "I'm just getting coffee for Lou. Can I get you another?"

"More coffee?" Adam looks up from the papers he's studying and frowns. "At this rate I'll have caffeine poisoning before dinner. No. Thanks."

*Ohhhkaayy.* I think I'm making my point.

"Emma, I need some help with this report for Adam." Lou places a file in front of me. It is for the Burgoyne campaign. Oh joy.

"We need to come up with some fresh new ideas. I thought you might be able to, you know, suggest something."

"Fresh new ideas—sorry, Lou, that's just not me. That would be your department, being an account manager. If you need anything typed, or fetched, that would be my department on account of being a secretary." I say all of this with such a sweet smile on my face, I don't think he realizes that I'm being sarcastic.

"Well, I've come up with a couple of things we can play around with. Maybe you could take a look? Read what I've proposed, see what you think. If anything kinda leaps out at you as you're reading them, just let me know. Oh, I also need you to check out the on-line video libraries—I want you to track down the type of photos I've stipulated for my proposals." Before I can tell him no, he strolls back to his desk.

I open the file.

These are Lou's "original" ideas.

1. Cute animals in funny ass-turned-toward-camera poses, with clever captions underneath (he hasn't specified what these clever captions are; he's just written "clever captions").

2. Supermodels dressed as puppies. They are joyfully cavorting around the house, pushing rolls of Burgoyne toilet tissue.

As I sit here amazed by his audacity, the boy genius strolls past me, attaché case in hand.

"See you tomorrow, Emma."

If he can leave at five on the dot, so can I.


Thank God it's Friday!

Ten more minutes of this horrible week to go and then I'm free for the weekend.

I have to start hunting for an apartment tomorrow, I really do. Maybe I should call at a couple of real-estate agents on my way home from work. Maybe I'll go to the gym instead. Maybe I'll go shopping . . .

I am trying to distract myself.

Stella has been closeted in Adam's office, with Adam, for the best part of an hour. The door is closed, and I think I heard it click as Adam locked it from the inside. I *just know* they are having wild sex on his desk. Why else lock the door?

I am still yearning for the old days when Adam was still an unknown, Godlike quantity, and Johnny was still butt-patting me when the telephone rings.

"Emma, babe?" Norbert.

Oh. Peri obviously gave him my work number. After the Helmut disaster, I'm not in the mood for Norbert.

"Just callin' about that date. You know how you said . . ."

As the door to Adam's office opens, and Adam and Stella come out looking fuck-drunk, I stop thinking about how to nicely but firmly say no to Norbert.

"How lovely to hear from you," I say brightly down the telephone. "I'd love to go on a date with you."

Adam looks across and frowns. Serves him right.

"That's cool, babe," Norbert tells me. "I got Plant tickets for the Hammerstein Ballroom on the twenty-fourth."

*Robert* Plant? My God-among-men *Robert Plant?*

I instantly forget Adam and Stella (and Norbert) as I fall into daydream mode. I casually wait at the stage door as he leaves (after a sublime performance, obviously). Our eyes meet across the throngs of other fans. Robert smiles at me. I smile back. Violins play in the background as the crowds disappear and Robert whisks me away in his limousine.

"That's great," Norbert tells me. "I'll call you next week, babe." Norbert hangs up.

I can't believe it. I'm going to see *Robert Plant.*

"Emma." Adam pauses in front of my desk. "That wasn't a personal call, was it?"

"Of course not," I lie. "I'm totally familiar with company policy," I tell him primly, but can't help the smug smile.

On this triumphant note, I head for Hoboken and the gym to work off my Lou/Adam/Norbert-related stress. The apartment hunting can wait until tomorrow. *Robert Plant! Y-e-s!*

I am pounding on the treadmill.

I am wearing a washed-out tank and shabby sweat pants.

I am totally out of breath and plastered in sweat from my exertions.

This is not a good look for me.

So, of course, this is the perfect time for me to bump into someone I really don't want to bump into.

"Emma."

It's Jack.

# 13

......................................................................................

## Polydating

### TO DO

1. Purchase new, sexy gym clothes.

2. Ensure makeup is perfect before going to gym.

3. Ensure hair is perfect before going to gym.

"Jack," I gasp, hopelessly out of breath but trying not to show it. "So, you've joined the gym? This is my gym. What a coincidence."

What an idiot. Babble, babble, babble. Why am I even bothering? This is only Jack. It's not like I want to impress him or anything.

I push back a lock of my damp bangs in a vain and point-less effort to make myself look better, and nearly fall off the damned machine, because I've forgotten that I haven't mas-tered it without hands yet. Clumsy is not the effect I was try-ing for but it seems I am fated to embarrass myself in front of Jack.

"Whoa, there." Jack steadies me, placing one hand on my spine, and the other on my arm. Actually, that feels rather nice . . . Hang on just a minute. This is Jack. It must be my lack of sex . . .

"You okay?"

"Sure." I beam back at him without slowing my pace. I am

really struggling to control my breathing now, because I'm surrounded by physically perfect people who can probably run for hours on this machine without even breaking a sweat. I am *so* not going to pant and show myself up for the couch potato I am.

"Because for a moment," he says, "I figured you were so impressed with my masculine physique you were going to fall at my feet."

Trust Jack to assume he's just so appealing that all women will instantly want him. But he does look really hot in black Lycra and I am not the only one who thinks this. It hasn't escaped my notice that most of the women in the gym are eyeing him like hungry lionesses who've just spotted a meaty buffalo.

*And he knows it.*

"Actually, Jack, I joined the gym to get fit—not to check out the prime rib." I know I sound prissy, but really, the ego on this man is unbelievable. "You're not that irresistible."

"I have my moments," he says, as his eyes follow the shapely brunette who is strutting her stuff for all she's worth. As she passes Jack, she turns and smiles at him.

"Hi," Jack says to her, and she nearly swoons.

I mean, *really.*

"Jack, you ready for your fitness assessment?" Shelly, the pretty, blonde personal trainer, beams at him.

"You bet," Jack says, then winks at me.

"God, you're such a slut," I tell him.

Two women in as many seconds. How lucky is that?

"Slut works for me every time. See you around."

*Oh, I hope not.*

"Is that a threat or a promise?" I quip, as he walks toward the weight section.

"Depends on your point of view," he says.

This is the perfect end to my day. I refuse to stay here and watch Jack charm the birdies out of the trees, so I give up on the gym and go back to Tish's place.

.................

## Saturday afternoon

God, it's so hot I can barely breathe. Humidity is high, my stress levels are even higher, and I have spent the day depressing myself by checking out apartments that I cannot afford.

My last appointment was to view a great, but very tiny, two-bedroom apartment. It's totally perfect for me. Nicely finished floors, close to the PATH and the ferry, close to all my friends. Light and airy, the kitchen has all new appliances. The only problem with this apartment is that I *cannot afford it*. The rent is more money than I make each month. And even if I could find a roommate to split the costs, I would barely have enough to pay bills, and food would be a luxury.

This is the same story for all of the apartments I have either viewed or seen details for. I mean, I knew Hoboken had become more expensive in recent years, but these prices are just so . . . so unfair!

Oh, but I yearn for the old days when Tish and I shared the apartment upstairs from Mrs. Hocksted, our landlady. It was a perfect arrangement. Nicely situated on Park, the apartment was spacious, convenient, and most importantly, it was only eight hundred dollars a month. And that was between the two of us. *Four hundred dollars each a month*. I can't believe I was so stupid to give it up completely. Oh, how I *wish* I'd kept the apartment when I moved in with Adam. Even paying the full rent by myself is less than half of the rent I would currently have to pay. I wish I hadn't spent so much on expensive dinners with Adam.

Mrs. Hocksted's apartment was a unique opportunity, though. Dad knows her son, and Mrs. Hocksted was more interested in renting the apartment to reliable, professional, well-behaved adults than making a fortune from us. So of course, Tish and me immediately sprang to Dad's mind. Being nearly deaf, Mrs. Hocksted thought we were wonderful, quiet girls. I wonder if she's rerented the place? Of course she's rerented the place, why would she not rent it at that price?

As I trudge down Washington, I decide that I really need one of Rufus's banana-granola muffins. I know he is *The Enemy,* and that Tish has declared his deli no-man's land, but desperate times call for desperate measures. I glance around furtively to check that I have not been spotted, and duck into the cool, air-conditioned interior.

Rufus is in his usual place behind the counter. He barely glances up from his newspaper as I approach.

"Hi, Rufus," I say.

Now, although we are boycotting the deli, technically this has not been my local deli for the past three and a half months, so I don't feel uncomfortable that Rufus might have noticed my part in our one-week boycott.

"Emma. The usual?"

"Yeah, please."

You see? This is what I want. Rufus knows my needs. He doesn't have to be told that the banana-granola muffin with the skim-milk, chocolate cappuccino is what I want. Why can't everything in this life be as simple?

I sit in the corner at a table for two, and dig out my notebook and pen. I have to do some math and see just exactly what I *can* afford. But the main problem is just how much money I need for the deposit (usually one and a half month's rent) and the agent's fee (again, one and a half month's rent), plus one month's rent in advance.

Okay. If I want this apartment, I need to come up with ten thousand dollars before I even get the key. *Ten thousand dollars.* I mean, that's just not the kind of money you have lying around, is it? And even if I find a roommate to share the costs, we'd still have to pay five thousand each.

Actually, there is one person I know who has this kind of money lying around. My dad. But I will *not* ask him, because (a) I'm too old to ask my parents to bail me out—that is just too pathetic, (b) he has Peri and the twins to take care of—orthodontic bills and college funds to pay out for, and (c) he's fifty-six and getting close to retirement age.

I'll just have to figure out a way to do this by myself.

Of course, my car will have to go. If I have to spend such a fortune on rent, car loan payments are out of the question. I really *hate* this idea. My car is the last symbol of my adult achievements. I have no home and no boyfriend, and my career is down the drain. But I do have my car. I *love* my car. If I have to sell it, I will have *failed in everything!*

I lay my head on the pad and close my eyes. This is so much worse than I imagined.

"Here," Rufus says, placing my food on the table. "Y'okay? Only yer don't look okay."

"I'll live. Unfortunately." I take a sip of the cappuccino and feel instantly better.

"Not the trouble with yer man, is it? Only I saw his picture in the paper with that other one . . . don't mean to intrude, just, you know . . ."

I love his Irish accent. And I'm touched that he cares so much about me.

"Thanks, Rufus, but Adam is the least of my worries," I say. "I'm just so—so—pissed. I mean, I just didn't realize how high rents are around here."

"Yeah, tell me about it. Mind if I sit?"

It is then that I notice that Rufus has brought two cups of cappuccino. It seems he's feeling chatty, and I'm curious. And let's face it, I don't have anything better to do.

"Sure, be my guest."

We sit companionably for a few minutes while I attack my muffin and Rufus sips at his cappuccino, occasionally shaking his head with gloomy resignation.

"It's all the Manhattan yuppies," he says, finally.

"Sorry?"

"That's why the prices are so shite high. S'all them new developments along yer Hudson River, there, don't ye see? Easy access by PATH and ferry to Manhattan. Had to happen sooner or later." He scowls as if it is the end of the world. "I mean, it's good for business and all—got a lot of new customers. But it's changing the feel of the place. Hoboken used to be like a family town, now it's full of all the upwardly mobile types. It's a shite deal, so it is."

"There's nothing wrong with being a Manhattan yuppie," I tell him. "I aspire to Manhattan upwardly mobile myself, but now it seems I'm doomed to sleep on Tish's sofa forever."

"Oh, sorry. Didn't mean no insult to yer. I like yuppies, really. . . ."

"It's okay, Rufus, I was just teasing you."

"Oh, right then. You staying with Tish, then?"

"Yes." I take another sip.

He's definitely interested in that piece of information. I thought he might be, which is why I mentioned it. I may be wrapped up in my own woes, but I can see the obvious when I want to. This is probably one of the longest conversations I've ever had with Rufus. And I know it's not just for the pleasure of my company.

"So she's all right, then? Only I haven't seen her around a deal recently."

"No, she's been busy. You know, with the store and everything."

"Oh." He sips thoughtfully for a few seconds. "I've seen her in O'Malley's a few times."

"Is that right?"

"Yeah."

Oh, call me sadistic if you like, but I'm loving every moment of this. It's obvious that he's really into Tish, and that he misses her, so that's good, isn't it?

"With a guy," he says, rather pointedly.

"Yes. Well, she's a very attractive woman. No reason why she shouldn't be in there with a guy, is there?"

"So she's got a new boyfriend, then?"

"No, not exactly," I say, wondering how much to tell him without being disloyal to Tish, but enough to give Rufus a good, hard nudge in the right direction. "But she won't find Mr. Right if she stays home every night, will she now?"

"I suppose not. Pretty girl like her. I guess she gets asked out a lot."

"Yes."

"Okay, well, nice talking to yer," Rufus says as he gets to his feet. "Take care of yerself, girl."

"Thanks."

"Oh," Rufus adds. "I dunno if this is a good idea, but . . ."

*Come on Rufus, spit it out. Ask me more about Tish.*

"If yer desperate, like, I've got a spare bedroom in me apartment upstairs. I own the whole building, so there'd be no trouble with landlords and the like. S'probably a bad idea . . ."

Now that's one I wasn't expecting!

"It's really kind of you," I say, "but I'm sure I'll find something."

"Right you are, then. But if you're stuck—"

"I'll bear it in mind."

Well, that was a very interesting little chat. I wonder if I should mention this to Tish? Of course, that would be tantamount to admitting that I've ventured into enemy territory, but I could make out like I did it on purpose, just to gauge Rufus's feelings.

I think it best not to mention that Rufus asked me to move in with him, though.

But I forget about Rufus and Tish a few moments later.

Just as I turn into Tish's street, I see Katy, with Alex in his stroller, outside Tish's door. Alex, oh sweet and perfect child, is sleeping under his canopy. But Katy is crying.

"Katy," I say as I cross the street. "Whatever is the matter?"

"Emma, I'm so pleased to see you." She blows her nose on a tissue. "Can we go inside? I'm hiding from Marion Lacy and the MASS mothers."

Fifteen minutes later, she's calmed down enough to tell me the tale. Because there's always a tale when Marion's involved.

"She's just so . . . so pushy," Katy says, and I sigh. "I feel like she's hijacked my life," she adds, and I sigh again. "It's not that I want to ditch the MASS mothers completely, but I do have a life. And I don't want to spend every waking moment either planning the latest campaign or dragging poor little Alex off to his next class. I'm a terrible mother."

"No, you're a great mother," I tell her, because she is. "All you have to do is to look at Alex to see what a great mother you are." It's true. He's a completely fab kid. "But . . ." I feel my way carefully, "but, well, maybe Marion is just a little bit intense . . ."

I don't want to say too much. I don't want to offend Katy.

"But Marion Lacy's a complete *nightmare*," Katy says, and I giggle with her, because she's right.

"Well, maybe just a bit." I should be a diplomat.

"You know what? She's completely awful. Alex really doesn't need all those classes," Katy says.

"Well . . ." I don't want to give her the wrong impression. "I think it's great he has so many activities to stimulate him—but maybe a few too many . . ."

"He loves the art class," Katy announces, suddenly. "I think I'll just keep that class for him. But everything else goes. The e-mail account definitely goes. Who ever heard of a two-year-old needing e-mail?"

My point exactly, but I don't say this.

"But what about Marion?" I ask instead.

"I'll just have to face up to her, won't I? I just don't get it. How could I let her run my life like this? And poor Tom— he's working such long hours at the moment, I don't want to worry him. But what do you think I should do?"

. . . . . . . . . . . . . . . .

**Saturday night**

Despite wanting to stay in and mope, Tish and Rachel decide that we will hit the hip Hoboken bars because, after all, we are hip young women. And this is what hip, happening

young people do on Saturday night. Plus, they are deadly serious about the polydating thing, and are determined to
meet as many men as possible (I think they may have made
a bet with each other). Unfortunately, it seems they cannot
meet men unless I accompany them.

"It won't be the same without you," Tish wheedles.

"You're coming, okay? Because we're your oldest, closest
friends and we will never speak to you again if you don't,"
Rachel says, leaving me no option but to comply.

I could argue if I really wanted to. But I also don't want to
mope alone. I prefer to mope in packs, so I'll just do it in the
hip bars instead of at home.

It is definitely a casual night, and I am wearing khaki pants
and a black tank. Tish has done something spiky-but-hip with
my hair, and something dramatic with my makeup. (Also
hip—how come I can't manage this look when I do it myself?)

This is a *fab* look for me.

So while I feel like an emotional punching bag, I know
that I look good. *Man, am I hot!*

But I'm still worried about Katy.

"But what do you think she should do?" I ask, as I glug
down my wine.

"Will you stop obsessing?" Rachel tells me. "Katy is a
strong, sensible woman. She has to stand up to Marion herself. And she'll do it, too, when the time's right."

"You know, I think it's the stress of having children," Tish
says thoughtfully. "I mean, Katy's stuck at home all day with
Alex, and delightful though he is, it must be hard for her. She
used to be so career-minded. You can't just switch off all that
ambition when you stay home to have a family. I mean,
where does it all go?"

"Remind me never to have any brats," Rachel says, wrinkling her nose.

"Don't think anyone *needs* to remind me," I add, glumly
envisioning my future years of man-free, baby-free spinsterhood.

"Remind me never to get married, either." Rachel drains her drink. "Men have it all ways. They get to have careers and families, without any disruption to their little routines. And what happens to their wives?" she asks rhetorically.

Tish and I have more sense than to actually answer this, because after a significant pause, she's off again.

"I'll tell you what happens to these unsung heroines of domesticity. Twenty years down the road they've sacrificed their promising careers in favor of child-rearing. They've cooked, cleaned, soothed, wiped shitty asses, cleaned up vomit. And what do they have to show for it?" Rachel, after a couple of drinks, is once again in full rant mode.

"I'll tell you what they're left with," she says. "Stretch marks, bags under their eyes, and cellulite. Unless they happen to be married to a plastic surgeon, which is even worse, because then they're all getting face lifts and liposuction, and pandering to society's ideals. But my point is, all they're left with is an ungrateful fucking spouse, who more often than not leaves them in favor of a younger fucking model, and they don't even have a 401k to show for it. Remind me to send my mother some flowers. Another fucking round, girls?"

"Whew." I grin at Tish. "I thought for a moment there that we were about to get the 'why women should rule the world' speech again. Not that women shouldn't rule the world, because I do believe it would be a better place—"

"So tell me again," Tish says.

"Well, she's basically going to tell Marion that she needs to spend more time with Tom and Alex—"

"Not Katy. I mean Rufus."

"Oh, I *see*."

We've done this at least ten times already, but I expect we'll do it another hundred so she can extract every possible nuance of meaning from his words.

"Not that I'm interested in him anymore," she lies.

"Course not."

"Come on. Quick, while Rachel's getting drinks."

So I launch into another telling of what-Rufus-said-next, but remember not to include the part where I get asked to move in with him.

"I can't believe you know more about him than me. I didn't even know he owned that building."

"Yes, Tish," I tell her patiently. "But you don't speak to him. If you want him, go in for muffins and coffee and just speak to him. Ask him out. Take him on a date, then sleep with him. See? It's simple."

God, I'm so good at giving advice, what a pity I don't listen to myself more often.

"I told you, I'm not interested," she says, blushing slightly because we both know this is not the truth. "He's missed his chance. I'm seeing Julio again on Tuesday."

"The café guy? Nice pecs. Nice body, generally."

"Yup. Oh, but don't call him that. He's very sensitive about being classified as a waiter. He's a biology student, he just works in his uncle's shop to earn extra money."

"Well, if he's a biology student, I suppose that means he must know his way around the female anatomy," I say.

"That's what I thought." Tish giggles. "So, I figured I might even get as far as four dates with him. It's been too long since I had sex."

"Well, you can always borrow my mechanical friend, if the need takes you. Talking about sex, take a look over at Rachel. I think she's solved her Saturday night no-date problem."

Rachel is happily flirting with a dark-haired guy in Ralph Lauren. I just hope she remembers to order our drinks. Thinking of drinks reminds me that I really need to fight my way through the crowded bar to the restroom.

The music is loud, but this is a great bar. Maxwell's, on Washington, is the hip place to be on Saturday night. It is heaving with packs of beautiful young things, all out to have a good time.

And as I fight my way back through the packs of beautiful young things (of whom, thanks to Tish, I am one), a familiar hand grabs my arm. Jack, of course, because I can't seem to move these days without bumping into him.

"Hi," he shouts above the din. And he seems so pleased to see me that for a moment I forget that this is Jack. Plus several glasses of wine have added to my general euphoric do-you-think-I'm-sexy frame of mind.

"Hi yourself. You having a good time?"

"Sure. This place is great. Can I buy you a drink?"

It's not every day of the week that attractive young men dressed in black Calvin Klein offer to buy me a drink, so I am just about to say yes, and to hell with the consequences, when he adds a disclaimer.

"You know Kelly, don't you?" He points toward the bar, where the brunette from last night's gym encounter is pointedly waiting for him to return. She is also pointedly sending me daggerlike "get your own man, girl" glares.

"Actually, I'm here with friends," I say.

For a moment he looks disappointed. At least I think he does, but then he smiles his Jack-the-Wolf smile.

"Okay, Emma. Maybe another time."

When hell freezes over, sure, because I can think of nothing I'd like better than to play third wheel on one of Jack's dates.

"Sure. See you."

I decide not to say anything to Rachel or Tish about Jack, because I'd only have to introduce them to him, and that would complicate things, wouldn't it?

When I get back to our table, Rachel has returned with our drinks, plus her handsome guy. Plus his two handsome friends. Marco, Steve, and Tony. Tony, it seems, is for me (on account of being the shortest, but still very handsome—all dark and Italian). Tony is dressed in black Calvin Klein and he's bought me a drink.

*Hel-lo.*

Unfortunately, Tony's conversation does not match up to his looks. After we have done the "hi-it's-nice-to-meet-you-do-you-come-here-often" thing, his next line is not promising.

"So, you're British?"

"Yeah, kind of." Explaining about my mother and father, and how they got divorced before I was born, but my mother is an equal opportunities parent so she made sure I spent equal amounts of time living and studying in America so I'd know my dad, is complicated. I usually save it for at least the third or fourth date.

"So, have you ever, like, met Tony Blair? Hey, I've got the same name as him, what a coincidence."

God. How many men in the world are there, do you think, who are called Tony? I ask you! This guy is definitely arm candy, but I get the feeling he's not the sharpest knife in the kitchen. And I really hate this particular question. Trust me, I have been asked this several times before because men think it's a really funny chat-up line.

Now I could be mean and say, (a) "Well, Tony, the population of London is, according to the National Statistics Office, about seven point four million at the last count, so the chances of my having bumped into Tony Blair are pretty slim, don't you think?" Or (b) "Of course, and I have tea at Buckingham Palace with the Queen every time I visit London." Or I could say (c) "Of *course!* I went to school with him." You see, I *did* go to grade school with a snotty little kid who just happened to have the same name. Or I could even say (d) "No, but my mother knows Tony and Cherie."

Because she does actually know them. I'm not sure how it happened, but shortly after Tony was elected for his second term of office, she got invited to tea at Number Ten Downing Street (along with a gaggle of other top-left-wing barristers).

Anyway, while I'm pondering my reply, I glance across at the bar and see Jack watching me. As I catch his eye, he gives me a huge grin and winks, so then my answer is sealed. It's got to be either (c) or (d).

"Actually, I went to school with him," I tell Tony.

"Get outta here."

Yes, I would like to get out of here.

"No, really." I bat my eyes at him and launch into the tale of how it was all just a big coincidence, and before I know it I am in full flirt mode. I can't have Jack thinking I'm some loser spinster without a sex life, can I?

Later, much later, after several more glasses of wine, Rachel has disappeared back to her apartment with Marco. Steve is walking Tish home, and Tony and me are following several paces behind them. The wine has definitely made Tony more attractive, intellectually speaking, because my brain has definitely taken a vacation at this point.

When we arrive at the apartment, Steve and Tish are kissing goodnight. So Tony and me kiss goodnight. And although Tony is not exactly Einstein, he certainly knows how to kiss. And just as things are getting more than a little heated, he pauses.

"Can I come in?"

Now, although not a prude, I'm with Tish on the four-dates-before-a-fuck principle.

"Not tonight," I say. "Tish and me share a very small apartment. No privacy."

"Oh, that's no problem," he says, kissing me again.

God, can he *kiss*. It's ages since I just had a good old make-out session, with no more expectation than tongues, and hands on my butt.

"Me and Steve, we've done this before."

"Hmm?"

*Kiss me more*, I think.

"You know. A foursome. It's kinda sexy, you know?"

## 14

.....................................................................

# Misery Loves Company

### TO DO

1. Drink less.

2. Get Caller ID for Tish.

3. Become a lesbian? Would certainly remove need for larger breasts (unless lesbians also prefer women with bigger boobs). Would also avoid kinky foursome suggestions from men named Tony (unless lesbians also like foursomes).

**Sunday morning, 8 A.M.**

Heath Ledger is about to dehorse the bad guy, win the tournament, and kiss the girl (this would be me, on account of this being my dream).

"Kiss me, Heath, kiss me," I tell him, as he gathers me in his arms and lowers his head. Mmmm . . .

And then I'm rudely awakened to the reality of my hangover by the ringing telephone.

God, I *wish* I hadn't drunk so much wine last night. God, I *wish* Tish had an extension in the bedroom, so that she could answer it. God, I wish *even more* that she had Caller ID. She's been in this place six weeks and hasn't even arranged for voicemail yet. Maybe I should do that for her as my way of saying thanks for letting me crash here.

I drag myself off the sofa, careful not to move my head too much on account of all the large hammers banging on my brain, and pick up. As I do this, I stub my toe on the end table, but manage to save the lamp, which is good.

" 'Lo," I croak, carefully steadying the mock Tiffany lamp.

"Hello, dear," says the older, feminine Irish voice on the other end. "Would this be Miss Emmeline Taylor I have the pleasure of speaking to?"

"Yeah. Whosis?"

"Emma, dear—oh, is it all right if I call you Emma?"

"Sure." I yawn, wondering if this is part of my dream, because if it *is* part of my dream, it is very rude of her to interrupt before I get to properly kiss Heath. I am also thinking that at this time of the morning she can call me anything she likes.

"My name is Sister Mary Immaculate from the Convent of St. Staples. How are you today?"

I am immediately overcome with waves of guilt, because I am speaking to a woman of God, and am wearing only a pair of panties and a tank. And what is more, last night's wine has turned my blood to alcohol. I'm truly sorry for all the blasphemous *oh God* thoughts I had just seconds ago, too. Just as well Tish and me didn't have a foursome with Steve and Tony last night . . .

Euch! The very thought of it increases the acid buildup in my stomach.

"Er, I'm fine, Sister," I tell her, straightening, because although she cannot see me, and although I am not a Catholic, I am very respectful of nuns in general. "And how are you today?"

"Well, it's very sweet of you to ask. I can tell from your voice that you're a very kind young lady. And actually, apart from the trouble with me arthritis, I'm grand."

"Er, well that's very good to hear. Er, what can I do for you?" I make a mental note to stop preceding everything I say with "er"—sounds so like I have no brain cells. Actually,

I probably don't have many of those left on account of the alcohol. Oh, God, I need some water. Oops. Another blasphemous thought. *Concentrate on the nun,* I tell myself.

"Well, Emma, it's more a case of what you can do for God.
We at St. Staples are having a wee problem with our roof
fund, and were wondering if you might see your way to helping us raise the money by pledging your support."

It takes a few moments for her words to sink in.

I do not believe it.

I have been here for only two weeks and the telemarketer
crowd have *tracked me down.* My *mail* hasn't even found me
yet! And what's more, after all the times I have been rude to
them, they are punishing me with a nun.

*I can't be rude to a nun!*

"Er, actually, Sister, it's a bit of a difficult time for me at
the moment—"

"Oh, but St. Staples needs you, dear. You see, if we don't
fix the roof, we can't have all the poor, homeless, battered
wives sleeping in the vestry. You do have a roof over your
head, don't you, dear?"

"Yes," I say, very quietly.

"And no abusive husband?"

"Nope. No husband of any description."

"Well, then."

She doesn't prompt me any more, she just waits for my
guilty conscience to kick in. Which of course, it does.

"Well, I could manage five dollars . . ."

"Actually, Emma, our bronze donation, the minimum donation, starts at fifteen. Would that be all right, then? And if
you like, we can even do it now, over the telephone. We take
Visa and Mastercard, and any other major credit and debit
cards, so if you could just give me your details . . ."

At this point my guilt begins to seep away. I have just offered, of my own free(ish) will, to donate five dollars to her
charity. But is my five dollars good enough? Oh, *no.* Because
the minimum *acceptable* donation is *fifteen dollars.* Plus, giv-

ing out credit-card information on the telephone to unknown third parties is stupid. Even if it *is* to a nun.

"Er, sorry, Sister, my credit card is maxed out."

It's very embarrassing to confess this to a nun.

"Oh, well, I'm very sorry to hear that. You know, 'tis the
Devil's own influence, persuading young women to spend
money they don't have. You must be more careful in future,
Emma."

"Oh, I will."

"So I'll send you the details through the mail, and I can
rely on your check for fifteen dollars by return?"

"Absolutely," I lie. And cross my fingers.

"You have a lovely day, now."

"Definitely a scam," Tish tells me as she gets ready to go to
the gym. I could do with a good workout myself, but I have
to look at more apartments.

"I've never heard of nuns canvassing for money on the
telephone. Anyway, see you tonight," she tells me, then
pauses at the door. "So you really think Rufus might be
kinda interested in me?"

I throw a pillow at her.

My morning is not a success. I have targeted the lower-
budget apartments, which seem to be occupied by students.
I have seen four apartments. This is my impression of them:

1. Dungeon. Basement bedroom, shared with another person. No window. Communal kitchen, communal living
   room, communal shower to share with three other girls. It
   is dank, smelly, and the three other girls have nose rings,
   belly button rings, and eyebrow rings. I wonder if they are
   forming a cult.

2. Prison. But it would be *my own* prison, as I do not have
   to share the six-by-six room with anyone, thank God.

However, the three other occupants of this very unde-lightful apartment interviewed me very carefully, and will let me know next week if I am the lucky applicant. I don't think they liked my answer to "how do you feel about al-cohol?" I said, "Oh, definitely favorable. Actually, I could use a drink now to cure my last-night hangover. What have you got?" I feel, somehow, that they won't be calling me.

3. No. The apartment was quite nice, but I refuse to share with three jock types who think I am the answer to their domestic cleanliness problems.

4. Perfectly nice, if small. But I'd still have to share a room with Denise, and I think Denise quite fancies me. I have nothing personally against her, or any other lesbian for that matter, because I know some very nice lesbians. Denise is a very attractive blonde girl and I wonder for a moment if I should become a lesbian, too. Life would be much simpler. No more need for men, for a start. Hmm . . . But try as I might, I cannot imagine wanting to kiss her (or do anything else with her, either). Sorry, Denise. I'm just not a lesbian.

I really should think about the job problem, too. I flick through the *Times'* Sunday classifieds. There are quite a few openings for admin assistants/secretaries but the money is similar to what I'm already getting—by that, I mean pitiful.

It's not that I'm ecstatic in my current job, as you know, but at the moment I can't face the task of job hunting—this rates even more highly on my stress scale than apartment hunting. No, I'll solve the apartment problem first, and then everything else will fall into place.

"*No!* My God, I don't believe it!" David laughs. "A four-some. So what did you do?"

I groan. Tish is telling the tale of last night's near-orgy.

Rachel, however, looks like the cat who got the cream. She's seeing Marco again on Tuesday night . . . wonder if he'll take Tony and Steve along . . .

"I think I've solved it," Tom confides. "You know, Katy being so tired. Our main problem is that we just never get any time alone. So I've arranged time off from work and I've booked a trip for the three of us to go to Disneyland. We can spend time together as a family, and Katy and me can spend time alone in the evenings. So what do you think?"

"Tom, I think that's a great idea. When are you going?"

"End of this month. A week from Thursday, for five days. I can't really take off any more time than that."

"Have you told Katy yet?"

"No. It's our wedding anniversary next Friday so I thought I'd surprise her."

What a lovely man. If Tom were single, I'd marry him in an instant. Actually, much as I love Tom, maybe not. He just doesn't give me that—you know—*zing.*

"*Ma mère,*" Sylvester hisses to me. "She is coming to visit for *two weeks.* Zis, I don't need."

"But your mom's great," I tell him.

"Yes, but not now. Not wiz . . . you know," he says, glancing across at David. "I follow him zis week. He goes to Greenwich Village to see *Simon.* He is zere two hours. *Two hours. Merde!* I told you he's having an affair. . . ."

"No, I'm sure it's not that," I say, hoping that I sound more certain than I feel.

Could I have been wrong? Is David having an affair with his designer friend, Simon? God, I hope not.

"I'm not putting up wiz it," Sylvester says. "Now I go check on the dessert, *non?*"

"Here," David tells me as he motions to refill my wineglass.

"No, none for me," I say. I need to stay sober, just to keep up with all the intrigues going on around me. Obviously, I don't say this. I'm dying to ask David about Simon.

I wonder how I can broach the subject of Simon.

"So, Sylvester tells me Hélène is coming for a visit."

"Yeah, he's like, totally freaked out about it. It's really not like him at all. I love his mother. She's so—so *French*. You know." David leans closer to me after glancing around to make sure that no one is listening to our conversation. "He's acting kinda weird generally. He's, like, *totally* off sex."

Oh, boy. Here we go. I grab the wine bottle and refill my glass. I feel I need to anesthetize myself before I hear any more.

"He's like a friggin' prima donna in the kitchen. I mean, I just can't say a thing without him overreacting. Has he said anything to you?"

How to phrase this with delicacy and diplomacy? Hmm . . .

"Have you been doing anything differently lately?" I ask. This is very discreet of me. "You know, any changes to your normal routine?"

"Well actually." David leans even closer. "I have been working on something special. No! No," he says, raising his hands, "I can't tell. Won't be a surprise if I tell you. I still think it's the forty thing. He's trying to pretend it's not his birthday in October. He doesn't want a party or anything. I mean, you can't turn forty without a party, can you?"

"Maybe he's a bit, you know, worried that he's too old for you."

"That's, like, so *dumb*. It's only eight years. What's eight years? I don't care how old he is."

"I know that. But maybe you should tell him—you know—to reassure him."

"He *has* said something to you. I knew it. Come on. Spit it out, girl."

Oh, God. What do I say now?

"Well, he hasn't exactly said . . ."

"Emmeline, don't tell me porkies, now." David folds his arms across his chest and leans back in his seat.

I'm obviously not going anywhere until he's extracted information from me—David is very good at extracting details about *anything* from *anyone*. He should have been a spy. But maybe I should tell him . . . I don't want David and Sylvester to part company just because I'm too anal about keeping secrets, do I?

"Okay," I say. "I think he's a bit worried about you disappearing in the afternoons. Not that he thinks you shouldn't have time to yourself or anything," I add, because I don't want to make the situation worse. "I think he's just a bit worried that you're—"

"I knew it! He's worried I'm planning him a party. Well, I *am*. Oh, but you must promise to keep it a total secret."

"Oh," I say, totally taken aback.

And relieved. No affair, just a surprise party. This is very good. I take a good gulp of wine. This is *very* good.

"I'm not saying another word on the subject," David says. "I'm planning something really spectacular with Simon. You'll find out soon enough." And then, "He thought I was having an affair, didn't he?"

"Oh, no," I say quickly. "Not that. Hahaha. Can't imagine anything more ridiculous than either of you having an affair. . . . hahaha . . ."

"God, he is such a *queen*."

It's getting late. After we've eaten Sylvester's *petits fours*, it's time to go (stagger) home.

But Sylvester pulls me to one side. Rather obviously, actually.

"So what did he say to you?"

"Sylvester, I promise you he's not having an affair with Simon. He's crazy about you."

"Thank God. Zat is a relief. Zank you, Emma, zank you."

"My pleasure." I preen, pleased with myself.

"But zere is a secret, *non?* Yes zere is. Come on, you tell me."

"I . . ." *Oh, God.* "I can't. I promised. It's a surprise."

"I knew it. He's planning a surprise party for me. Oh, zis is so exciting!"

"I thought you didn't want a party."

"*Non,* but is much better zan David having an affair, *n'est-ce pas?* Anyhow, I say I don't want ze party, but he knows I *love* parties."

Sometimes I think I worry too much, I really do.

I give up. I'm going home right now.

At least, I'm going back to Tish's sofa.

................

**Tuesday, July 23**

I am so whipping Lou's ass!

*Y-e-s!*

You see, for the past week and a half, I have been perfecting my strategy (with help from Angie, who is actually quite nice when you get to know her—not like Cruella at all, she just has unfortunate facial muscles).

After the debacle with the Burgoyne report (me leaving on time, for once, Friday before last, and not actually *doing* the report, because *Lou* should have done it), Adam called me into his office. Lou smirked at me all the way across the office as I followed, like a lamb to the slaughter.

"Emmeline, I asked you to help Lou any way you could. What's going on? Why isn't this report ready?" Adam asks, waving the folder at me. "Why hasn't this research been done?"

"Oh, hasn't it?" I say, feigning innocence.

"Of course it hasn't. Lou tells me he asked you to do it, but you had to leave early on Friday because of private plans. This isn't good, Emmeline."

The injustice of it all sticks in my craw. This is so petty and grade school.

"Adam, I left at five on Friday. Along with the rest of the *secretarial* staff," I tell him. "And of course I'm helping Lou as much as I can. But technically, he needs to do the research himself, doesn't he?"

"Technically, yes, but—"

"It's not really within my job description, is it? Doing the account manager's job, instead of the account manager doing it himself. I mean, I'm only a secretary."

Have I mentioned to Adam that I am only a secretary enough times, do you think? The words hang in the air between us.

"You're doing this on purpose, aren't you? I thought we'd cleared the air between us. Are you deliberately trying to sabotage this campaign?"

"Of course not." *Yes.* But I don't say that.

"Have you had any ideas for the campaign yourself?"

"No." *Yes.* But I don't say that, either. He has six other account managers. Surely they can come up with something between them? Grady Thomas is usually pretty solid. And what about Adam? He was brought in to give the company some new blood. He has a list of prior achievements as long as your arm.

"Emmeline, Emmeline." Adam sighs and leans back in his chair. "You're not helping yourself."

"I'm doing a good job," I tell him, indignantly. "I'm a really efficient *secretary.*"

"Y-e-s. But I expect more from you. You're a very intelligent young woman. I want *you* to do the research. That's an order, okay?"

I slink back to my cubicle. I do not look across the office at Lou, who I think is still smirking.

But I am not defeated. Oh, no. Lou may have won this round, but one battle does *not* win the war. After all, I *am* named after a famous suffragette. I'll *do* the research, since I can't avoid it. But that doesn't mean it has to be *good,* does it?

And so I do it. In between getting coffee and food for Lou, and actually doing my own work, I find the kinds of photos Lou wants. I stick exactly to his outline. I do not add any improving suggestions of my own. I list the photos, the web sites where they can be found, and the costs. But I'm sloppy. I don't worry about the expense or the quality of the photos in the same way that I would if it were *my* project.

Oh, and because I'm so tied up doing Lou's work, I can't possibly do all of Adam's stuff too. Every time he asks "where's this, where's that?", I produce urgent work that Lou has assigned to me. I think Adam's honeymoon with Lou is quickly reaching its end.

And I know Stella hated the report. I don't think she liked anyone else's ideas, either, because she stormed out of the meeting last Friday. Take *that*, Lou Russo! And I hope Stella and Adam had a shit weekend, too, because I still haven't found anywhere to live. Come to think of it, Adam's not been in a very good mood for the past couple of days . . . Maybe Adam's honeymoon with *her* is waning, too . . .

*Wishful thinking.*

My telephone rings and it is Rachel. I am expecting her to call, because she had a second date with Hugh last night. He waited nearly *two whole weeks* before asking her out again, despite her flirting and brushing against him at the office, so I'm dying to know what happened.

I immediately hang up and call her on my cell phone from the restroom, as per her instructions.

"Motherfucking bastard!"

Oh, so it was that bad, was it?

"Okay," I sigh. "What happened?"

"He virtually fucking accused me of sexually harassing him at work." Another string of curses follows this statement.

"Oh dear. Maybe you shouldn't, you know, brush up against him. I suppose if a man did that kind of thing—"

"So you're on his side, are you?"

"No, of course not. I'm totally with you," I hastily reassure her.

I do *not* want a repeat fall-out with Rachel.

"Well anyway, I got my revenge." Rachel laughs. It is not a

pleasant laugh. "After we do the dinner thing, and he tells me that I have to show more restraint at work, he only friggin' makes a move on me."

"No."

"Yeah. It was magnificent. We're at my front door, and he's kissing me—"

"With tongues?"

"Yes, with tongues. Will you let me finish?"

"Sorry."

"So we're getting pretty into each other, and then he asks if he can come in." She pauses, for dramatic impact.

"And?"

"Hey, who's telling this story? Patience, sweetie, patience. So anyway, there we are, and he's all over me like I'm the best thing since the cure for smallpox, and he's really *hot* for me. So I open the front door, push him away, and tell him not to sexually harass me anymore. My God, you should have seen his face just before I slammed the door on it."

"My God, you've got balls."

I can't help but feel sorry for poor Hugh, and I'm wondering if Rachel has painted a subjective, warped picture of him. Not that she'd do that, of course. . . .

Rachel chuckles, and something occurs to me.

"Did he actually use the term *sexual harassment?*"

"Not exactly, but that's what he meant."

"Oh." *Maybe he just likes you,* I don't say. "So how are things at work today?"

"He's learned his lesson."

I'll bet.

"He won't be bothering *me* anymore."

"No, that's for sure," I agree. If I were Hugh, I'd avoid Rachel at every opportunity.

"What? Don't you think I'm attractive? Don't you think he wants me? You think I'm a, and I quote, 'hardhearted, callous bitch,' don't you?"

"Rachel. Stop jumping to conclusions. I never said that.

Anyway, I thought you didn't want him. So if he leaves you alone from now on, well that's good, isn't it?"

"Yeah," she says. But she doesn't sound sure. "Look, I've gotta go. See you tomorrow night for pizza?"

"Sure. Have a good time with Marco tonight."

When I get back to my cubicle, Adam is waiting for me.

"Do you need to spend so much time in the restroom, Emmeline?"

"Yes, I do. Urinary infection," I lie.

Adam does not say another word, but hands me a cost report to type. I'll start it after I get Lou's doughnut.

"Adam," I say around the door of his office. "I'm getting Lou a doughnut. Do you want one?"

# 15

## All Packed Up with Nowhere to Live

### TO DO

1. Purchase new Robert Plant CD to prepare thoroughly for Robert Plant Night.

2. Purchase new (but casually grunge-chic) outfit to prepare thoroughly for Robert Plant Night.

3. Get hair done (also casual grunge-chic) to prepare thoroughly for Robert Plant Night.

**Wednesday, July 24**

Robert Plant Night. *Y-E-S!*

**6:30 P.M.**

Right—I'm just about ready for my evening with Bob (and Norbert). My hair is casually grunged with wax, courtesy of Tish. I'm wearing Calvin Klein faded jeans, with a peasant-style black top (don't want to be overdressed) and I'm looking pretty babelike, in a Courtney Love kind of way. My lips are pouty and red, my lashes are long and flirty in case of fluttering-eyes-at-Bob opportunities (thanks to Tish's lash-thickening mascara).

This is a really great "Bob groupie" look for me.

You know, I've been thinking about Norbert rather a lot over the last few days. Maybe I've been a bit unkind to him in the past. Maybe I just haven't given him a chance, and have dismissed him because he doesn't conform to society's ideals re: the perfect alpha male. And let's face it, I know all about not conforming to society's ideals. I'm not exactly perfect myself.

*How shallow am I?* To make assumptions about someone without getting to know them properly. I think I'm going to really try to dig deeper and seek the *inner Norbert* tonight.

Ah. Telephone. It's probably Norbert again—he's called me three times this week already to make sure I'm still going to the gig with him. How insecure is that? Bless him, he's obviously had such a hard time with women that he automatically *expects* rejection. I think that all he needs is the love of a good woman.

Not that I'm ready to love again yet, of course, because I am (obviously) still getting over Adam. It's only been a few weeks, after all. Actually, I don't feel broken-hearted at all, but I must be, mustn't I? But in time, after our friendship has deepened and we've gotten to know each other as individuals, maybe *our love will grow.*

Plus, Norbert hasn't mentioned small breasts at all recently, which is a good sign. Maybe he was just using the small breast thing as a way of making conversation—he is a plastic surgeon, after all. Of course he wants to discuss implants—it's only part of his job. Better pick up the telephone . . .

"Hello," I say, in my best "I am a caring person, you can talk to me" voice.

"Hi there! This is Hal, how's it going?"

I don't know anyone called Hal. And no one called Hal knows me, either. Maybe it's one of Tish's new men.

"I'm calling on behalf of the Mothers Against Sexual SPAM Hoboken group. You've probably heard of us, we've been pretty active. You may have seen our march on Independence Day? Anyway, my call tonight is to tell you more about us, and our efforts to raise money to help fight our campaign against the ruthless companies who . . ."

Well, Hal isn't giving me any opportunity to be mature and kind here, is he? I mean, he's hardly drawn breath and is now telling me that the bronze donation starts at thirty dollars. *Thirty dollars!* I can't believe another bastard telemarketer has caught me unawares. I didn't know the MASS mothers were into this kind of thing. God, I hope Katy won't have to do this.

I instantly forget my caring-person voice and decide on tonight's method of getting rid of this irritating person who is trying to extract cash from me. And let's face it, my feelings towards the MASS mothers are not exactly friendly at the moment. As Hal continues to drone on at me (bearing in mind he hasn't stopped talking since I picked up), I can't help it. I know what I'm going to do.

*"Ich habe eine grosse Bitte an dich,"* I say (no, I am not calling Hal a big dick, although I am sorely tempted to call him something very rude, indeed).

"Say, what was that? Do you wanna do the silver option?"

Do you know what? I'm really not in the mood to do this tonight. I mean, how childish is it, torturing poor Hal just because I can't stand Marion Lacy?

"Or do you want to go for the premium gold option of ninety dollars? You can give me your pledge now, we'll get the paperwork in the mail—"

*That's it.* I've had enough. I'm so glad that Sylvester spent a year in Austria as a pastry chef.

*"Und nun verpiss' dich endlich und lass' mich in Ruhe."*

Okay, so I couldn't resist it. I have just told Hal to fuck off and leave me alone.

................

**10:30 P.M.**

I am in *love.*

Robert Plant is totally *sublime.* And I know *exactly* how to solve all of my problems—I have a completely *great* plan. I just have to (a) quit my job, (b) give away all my possessions, and (c) become a groupie and follow Bob around the world.

Also, I'd never have to see Norbert ever again.

Our evening has not gone well. This is what happened.

When I arrive at the great new wine bar where we have arranged to meet, Norbert is not alone. He has already started making friends and influencing people—two people, in fact. Two very attractive twentysomething girls.

"Emma, good to see you," Norbert says. "Meet Shelly and Nicole. We just kinda got talking."

"Hi," Shelly and Nicole tell me, checking me out thoroughly. And then they return all of their attention to Norbert, as they giggle and fawn all over him.

Although I try to be interested in the conversation and make one or two attempts to join it, they really are not interested in me. More in what surgical procedures Norbert thinks they would benefit from. But they're lovely, for heaven's sake. Why would they *want* to do anything to themselves? I'm happy for Norbert, though. I really am. Because this will give him the self-confidence he needs to *overcome* his *insecurities.*

"Take Emma, here," Norbert tells Shelly and Nicole. "I've been sayin' to her for ages that she should get hers done. It really gives a woman the confidence she needs to *overcome* her *insecurities.* I see it all the time."

"Oh, you're so lucky," Nicole or Shelly giggles to me.

"I'd love to date a plastic surgeon," giggles the other Shelly or Nicole. "Someone just like Norbert."

"Oh, we ain't dating," Norbert tells them. "We're old pals, me and Emma. I work with her dad."

"Oh," they both say, then forget about me.

Anyway. I'm forgetting all about Norbert for now. Apart from the fact that he has left me alone all evening to flirt with other women, Bob is just starting to sing "Whole Lotta Love." *Truly, truly sublime.*

"Emma," Norbert yells in my ear. "Do you wanna go now? I mean, Plant's not what he was, is he?"

No, I do not want to go. And he is right about Bob.

"You're right," I tell Norbert as I watch Bob. "He's like a fine wine—just gets better with age."

"Oh. Well, we gotta go soon. Only I got five ops tomorrow and I need to get my sleep."

I don't make it to the stage door. I do not get to make eye contact with Bob, and he does not sweep me away in his limousine.

Instead, Norbert sweeps me away as soon as Robert finishes his encore. As the cab pulls up outside the apartment, I wonder how I can get out of kissing Norbert good-night. I really hate this about first dates. To kiss or not to kiss. Especially when you know you're not going on a second date with them.

"Emma, don't take this the wrong way," Norbert says, just as I am bracing myself to endure. "But I don't think it's gonna work between us. I mean, there's just no chemistry."

"I was just about to say the same thing," I say, relieved.

"You're a nice-looking chick, and all," Norbert continues. "But you just ain't the right type for me. Sorry, Emma, but you just don't do it for me, babe."

Oh God. I'm old and ugly and unattractive.

................

**Thursday evening**

Girlie night in Tish's overcrowded living room. The video of choice tonight is *What Women Want,* because, apart from the fact that Mel Gibson is hot, it is Tish's favorite movie and it's her turn to choose. Plus I think they're sick of hearing about Robert Plant, and how wonderful he is, and how fabulous the planet would be if *all* men were Robert Plant.

Mel is just about to try on pantyhose when the front door

buzzer buzzes. I have a mouthful of four-cheese pizza, but am also the nearest, so I pick up.

"Hewow," I say, chewing madly.

"Emma?" It's Katy.

"Yef." *But I thought you were on your way to Disneyland,* I nearly say, but I don't because (a) my mouth is full, and (b) she obviously isn't on her way to Disneyland. But I press the buzzer to let her in.

"I hope nothing's gone wrong," Tish frets. "I wonder where Tom is? Do you suppose they had a fight and now the whole vacation is off?"

Oh no. Surely it hasn't come to that, has it?

"Marion Lacy better not be involved," Rachel says, taking a hefty swig of her wine. "That woman is a public menace."

God, if Tom and Katy split up because of some stupid, pushy, arrogant, bitchy broad, what will happen to poor Alex?

"You should have heard me, girls," Katy says as she comes into the room, her face flushed and triumphant. "I was great. I was empowered. Boy, did I kick ass. Can I get some wine?"

"But why aren't you on vacation?" Rachel asks. "You've had a fight with Tom, haven't you? I *knew* it. You *have* had a fight with Tom." And she's off in full rant mode. "You are so lucky to have him," she continues. "Not only is he support-ive and kind, he's also intelligent, which is rare for a guy. I can't believe you'd be so *stupid.*"

This stops us all in our tracks. Is this really Rachel speak-ing, or has her brain been hijacked by aliens?

"What are you talking about? Tom's a complete angel," Katy says. "Why would you even *think* I've had fight with Tom? After he planned such a wonderful surprise for our an-niversary? We're leaving in half an hour. I just had to stop by and tell you about my fight with Marion Lacy."

Oh. That takes the wind out of Rachel's sails. And out of mine and Tish's, too.

"It was great," Katy says, pouring some wine. "Marion came up with a fundraising plan. She expected me to spend the *whole weekend* calling strangers and asking them for money. Can I get a slice of that?" she asks, stuffing pizza into her mouth. "I mean, can you believe that?"

"But you've never said no to her before," Rachel reminds her.

"I know." She pauses midchew. "I was a wuss. What can I say? But I'm not anymore."

"Yes, but what actually happened?" I ask. "Get back to the story."

"Okay. Well, she dropped by unexpectedly this afternoon so I made Tom answer the door." She blushes just a bit and then pushes on.

"I know that was weak of me. *Weak.* But when Tom told her I was unavailable this weekend, she really laid into him. Right on our own doorstep." She pauses, then pulls a face. "Okay, I was hiding in the living room so I heard every word."

"I'd hide, too, if Marion Lacy came knocking on my door," I tell her loyally. Because it's true.

"Thanks, hon," Katy says. "I appreciate the support."

"So how exactly did you kick ass if you were hiding?" Rachel prompts her.

"I'm just getting to that. You see, it was when she laid into Tom about how he dominates me, and how controlling men are in general that I got real mad. How could she pick on Tom? That was the final straw. I came out, all guns blazing, and told her what a cold, interfering bitch she was and what she could do with her PPPTA and her MASS mothers."

"Atta girl," I tell her.

"Wow. I wish I'd been a fly on the wall," Tish says.

"Fucking fabulous, darling," Rachel says. And then, "Speaking of flying—you'd better go. Much as we all love you, and this may come as a shock, the airline doesn't feel the same way about you. They have flight schedules to worry about."

"Thanks." Katy hugs us all on her way out of the door. "You're such good friends."

...............

## Friday night

I'm pumping iron in the gym. I'm not doing the fat-burning aerobics, because I don't want to burn fat—I want to encourage it as much as I can. In a nation obsessed by obesity, we thinnies tend to be forgotten—I mean, how often do you hear people *bragging* about how many pounds they gained over the vacation? Personally, I think a little extra weight on women is lovely. I'd love to be a nice, curvy size ten.

And the disgusting shakes and the exercise are starting to work. I put on three pounds this week, which means I'm no longer officially underweight, according to my body mass indicator. So that's good, isn't it?

But I *am* officially homeless for the weekend, which is not good.

Last night, Tish ordered me out of her apartment. Actually, she didn't order me out at all. She very sweetly and kindly asked if I'd mind spending this weekend at Rachel's instead, because she wants to invite Julio back for breakfast in bed. They've already been on four dates, so it's time to progress to the next stage.

"I know you're allergic to Rachel's cats, but it's only for two nights," Tish tells me. "Sorry, Emma, I wouldn't ask, but we can't go to Julio's because he lives with his uncle. I should have mentioned it earlier this evening, but with Katy and her kicking-Marion's-ass story, I forgot."

"Course I don't mind. Stop apologizing," I say, wondering how much allergy medication I have left. "No problem."

"Oh, sorry, but would you mind storing some of your stuff at Rachel's too, to make some space in the living room? Maybe you could take the huge plant?"

So I call Rachel straightaway and ask if I can store some stuff in her storage room for the weekend. Before I ask if I can store *me* on her sofabed for the weekend too, she interrupts me.

"Sure. But can you bring it round now? I have weekend breakfast-in-bed plans with Marco."

So I can't stay there, either. Obviously.

So what's going on? Everyone but me suddenly has weekend-breakfast-in-bed plans? I feel left out. Why don't *I* have an overnight date?

Katy and Tom are still in Florida, so that's good. But they didn't leave a spare key, so I can't even squat at their place. Plus Sylvester's mom is visiting, so their spare room is also out of the question. It seems pathetic to call Dad and ask him and Peri if I can stay with them. They'll only worry, and maybe they'll force me to move back in with them permanently. Then there's the terrible twins . . .

On the bright side, Dad ordered new car keys for me, so at least I have my car back. He and Uncle Derek drove down last weekend, because Dad insisted that I shouldn't be put to any trouble, seeing as it was the twins who caused the problem in the first place. I think he just wanted to get out of the house and away from the twins for a while. And Uncle Derek only mentioned breast implants once. Which is good, for him.

I wonder if the backseat of my car is comfortable? I mean, lots of people sleep in their cars, don't they? And if I hunker down, no one will be able to see me, will they? I'm parked half a block from Tish's apartment, and it's a nice part of Hoboken, so it's not like anything could happen, could it?

I *could* check into a hotel, but the whole point of not doing that is so that I can save money. I *have* to save money—I can't stay with Tish much longer. I've got eight hundred dollars in my savings account. So once I save approximately double that, and trade in my car, I should be able to afford to move into a really dreadful, cramped apartment.

The thought of living in any of the apartments I've seen is depressing, so I abandon my weight training and take a leisurely sauna and shower. Actually, I think my muscles are getting bigger. I'm sure I've got more definition. I check my watch again. It's still only 9:15 P.M.

I decide to retreat to the juice bar to while away more time. It is nearly empty. Obviously, everyone else has something better to do on Friday night. Apart from me. I think the gym closes at eleven.

Just as I am drinking my second carrot juice and wondering how much more of it I can stomach, someone sits at my table.

"No hot date tonight?" Jack asks me.

His hair is still damp from the shower. He's wearing shabby old jeans and a faded white T-shirt. His biceps gleam healthily, and so do his teeth as he smiles at me.

"No," I tell him, stirring my carrot juice. "You?"

"No. Didn't finish work until eight thirty—too late to set something up. Mind if I join you?"

Oh, so he's alone through *choice* then. This does not make me feel better. This makes me feel even more belligerent toward the whole world in general, so my reply is not very friendly.

"It's a bit late to ask, isn't it? Seeing as you've already got your feet under the table."

"Okay. I'll leave." He scrapes back his chair and I panic. It's only Jack, but at least he's human and breathing. Someone to talk to. Someone with whom to while away the lonely hours before bedtime.

"No. No, it's fine. Stay if you want to."

"Gee, thanks," he says, rather dryly. "Try not to be too enthusiastic." But he sits back down, so he can't be that pissed with me.

For a couple of minutes we drink our liquidated vegetables.

"So how come you're not out on the town?" he asks.

It sounds like a challenge. It sounds like, "So what's wrong with you? No one like you enough to ask you for a date?"

"Didn't feel like it," I lie. "Work's hell at the moment."

"Yeah. Me too."

"Well, good," I say. "I'm glad we got that sorted out. We're both young, attractive, educated people who prefer to spend our Friday night without Friday-night dates."

And when he looks at me in that who-are-we-kidding-here way, I can't help but smile, and then he's smiling back at me.

"You didn't get asked, did you?" he says.

"No."

"Me neither."

We grin at each other in a conspiratorial kind of way.

"Have you eaten yet?"

"Only veggies," I say, pointing at my drink. "Very nutritious."

"I hate eating alone. You want to come eat with me? You look kinda hungry."

"What? You mean like a date? You must be desperate."

"Desperate for sustenance. This is a nondate. Just two hungry people. You look like you need to eat."

"Gee, thanks." *A nondate?* Well, it's better than sitting here alone, isn't it? "For your information, I've put on three pounds this week," I tell him.

"Well, see? You gotta keep up the good work. Come on. I know this great Thai place. You like Thai food?"

"You've only been back in Hoboken for a month and you already know the great places to eat?"

"Hey, man cannot live by love alone, you know."

"Please don't feel you have to share those details with me." I giggle.

Surprisingly, I have a really good time on my nondate with Jack. I think it's liberating to have dinner with someone you don't like and who doesn't like you. You don't have to pretend to be something you're not to impress him, and you don't have to worry about saying anything to hurt him. I'm dying to ask about his ex-fiancée though, but think that may be going a little too far.

"So let me get this straight," Jack says, as he devours another bite of spicy chicken. "Adam is your ex-boyfriend and he's also your boss? Jesus, that's not good. Not good at all."

"Yeah. I know, I know," I say, waving my hands. "Don't give me the lecture. I already had it from Rachel."

"Nope. No lecture. You want any more of this noodle?"

"I can't," I say holding my hand to my throat. "Too full."

"Okay, if you're sure. This is great. I told you this place is great, didn't I?" Jack says, finishing it off in two mouthfuls. And then, "I dated my boss once."

He did?

"You did?" Wonder if I should ask him what happened. Would that be too nosy? "What happened?"

"Oh, same old, same old."

Obviously he doesn't want to talk about it, so I won't push. I'm not that interested, anyway.

"We got engaged. Then she met someone else."

"Oh, I'm sorry," I say. "That's terrible."

Interesting. It explains a lot about Jack.

"It happens. I was too young to get married, anyway. At least she left me before the wedding. She did me a favor. Can you pass me the shrimp?"

And although I want to hear the whole story, Jack obviously doesn't want to tell it, and we chat about stupid stuff. After he's vacuumed the rest of the food from the dishes, we realize that the restaurant staff are anxiously hovering because it is now 11:30 and they want to close up.

Jack insists on paying for the food, and since it is only twenty-five dollars for the two of us, I let him. It's when he insists on walking me home that I balk.

"It's a few blocks—it's out of your way—I do it all the time." I hedge.

"Yeah, but I need to know you're safe. Your dad would kill me if anything happened to you after you'd been out with me."

Oh, so he's worried about my dad. Not about me, then. How can I get rid of him?

"But you live in the opposite direction," I say.

"Come on," he says, and I know that it is pointless to protest. Besides, if I protest too much, he'll smell a rat.

What do I do when we get to Tish's? I can't tell him I'm sleeping in my car. How pathetic does that sound?

Oh, here we are already, outside Tish's!

And the living-room light is on, which means Tish and Julio are up there. Which means I can't let myself in, then cunningly slip out once Jack's gone.

"Actually, I feel like a drive," I tell him, as I hesitate, key in hand. "You know what? That's just what I'm gonna do. Go for a drive."

"At this time of night? Are you serious?"

"Yes. I like driving at nighttime. By myself. On the turnpike. I'm helping my friend Katy with her MADD campaign." I open the car door and climb in.

"*You're* mad," he says, shaking his head.

"Can I give you a ride home?" This would be a cunning way to get rid of him.

"No, I like to walk," he says, obviously perplexed.

I have now confirmed his earlier suspicions that I am a crazy, deranged woman. But this is better than him thinking I am a pathetic sleeping-in-a-car person.

"So, thanks for the nondate," I tell him. "You were right— the food was great."

"You're welcome. Good-night, then."

But after I close the door, he's still waiting on the side-walk. Oh, God, he's waiting for me to leave. I'll have to drive around the block a few times until he's gone. But if I do that, maybe someone will take this parking space. But what else can I do?

Engine on, lights on, he's still there. I wave, smile, and pull out. Once around the block should do it. I go around three blocks, just to make sure.

Five minutes later there's no sign of Jack. And my space is thankfully empty, so after five attempts, I manage to reverse back into it without bending any fenders. I get out of the front, after checking there's no one around, then climb into the back. I lock the doors and try to get comfy.

I'm glad I had the foresight to throw a comforter and cushion in here. I hope no one can see me. I cringe as I hear a crowd of Friday night revelers pass on the other side of the street.

*I'm fine. It's okay.*

This is actually quite comfortable.

Five minutes later, just as I am imagining all kinds of dreadful scenarios and generally working myself up into a bundle of nerves, I nearly die on the spot when someone knocks on the window.

*Oh God. What do I do now?*

I pull the comforter over my head and pretend to be a pile of old clothes. But then they knock again. I'll just have to leap into the front seat and make a dash for it. I brace myself and throw back the comforter.

It's Jack.

Oh God. And he's knocking again. I open the window just a little. He doesn't look very happy.

"What the hell are you doing?"

"Taking a nap," I say, folding my arms across my chest. I feel so stupid.

"I thought you were going for a drive."

"I was, but then I got tired and decided to take a nap first." Okay, so that sounds lame.

He runs a hand through his hair, and sighs.

"What's going on, Emma?"

"Nothing. Nothing at all. Just go home. I'm good."

"You're *crazy*. You were going to spend the night in your car, weren't you? How come you can't go into your apartment?"

It's obvious he's not going anywhere until I give him an explanation.

"Look, Tish has a guy in there. They're having a romantic weekend, and they don't need an unromantic third wheel in the living room, and the walls are really thin. Okay?"

"Don't you have other friends you can stay with?"

"Of course. I have plenty of friends. *Plenty.* They're just . . . all busy."

"Give me your keys. Come on, give," he says, as he pushes his hand through the window.

"No, I'm fine. I'll go check into a hotel right now."

"I don't trust you."

"That's your problem."

He doesn't say a word, but pulls out his cell phone and starts punching numbers.

"Who are you calling?"

"Peri."

Oh God, not Peri. I will never hear the last of it.

"Okay," I say, handing him my car keys. "You win."

...................................................................................

# 16

# Home from Home

### TO DO

1. Figure out a way to move in with Jack.

2. Figure out how to get a new boyfriend. Apart from missing sex, I cannot attend Colleague of the Year alone.

3. Make sure am completely alone before next impersonating Cinderella making entrance at ball.

**Saturday night**

Jack's house is lovely!

When I say lovely, I mean it has great potential. At the moment it mostly resembles a building site, because two of the second-floor bedrooms are undergoing floor restoration and are sealed off with thick plastic sheeting. Strange machines and toolboxes lurk in corners. The master bedroom, Jack's room, is next on the list, but he says he has to wait awhile until he's saved more cash. But even in its unrestored state, it's beautiful. He has so much light and space! He has *three whole floors* to himself.

He's put me in the huge attic room, which is great, because apart from the fact it is so spacious and light, it has an en suite bathroom—or at least it will once the shower's been installed. But there *is* a toilet and basin, so at least I can pee and brush my teeth in peace. And there's an air-conditioning unit.

*Bliss.*

I'd forgotten what it was like to have space.

It's so great to be on my own. *By myself.* No one to disturb my solitude.

I wonder who I can call?

Hmm . . . Tish and Rachel are possibly (depending on how last night went) entertaining Julio and Marco. (Though obviously, not all in the same bed. At least I hope not. Marco's friends were very odd.) Sylvester and David—nope, no time to chat—the restaurant's probably heaving. I'll see them tomorrow night, anyway . . . I hope Katy and Tom are having a good time in Disneyland.

I'll just have another walk around the house, but obviously will avoid the master bedroom—I don't want to invade Jack's privacy. Maybe I'll just peek around the door . . . My God, the size of his bed! No, I'm not even going there. Do not even *think* about it.

Jack doesn't have much furniture yet (apart from beds)—it makes sense to wait until the renovations are completed before filling the rooms. But the living room is finished. The floor is a beautiful rich cherry brown, and although the walls and drapes are cream, it's not cold in the way of Adam's apartment. Jack believes in color and texture. Lovely green sofa and chairs, with russet and yellow cushions. The central rug is pale-green-and-white check. I can just picture the color and light that will fill the rest of the house . . .

Jack's got a date tonight. But he told me to make myself at home, so I am. I'm currently making myself *very* comfortable on the squishy sofa. I'm wearing pajamas, I have grilled cheese sandwiches, and I've rented *The Wedding Planner* from Blockbuster. I love this movie. It's a really *feel good* movie. Plus Matthew McConaughey is extremely hot. I wish he'd been around to save my Manolo Blahnik shoes . . . Wonder if they're fixable? I can't quite bring myself to throw them away.

The only problem is that Jack's house has totally ruined me for apartment hunting. I really have to explore more apartment opportunities. There must be *something* out there for me, surely? But the ones I saw today were no improvement on the previous batch, and all the time I was trying to be objective about small, grotty bedrooms, I couldn't help but envision Jack's attic.

Jack was very unamused last night after blackmailing me with Peri. He didn't give me any lectures, but he barely spoke to me as he drove my Beetle to his garage. Typical man—I mean, I *do* know how to *drive*. It *is* my car. Still, he was okay this morning.

I thought I'd slip out of the house early and get breakfast at Rufus's deli to cheer me up before checking out today's list of apartments. But as I came down the stairs, the smell of bacon wafted up to greet me. And then Jack wafted to the kitchen doorway to greet me.

This is what happened.

"Hi. You sleep okay?" he says. "Come and have breakfast."

Oh. Thank God he's not pissed at me anymore.

"You sure there's enough? I don't want to steal your food," I say, because my stomach is now growling and I *do* want to make peace with Jack.

"You kidding? You don't eat enough to keep a bird alive. There's coffee in the pot and mugs in the cupboard."

"Thanks."

"Here," he says, as he pushes a huge plate of bacon, scrambled eggs, and toast under my nose. "Eat."

"This is way too much."

"Knock yourself out. So where are you planning to stay tonight? You want me to check out the park for a bench? I hear the graveyard's very popular—loads of benches and comfortable tombs there."

"Don't exaggerate. I would have been fine in my car."

"Sure. I can just see the news headlines now," he says, taking a bite from his toast. "I can't believe you have *flowers* painted on that car. I can't believe *I* drove that car. I'm sure glad it was dark—I'd never live it down if someone saw me driving that car. It's so—so *girly.*"

"Well, I *am* a girl. I *love* that car." Obviously, he has no taste.

"It's okay to *love* the car. Just don't *live* in the car. Do you know how stupid that was?"

"Yes," I say, indignant, because he's right. "Look." I wave a fork of bacon at him. "I don't poke my nose in your business, so you keep out of mine. I'm saving money, okay? Because if I don't, I might be spending a lot more nights sleeping on that backseat, flowers or not."

"I'm *so* not poking my nose in your business. We're family. Interfering is compulsory. That bacon's about to make a bid for freedom—I'd eat it quick if I were you."

"You are *so* like Peri," I tell him as I push the fork into my mouth.

There's silence as we eat. But it's not uncomfortable, because I'm not really pissed at him anymore. Before I realize, I've eaten three quarters of the food on my plate.

"You finished with that?"

"Yeah. Thanks."

"Pass it over."

As Jack finishes my breakfast, I stack dishes in the dishwasher, because Jack cooked, so it's only fair that I clean up, isn't it?

"Okay," I say, grabbing my purse. "I've got to hit the real-estate agents. Thanks for breakfast. And thanks for letting me stay."

Wonder if I could stay tonight?

"Hey." Jack follows me into the hall and dangles a bunch of keys in front of me. "I have a date tonight so you'll need these to get back in," he tells me with a wry smile. "See you later. Or maybe tomorrow morning."

Whew.

How kind is that?
*Wonder what it would be like if I lived here?*

................

**11:30 P.M.**

I wake up to the sound of voices, and for a moment I can't remember where I am. Oh. Jack's house. I meant to head up to bed before he got back, because I wanted to avoid a sticky I've-brought-a-date-home-for-the-night situation. But I'm too late. I jump off the sofa just as they head into the kitchen. Don't want to cramp his style. I want him to realize how easy I am to live with. I've already disinfected the bathroom and cleaned the kitchen floor. Wonder if I can make it up the stairs without them noticing me?

I am just about to climb onto the first stair when they come out of the kitchen with drinks. The immaculate, well-stacked blonde stops in her tracks as she spots me, and raises a beautifully plucked eyebrow. I am self-consciously aware that not only am I wearing my oldest, ugliest pajamas, but my hair is sticking up, and I am not wearing a scrap of makeup.

This is *not* a good look for me.

I give her a huge grin.

"Hi," I say brightly. "Don't mind me. Just going to bed. In the attic. I won't hear a thing. That is, I won't hear a thing if you make any noise." I shut up, before my tongue can get me into any more trouble.

"Jack, who is this?" she says, after giving me a thorough once-over.

"This is Emma. Emma, this is Laura," he says, grinning wryly.

He's very good at those wry grins. I wonder if he spends hours practicing them in front of the mirror for varying degrees of wryness. He obviously thinks this is funny, but at least he's not embarrassed or pissed off at me.

"Oh, nice to meet you, Laura," I say, retreating up the stairs. "I'm Jack's niece. Er, well, have a good time—I mean, a pleasant evening . . ."

I shut my mouth and flee before I can further embarrass myself by telling her to enjoy her night of hot, unbridled sex with Jack.

.................

### Sunday evening

I've packed what little I brought with me. My overnight bag, my comforter and cushion are all safely back in my car. All the dishes are neatly stacked in the dishwasher, and I've vacuumed the living-room rug. Okay. Time to go. Better go find Jack and tell him good-bye.

He's working on some architectural plans in the dining room. Well, it will be a dining room once it's finished and he puts a table and chairs in here. At the moment, he just has a desk and a computer.

"Er, sorry to disturb you," I say from the door. "Thanks for, you know, everything. I'll leave the keys in the kitchen, shall I?"

"Emma," Jack says. Those glasses really suit him. He's a bit Clark Kentish. Bit of a babe, actually. Not that I like him or anything.

"Hmm?"

"I've been thinking."

"Yes?"

So have I. I really want to live here. I know Jack's part of the package, but I can stay out of his way. He's probably not here much, he's probably out every night with a different woman.

"Peri has a point. About you moving in here."

"Oh, no." I laugh, waving my hand in front of my face. "Don't give it another thought. You know what she's like . . ."

*Please ask again, please make me an offer I can't refuse.* I can't bear the thought of living in any of the terrible places I've seen.

"I could use the extra money—you know—toward the cost of refurbishing this place, and paying off the rest of the loan to your dad."

"You don't have to do this just because my dad lent you the money, you know. I'm sure I'll find something . . ." *Convince me, convince me.*

"You could live here just temporarily, until something else comes along. It's gotta be better than the backseat of your car."

Okay. So how long is "temporarily"? A month? Six months? A year?

"I figure it'll take me another few months to fix this place up, then I'm going to put it on the market."

If I owned this house I'd never sell it. It's gorgeous.

"We'd be doing each other a favor," he tells me. "I don't want the hassle of a tenancy agreement, you need somewhere to stay. I could really use the extra cash."

"But we don't like each other," I say. Then, "How much rent do you want?" I don't want to sound *too* negative or disinterested, do I?

"Five hundred a month?"

"A thousand." Yes, I know this is stupid of me, but I can't cheat the man out of a fairer rent.

"Let's split the difference."

"But that's not—"

"You're gonna save me a fortune in housecleaning services, anyway, so let's say seven fifty."

Oh, he noticed that I cleaned. Good.

"So when do you want to move in?"

"Tomorrow?"

"Fine. Keep the keys."

This is fabulous. I'm no longer homeless! Can't wait to tell everyone my news.

★   ★   ★

"Hi everybody," I trill, as I step through the door of Chez Nous. "Guess what? I've found a really great place to live . . ."

I close my mouth as all eyes descend on me. Tish, Rachel, Sylvester, David, and Sylvester's mom, Hélène, are all looking at me like they just saw a ghost.

"What's going on? Did something terrible happen?"

"Where the hell have you been?" demands Rachel, the first to reach me. She surprises me by hugging me fiercely, then just as abruptly lets me go. "We were going to call the cops and report you missing."

"Thank God you're safe." Tish hugs me.

*"Chérie,* you took years off our lives." Sylvester kisses me. "Don't do zis again."

"Hon, we were about to get the Hudson dredged." Now David kisses me. "But we figured we'd give you until tonight before we really panicked. You got lucky, didn't you? You spent the weekend with a guy, I just *know* it. See everyone, I was right."

"You give everyone *beeg* fright," Hélène tells me, squashing me to her ample bosom and slipping into a stream of incomprehensible French.

"God, I never thought you'd all worry about me. It never occurred to me . . ."

I *love* my friends.

"Peri called yesterday afternoon to speak to you, so I gave her Rachel's number," Tish says. "And when she called Rachel's, you weren't there, either. And your car was gone. And then you weren't *here* at Chez Nous, either."

"Does Peri think I'm missing? Because I'd better call her—she'll have the state police out en masse."

"Relax," Rachel tells me. "I told Peri you were out. She knows nothing. You *idiot.* Didn't it occur to you that we'd worry? Why didn't you tell either Tish or me that you had nowhere to stay? Why didn't you call David or Sylvester? Nope, don't answer," she says, holding up a hand. "I already know why. Emma, stop being so—so fucking *nice.* It's bad for my nerves." She takes a gulp of her wine. "We're your *friends*. We'd have changed our plans."

My friends are *so* wonderful.

"Oh God," Rachel continues, slapping her forehead with her palm. "Please don't tell me you slept in your car. *Do not* tell me that's what you did. That *is* what you did, isn't it?"

"Of course I didn't sleep in my car," I say, but I know that I'm blushing just a bit because my face is hot. "I stayed with Jack. In fact, I'm moving into his house tomorrow."

There is an incredulous silence. I may as well have told them I'm moving to Venus.

"But you hate Jack," Tish says.

.................

## Sunday, August 18

You know, living with Jack is okay. It's weird, I thought we'd be at each other's throats all the time. But over the past three weeks we've settled into quite a nice routine. No real flies in the ointment.

Apart from the telephone.

I think he got really pissed about that, actually. It's not my fault, is it, if I have such great friends and family who need to speak to me continually? Anyway, this came to a head last weekend. I was scrubbing the shower along to *Led Zeppelin IV* when Jack called me to the phone. As I took it, he gave me a very pointed, disgusted look.

"What can I say?" I ask him. "I'm a popular girl with lots of friends. Hello?"

"Hi, Emma?"

"Yes?" I don't recognize this person.

"How are you today? My name is Greta and I'm calling on behalf of—"

A telemarketer! I don't believe it! Will these people never

leave me alone? What do I have to do? How do they find me? How?

Anyway, after I get rid of Greta, who wants to be my new best friend, plus she wants a minimum fifteen-dollar bronze donation for her very worthy charity, I am not happy.

"That was cruel," I tell Jack, after promising to send Greta my money by return mail. "You could have said I was out or something."

"Hey, can I help it if you're popular? Everyone loves Emmeline," he says, whistling as he heads back to varnish a floor.

Anyway, we've resolved the issue. Or rather, Jack has. On Wednesday night after he got back from the gym, he handed me a piece of paper with a telephone number scrawled on it. Plus a plain, brown box.

"Here. Give this number to everyone you know. Please. For my sanity. And my social life."

"What's this?"

"Your new line. And your new telephone. There's an outlet in your room."

How nice is that?

Well, during the week, I head straight for the gym after work (to work off the Adam/Lou-induced angst—but to be fair, they've been okay just recently), arriving home around eight. I make myself something to eat. And okay, so I make enough for Jack to stick in the microwave when he comes in. Yes, I know this is very domesticated of me, and I shouldn't be doing the me-woman-me-cook thing. But I don't mind. I need to eat something other than noodles, and if I'm just cooking for myself, I can't be bothered with anything more complicated than grilled cheese. So it's good, cooking for two, see?

Actually, I've been very good, foodwise. I'm drinking the shakes and eating healthily, and I've put on three more pounds—my face is filling out, and my muscles are definitely improving.

This is a very good look for me.

Jack finishes work much later than me. He's working on

some big warehouse conversion project at the moment, so they're all under a lot of pressure. He goes to the gym around eight to get his workout, then arrives back at the house around ten. As he's arriving, I'm taking a shower so that I don't get in his way in the mornings, after which I head to bed with some herbal tea and a good book. So you see, we hardly see each other.

Friday nights are a bit different. I meet Tish and Rachel after work for coffee and a general catch-up on the week's news (despite the fact that we speak at least once a day on the telephone), so I get to the gym around eight. Which, co-incidentally, is the same time as Jack. So we work out, and then we go for a Thai meal.

It's not like a date or anything, we just have to eat. So we may as well eat together, see? Plus, Jack says that he wants to feed me once a week, because it's only fair on account of me cooking for him. And you know, it's nice—he's not quite the jerk jock I thought he was. Although he *is* still an ionic bonder. I don't think he dates (sleeps with) the same woman more than once.

Saturdays, after yoga class with Tish and Rachel, I do chores. Laundry, food shopping, cleaning. And Jack works on the house. I didn't realize what a skilled craftsman he is—he's doing most of the renovations himself. Saturday night is Jack's hot date night, and my hot-movie-at-home-by-myself night. This is lovely. This is good. Tish and Rachel are both pretty vague about how they're spending their Friday and Saturday nights at the moment, because I suspect they don't want to make me feel jealous by admitting they're having lots of sex, and I'm, well, I'm not having any sex.

Sunday nights, of course, I meet my lovely friends at Chez Nous and Jack usually has another hot date. So all in all it's working out pretty well. It's a bit like having a husband, but without the sex. Or the rows.

I miss *sex*, though. Although I know Adam is a bastard, I kind of miss *him* . . . But I think it's maybe time for me to start dating again. Not only for the sex. Next week is Cougan & Cray's annual Colleague of the Year dinner, and it would be great if I could find a boyfriend before then. You see, Bastard Adam is the Colleague of the Year.

It's very formal. Everyone talks about it the whole year around. It involves new gowns, manicures, pedicures, facials, hair—the *works*. Most of the women take at least the afternoon off work to be beautified before the evening's revelries (food and drink all free). I have my invitation. But I'm not going.

I refuse to go alone, a sad, dateless spinster, while Adam and Stella make nice with each other. Object of Pity is not my style at all, and I'd rather eat Thai with Jack than eat humble pie . . . Still, if I could magically produce a good-looking guy to take with me, I think I'd go just to spite them.

Anyway, tonight I'm looking pretty hot. I'm wearing a long, floaty skirt that skims my ankles, and a sheer, pale blue, peasant style blouse. The tiny silver stars on my (very slightly padded but only a bit) bra glitter through the sheer material of the blouse. My skin is glowing with good health and my hair is gleaming with highlights (went to the salon yesterday morning after yoga with the girls). Pity I'm not likely to meet any eligible men in Chez Nous.

I slip into pale blue sandals, grab the matching purse and walk down the stairs, imagining I'm Cinderella making an entrance at the ball. I smile, and float elegantly down, sliding my fingers along the newly finished banister rail.

It is then that I notice Jack *watching* me from the hall.

So I stop graciously waving to imagined throngs of admirers and clomp down the rest of the way. Some things we do are just not *meant* to be witnessed by others.

"Wow, *baby*," he tells me, shaking his hand. "We are lookin' *hot!*"

"Shut. Up." My face is very hot. Actually, Jack looks pretty hot too, in black Calvin Klein jeans and a white DKNY T-shirt.

"Wave to me, princess, *wave* to me," he says, falling to his knees in mock James Brown style, raising his hands to the ceiling.

"Behave yourself, idiot," I say, pausing to check my makeup and hair in the hall mirror. "See you."

"Hey, you got a hot date tonight?"

"No. It's Sunday. I'm meeting friends for dinner."

"Oh," he says, then gives me the little-boy-lost look. I know he's just teasing.

"Have a good time," he adds. "Don't, you know, worry about me being home alone."

"Don't tell me macho man has no date tonight?"

"Nobody asked me. Nobody loves me. Nobody cares. Guess I could order pizza and watch the news."

I know he's manipulating me for an invite. I just *know* it.

"What about Laura? Or Susan? Or Ann?" I ask, raising an eyebrow.

"Nah."

He really is an ionic bonder. But at least he doesn't string them along like Adam strung me along . . . And I'm not taking him to meet my friends.

*Definitely* not.

But it does seem mean. He's spoken to them all frequently on the telephone, anyway.

"Okay," I say brightly as I head for the door. "Have fun."

"You're a hard woman, Emmeline Taylor."

"It's the new me."

Actually, they're all dead curious to meet Jack. But I sort of don't want them to meet him, because then it will make him like a—a friend, or something.

"Well, say hi to everyone for me. Tell Katy to keep up the pressure with Marion Lacy. And tell Sylvester not to worry too much about the wrinkles."

He *knows* about these things? He spoke to them like once or twice and already they're best buddies?

"I really miss them since you got your own line."

I am going to regret this. I just *know* it.

"Okay," I say. "But if you mention the napping-in-the-car business, you will be a dead man."

"Hey, I can be discreet."


"Emma." Tom kisses my cheek. "Thanks," he whispers. "Whatever you three girls said to Katy, it worked."

"No, we didn't really do anything," I tell him. "It was all Katy."

"She was great, you should have seen Marion Lacy's face when Katy laid into her," he says, beaming with pride.

This is the first time we've seen Katy and Tom since their trip to Disneyland. Obviously, they sorted out their problems because we think they've spent the past few Sunday nights in bed. They certainly look fuck-drunk, and although I'm delighted for them, I can't help but feel a bit jealous.

"I like your Jack," Tom says, as he heads back to Katy and kisses the back of her neck.

But he's not *my* Jack. He's just a friend. I don't want anyone thinking that I *like* him, or anything.

"Wow," Tish whispers to me as she glances across at Jack. He is talking to Rachel. I think that she and Jack look really good together. Really *great* together. He's gorgeous, she's gorgeous . . .

*I am a bitch.* How can I feel jealous of my best friend?

"You never told me he's hot—sort of like an older Heath Ledger with dark hair."

"Shut up," I say. "He's not a bit like Heath."

"He seems really into you." Rachel joins us, sipping on her Chardonnay.

"No he's not," I protest. "He's into any woman under fifty. But he loses interest after one fuck."

"Yeah, but it would almost be worth it, don't you think?" Rachel says.

Oh God. I hope she doesn't have any ideas for Jack. It's

not that *I* want him, of course, but I'd rather he didn't sleep with all my female friends. That would be really icky.

"I'd really prefer it if you didn't . . ." I start, very uncomfortable with the idea of Rachel and Jack in his king-size bed.

"Not me. I'm fixed up in the fuck department," Rachel says, a little coyly. And she blushes, which is completely odd, and I wonder what's going on.

"I mean you," she says, artfully turning the attention away from herself.

"No. Bad idea," I say, my cheeks flushing because I can't help but wonder what Jack looks like minus his clothes . . . "Really bad idea," I insist. "He's my landlord. It would be like sleeping with my boss. Done that, got my heart broken. Anyway, who are *you* sleeping with these days? Is it still Marco?"

"No." Rachel flushes even more. "It's . . . kinda early to talk about it. I just want to see how it goes."

*My God.* She's in love.

"My God," Tish says, "Rachel's in love. You are, aren't you?"

"Shhh," Rachel hisses. "I—I don't know—"

"How the mighty have fallen," Tish crows. And then, "I'm sorry, honey, I shouldn't be so smug and superior about it."

"Why not? I can't remember how many times I've been smug and superior with you two girls. You crow all you like."

"Who is he?" I ask.

"Can I tell you another time? It's not that I don't want you to know, I just don't want to jinx it."

Wow, this sounds serious.

"Anyway, back to Heath." Tish grins. "He'd be perfect to take to the dinner. Tell me you wouldn't love it. All the women drooling over him, all the men green with envy. Adam green with envy."

"No. Absolutely not. I am not going to do this. Promise me neither of you will suggest it, or I will be your ex-friend."

"I think the lady's protesting too much," Rachel says. "What do you think, Tish?"

"Definitely."

"Promise me."

"Okay."

"Darling," Katy calls to me across the table. "Who are you taking to the dinner on Friday night?"

Rachel and Tish smirk, and I make a mental note to cross them off my Christmas-card list. Trust Katy to remember!

"What dinner?" Tom asks, and David tells him (and Jack) about Colleague of the Year. I drink my Chardonnay more quickly than is good for me, and cough so badly that David has to slap me on the back.

"I'm not going," I say, after I've recovered my breath.

"*Chérie,* you have to go to show Bastard Adam zat you are a desirable, beautiful woman. Because zat's what you are. *N'est-ce pas?*" Sylvester turns to Jack for agreement. Oh God.

"Sure." Jack grins at me. "Emma's a complete sex goddess."

I know he's only being nice. After all, he's seen my breasts. Oh God, why did I have to remember that, now?

"If you don't go, what will people think?" David asks. "They'll think you're a scaredy-cat. Adam's the Colleague of the Year," David adds to Jack.

"I'm *so* not a scaredy-cat," I say, flushing. "I just don't want to go."

"She doesn't have a date," David tells Jack. "We need to get her a date. What are you doing Friday night, Jack?"

"No!" I say.

"Why not? I scrub up real nice. I look good in a tux," Jack says, and my heart skips a beat. Which is ridiculous, because I'm so not interested in him that way.

"I'll just bet you do," David says, giving him the once over. "But not as handsome as you, darling," he adds, to Sylvester.

"But—" I say.

"Well, I think it's a great idea," Katy says. "Don't you all think it's a great idea?"

There is a general consensus of head nodding and yesses and I know that I've been outvoted. Seems I'm the only one who doesn't. Besides, I don't have anything to wear.

"I don't have anything to wear," I say. Yes, I know this is pathetic.

"Don't be pathetic, sweetie. You have four shopping days before Friday. We'll find you something to wear," Rachel says. She is enjoying every minute of this.

Everyone loves Jack.

As we leave the restaurant, he is thronged with invites to come back the same time next week. And every following Sunday night. This is not fair. This was supposed to be a once-only thing. I want my Sunday nights with my friends. I don't want Jack complicating things.

"You don't have to do this," I tell Jack as we walk home. "Really. My friends mean well, but they really put you in a corner there."

"You turning into a wimp on me?"

"No, I'm *so* not a wimp. I just don't want to go to the stupid dinner, is all."

"Liar."

# 17

32AA

## TO DO

1.  Do not sleep with Jack.

2.  Forget Jack and concentrate on new role as intelligent, perceptive, wise, great advice–giving goddess.

3.  Do not even *think* about sleeping with Jack.

### Friday, August 23

God, I'm nervous. I check myself in the full-length mirror one more time and fuss with my hair.

The black tank and skirt I found at the Calvin Klein outlet are fabulous, although I had to seriously ravage my savings account. (But Tish and Rachel assure me they are well worth it.) The tank has three straps on each shoulder that graduate down to the top of my (beautifully defined, thanks to the gym) arms. The skirt is long and flowing, skimming my ankles. I've clipped tiny, glittery barrettes in my hair.

And I'm wearing my Manolo Blahnik shoes. I'm so glad they could be repaired!

"Emma," Jack calls up. "Cab's here."

With a final glance at myself, I drape the chiffon wrap over my arms and pick up Rachel's Dolce and Gabbana evening purse.

Time to go.

I hope I look all right. What am I obsessing for? I know I look all right because this is a—

"Wow. That's a *gorgeous* look for you." Jack smiles at me as I reach the bottom stair, and I gasp, because I can't believe he's just finished my thought.

"You look beautiful, Emma," he tells me, and I get a warm feeling in the pit of my stomach because he's eating me with his eyes.

"You look beautiful yourself," I tell him, because he does. In fact, he's looks so good, I'm getting the strangest urge to ravish him right here, on the hall floor. I must stop doing this. I concentrate on the suit instead. I'm pretty sure his tux is Versace.

"Come on, princess, let's go dazzle them," he says, holding out his arm. His smile dazzles *me,* and tugs at my heartstrings.

As we ride through the Lincoln Tunnel and into Manhattan, I force myself not to keep looking at him. Not Jack. I can't be harboring illicit thoughts about Jack, for heaven's sake.

God, but he smells so good . . .

Cocktail hour is in full swing by the time we arrive, and the foyer is full of glittering gowns and black tuxedos. I see Lou Russo chatting to two of the secretaries. He looks about ten years old—but I wish him well, because for once, I can't muster the emotion to be mad at him. I'm too intoxicated by Jack. But then Lou sees me, and gives me a funny sort of half wave, so I smile. I can afford to be generous. And then Lou glances at Jack in disbelief, then back at me again. This does not make me feel good, and I start to worry that I've chosen the wrong outfit.

"Relax," Jack tells me. "You look fabulous, just enjoy yourself."

So I do relax. And I do start to enjoy myself. As we wander toward the far end of the foyer, we stop and chat to people I know, and Jack is the perfect date. Charming, witty, attentive. Completely fuckable . . .

*Reality-check time.*

I must remind myself that Jack is not my real date.

"Emma," Grady Thomas calls to me. "How lovely to see you."

Grady and his wife are nice. I wish Grady had got dear old Johnny's job, instead of Adam. As I chat to them, Jack goes to get us some drinks and I see Adam and Stella arrive.

They are heading straight toward me, so I cannot avoid them. After they greet Grady and his wife, their attention turns to me. Grady and his wife move on to say hi to some other people and so leave me to Adam and Stella's not-so-tender mercies. But at least I look good, so I give them a friendly smile.

"Emmeline," Adam says. "Good to see you."

For once, oddly, the sight of them together does not upset me. I wait for the familiar knot in my stomach, but Adam's beautiful smile does not make me wish for him back. I wonder if I'm over him?

"Emily," Stella gushes, waving her ring hand at me. I swear the rock on her finger is the size of Gibraltar. "How *sweet* you look tonight," she says, but her voice is insincere and she makes it sound like an insult.

Stella is divine in cream silk Ralph Lauren. Her hair and makeup are flawless, and if I didn't know better, I'd place her in her early thirties. And her cleavage. Wonder if it's natural? She's so beautiful, so elegant, so rich . . . No wonder Adam prefers her to me. But I don't care, I really don't, because Jack thinks I'm beautiful.

"Adam tells me your father's a plastic surgeon, dear," she says, pointedly glancing at my braless (because I cannot wear a bra with this top) breasts. "I'd never have guessed."

Oh. No. Not this again.

I feel my self-confidence shrivel and die, because her meaning is completely clear. Why are people so unkind? She got the man. She got the ring. She *won*. Why does she have to rub my face in it? I am just about to excuse myself and head to the ladies' room in search of a friendly plant to chat to when Jack comes charging to the rescue.

"Yes, that's right, isn't it, darling?" He smiles, placing a possessive hand on my shoulder. "Joseph Taylor's one of the top guys in the area, so if you need a good plastic surgeon I can highly recommend him," Jack says, pointedly examining Stella's flawless throat for signs of droop.

Stella's smile falters very slightly.

I love Jack's white knight act, even though it is only an act. Isn't it? Well, anyway, whatever it is it's really nice.

"She's really lucky she doesn't need her father's skill with a scalpel," Jack continues smoothly. "And her skin—her skin is wonderful. So fresh, so young—don't you agree? That's something not even the surgeon can plastically enhance, don't you think?"

I think Stella will have a fit, right here on the plush carpet, in a minute. I half expect her to start foaming at the mouth, because Jack's meaning cannot be lost on her.

God, I *love* this.

Even if she does find some way to extract future revenge.

"I'm Jack, by the way," he finishes, holding out his hand.

"Jack, er, this is Stella Burgoyne," I say, and then, "And this is Adam, my boss."

"Great you meet you." Jack shakes his hand, and I think Adam is wincing. Adam is in fairly good shape, but Jack is much more broad and muscular.

"Emma's told me all about you." Jack smiles his wolf smile. "Congratulations on the engagement."

"What is it you do, Jack?" Adam asks, his eyes narrowing as Jack pulls me even closer to his side.

"I'm an architect. I'm currently working on the Hendon development in Hoboken."

"Oh, how interesting," Stella says, her eyes flashing daggers. And then to Adam, "Come on, darling, we have to circulate. Nice to meet you."

And then they're gone.

"That was a really nice thing you did," I tell Jack.

"I'm a nice guy. My God, that broad's a bitch. I'm sure glad I'm not in his shoes. Come on," he says, taking my elbow. "They're calling us into dinner."

Fortunately, we are not at the same table as Adam and Stella. They are sitting at the top table, with all the other top executives. I think Stella has had too much to drink, because she's flirting heavily with William Cougan, and Adam looks decidedly pissed.

As we take our places, I'm glad to find myself seated next to Angela and her husband (whose black wig is obviously a black wig).

"Adam's pissed," Angie says to me. "Stella ain't behavin' herself—think she's after fryin' a bigger fish."

"What? You mean William Cougan?"

"Yeah—I heard it from Tracey in Human Resources."

This thought cheers me immensely. Although I don't want Adam back (at least I'm pretty sure I don't), it would serve him right to have the tables turned.

"Glad you're at our table," Angie says. "Some of the pricks at our place make me sick." And then she adds in a whisper, "Who's the gorgeous hunk?"

"Just a friend," I whisper back.

"Wish I had friends who looked like that."

"Jack, this is Angela and her husband, Morrie."

"Delighted," Jack tells them, and we exchange names around the table.

As we eat the first course of salad and pâté, the blonde from Marketing on Jack's other side flirts madly with him. And of course, I'm not jealous, because he's just here as my friend. If he meets someone, then that's great, isn't it?

As we eat the main course, Blondie is all but ready to climb into Jack's lap. My God, would you just look at her makeup? She'll need a hydraulic drill to get all that stuff off her face . . .

Angie, who I'd thought quiet and morose, talks at me non-stop, so I don't get the chance to interrupt the tête à tête between Jack and Blondie. Not that I want to, of course.

"Grab your favorite partners, all you rock 'n' roll fans," the band leader announces. "We're gonna heat up this place with Van Morrison's 'Brown-Eyed Girl.' "

I love to rock and roll. I wonder if Blondie will ask Jack to dance?

"Come on," Jack says, tugging at my arm. "Let's show them what we're made of."

"You dance?"

"Sure. I'm a man of hidden talents."

"Obviously." And I want to know what they are, I think, but obviously don't say. "Don't you want to dance with your new friend?" I ask instead. Which is pretty dumb of me, because it sounds like I'm jealous.

"Heather? No. Why, do you *want* me to dance with her?" He smiles at me. "You jealous?"

"Of course not. What's to be jealous about?"

"Okay," he says. "Glad we got that sorted out. So can we dance now?"

Surprisingly, Jack is a great dancer, and as he whirls and twirls me around the dance floor with panache and grace, I am having a lovely time. The party is lovely. Jack is lovely. As the music moves into an eighties medley, we dance and shake our stuff, until finally, to accompany the dessert course, the band slows to a soft, romantic song.

"You game for this?" Jack says, holding out his arms.

I'd love to, but I daren't. I'm liking Jack far more than I should. There's nothing I want more than to be held by him, just to see what it would be like, of course. And so I mustn't.

"Actually, I'm beat from all the dancing," I lie. "I'm gonna head back to the table. I want my dessert."

"You sure?" he asks, and I don't know if I'm just reading too much into this, but I almost think he looks sorry that I don't want to slow-dance. I'm so tempted.

"Sure," I tell him, before I throw myself at him. "I need my sugar fix. Maybe Blondie likes to slow dance."

Why did I say that? That was dumb. Jack lets go of me and drops his arms to his sides, as if I've just slapped him in the face.

"Maybe I'll ask her," he says.

And then it happens.

As we make our way back to our table, just as we are nearly there, just as we are in full view of our fellow diners, Lou Russo stumbles into me with his drink. In slow motion, the glass tips toward me and his white wine empties onto my breasts. As the liquid soaks the fabric of the top, it clings to me and the outline of my nipples are jutting clearly against the fabric. I might as well be naked.

"Whoa, there," Lou tells me, smirking. "Sorry about that, Emma, accidents will happen. You need to watch where you're going."

As I glance down at myself in disbelief, the two secretaries giggle. All conversation at the table stops as everyone looks at me. Blondie tries to hide a smirk as she looks at my non-breasts, but she doesn't quite manage it.

"Don't worry, Emma," Lou says. "One of the good things about having no breasts is that you look the same wet or dry. No one's gonna notice."

And I know that Lou is just a juvenile, idiot boy, but I cannot help it. I am transported back in time to Peri and Dad's wedding and the unkind comments of two other juvenile, idiot boys.

"Do you have a problem?" Jack, the idiot boy, says, stepping up to Lou. He towers over Lou by at least six inches, and Jack is so angry that I think he's going to punch Lou. I don't want this. I don't want to make a scene.

"Leave it, Jack," I say, grabbing my purse and clutching my wrap in front of me. I turn on my heel and head for the restroom, hoping that not too many people will notice my dripping clothes in the dim lighting of the ballroom.

For a while I just stand inside the locked cubicle with my forehead pressed against the cool plastic of the door, tears streaming down my face. I can't do this anymore. I'm sick of all the comments about my breasts. Why don't people say nice things about my intellect, about my kindness? Why are men obsessed with breast size?

"Emma? It's me." Angie. "Come on out of there, honey, that little dick ain't worth it. He's just sour because he knows a girl like you will never date a prick like him."

I open the door and Angie clucks over me like a mother hen, which is really comforting.

"Come on. Let's fix your face and get you back to your man. He's outside the door waiting for you. He's really worried about you, honey."

"Jack? But we're just good friends," I say, as she wipes away my smeared mascara and expertly applies more.

"Sure. Tell it to the Pope."

"No, really . . ."

"Trust me. I know these things. There. All done. Not a tear left in sight. You okay now?"

"Yeah. You go back to Morrie. I'll be fine."

"Okay. Don't keep Jack waiting too long."

I can't stay in here forever. The restroom is thankfully empty. I take a really good look at myself in the mirror, hating my small breasts, and then I pull my wrap around my shoulders, holding it in front of me to hide my 32AAs. Cinderella has turned into a pumpkin and it's time to go home.

"Emma, are you in there?" It's Jack. "Emma, I know you're in there. If you don't come out, I'm coming in."

I don't want to see Jack. I don't want to see the pity in his eyes, because just for a while there, I thought it might have been desire. But I think it was just pity. Take the poor, dateless, jilted, breastless girl to the party.

"I mean it. I'm coming in right—"

"I'm here," I say, opening the door. I don't look at him.

"You okay? Man, that kid's a jerk."

"Yes," I say, staring at the floor.

I hope Lou's impotent and can't get it up. I hope his penis is three inches long. I hope all his girlfriends poke fun at his tiny little penis.

"Just a stupid, insecure, jealous little jerk."

"Did you beat him to a pulp?" Stupid question, but I half hope he did.

"Nah. He's not worth it. I just put the fear of God into him, that's for sure. I don't think he'll bother you anymore."

And when I say nothing, Jack grasps my chin so that I have to look into his eyes.

"Emma," he tells me. "He's just a stupid kid."

"Yes, I know," I say, pulling my face away. "I remember a similar occasion when some other stupid kids said something unkind about my breasts. But I guess they were just being, you know, guys. Jocks."

This stops him in his tracks and he rakes a hand through his hair.

"Look," he says.

"No," I tell him. "I'm going home."

I am just climbing into a cab when I realize that he is right behind me.

"You don't have to leave the party on my account," I say, because instead of being angry with Lou, all of my fury is directed at Jack. For what happened at Dad and Peri's wedding. And because I've allowed myself to be lulled into a false sense of security. I like Jack too much and it scares me, because I know that he's a one-fuck kind of guy. Not a forever kind of guy.

"I'm sure you'll find a chick with breasts who wants to sleep with you. Don't let me ruin your evening." Yes, I know this is bitchy. I just want Jack to stop being nice to me.

"Emma, that's not fair."

"It is *so* fair. Heather's really into you."

"Will you stop?" he says, and I know that I am pushing it too far.

He gives our address to the cabdriver and neither of us says a word until we are inside the house. I am going straight to bed, because I am going to have a really good cry. But as I step up onto the second stair, Jack is right behind me.

"Emma," he says, softly grasping my upper arms. "There's something you need to know about what happened at the wedding."

I don't move, because I can't. I'm frozen to the spot.

"Chip and I . . ." He sighs, and I shiver as I feel the warmth of his breath on my nape. "Look, if I did something, Chip had to do it better. If *I* liked a girl, Chip had to prove that she liked *him* better. The things we said on the terrace that night, well, I didn't mean them. I thought if he knew I really liked you, he'd have to have you."

I don't know what I was expecting, but it wasn't this. Is he admitting that he liked me, all those years ago? Have I carried a stupid grudge all this time for the wrong reasons?

And then he turns me gently around to face him.

"Chip slept with my fiancée in Hong Kong," he tells me. "That's why we split up."

"Oh God, that's terrible. He was your best friend," I say, finding my voice. "Jack, I didn't know. I'm so sorry . . ."

"Yeah," he says, almost whispering. "Here," he says, tugging the wrap from me because I'm still clutching it like a security blanket. But I let him take it, because in that moment I trust him.

As the wrap flutters to the floor, Jack places his hands on my midriff, over the still-damp fabric.

"You are so beautiful," he tells me, his eyes on my breasts. "Your breasts are perfect, just like the rest of you. Promise me you won't do anything stupid?" He looks up from my breasts and we are nearly at eye level, because he is still standing on the hall floor.

And then I know he's going to kiss me.

As he silently asks permission with his eyes, I lean toward him to show him I'm receptive. I don't care if he's my landlord. I don't care if he's Peri's brother. I don't care about anything, except that this is Jack and that I want him so badly to kiss me.

And just as I close my eyes, just before our lips meet, the kitchen door is pushed open.

"Jack, Emma, where have you guys been?" It's Peri.

Our eyes fly open and Jack can't let go of me quick enough. Fortunately, Peri does not seem to notice.

"Oh, Jack." Peri runs the length of the hall and throws herself into his arms. "I've left Joe. Me and the twins are moving in with you."

"I just can't believe what he said." Peri sniffles as she drinks her tea. "After I told him he had to spend more time at home, he said that he couldn't stand being at home because—because—because the boys are a *nightmare*. He said that about his own children."

I give her another tissue and wonder what to say to be diplomatic, because I totally understand where Dad is coming from.

"He said that I'm ruining them by not disciplining them. I'm sorry, Emma, I know he's your dad too, but he doesn't have any idea about child-rearing. So, it's okay if we stay here, isn't it Jack? Until I figure out what to do?"

"Sure, of course it's okay," Jack says, sliding me a glance which I totally ignore.

"So why are you guys all dressed up?" she asks, noticing our clothes for the first time. "You been on a date or something? You have, haven't you? Oh, it's—"

"No, no date," Jack interrupts her quickly.

So quickly that I just know that he's regretting our near kiss. I'm surprised at the depth of my disappointment. But it's a good thing Peri interrupted us, isn't it, because if we'd had our one fuck, where would that leave me in the morning?

"I think we all need to get some sleep," I say, placing my cup on the table.

"Oh, I put the boys in your bed," Peri tells Jack. "The other two bedrooms are too smelly with varnish and paint— and there are no beds in them, anyhow. I can sleep with the boys, there's plenty of room for me in there. So I guess I'll see you guys in the morning."

And she leaves, before I can sneak up to my own bed, and I'm alone with Jack. The silence is heavy and loaded. I know Jack is watching me.

"I'm, er, I'm going to head off to bed now, too," I say to the floor.

"Emma?"

"Hmm?" I say to the table.

"About earlier—"

"Er, I'll see you in the morning," I say, and flee.

Yes, I know this is pathetic and cowardly.


I do not sleep well. I toss and turn, and am torn between (a) wishing I'd slept with him, and (b) thanking Peri for my narrow escape. This is what I get for having illicit thoughts about Jack. This is what I get for nearly letting him kiss me.

The following morning, I am exhausted, and sleep until after nine so I miss my Saturday-morning yoga with Tish and Rachel. I don't mind missing the yoga, because I feel like shit, but I do miss my friends. I'm not going to tell them about me and Jack nearly kissing, I think I'll leave that alone.

By ten, I decide to get up and face the music downstairs. If possible, I will slip quietly out of the front door and thereby avoid Peri, the terrible twins, and Jack. I'm so embarrassed by our near-kiss situation . . .

"Hi, Emma, you want some breakfast?" Jack calls from the kitchen. He sounds very cheerful.

He sounds like *old* Jack.

He is not nearly-kissed-me Jack anymore, and just for a

moment I am overwhelmed with regret that he will never be nearly-kissed-Emma Jack again.

"I'm making bacon and eggs for Peri and the boys. You want some?"

"Oh," I say as I pause at the kitchen. "Er, no thanks, Jack. I have stuff to do . . ."

Jack looks fabulous. Although wearing a faded T-shirt and cutoff shorts, he looks well rested. This is not fair, because (a) it means he didn't obsess all night like I did, and (b) he slept on the sofa. How can he look so great when I feel like shit. How?

"You must eat," Peri says, pressing a cup of coffee into my hand. "You look ill. Doesn't she look ill, Jack? Are you okay? You don't look okay. You definitely need to eat."

"She looks good to me," Jack tells me, flashing me his old-Jack friendly grin.

This is a bit of a relief, but would it hurt him to show the teeniest symptoms of disappointment about last night?

"Thanks, guys," I say, eyeing the twins, who are eating messily with their fingers. This is enough to put me off food for life, but at least they are marginally well-behaved when stuffing their faces with food. It is the only time they are quiet.

"I have stuff to do. I think I just need some fresh air," I say, putting down the coffee cup and heading for the door. "See you later."

It is very cowardly of me leaving Jack with Peri and the boys, but she is *his* sister . . . I think I'll go smother my sorrows in one of Rufus's banana-granola muffins.

As I reach for the door handle of the deli, I pause because I see Tish inside. She is seated at a table, and she is not alone. Rufus is sitting with her, and they are actually talking to each other. In fact, Tish is flirting with him. I can tell by her body language, plus, she's wearing that sexy little red *fuck me* dress. And Rufus is laughing and leaning closer to her.

Okay, they do not need me to play third wheel. I think I'll go see Rachel instead.

*You go, girl,* I think, sending silent, encouraging vibes to Tish.

When I reach Rachel's apartment, I ring the doorbell and am startled when a man's voice answers. Oops, this must be her new man. I don't want to interrupt. Okay, so this is not a good time for Rachel, either.

"Oh," I say. "Sorry. I'll come back later."

"Hold on. Are you a friend of Rachel's?"

"Er, yes."

I can always go and play third wheel with Tom and Katy instead—at least, I could play with Alex so that they can go back to bed for more hot sex.

I really must do something about my lack of sex. I think it's having a strange effect on my brain.

"Well, come on up," he insists, pressing the door-release buzzer.

I'm curious, so I get in the elevator, and as I reach Rachel's door, I am shocked by the man who opens it and smiles at me, because never in a million years would I have placed him as Rachel's type.

He is in his late thirties and is several inches shorter than Rachel. He is also rather cuddly (but in a nonfat way) and has a beard. He smiles, and his blue eyes crinkle nicely. He has a kind face.

"Hi," he says, holding out his hand. "I'm Hugh. Come on in."

Well, knock me down with a feather. This is Hugh?

"I'm Emma," I say, shaking his hand and grinning like an idiot.

"Rachel won't be a minute, she's just getting dressed. Come in, come in, I'll get you some coffee."

"That would be great," I say, following him into Rachel's kitchen. Her cats know instinctively that I am allergic to them, because they immediately start rubbing themselves around my ankles, and I sneeze.

"Bless you," Hugh says. "They have the same effect on

me. I'm doomed to weekly allergy shots in my butt. The things we do for love."

Oh. *That's* interesting.

Oh God, talking of love, what if they were, you know, having sex when I rang the doorbell?

"You sure I'm not interrupting . . . anything . . . ?" I tail off, because it sounds like I'm suggesting that I've just interrupted a bout of hot passion. Because that's exactly what I'm suggesting.

"No, not at all. We weren't in bed." He grins and I blush a little, but grin back. He really does have the kindest face.

"It's good to meet one of Rachel's friends," he says. "I was beginning to think you're all figments of her imagination. Or that she's scared you'll tell me all her secrets, because she won't let me come to Chez Nous on Sunday nights. Or that you're all embarrassingly odd. But you look lovely—not an oddness in sight."

"Why, thank you. So do you."

"Do not listen to this man," Rachel tells me from the bedroom door. "He's an idiot." She kisses me.

And she is glowing with that rosy hue of someone who's getting a lot of great sex. I can practically smell the pheromones oozing from her pores.

"Er, hi," I say. "I'm sorry I missed yoga this morning, I can come back later. Or maybe I should call you."

"Oh, I missed yoga, too, because—" Rachel pauses, and blushes. They *were* having sex.

"No, don't stop on my account, honey," Hugh tells her. "I'll leave you two girls alone, then you can talk about me in peace. I'll call you later, Rachel," he says, then he grabs her and kisses her very thoroughly. "Nice to meet you, Emma." His blue eyes twinkle. "Maybe she'll let me meet her other friends, now. I'm really well housetrained."

"I'm sure you are," I say, and I cannot help but smile back at him. He's just really, really infectious. "Nice to meet you, too."

As soon as the door closes behind him, Rachel turns to me.

"What do you think? Do you like him? Don't you think he's cute?"

"Rachel, he's lovely," I say, because he seems lovely. "But how did you guys get it together? I thought you hated him."

"Oh no, I never *hated* him. Not *hated* him, exactly."

I do not remind her of all our telephone conversations regarding motherfucking, bastard Hugh, because obviously love has given her a selective memory.

"He just sort of—I don't know. Broke down my barriers, wouldn't take no for an answer. He's really clever, you know, he has a doctorate, and he's kind and good-looking. . . ."

Beauty is in the eye of the beholder, I suppose.

"Anyway," Rachel says, blushing again. "He's asked me to marry him. And I've said yes."

## 18

.................................................................................

# Mother Love

### TO DO

1. Buy tampons.

2. Tell Jack to buy condoms.

3. Sleep with Jack (after all, will only be following motherly advice as all good daughters should).

**Friday, August 30**

God, is it really only a week since Peri and the boys arrived? It feels like longer.

It feels like an eternity.

Last night, when I got home from the gym (I spend as much time there as I can at the moment so as to arrive home after the boys are safely asleep), Peri was waiting for me.

"Emma, darling," she says as she places steak and fries in front of me. "You're so *late*. I was worried about you. Are you really busy at work?"

I mumble a feeble excuse, but Peri isn't really listening.

Ugh. Peri, bless her, cannot cook anything except steak or burgers and fries. Does she know what red meat does to your veins? Still, if someone takes the trouble to cook you a meal (despite the fact you've told them you'll grab something at the gym), the least you can do is try to pretend to eat it.

I pretend to eat a soggy fry as Peri starts to tell me today's tale. Because there's always a tale.

"You know, you must be more careful where you leave your personal stuff," she says. "The boys were playing upstairs today and they found your tampons. But you shouldn't leave stuff like that where little ones can stumble across it."

"Peri, I don't have kids," I start. "I don't—" *need to worry about where I put my stuff,* I nearly say, but don't because Peri jumps back in.

"Yes, and that's the problem. I know you don't have kids, but one day you will, and then you'll know what I mean. So kindly think about it, will you? I had to make up a story for the twins. I told them that the tampons are for cleaning makeup off your face and I think they bought it."

"But maybe they shouldn't, you know, be playing in my room when I'm not there," I say, cautiously watching her reaction.

"Emma, I don't have eyes in the back of my head," she says with an indignant sniff, and I'm sorry I said anything.

"I only let them out of my sight for a couple of minutes, so if you could just make sure you don't do it again, then we'll all be much happier. Okay?"

" 'Kay," I say, pushing a bite of steak to one side.

"Good, I'm glad we got that cleared up. Where's Jack? It's nearly ten, is he always this late? You'd think he'd make more of an effort to come home early and see the boys, wouldn't you? He's just like your dad. Sorry, Emma, but he is. You wouldn't believe what I had to tell the twins about the king-size box of condoms they found in his bathroom. They thought they were balloons—they opened every single one in the box. Anyway, I'm tired, so I'm going to get an early night. I'll see you tomorrow. Good-night. Enjoy your meal."

"Yes. Thank you. Good-night," I say, then the moment I'm sure she's upstairs, I empty the food into a supermarket bag and push it to the bottom of the trash.

A king-size box of condoms, huh? Jack obviously has high expectations, sexually speaking. This thought depresses me and I try not to think about Jack and condoms. Or sex.

But this can't go on. I mean, I know Peri is Jack's sister, but this is supposed to be my *home*. I *do* pay rent. Okay, so a reduced rent, but I should have *some* say here. Dad has *got* to come and take her home soon or I'll need therapy. I grab the telephone and punch in the numbers.

"Dad, it's me," I say. "When are you and Peri getting back together?"

"Honey, she just won't listen," he says. "I *do* love her, you know? And I love the boys. But every time I try to explain to her that she's setting them on a path to infantile delinquency, she accuses me of child abuse. I'm not saying she should smack them, or anything, but she lets them do exactly what they like."

"I know," I say, glumly. Obviously Dad is not going to be a big help here, so we finish our conversation just as Jack lets himself in the back door.

"Is it safe?" he asks.

"Yes. Although your condoms didn't survive," I tell him. Oh, I didn't mean to mention condoms. Not after Friday night. I quickly change the subject before he can make a smart reply.

"Peri's made you dinner. *Bon appétit.*"

"Not steak again?"

"Yes."

"What did you do with yours?"

"Hidden at the bottom of the trash can."

"Good plan."

"Good-night."

"Emma?"

Oh God, I hope he's not going to get too personal. Although mentally harassed by the twins, he's been back to normal this week. I like old Jack. Old Jack is safe Jack.

"Hmm?" I speak to the door.

There is a long, loaded silence, and then finally he sighs and runs a hand through his hair.

"Nothing. Good-night."

This does not make me feel good, so I go to bed and lie awake for hours obsessing about him.

Anyway, I comfort myself, at least work is not stressing me out. This week, Adam has been surprisingly nice to me. He's very interested in my welfare, because he keeps asking me if everything is okay. And a number of times he's stopped at my cubicle just for a friendly chat. A kind of "How's Jack? How did you meet him? You guys are living together then, huh? Oh, great, I'm happy for you," kind of chat.

So maybe I did let him think Jack and me *are* together. I didn't lie, or anything, Adam just assumed so I let him assume more.

Lou has kept his distance all week, which is also good. I suspect I have Jack to thank for that. Plus, I think Adam is really pissed with Lou, which is great. But earlier today, Lou was feeling brave (foolish boy—I can't believe I let him get away with bossing me around before) and tried to get us back onto our old footing. Him Account Manager, me Humble Secretary.

I am just chatting to Angie when Lou comes to my cubicle. He stands there for a couple of minutes as Angie tells me about her plans for the weekend, and finally (but only after we've let him suffer), we both turn to look at him.

"Hi, ladies," he says.

"What can I do for you, Lou?" I ask politely.

"Er, I was just thinking that maybe it's doughnut time. I'm a little hungry, so—"

"I'd love a doughnut." I smile. "Would you like one, Angie?"

"Sure. Cinnamon with frosting."

"Make mine apple." I smile sweetly. "It's so nice of you to treat us, Lou, we really appreciate it. Oh, and I'll have coffee, too—just milk, no sugar."

"Very nicely done, Emma," Angie says after Lou heads down to the doughnut store. "You learn quick. See, you just gotta apply Zen. You just gotta think how you want the situation to turn out, and make it so."

"Angie, you should give seminars. If ever you decide to do that, I'll sign Peri up straightaway." And then I tell her the tale of the tampons and condoms.

God, I wonder what they've done today.

I open the front door to chaos. There are papers all over the floor. Jack's papers. Bank statements, credit-card statements, architect plans . . . If someone told me a freak tornado had somehow only hit the inside of our house, I would not be surprised.

"Jack, you shouldn't just leave your papers lying around any old where." Peri's loud voice carries from the dining room.

Jack's home early. It's only eight. He's usually on his way to the gym by now. I wish I'd stayed longer, but have been feeling pangs of guilt for avoiding Peri and the boys. They are my family, after all.

"But the point is, I didn't leave them any old where, Peri. They were in files. In the dining room. On the bookshelf."

"But your bookshelves are too low."

"For fuck's sake, Peri—"

"There's no need to use language like that. The boys might hear you."

"Where are the little brats? No doubt wrecking the kitchen. Or my bedroom. Peri, you have got to exercise more control over them—they're turning into monsters."

Oh dear, maybe I should just slip upstairs to my room . . . Oh. My. God.

"What have you done?" I ask, as I regard the remains of my bedroom. Every item of makeup has been tested on every available surface. My underwear is scattered over the floor. The pink vibrator is currently doing its party piece in Jack Junior's hand, and Joe Junior has found my Goals by Thirty lists.

"Give them to me." I lunge for Joe Junior, but he evades

me and makes a break for the door with my papers in his grubby little hands. "And you." I try for Jack Junior, instead, but he screams so loudly that I stop in my tracks. Anyone would think I'd just beaten him black and blue. While I am still stunned by the decibels he has managed to achieve, he slips down the stairs with my vibrator still vibrating.

This has got to stop. I know they're only three. But I'm sure I didn't do this kind of stuff when I was three, Julia wouldn't have let me. Right, Peri has to sort this out for once and all. I'm going to speak to her. I'll apply Angie's Zen advice, that's what I'll do.

"Jack Junior, Joe Junior," I yell as I come running down the stairs. I want blood. But only metaphorically speaking, of course.

"Emma, don't shout like that, you'll frighten the twins." Peri's waiting for me at the bottom of the stairs. "How did Jack Junior get this?" she demands, wielding the throbbing, pulsating, vibrator (which, I have to add, I have still not used).

"Didn't I ask you last night to put your personal stuff in a safer place?"

This is so unfair. How come they get to be naughty and I'm the one in trouble? To add insult to injury, Jack appears in the dining-room doorway holding some papers. I think they are *my* papers.

"You should have more consideration. They are your brothers, after all."

"But they should have some consideration for me, too. My bedroom should be a *safer place*," I protest. "Can't you keep them out? They've wrecked it. They've destroyed every piece of makeup I possess, and my underwear is all over the place."

"I can't believe you're being so difficult," Peri says, bursting into tears. "If only you knew how hard it is bringing up two children, but you don't, because you don't have any—"

"Peri, what Emma means—" Jack, the peacemaker, puts an arm around her shoulders but the lady is not for turning.

"And you," she says. "You're just as bad. You hate them, don't you? And you hate me. I should never have come here."

Oh God, if this is what Dad has to go through every time he puts his foot down, it's a wonder he hasn't had a heart attack. But Peri, ditzy as she is, is usually lovely. So why is she behaving like a bitch to us? She knows we love the boys, and some part of her must realize that she cannot go on like this.

*This is good, Emma,* I tell myself, *this is what you should be doing.* Not looking for who to blame, but looking for solutions. I think back to what Angie said about Zen, and wonder how I can apply it to Peri. What would Angie do? What would Julia do?

As Jack tries to comfort the sobbing Peri, and as I am standing on looking, trying to think of a way to comfort the sobbing Peri, I have an epiphany, and I know what I'm going to do.

"Jack, go see what the boys are doing," I tell him.

"Don't you hurt my boys!" Peri shrieks.

"Peri, stop this," I say, in such a firm, commanding voice that she actually does.

"We're going to find the boys, clean them up, Jack is going to take them to bed and read them a story—"

"I am?"

"Yes, Jack. Don't interrupt. And then we're going to talk. Properly, without shouting, without accusations. Okay?"

The twins are halfway through smashing a box of eggs on the kitchen floor.

"No," I say to Peri. "Don't say a word. Jack Junior, Joe Junior, stop that *right now.* That's naughty." They look at me in disbelief.

But they do stop.

We clean up the mess, the boys are bathed and put to bed (amidst protests, but once Uncle Jack promises a bedtime story to only good boys, they succumb quickly enough), and Peri and I are at the kitchen table. I'm drinking a glass of wine, because I figure I deserve it. Peri is drinking soothing herbal tea.

"Peri," I begin. "No one hates you. No one hates the twins. But you have to see how badly they behave."

"But they're just exploring—"

"Their boundaries. I know. But you haven't set any for them. Boundaries, I mean. And boundaries are very important to a child."

"But what do you know about bringing up children?"

"I was a child myself. And Julia was very firm about what I could and could not do, but not to the extent where she discouraged me from exploring my environment. She encouraged me to reach for the sky, if I could get there. So did Dad. And you're wrong about him, too. He helped to raise me and I don't think I turned out too badly. A little demented around the edges, maybe," I say, and Peri gives me a weak grin. I take another gulp of my wine.

"I'm doing it all wrong, aren't I?" Peri starts to head toward another bout of tears, but I head her off at the pass.

"Not at all. You're a lovely person, and a good mother."

"I'm a terrible mother."

"That's not true. You're kind and loving. You just need to be a little more strict with the boys. If they're good, reward them. If they're naughty, don't let them watch television or have play dates. They're really smart kids. I bet you could turn all their excess energy around into something good, instead of tornado disaster time."

Then Peri begins to giggle, surprisingly, because I thought she might get pissed at me for giving her advice.

"Oh, Emma, it was so funny when Jack Junior came running into the kitchen with that terrible pink vibrator—"

"Yes, it was," I say, laughing with her. "You know, I didn't like them trashing my room the way they did, but at the end of the day, the mess can be cleaned. But what if I'd had something in there they could really hurt themselves with?"

"You're right," she tells me, looking tired. "When did you get to be so smart?"

"I'm not smart," I say. And then, "Peri, is something else worrying you? I mean, I know you've had a stressful week and everything, but you're not yourself at all."

"You're right. I *am* tired, I *am* washed out, I *am* on a short fuse. You see, I'm pregnant. It's playing havoc with my hormones."

*Oh God.* I hope she gets the hang of child-rearing with the twins before the new baby makes an appearance.

"Oh. Does Dad know?"

"I haven't told him yet. How will I cope when I have the new baby? I can hardly manage now," she says, and I stuff a tissue in her hand.

"Well, you could always get a nanny. And a cook," I add, because she should eat more vegetables if she's pregnant.

"Well, I don't know . . ."

"Maybe you wouldn't be so tired if you had help with the twins."

"I wouldn't want them to feel like I'd abandoned them."

"But you wouldn't be abandoning them," I tell her firmly. "It would just mean that you get some time for yourself. And for Dad," I add. I think that was very nice and subtle of me. Bringing Dad into the equation.

"I miss him." Peri sniffles into her tissue.

This is good. This is very good.

"And he misses you, too," I tell her. And then, "So, you're going back to Dad, then?"

"Don't worry." She gives me a watery smile. "I wasn't planning on destroying your lives forever. I think I should give Daddy a call."

"Good plan." And she's calling him Daddy again, which is a good sign.

Peri uses the phone in the living room, so that she can talk privately to Dad. I hope it goes well.

"When *did* you get to be so smart?" Jack asks me from the hall door.

"You heard all that?"

"Yeah." He grins at me, and pours himself some wine. "I liked all that stuff about boundaries. So tell me Emma, how do you set *your* boundaries?"

I think *new Jack* is rearing his head. And while I'm happy to help Peri in any way I can, I do not want to apply my advice to myself.

"These are yours, Madonna," he says, as he sits down opposite me and hands me my Life Goals.

"George Michael? Jon Bon Jovi?"

"Hey, you read them?" I feel so stupid. I should have thrown these out. I try to remember what I wrote just before my thirtieth birthday, and then I cringe, because the closest I come to achieving any of my goals is having great friends.

"Only by accident when I was clearing up. I loved the slut-in-the-bedroom part."

"You are such a—such a *guy*," I tell him.

"I do a great Jon Bon Jovi. Did you know I play guitar?"

Oh, the doorbell. Thank God!

"I'll get that," I tell Jack, happy to escape. "It might be Dad." Yes, I'm a coward. I admit it. I'm happy to escape Jack, but don't want to think too closely about *why* I want to escape Jack.

When I open the front door, it's not my dad at all.

It's my *mother*.

Who is supposed to be three thousand miles away in London.

"Mum," I say, because I'm—well—because I'm completely shocked to see her. "Julia. What are you doing here?"

"Emmeline, darling." Julia kisses my cheek. "It's nice to see you, too. Can't a mother come and see her daughter without a reason?"

"They don't usually fly three thousand miles to do it. Where's George?"

"George and I are not attached at the hip," she tells me.

"Just because we *live* together does not mean we have to spend every waking moment of every day together."

I think they've had a fight.

"You've had a fight, haven't you?"

"Of course we haven't had a fight," Julia tells me the next day as we wave off Peri and the boys for their reunion with Dad.

"Peri is so right for Joe, isn't she? Neurotic, ditzy—suits him perfectly. Sorry, Jack, I know she's your sister but it has to be said."

Julia is very proud of how she gets on well with her ex and his second wife. In fact, she treats Peri more like a daughter.

"Hey, I'm right with you. I love my sister, but God I don't want to live with her," Jack says. "Anyway, I'm going to finish painting the trim in the bedroom, now that I can do it without the twins wanting to help me."

"It didn't scar you for life, did it?" Julia asks me in an unusual display of uncertainty. "Joe and I getting divorced before you were born?"

"Of course not. I had a great childhood. You two have always gotten along." Which is true, but I think having the Atlantic Ocean between them helped. "Why are you worrying about that now?" Because, let's face it, they've been divorced for longer than I've been alive.

"Oh, I don't know. All the nasty divorce cases I handle, all those poor children—I see how hard it is on them. They'd rather have their parents together, and miserable, than happy and separated. I think marriage should be outlawed. It's far more sensible to live together."

"You *have* had a fight with George, haven't you?"

"George and I are perfectly fine."

I know this is a lie, because George has called three times today asking to speak to Julia, and she won't take his calls. This is not the Julia I know. This is not the Xena Warrior Princess I grew up with.

"We never fight," she says. "We just agree to differ on certain subjects. Anyway, I haven't come all this way to talk about George. Let's have a girly day in Manhattan. We'll go somewhere nice for lunch and catch up."

Unfortunately, Julia's idea of a girly day does not include any girly shopping. We spend our day visiting the Metropolitan and Guggenheim museums. Although I'm fond of art, by six in the afternoon I've had enough culture to last me until Julia's next trip.

Finally, we call into a café near Grand Central Station for subs and coffee.

"Did I tell you?" I say to Julia. "Rachel's getting married."

"What? *Rachel* Rachel? No, I don't believe it."

Thought this would interest her. Mum loves Rachel—she's exactly like Mum wanted me to turn out.

"Yeah. You'll meet Hugh tomorrow night. He's great—the way they are together remind me of you and George."

Okay, so I had ulterior motives for telling Mum about Rachel, but I think I managed to turn the conversation to her and George with great subtlety and diplomacy.

"Honestly, Emmeline, you're so transparent," she says, putting down her coffee. "All right, since you're determined to keep this up I'll tell you. We *have* had a disagreement. George asked me to marry him."

Oh. But that's lovely.

"But that's lovely," I say to her, because it is. It must be great to have someone love you enough to want to propose to you, mustn't it?

"No it's *not*. Don't you see? I don't want to get married again. We've been living together for seven years and I'm perfectly happy with our arrangement. Why does George need a bloody piece of paper? Why does he need to fix something that isn't broken?"

................

**Sunday night, Chez Nous**

Julia is flying back to England later tonight, so I'm not drinking because I have to drive her to the airport. I'm glad I brought her here—my friends are so nice. We're having an impromptu engagement party for Rachel and Hugh who, fortunately, is a great hit with everyone. Even Julia is impressed with him. She had a long chat with Rachel, and she's just been in the kitchen to call George, which is good.

"You know, maybe I should marry George," she tells me after consuming two glasses of champagne. "I *do* love him. And if he needs a piece of paper to make him happy, then would it hurt me to do it?"

"Julia, that's great," I tell her, hugging her.

"Don't get excited," she tells me. "No big wedding. Just me, George, and two witnesses. No fuss, no party."

I'm glad some things don't change. Alas, I am the only one not drinking champagne.

"But how did you know that Rachel was *the* one?" Jack asks Hugh, and I lean closer to listen to his reply.

"I guess it's all to do with diffusion," Hugh tells us. "You know, the spontaneous mixing of the particles of two substances caused by their random motion. Our particles just mixed, and that was it."

I completely understand why they're together. He speaks the same language. I wonder why Jack asked him that question? Has Jack met someone, or is it just curiosity?

"So when's the wedding?" Katy asks. "Because I'd love to help organize it." And then, "Don't worry, Tom, I won't turn it into another of my crusades."

"Darling," he tells her, affectionately kissing her cheek. "You're my maid in shining armor, you crusade all you like— just remember to be home for dinner."

"Thanks, Katy, but my mother's taken charge of the whole thing," Rachel says. "Trust me, you do not want to mess with her—she's been waiting for this her whole life."

Rachel's mother is planning a huge wedding, with white dresses and tiered cakes, the lot. The only stipulation Rachel made was that Tish gets to dress the bride, the bridesmaids, and matron of honor (coincidentally enough, that would be me, Tish, and Katy). This is a relief, because Tish will not torture me with something fluffy and vomit colored, with bows and frills everywhere.

It's funny. Out of Rachel, Tish, and me, I never would have guessed that Rachel would be the one getting married first. But then I thought she'd never get married at all. All it took was the right guy, and the rest has fallen into place. I hope she still rants occasionally, but not too much . . .

"Did you see *The New York Times* yesterday?" Rachel asks me.

"No. Should I have?" I was too busy admiring art with Julia and clearing up after Peri and the twins. Hope Peri and Dad will be okay. I think they will be. Dad was over the moon about the new baby. He called me last night—he loves the idea of a nanny and cook, and he tells me that the boys haven't been *quite* as bad as usual. Oh, well, Rome was not built in a day.

"There's a picture of Stella Burgoyne at a charity event with William Cougan," Rachel says.

"Oh?" That *is* interesting.

"Yeah, I thought you might find that interesting. I wasn't going to mention it, but I thought it would be better if you found out from me, rather than at work."

"Thanks."

"Don't go doing anything stupid," she tells me. "I know you, Emma Taylor. You leave that man alone." And then, "I hope she dumped him, I hope she broke his ionic-bonding heart to fucking pieces."

Me too, I think, but am distracted by the lovely picture Jack and Tish make. As Tish talks, Jack smiles and is hanging on to her every word. I wonder if he asked Hugh all those questions because he's in love with Tish? He *can't* be in love with Tish. Tish cannot do this to poor Rufus. Rufus will be broken hearted.

Not that I'm jealous, of course. Because it's horrid to be jealous of one's best friend.

I am still distracted by the thought of Jack and Tish, and poor broken hearted Rufus, as I drop Julia outside the departures gate.

"Darling," Julia says, hugging me across the stick shift. "It's been lovely. You must come to London more often."

"I'll try," I say. "Good luck with George."

"Oh, I don't need luck," she says, smirking. "Just a bottle of wine, a couple of candles, and an early night."

Okay. This is depressing. Even my mother, who at fifty-three is more beautiful than ever, is having more sex than me.

"Just a word of motherly advice before I go." She pauses as she's climbing out of the car. "Do yourself a favor and sleep with Jack."

## 19

*A New Life*

### TO DO

1. Be nice and stop having horrible thoughts about best friends.

2. Become wanton sex-kitten goddess.

3. Work on sex-kitten-in-morning look to assist plan to lure Jack into my bed.

**Saturday, September 7**

Thank God everything is back to blissful normalcy!

When I say normal, I mean me-and-Jack normal. Since I dropped Julia at the airport last Sunday, we've had the house back to ourselves. And we're back in our old routine—Jack is completely *old* Jack, my *pal* Jack. Actually, I can't remember when he stopped being just Jack and turned into pal Jack. When did I start liking him? Anyway, pals is good. Pals is what I want. (Although I can't stop thinking about what Julia said. You know, about having sex with him.)

Anyway, the only change in our routine is that he's not working late anymore. His team hit their deadline, so for now he can ease off a little. Several times this week we've bumped into each other at the gym, then come back home together for dinner.

It's nice to cook for two, and it's also nice not to eat alone. Last night, Friday night, we met at the gym as usual. And went for a Thai meal at our usual restaurant. So that's good, isn't it?

Peri and Dad are fine. They call regularly to give me updates on the nanny/cook situation.

Dad contacted an agency first thing Monday morning, and they've already met with a nanny they like (apparently she can cook, too). I think Dad's working fast so he can present Peri with a *fait accompli* before she can change her mind.

Julia and George are getting married in three weeks' time. Julia's booked Marylebone Registry Office in Westminster, which is a lovely, impressive, old building. Lots of pop stars get married there, apparently, and it just happens to be Julia and George's local office. She hated having to list herself as "spinster of the parish," because it sounds so awful.

In England, that is how an unmarried woman is described when completing marriage paperwork. I think it appears that way on the marriage certificate, too. Hmmm. Well, George gets to be "bachelor of the parish," and Julia, apparently, kicked up a fuss and insisted that she wanted to be "bachelorette of the parish." The registrar was not amused, but *spinster* is such an awful word, isn't it?

Anyway, Julia insists she's wearing cargo pants and a T-shirt for the happy occasion, because she doesn't want to conform to society's stereotypical expectations of a bride. Especially an older bride. But George has other plans. Unbeknownst to Julia, and with the help of the Internet and a credit card, he's taking her to Barbados and they're going to be married on the beach there. How romantic is that?

Meanwhile, Adam and Stella have definitely broken up . . .

Yes, it's true. I got it from Angie, who got it (naturally) from Tracey in Human Resources. I'm dying to say something to him, but obviously I can't, because that would be cruel and insensitive. Although he broke my heart, and although he is an ionic bonder, I have been sensitive and caring with Adam all week. I can't help but feel a bit sorry for

him. I wonder if he's still doing her advertising campaign?
I wonder if Stella kept the twenty-five-thousand-dollar
ring?

Anyway, he doesn't appear heartbroken. I suppose getting
Colleague of the Year has softened the blow of personal rejection. He's been rather flirty, actually. But I'm not falling
for that old routine again. *Definitely* not.

Rachel and Hugh are immersed in wedding plans. Tish
has moved in with Rufus . . .

Yes, it's true. She finally told us about their blossoming romance yesterday. Since I spotted them flirting madly in
Rufus's deli, Tish has not said a word about him, so neither
have I. Didn't want to be too nosy. And Rachel didn't mention it either, so I wasn't sure if she knew.

*I'm so relieved she's not in love with Jack.*

But it all came out yesterday when I met them for coffee
at Tish's apartment after work. We don't go to the Spanish
café anymore, because Tish doesn't want to run into Julio.
Apparently, he was heartbroken when he realized she was
just using him for sex. That is definitely a downside of sleeping with waiters. Sooner or later you're going to run out of
coffee shops and restaurants to frequent.

Anyway, we have coffee these days because neither of
them has time to go to the gym. *Traitors.* No, I don't really
think that. I'm truly happy for them both. Anyway, back to
Tish and Rufus.

This is what happened.

"How about Vera Wang?" Tish asks, pointing to the picture in *Vogue* magazine. "Very chic, but entirely practical.
Very New York. You could get it dyed after the wedding and
wear it again. I see you in Vera Wang."

"Sure," Rachel says, taking a bite of her cheesecake.
"Whatever."

"Come on, you have to be more interested in your wedding gown. It's the most important day of a girl's life," Tish
says, shocked by Rachel's lack of interest.

I'm a bit shocked myself, but not altogether surprised. Don't get me wrong, Rachel likes fashion and outletting, but weddings are not really her thing.

"Look, sweetie, I appreciate what you're doing," Rachel says. "But this wedding thing isn't really me. Just choose what you think would look good. Really, I trust you."

I wish I were getting married. I wish I could wear a beautiful Vera Wang dress. Or Stella McCartney would be good, too . . . I wonder if Tish and Rufus will get married . . .

"How goes the world of polydating?" I ask Tish in an attempt to subtly turn the conversation to her love life.

"Oh, I've given that up since I moved in with Rufus," she says.

Rachel chokes on her cheesecake. If I were eating cheesecake, I would choke, too. Instead, I just sit there with my jaw hanging open in a very slack, fly-catching way.

"Oh," I say, after recovering control over my jaw. "So you've moved in with Rufus. Well, that's nice, isn't it?"

"You sneaky bitch," Rachel says, taking a gulp of her coffee to wash down the remains of the offending cheesecake. "You kept that one quiet. How did you get from adoration from afar to the bedroom, Miss Tish? And how come you didn't tell us before?"

"I'm telling you now," Tish says, flushing. "I wanted to be sure of him before I said anything to you both. I didn't want to jinx it. I didn't want any I-told-you-sos."

"We wouldn't have done that, we're your best friends," Rachel says. And then, "Okay, maybe just a little. So come on, give us the dirt, girl."

"I just did what you both said. I just turned up by myself at O'Malley's, looking totally hot and babelike. I plied him with Guinness, took him home and seduced him. Life's too short. You have to go after what you want, or it'll pass you by."

"Wow. That's terrific, Tish. It really is," I say, envious. "But how can you live with him? You're a Catholic. The Pope will choke on his false teeth. If he has false teeth."

"Since when were you so interested in the Pope's dental arrangements?" Tish asks. "The Pope won't know. Anyhow, Rufus is Catholic too, so I should think the Vatican will be delighted. I haven't told my mother yet."

"But—but aren't you getting married?" Tish has always wanted to get married.

"God, I hope so, in time. But Rufus has to get used to the idea of me living with him first, before I ask him to marry me. I don't wanna scare him away before we get to third base."

"What will you do with your apartment?" Rachel asks, ever the practical one.

"I don't know. Keep it, for sure. Maybe I'll rent it."

"Good plan." Rachel nods. "It's a good investment. Something to fall back on if the living together doesn't work out."

"Hey, don't be such a pessimist," I say. "Of course it'll work out. Rufus and you are meant for each other."

"Thank you, honey. So what's going on with you and Jack?"

"Yeah, have you slept with him yet?"

"No. Of course not. It's not like that."

"Sweetie, it's *so* like that," Rachel tells me. "The man eyes you like a juicy bone. You froth at the mouth whenever he's in the room."

"I do not."

"The sexual tension is really getting to us all."

"Oh."

They've obviously been talking to my mother. Naturally, being a coward I just change the subject and ignore their pointed stares and grins.

Anyway, talking about back to normal, tonight is Jack's usual hot date night, and my hot-movie-at-home-by-myself night. I'm wearing my favorite old ratty robe, my pizza's just arrived (large, thin crust, extra cheese), and I'm just about to settle down to watch *Chocolat,* tonight's viewing choice. I love Juliette Binoche—she's so beautiful, so chic, so French . . . Plus, Johnny Depp is hot.

"Hey," Jack says, coming into the living room.

I'm a bit surprised, because he's wearing cutoff jeans and a ripped old T-shirt. He's still covered in paint.

"Hey, yourself," I tell him, through a mouthful of pizza.

"So what you up to tonight?"

"The usual." I bite into more pizza. "Movie, pizza, wine."

"Oh pizza, great," he says, grabbing a slice.

"Hey, that's my dinner," I say, but I don't mind because I know I won't eat it all tonight. But I do like it cold for breakfast. I'm just complaining out of habit, really.

"Little thing like you can't eat a huge pizza like this." He grins at me. "You want more wine? I want some wine."

"I do *so* need more pizza. I need to consolidate the good work—just two more pounds and I'll be happy."

"Did I tell you how refreshing it is to live with a woman who is actively trying to *gain* weight?" he says, demolishing the rest of his slice of pizza. "How about I get dessert? I have chocolate-chip ice cream in the freezer. Seems only fair to share."

"Won't you be late? Why aren't you getting ready?"

"For what?"

"It's your hot date night. You always go out on Saturday nights."

"Not this Saturday night. Oh, good. *Chocolat.* Juliette Binoche. What a babe. Mind if I watch it with you?"

Oh. Actually, I like the idea of Jack staying home with me.

"It's your house," I tell him, passing him my glass. "I'd love more wine."

It's nice. Just the two of us. Jack smells really good. He looks really good, too, despite the paint spots. And you know, maybe he isn't such an ionic bonder . . . Wonder if the love of a good woman could turn him into a covalent bonder? Do I care? Who am I kidding, I really can't stop thinking about sleeping with him.

It's time I forgot Adam and moved on. I will Zen myself into Jack's bed. Maybe I could Zen myself into his heart, too?

.................

**Sunday, 7 A.M.**

Oh, I fell asleep on the sofa. I wiggle into the cushions to get more comfortable, and then I realize that the reason I can't wiggle any further into the cushions is because Jack is at the bottom of the sofa with my legs on his lap.

He looks so sweet and vulnerable, asleep. And I don't think him being two years younger than me is a problem, is it? It's only two years. I quite like the idea of being the older woman. Seems to work for Julia. But how to let him know subtly that I have changed my mind? I will have to flirt with him more, send him Zen vibes . . . Oh, he's waking up.

"Oh, hi," he tells me, stifling a yawn with his hand.

"Hi yourself." I smile my most alluring smile, and then put my flirting into practice. "We didn't make it as far as bed last night." I try to flutter my eyelashes, for maximum flirt effect. I wonder if that is a little too obvious.

"No," he says, looking a little puzzled. And then, "I'll go put on a pot of coffee."

And then he gently moves my legs to one side, and stands up, stretching his arms up to the ceiling. He's definitely hot, I think, yearning to squeeze his biceps. He catches me watching, so I smile and flutter my eyelashes some more.

"Emma, have you got something in your eye?"

"No!"

"Only you're blinking a lot."

Okay, so maybe my sex-kitten look needs more work. My morning hair is not a pretty sight, and my ratty old robe is definitely not alluring. No wonder he didn't get it.

..................

**Tuesday, 9 A.M.**

I'm ready to go.

Today I am wearing comfortable black pants and a white T-shirt, proudly emblazoned with the words DON'T FORGET YOUR CONDOMS. And for once, I do not check myself in the mirror to see if this is a good look for me or not.

In the grand scheme of things, how I look is totally unimportant and trivial.

Today, Sylvester and David are hosting their annual AIDS fundraiser. Some of their closest friends have fallen foul of this terrible disease, and this is their way of fighting back. They've given the kitchen staff the day off so we're all helping out, either by cooking (under Sylvester's hawk eyes and sharp tongue—I would never work for him full time—not for a million dollars) or serving their multitude of customers. Apart from the entire gay community of Manhattan, they seem to know every one else on the island, too. Which is good, because it means lots of dollars for the fundraiser.

When I say we're all helping out, I mean Rachel and Hugh, Katy and Tom, Rufus and Tish, me. And Jack.

Yes, Jack. Since Sunday morning I've been working on my sex-kitten approach, but I don't seem to be getting anywhere. I've tried everything—full makeup at breakfast, complete with slinky robe at breakfast (tastefully arranged to slip over my shoulder in an alluring fashion), but Jack doesn't seem to have noticed. Either he's (a) blind, (b) not interested, or (c) I'm just not cut out for this slut-in-the-bedroom thing. I think (b) and (c).

Anyway, Jack and me are working the breakfast and lunch shift with Rachel and Katy. The others are coming down later to work the evening dinner shift. And we're busy. Rufus has brought mounds of his mouthwatering muffins, plus wonderful organic food supplies.

## 6 P.M.

The restaurant is full of drag queens and laughter and noise. And condoms. All kinds, all colors, blown up as balloons and hung from the ceiling. There are goody bags (donated by a pharmaceutical company) filled with condoms of every description. Everywhere I turn, there are constant reminders of my lack of sex. Everywhere I turn, Jack is right behind me reminding me constantly of my lack of sex. And the fact that I want to have sex with *him,* of course.

"Emma." Sylvester pointedly glances across at Jack and holds out a goody bag to me. "Did you get your condoms yet?"

"Like I need them," I mutter, blushing, as I try not to look at Jack.

"*Chérie,*" Sylvester whispers in my ear. "What are you waiting for? You need to take zat man to bed—ze sexual tension is driving us all crazy."

Fat chance of that. The man in question doesn't even seem to realize I'm a girl. I flush even more from the sexual frustration that's driving *me* crazy, too, and glance at my watch. Then glance at Jack, who is grating cheese. How quickly can I escape the kitchen? How can grating cheese be sexy?

"Emma," Rachel says as she collects omlettes. "You won't believe this guy out here. These green vibrators rival your pink one for tackiness."

Thank you, Rachel, for sharing that with me, I think.

"*Chérie,* you are a dark horse." Sylvester pauses as he whisks eggs. "Tell me all."

"What vibrator?" Katy asks, as she starts to load the dishwasher.

God, I really don't like Jack right at this moment. Smirking at my discomfort, he rubs the cheese up and down, up and down, up and down . . . I am in a very bad way.

"Just a joke present from Peri," I mumble, getting even redder with embarrassment and longing. This is too much.

"It has to be seen to be believed," Rachel says as she comes back into the kitchen. "Pink, long, very loud . . ."

"Wow. I've never tried one," Katy says. "Is it any good? Maybe me and Tom could—"

"Can we just drop the subject?" I ask in desperation. I really, really don't want to talk about sex.

As Jack goes back into the restaurant bearing bowls of garlic bread, Rachel and Katy stop what they are doing and look at me.

"What?" Do I really want to know what they are thinking? Probably not. Probably something to do with Jack.

"Jack's great," Katy tells me.

"Jack's hot," Rachel adds. "Although not as hot as Hugh."

"And sexy—but not as sexy as Tom, of course."

"Delicious." Sylvester rolls his eyes. "But not as delicious as David."

"Ohhhkaayy," I say, holding up my hands. "So we're all agreed that Jack is great. I get the message, guys, but he's not interested in me. And I'm definitely not interested in him, either."

"So why aren't you sleeping with him yet?"

"It's not like that," I say, wondering what they've all been saying behind my back.

"Emma, you are one blind chick," David adds his voice to the Jack fan club from the kitchen door. "Wake up and smell the *testosterone,* sweetie."

I can't help it. I have to laugh.

"This is a conspiracy," I say. And then, "So you really think I should—?"

At that moment, Jack comes back into the kitchen with more dirty dishes so of course everyone stops talking and watches him. Very obviously.

"What?" he asks.

"Nothing," Rachel says, smiling at me in a knowing, feminine way. "We were just talking about you."

Oh God.

"Oh, good. Well I hope it was an interesting conversation," Jack says, obviously confused.

"Definitely interesting," Katy says.

"Guys," I plead with them.

"Sylvester, dear, where are the lamb cutlets for table three?" David says, taking the hint. "They've been waiting fifteen minutes already. Chop, chop."

"*Voilà.*" Sylvester flounces past him, plates in hand. "A work of art, of perfection, exquisite. Zese zings cannot be hurried."

"He thinks he's the culinary world's answer to Monet." David rolls his eyes, and heads back into the restaurant.

I need to get out of here for a bit. Tish, Hugh, and Tom will be here very soon, anyway.

"I'm just going to take a few minutes, guys," I say. "I need a breather."

I make it halfway down to the waterfront when Jack catches up with me.

"Mind if I come with you?"

*Yes, I do mind. The whole idea was to get away from you.* But I don't say this, obviously.

"Sure," I tell him in what I think is a definitely uninterested way. "It's a free country." I march on, quickening my pace. Endorphins will surely help me. I'm self-conscious and tongue-tied, and Jack isn't exactly chatty, either.

"Hey!" Jack shouts as he grabs at my arm. And yanks me back from the road just as a black car squeals past, missing me by a hair's breadth.

"Stupid asshole," Jack yells as the car screeches around the corner. "Are you okay?"

"Yes," I say, trembling, as Jack pulls me into his arms. I could have been killed. If I'd taken one more step into the road, I would be hurt. Or worse. And then I hear a completely pitiful whining and glance toward the pavement.

"Oh, but this guy's not," I say, forgetting my fright as I pull away from Jack's lovely warmth. "Jack, look. Look at this poor little dog. We have to *do* something."

"Bastards," Jack says, squatting in front of the ball of black fur and red blood. "Hit and run. Motherfuckers."

The small mongrel whines again, then licks at Jack's hand. Its leg is injured. The hip bone is sticking awkwardly through the flesh.

"I'll go get my car," I tell him. "The vet's will be closed, but there's any emergency animal hospital about twenty minutes away from here. I went with Rachel when she took one of her cats last year."

"No," Jack says, pulling off his T-shirt and wrapping it carefully around the poor creature. "You stay. I'll go. I have longer legs. I can run faster."

How nice is that? How lovely is he to not care about his top being covered in blood?

I try to comfort the poor creature as we wait for Jack's return. I stroke its silky head, murmuring silly meaningless words. I think it's a girl. I'm pretty sure it's a girl. She has no ID tag or collar, though, which is not a good sign.

"Poor little girl," I croon. "Such a pretty little thing. I think I'll call you Beauty for now. Because you are one, aren't you? And all dogs deserve a name."

Jack pulls up and we gently load Beauty into the backseat.

It seems to take forever to get there but fifteen minutes later we hand Beauty over to the vet.

"From her general condition, I'd say she's been living on the streets," the vet tells us twenty minutes later. "She's very thin—her ribs are really prominent. She's young—about a year old, I'd guess."

"But will she be all right?" I bite my lip.

"We've made her comfortable, but as there's no owner . . ." the vet trails off and I know, instantly, that she means Beauty will have to be put down.

"But . . ." I mentally calculate the funds available to me in my savings account. Or on my credit card. Which is useless, because I know that I don't have the hundreds of dollars required to pay for Beauty's treatment. Tears well in my eyes and I swipe at them as I think of who could lend me the money. Rachel would. I know she would.

I look up at Jack and see the tears in his eyes, too. And I like it that he's not one of those men who thinks tears are for women. It makes him stronger. More compassionate.

"She's a lovely dog," the vet continues. "Such a friendly little thing, despite her pain. She'd make a really great pet."

"Okay," Jack says, pulling out his credit card. "Go ahead and do whatever needs to be done. I'll take care of it."

Oh God, but he's lovely.

By nine, Beauty is comfortable and due to be operated on the next morning. We drive back to Hoboken in silence.

I feel curiously shy as I mull over the possibilities of me and Jack. Together. As a couple. But I like the idea, I really do. I think back to the night of the fated dinner, I think about what he said to me on the Fourth of July. He thinks my breasts are perfect . . . Plus he's caring, sensitive, considerate.

And as we drive down Washington toward his house, I know. I just know that Tish is right. Life *is* too short. You *do* have to go after what you want, or it'll pass you by. It's time to stop dithering. It's time to *carpe diem*.

I'm just wondering about how to start the conversation and subtly turn it around to Jack and me when Jack (who has been doing a really good impression of a deaf-mute since we left the animal hospital), pulls the car over to the side of the road. And turns to face me. And takes my hand.

"Emma, we need to talk," he tells me. "Properly. No running away, no pretending like we both don't know what's going on here. Because it's time, princess."

And for once I don't direct my reply to some inanimate object, on account of no handy door, or floor being available. And because I don't want to.

"Yes, we do," I tell him, looking right back into his face. "About my boundaries. And how they've changed."

He smiles, and I breathe a sigh of relief that his thoughts are running to the same place as mine.

"Yeah. And other stuff," he says. "But not here. Let's go home."

Home. That sounds good.

"Okay," I say, and he keeps a hold of my hand as we continue on our way.

And I *do* feel scared. I *am* nervous. So as we pull into the garage, I try to practice what I'm going to say and how I'm going to say it. But I can't think of a damn thing, on account of my heart bumping in my chest, so I guess I'll just have to fly by the seat of my pants. Every now and then, Jack gives my hand an encouraging little squeeze, so I know it will be all right. And I squeeze his hand right back.

But when we get back to the house, there is an unexpected surprise waiting for me on the steps.

Adam.

Crumpled, but still stylish. He is holding a bunch of red roses. The roses remind me of Beauty, and all that blood.

"Emmeline," he says, getting to his feet. "I've been waiting for you for hours."

"Adam. What are you doing here? How did you get this address?"

He gives me his lopsided Adam smile, the one that used to make my heart pittypat, and I have to admit, there is a small pitty. But only a very tiny one.

"Human Resources," he says. "They have your address on file."

Of course they do.

"Emmeline, I really need to talk to you. In private," he says, for the first time acknowledging Jack's existence. Jack squeezes my hand.

"Maybe she doesn't want to talk to you," Jack says. "Emma, let's go," he tells me, tugging at my hand.

But he's wrong.

I do need to speak to Adam, to hear what he has to say. He was so important to me just a few months ago, and he disappeared from my personal life so suddenly that I didn't have a chance to resolve things. I need to know why he rejected me. At the time it was almost like Adam the lover died. I think I need closure, so that I can move on to a new relationship.

With Jack.

"Jack, it's okay," I tell him, squeezing his hand in a reassuring way. But he doesn't squeeze back. Instead he pulls his hand away.

My hand is cold, his face is stony and unforgiving.

He *has* to understand. He just *has* to.

"I'll see you later. We'll talk properly, I promise," I say to his back as he bounds up the steps.

"Sure," he says, closing the door. "Maybe."

Oh God.

# 20

## Mixed Signals

### TO DO

1. Give up men for good (all except Robert Plant, but since my chances of ever meeting him are zero, is safe to worship him from afar).

2. Despite allergies, get a pet. Allergy shot in the butt once a week seems a small price to pay for loyalty, love, and utter devotion.

"Emmeline, I'm leaving Cougan & Cray," Adam tells me as we sit on a bench in the park. "Sezuma Advertising want me back. They called me yesterday and made me a fantastic offer."

"That's great," I tell Adam, while I worry about Jack.

"Yeah. They want me to head their office in Hong Kong."

"Wow. Hong Kong," I say. Jack *must* know how I feel about him.

"The thing is . . ." Adam starts. "You know about me and Stella?"

"Yeah, I heard. I'm sorry about that," I say, and mean it.

"It's okay. It's a relief, to be honest. I was blinded by her money, her beauty, her power. And I'm man enough to admit I have my faults."

"That's very good," I say. "Self-awareness is very important."

"That's exactly what I'm trying to say," Adam says. "Self-awareness. You see, I've realized a lot about myself over the past few months. And one thing I know, is that I made a mistake with you, Emmeline."

"You did?" I ask.

I think I made a mistake leaving Jack.

"Huge mistake. Stupidest thing I ever did, breaking up with you. So the thing is, I want you to come to Hong Kong with me."

"What?"

There's one I wasn't expecting.

"Oh, Emmeline," he says, taking my hands in his. "I was a fool to ever let you go. I was a fool to let Stella turn my head—"

I was a fool to leave Jack.

"I love you, Emmeline," Adam says, and in that instant I know that I love Jack.

"I want you to marry me," Adam says, and I know that I want Jack, married or not.

"It'll be great. You and me. Mr. and Mrs. Blakestock, living the high life in Hong Kong. And you could be my assistant—I've made that part of the deal. You won't be a secretary, you'll be an account manager—just like you wanted. Isn't that great? We'll have to learn to speak Mandarin, but the company will pay for private lessons for both of us. And they've offered me a house as part of the deal. Private schools for the kids . . ."

It's weird, isn't it? If Adam had offered me all this three months ago, I'd have bitten off his hand right away. For sure, he's successful, handsome, and getting-to-be-rich. I'd never have to worry about orthodontic care for the kids, or college funds or anything. And I'd get to live in Hong Kong, with a great apartment in Greenwich Village.

But I've changed.

I think about my ridiculous list of what I wanted to achieve by thirty. In a heartbeat, if I just say yes, Adam can give me everything.

Except Adam would *never* ruin his clothes for the sake of a mongrel dog. He'd *never* pay several hundred dollars to save it. Even if I loved Adam, which I don't, I could never trust him again.

All the time I aspired to live in Manhattan, I couldn't see that everything I want is right here in Hoboken. My friends, Jack . . .

All the time I wanted to get a great career . . . Well, I still want that, but not because someone handed it to me on a provisional plate.

And sure I want kids . . . but not with Adam.

"Adam," I tell him. "Thank you. But I don't love you. I can't come to Hong Kong with you."

"But—but why not?" he asks in disbelief. "Which part didn't you like? Is it still the Stella thing?"

"Oh, it's a great package," I tell him, getting to my feet. "And I'm sure you'll find the right woman to share it with. It's just not going to be me. Good luck, Adam, I wish you well."

And as my feet carry me away from him, I know that I mean it. Even though he is a bastard ionic bonder.

I walk quickly, because I have to see Jack and tell him that I love him.

But when I get home, the house is empty. It is *Jackless.* Maybe he went for a walk to clear his head? I'll just make some herbal tea and sit and wait for him. But it's late—it's already eleven . . . I'll wait for him in the living room.

I wake to the sound of voices in the kitchen, and for a moment I can't think where I am or what I'm doing here. And then I remember I'm waiting for Jack. *Jack.* I must speak to him, I have to tell him . . .

As I hear the sound of feminine laughter, I pause at the kitchen door.

There's a woman. In the kitchen. *With Jack.*

I don't *believe* it. There's got to be some mistake. Maybe it's all perfectly innocent. I have to put my faith in him, I have to trust him. I push open the kitchen door.

"Princess." Jack laughs at me, his arm around Laura, or Susan, I can't remember which one she is. "Come and join the party. You remember Karen, don't you?" he says, planting a kiss on her cheek. "Lovely Karen."

At this point I should just head out and leave them to it. Obviously, I've read all the signs wrong. Jack wouldn't do this if he really cared about me. *Really* wanted me. But I can't move. My feet are rooted to the spot. I can't leave this unresolved, I have to know.

"I thought you wanted to talk," I say, "I thought you'd wait for me."

"Yeah, well, a guy can't wait forever. So where is good old Adam?"

"You're drunk," I say.

"Not drunk enough," he says, turning to Karen. "Let's have some whiskey."

"Now, honey, we don't want you too drunk," she tells him, laughing. "Too much of the sauce ain't good for the gander, if you know what I mean."

"What's going on?" I ask, which is stupid, because I know full well what's going on. Jack is back to his old ways. He's pissed at me, so he called Karen.

"I could ask you the same question, princess. So what did good old Adam want? Like I can't guess."

Pride, in the name of saving face, I think to myself. Got to salvage something.

"He asked me to marry him," I say. "He wants me to go to Hong Kong with him."

"Congratulations, princess. He's all you ever wanted. Hope you'll be very happy with him and your Tiffany ring."

Call me a dog worrying at a bone, if you like, but pride aside, I can't leave things like this.

"Jack, I don't understand," I say. "I thought we had a—a *thing* going here . . ."

"Hon, we never had a thing. See, the problem with you is

that you're too—too—*effusy*. You know. Hugh explained it to me. Smart guy, Hugh. Smarter than me, that's for sure."

"What? This is getting too weird for me," Karen says.

*"Effusy?"* I ask.

"Yeah. Gas particles. Lots of pressure. Passing through the eye of a needle, or something small, anyway. Tiny opening. See, that's you. You find a tiny opening and you run. Slightest excuse and you escape."

I don't have a clue what he's talking about, but then he is drunk so I figure that must have something to do with it. But he wasn't drunk when he left this house, desperately seeking Karen. Is this how it would be?

"So this is what you do when you're pissed at someone?" I ask.

"Don't know what you mean, princess."

"What I *mean* is that I had a lucky escape. If you go in search of the nearest skirt every time we have a difference of opinion, it doesn't hold much hope for us, does it?"

"Hey, I'm not a skirt," Karen says. "Me and Jack go back a ways."

"Princess," he says, taking a swig of whiskey straight from the bottle. "See, that's where you got it wrong. What is this *us* you keep talking about? There is no *us*. There never *was*."

Jesus, I really did get it wrong. I'm a fool. I'm an idiot. I want the ground to open up and swallow me.

"C'mere, beautiful," Jack says to Karen, then pulls her toward him and kisses her.

*With tongues.*

My humiliation is more or less complete. I have nothing more to say, or do. Except one thing.

"I'll move out first thing tomorrow," I say.

"Anything you want, princess," Jack tells me, then returns to kissing Karen.

I will not be dismissed like this.

I let Adam get away with this, I sure as hell am not going quietly into any sweet night this time. Not without having my say.

"If you could just put her down for a moment," I say, because my temper is kicking into gear. "I have a thing or two I'd like to say to you."

"Can't we talk later? That *is* your thing, isn't it, princess? Talking later? Why do it now if it can wait until tomorrow?"

"Hey, shall I leave you two alone?" Karen asks. "I don't get what's going on here, but this is the strangest uncle-niece thing I ever saw. I'll wait for you in the bedroom, sweetie," she tells Jack. "Don't worry, I know the way."

"She's not the only one, is she, Jack?" I say after Karen leaves. "The whole female population of Hoboken knows the way to your bed."

"Yeah, well you'll never find out what you're missing," he says, slashing my heart with his tongue.

"That's your trouble, Jack. You hide the real you with one-night stands, just because your *stupid* fiancée slept with your *stupid* best friend. You think we're all like that? You think I'm like that? You think I'll betray you at the first opportunity?"

It's true. I didn't see it before, but I know I'm right. Jack is saying nothing, he's leaning against the refrigerator with his bottle in his hand.

"You just don't know how to trust," I continue. "The slightest problem and you assume someone's going to cheat on you. The smallest glitch and you're off chasing skirts to preserve the good old Ionic Bonder Jack image. Well, you're lying to yourself, Jack," I say. "And now you'll never find out if we had a chance or not."

For long moments there is silence, and I'm just starting to hope that my words have sunk in.

"You sound like Peri," Jack says, finally. "You finished the lecture now? 'Cause I'm going to bed. See you around, princess."

Upstairs in the attic, I systematically gather my things together ready to pack into my car. I want to leave now, but it's too late to call any of my friends. I don't want to stay another night in this house, not with Jack and Karen making out only a floor below me, but I don't think I have any choice.

There's always the backseat of my car . . .

No, I didn't sleep in my car last night. I did think about it, then dismissed it as stupid and dangerous.

I was packed by five this morning, so I quietly crept up and down the stairs, carrying my possessions out of Jack's house to my car. Despite about twenty trips up and down the stairs, I carefully avoided looking at his closed bedroom door.

By six, I was done and out of there. I managed to get a parking space near to Tish's apartment, which is good, and then I whiled away the time at the station—the café there opens at some ungodly hour.

By my third coffee, I've had plenty of time to reflect on my life and it isn't pretty. Yet again, I'm back to square one. Boyfriend-less, homeless, hopeless.

But at least I have a job, I tell myself. Maybe I should just forget about men and concentrate on my career for a while. At least I have my excellent friends. Actually, I saw an interview with Will Smith on *E!* some time ago and it's kind of stayed with me. He said that achievement was all a question of math. All I have to do is imagine where I want to be, work out where I am now, and try to figure out what I have to do to get there. Now I come to think of it, math is exactly like Zen, isn't it? Will Smith and Angie are two very smart people.

Anyway, I shall start planning my career on Monday. I'm not going to work today or tomorrow. I'm taking time off sick, because I am sick.

I have Jack-itus.

I have a broken heart. I thought it was broken after Adam, but I was wrong. After Adam I was humiliated and hurt, but my heart was only bruised. A little ragged round the edges, maybe, but basically intact. It took Jack to worm his way into my affections and break it into a million tiny pieces.

I hang around the station until nine thirty, and a fourth cup of coffee, when I know Tish's shop will be open. I am glad to leave because the guy in the coffee shop is starting to think I'm a hooker looking for a client. I will not think about sex, I tell myself, because it's unlikely I'll get any in the foreseeable future.

Thank God Tish is here, I think, as I push open her door.

"Emma, what are you doing here, shouldn't you be at work? Oh my God, you look like shit. You look sick. Are you sick?"

"Yes," I tell her. "I have Jack-itus. It's incurable and I may never get over it. Can I rent your apartment?" I ask, then burst into tears.

................

## Friday evening

"But I don't get it," Katy says, for the umpteenth time. "I was so sure I was right about you and Jack. Don't you two agree?" she asks, looking at Tish and Rachel.

"No," Rachel lies. "Definitely not the guy for Emma— definitely a bastard ionic bonder."

"Well, maybe I thought that at first," Tish says, then after Rachel glares at her, "but not now, of course not now. Bastard ionic bonder."

My friends are so lovely. So loyal.

"He was in Rufus's deli earlier," Tish adds, and my heart starts its familiar pittypat. "He looked like shit."

"Serves him right," Rachel says, "It was probably his hangover and his guilty conscience. Anyway, the AIDS benefit was a huge success. Sylvester and David are still counting the proceeds. Have some more wine."

See what I mean? Rachel is swiftly changing the subject to save me from more pain.

We are having a girly night at my (Tish's) place. I must say, it's strange living here without Tish—but there is a lot more space, and it's nice not to have to sleep on the sofa.

The reason for the girly night, despite having men waiting for them at home, is because they are afraid that if left alone I will do myself harm. They should know by now that I am allergic to pain in any shape or form. Except *Jack* pain. I think I've cried me more than one little river . . .

Anyway, tonight we have pizza, because Tish, Rachel, and Katy worry that I'll undo all my good work and lose weight. Due to my broken heart. The pizza is large, thin-crust, with extra cheese, of course. We have wine (Australian Shiraz of a very nice vintage—we developed an expensive taste in wine after Tish stole six bottles of Adam's good stuff) and the video of choice tonight is *Men in Black*.

*Men in Black* because it is not a romance. They fear romance will only remind me of Jack. Plus Will Smith is hot. And extremely smart.

Just as Will is about to zap Tommy Lee Jones with his forgetful beam zapper so that Tommy can spend the rest of his life with the woman he left behind to join the MIB, I remember what Jack said to me about being effusy.

"What's effusy?" I ask Rachel, because she's bound to know. "Only Jack said I was effusy, and that Hugh told him about it."

Rachel chews for a moment on her extra cheese, her brow wrinkling as she tries to translate stupid-person science into intelligent-person science.

"Oh, you mean effusion," she says.

This is not enlightening.

"Effusion. Process by which gas particles under pressure pass through a tiny opening."

"Yes, he definitely mentioned tiny and particles."

"But what did he mean?" Katy asks, pouring us some

more wine, and we all stare blankly at Rachel for an explanation.

"I think he means that you find an out when you're under pressure," Rachel says, with careful consideration. "It means that you don't trust your feelings, so you run at the slightest sign of a black cloud. And if there is no black cloud, you invent one."

Oh. I'm not sure I wanted to know this.

"Which is a total lie," Rachel continues, "because you were all set and ready to marry Adam three months ago. You don't get more relationship committed than that. You were not the effusy one. You didn't look for an out."

"But what if I was settling for Adam because I thought he was safe?" I ask, because I've been thinking about this. "I mean, I didn't really love Adam, so I was never really in danger of having my heart broken by him, despite the fact he dumped me and got engaged to someone else."

The three of them are looking at me in amazement, and for a few moments no one says anything.

"No," Tish says.

"Absolutely not," Katy says.

"Not at all." Rachel agrees with them. "Emma, honey, you are unclassifiable."

I think that's a compliment, but I'm not sure.

"More like certifiable," I add, darkly. And then, "Oh God, what if he comes to Chez Nous on Sunday night? I think I'll stay away, just in case."

See? I am pathetic. And effusy.

"That's all fixed," Rachel tells me, grabbing another slice of pizza. "I called him already. I told him if he shows up, I'll cut off his balls with a pair of blunt scissors. We're *your* friends. We're on *your* side. We come as part of the *Emmeline* package, and if he messes with one of us, he messes with us all."

"Wow. You fucking told him, you go, girl!" Tish says.

It's still odd hearing her say *fucking*.

"Oh, my," I say, with visions of John Wayne Bobbitt. And then, "You really said that?"

"No," Rachel says. "Yes, actually I did say that. Except with more force. I don't think he'll come anywhere near you again."

I wonder what else she said. I'm too afraid to ask. I love these girls, they're so loyal.

## 21

# A Whole New Me

### TO DO

1. *Forget Jack.* Do not even mention his name.

2. Meditate. "Ohm—I will not think about Ja-"

3. Let's try this again. Repeat after me: "Ohm—I am totally focused on my career. Ohm—I have no need of a man."

**Saturday, October 26**

Seven weeks have passed since the debacle with Ja—, and I've got to say, I'm doing really well. I've done a lot of singing along to Robert Plant and playing air guitar to Jimmy Page. And I've eaten buckets full of Häagen-Dazs ice cream.

Actually, a lot of the time I feel like shit. A lot of the time I think about Ja—, I just can't help it. But sometimes I feel okay about things.

I'm good.

I really am.

I do have moments when I run the gamut of what-ifs, but every time they threaten to overwhelm my newfound source of Zen-style inner peace, I count my blessings. And lessons learned.

You know, the whole non-engagement-to-Adam and non-relationship-with-Jack episodes have really taught me a lot about myself.

I don't need to change myself for somebody else.

I don't need to alter my personality to accommodate someone else, like I did with Adam.

I don't need bigger breasts to please a lover, because the ones I have fit my body just nicely. Even if they are on the small side. But *I'm* generally on the small side . . .

Ja—said my breasts are perf—. I hold the thought right there.

*I* think my breasts are perfect for me.

In fact, one of the first things I did when I moved into Tish's apartment was to flush the breast-enhancing pills (sorry, Sylvester and David) down the toilet.

I'm not saying they're a good thing or a bad thing. They're just not for me. If you are a woman who really, really wants larger boobs, then you go, girl! When I really think about it, I don't want mine any larger. I just thought that they *should* be bigger, which is a different thing completely.

Although I'm still drinking those revolting shakes—I like me with a little extra weight. I feel better, and I look healthier.

I still go to the gym, too, except I go early in the morning these days on account of not wanting to bump into Ja—. Because it's convenient. Nothing to do with the unmentionable man at all. I just like my muscle definition, is all. And I *love* my yoga.

But you know, Ja—. That unmentionable man *did* have a point about me being effusy, despite what Rachel and Tish say.

I *do* look for the out.

I had some opportunities to start a relationship with Jack, and each time, I found an excuse not to. Nine years ago, I didn't give him a chance to explain about him and Chip tossing the coin for me, because I didn't want to know that Jack was a nice guy.

Because I liked him too much.

More recently, after moving into his house, I had several

opportunities to stay and face whatever might happen be-tween us. To *not* be that agitated, scared particle looking for a tiny opening through which to escape. Because I was afraid it might be the real thing.

But I'm not afraid anymore.

And if love comes knocking on my door, I won't turn it away. Not that I'm looking for love at the moment. I mean, I still do miss sex and all, but I'm perfectly happy on my own.

Well, maybe not perfectly happy. Quietly content. But that's enough for now.

Anyway, tragically, I sold my yellow Beetle just after I moved into Tish's apartment, because it's not like I really need a car, is it?

Plus, I needed the extra cash to make sure I could pay Tish a decent rent. Just because I'm her best friend is no excuse to sponge off her kind nature, is it? She has mortgage pay-ments to make, and if she rented through a real-estate agent, she'd make enough. So I have to give her enough, despite her protestations.

Still, I really *loved* that car. But it's only a *thing*, after all.

Yes, I'm really getting to grips with being a spinster of the parish of Hoboken *(spinster* is such an awful word, isn't it? Julia's right—bachelorette *is* much nicer). No, really, *I am*. And despite the fact that my personal life is down the tubes, things at work took a decided turn for the better.

You see, Adam left for Hong Kong fairly immediately after he announced it to William Cougan. About five minutes after. If you're someone fairly important at Cougan & Cray, then you pretty well leave immediately, accompanied by a se-curity guard just on the off chance you might try to acciden-tally take a few company clients with you. I got this from Angie, who witnessed the whole thing—I wish *I'd* been there. Grady Thomas was promoted to Adam's old job.

I've always liked Grady. Actually, it was Grady who came up with the new campaign for Stella Burgoyne. (Her engagement to William Cougan was announced last week—I think she only does it to get expensive jewelry from Tiffany's.)

Grady's campaign features rugged, outdoorsy types with their rugged, outdoorsy SUVs—and of course, Stella's exceptionally rugged, outdoorsy toilet paper.

It was a great idea, but not as good as my idea. Picture this: babies dressed in Baby Gap–meets–National Guard combat gear. Assault courses built from—you guessed it—Stella Burgoyne's toilet paper.

But it doesn't matter. You see, the thing is, I'm now officially a junior account manager. Lou got fired straight after Adam left, and Grady recommended me for it. And Angie got my job, which is great.

I'm only on small accounts at the moment, but I'm keen, and the pay raise was fairly significant, which is a plus. I'm currently working on a campaign for a new range of thigh- and tummy-diminishing creams, which frankly gives me a lot of scope for comic content, don't you think?

The only downside is that I've already sold my Beetle. I wish I hadn't taken it back to the dealership, but I didn't know about my promotion at the time. Two weeks after I sold it, I went back to try to reclaim it, but it had gone. Some lucky person had snapped it up already. The salesman tried to interest me in another Beetle, but it wasn't the same.

If there's anything I've learned, it's that it has to be the *right* Beetle, not *any old* good-looking Beetle.

Anyway. Everything is fine.

Tish and Rufus—fine. (Although Rufus wears an expression that is halfway between delight and confusion. Tish, on the other hand, is just unbearably smug.)

Rachel and Hugh—fine. (Although Rachel's mother is driving them both nuts with menus and flowers. They're more interested in molecules than salmon mousse.)

Katy and Tom—fine. (Actually, Katy took over the PPPTA in a rather marvelous *coup d'état*—apparently she wasn't the only one who felt intimidated by Marion Lacy. The other mothers were delighted to hear a voice of reason amidst MASS chaos.)

David and Sylvester—fine, in their own special way. (Although the secret preparations for Sylvester's surprise birthday party are driving him mad with curiosity.)

Julia and George—ecstatic. (Julia called me last night—"can't think why I didn't marry him years ago, darling.")

Peri and Dad and the twins—better. (The twins are still difficult, but the new nanny is definitely getting a handle on things and Peri is too stricken with all-day morning sickness to interfere with the good work.)

Anyway, tonight is Sylvester's long-anticipated surprise fortieth birthday party at Chez Nous. I am wearing the lovely Calvin Klein tank and skirt that I bought for the Colleague of the Year dinner, because it cost me a fortune and I need to justify spending that much money on one outfit. The wine didn't ruin it, on account of its having been white wine, so that's good, isn't it? Plus, I'm wearing my lovely Manolos.

I check myself in the mirror one last time before I leave. My hair, newly trimmed and highlighted, is soft and pretty. My skin glows with good health and expensive makeup.

The last time I wore this, Ja— . . . I ruthlessly push aside thoughts of him.

*This is a great look for me,* I tell myself.

Not that I'm expecting to meet any single men, because the only single men at this bash will be gay, and will therefore be more interested in my designer clothes than me. But that's cool. I can look great just for myself.

When I arrive, the party is already up and swinging. Oh, God, it's karaoke. I hope no one makes me sing. The sound of my voice has been known to make grown men weep with pain.

"Darling, happy birthday," I say, handing my card to Sylvester. I've bought him a gift voucher for Kenneth Cole, because he loves Kenneth Cole.

"*Chérie,* you are breathtaking." Sylvester kisses me on both cheeks. "Come on, you are about to miss David—he's on next." Sylvester leans down to my ear. "You know zat time I zought he was having an affair wiz Simon? *Oui?* Well, Simon's boyfriend is a music teacher—he's been teaching David to sing. David did it so he can sing to me tonight."

"How romantic is that?" I say, because it is.

The room is filled with drag queens, and all the usual gang are here.

As I join them, I am kissed and hugged, and I feel truly thankful to have such a wonderful extended family, and I settle down to gorge myself on Sylvester and David's wonderful food, and drink too much of their wonderful wine.

"So, how's it going with Rufus?" I ask Tish. Obviously, this is a stupid question, because she's never looked happier.

"You know the old saying, 'You can lead a horse to water, but you can't make it drink'?" She smiles a very secretive smile.

"Yeah?" What does this have to do with true love?

"Well, it's wrong. My horse just needed to be gently led to the water, so he could taste how sweet it was. Remember that day after your birthday, when Rufus went missing from the deli and I thought he'd stood me up?"

"God, that seems like a lifetime away." And yet how things can change in four months.

"Doesn't it? Well, anyway, he went to book a course to help him with public speaking. So he could overcome his shyness and talk to me."

"Wow. Greater love hath no man, and all that."

"I know. He just didn't have the confidence to believe in himself. And I just didn't have the courage to ask him on a date. How stupid is that? I asked other men on dates, but then I didn't have feelings for them, so it was easy."

"You've both come a long way. I'm sure you'll be really happy together."

"I hope so. You know, there are no guarantees in this life.

Sometimes you just have to be brave and expose your inner self to get what you want. Anyway, back to horses. There's one over there who looks positively dehydrated," she says, glancing across the room. At Jack.

*At Jack?*

"What's he doing here?" I hiss, thinking how wonderful he looks, and how much it hurts to see him.

He's wearing his black Calvin Klein jeans and top, and chatting to a Barbra Streisand queen. He's very comfortable with his own masculinity, it seems.

"David invited him," Tish says, then smiles at me. "Apparently, Jack's been really miserable since you moved out. Tom thinks he's missing you, and so does Hugh. Sylvester just thought it would be romantic to get you both in the same room."

"But Sylvester's French. He thrives on romance and drama," I say.

"I think we should keep Rachel away from sharp objects," Tish adds. "After what she said about Jack and blunt scissors."

"I need to go home," I say. Why do men always stick together?

"No you're not," Rachel says, joining us. "I can't believe Hugh would be party to something so fucking outrageous. I may not have sex with him for a week. Here," she says, thrusting another glass of wine into my hand. "Have another fucking drink."

I gulp the wine like a condemned woman having her last taste of alcohol. But, I think, I can do this. I'm a civilized, adult person. I can cope. *I feel sick.*

"Sorry about Tom's involvement," Katy says as she joins us. "Believe me, he will suffer."

"No, it's fine. Truly. I'm fine," I say. I do not want to be the cause of disharmony, marital or otherwise.

"But he did adopt Beauty," Tish adds. "A three-legged mongrel isn't everyone's ideal pet, so he can't be all bad, can he? Obviously he's still a bastard ionic bonder," she adds, when Rachel scowls.

He adopted Beauty? Oh. I didn't know that. She had a leg removed? Poor baby. What a hero Ja—.

*Stop right there.* I harden my heart. He could adopt a million desperate, three-legged dogs as far as I'm concerned. Rachel's right. I don't need another ionic bonder. But still . . .

Tish, Rachel, and Katy stick staunchly to my side like bodyguards, occasionally throwing dark glances across to Jack.

I ignore Jack completely.

I'm totally enthralled by the karaoke. I love David's rendition of "I Only Have Eyes for You," as he only has eyes for Sylvester. How sweet is that? I'm totally into up-and-coming-designer Simon's Cyndi Lauper impersonation with "Girls Just Wanna Have Fun." And Sylvester's Streisand version of "Evergreen" is totally great.

Yes, all in all I do a completely great job of totally ignoring Jack, and hardly ever looking around the room for him. Even though I'm desperate for another look at his sweet face. Even though I can think of nothing but him.

It's the next act that really brings me to my knees.

"And now, Hoboken's answer to Robert Plant," David announces from the impromptu stage at the front. "Please raise your hands for our very own Jack Brown singing 'Rock and Roll.' "

I freeze. Both hands grip the stem of my wine glass with such ferocity that it's a miracle it doesn't turn back to sand. My mouth is dry. My legs are shaking.

And then Jack is in front of us, complete with long, blond, curly wig. And he's dancing around the small podium playing Jimmy Page air guitar to the intro to the song. He is a complete idiot. But boy, can this man dance.

And then he starts singing. Directly to me. And my heart thumps painfully in my chest.

He's telling me that it's been a long time, a lonely time. And as he sings "lonely time" directly in front of me, *to me,* I can't help myself. I echo the lyric for him.

"Yes it has," I say.

It's so romantic. He can't sing worth toffee, but it *is* romantic. And he brings the house down. Everyone cheers and claps as he finishes.

And then he's standing in front of me.

How can I possibly resist a man making such a fool of himself for me?

How can I possibly resist a man who adopts pathetic, condemned dogs?

"Hi," he says.

"Hi yourself," I say, wishing I could think of something more clever. But this is Jack. I remember my vow to just be myself.

My bodyguards have mysteriously disappeared. Even Rachel. I see her across the room with Hugh, and as she smiles encouragement at me, I smile back. Not that I need her encouragement or approval, but it's nice to have it, isn't it?

"Emma," Jack says, and he's really awkward. Really nervous. "Can we talk, do you think? Please?"

Now I could say (a) "How's Karen?" or (b) "It's too late for talking, baby, you sure missed your chance" or (c) "Yes."

But he looks so scared and miserable.

(c) it is.

"Yes," I say.

"Do you mind if we take a walk? There's something I want to show you."

"Okay."

As we leave the restaurant, our progress is followed by at least ten pairs of watchful eyes, and I am glad to get away.

We walk in silence. We are not doing a good job of having even a basic conversation. But I am so nervous that my tongue has swelled to gigantic proportions in my mouth and

I cannot even *open* my mouth. And then I realize where we're going.

"Why are we going to your house?" My voice comes out like a frog croak.

"I didn't sleep with her, you know," he says, quickly.

"What?"

"Karen. The night we found Beauty. You were right."

"Oh?" I must stop speaking in words of one syllable. How stupid do I sound? How relieved am I? He didn't sleep with her!

"I *was* looking for an out," he continues, looking at his shoes. "I *was* waiting for betrayal. I've thought a lot about what you said."

"I didn't betray you," I say. And then it all comes out in a garbled rush. "I just needed closure with Adam. I didn't love him anymore, but I had to hear whatever it was he had to tell me. And when he asked me to go back to him, I needed to tell him no and feel that I really meant no. And all the time he was talking, I couldn't concentrate and I was thinking about you. So I told him no, and came back home looking for you. Is this making any sense?"

"Yeah, and I brought back a broad. Very grown-up of me, so I've been told," he says, smiling wryly.

And I can't help myself. I smile back.

"You have very protective friends—great friends."

"I know."

"So what were you coming back to talk to me about that night?" he asks, and he's nervous, but so am I.

"Mutual boundaries," I say, smiling. "I thought something like an alliance . . ."

"A treaty of intent."

"Yeah." I laugh manically, my anxiety obvious. "God, we sound like two politicians discussing borders."

"I know. It's easier, isn't it, though? To avoid the personal, mushy stuff. I'm no good at mushy stuff," he says, pushing a hand through his blond wig. "Oh, I forgot I was wearing this."

"It's very becoming," I say. "I bet you're really good at mushy stuff." And then, because I'm getting more confident with each passing moment. "Tell me something mushy."

"I love you."

Oh God, he said it. He really said it, and he looks like he's going to cry.

"I love you, too."

"Good," he says, faintly, looking relieved but at the same time disbelieving. "I'm glad we got that out of the way."

"So are you going to show me your etchings?" I ask, as we turn onto his street.

"Later, princess, later," he says to me. "But first, I want to show you this."

He takes my breath away again.

There, parked in front of his house, is a yellow Beetle.

*My* yellow Beetle.

"I thought you said it was too girly," I say, but he can see that I'm happy, because I'm dancing. I'm so happy I'm pirouetting in my Manolos.

"Hey, I'm in touch with my feminine side," he says, catching my hands and spinning me around on the sidewalk.

"So what do you think, Emma Taylor?"

"I think," I say, pulling his head down toward mine. "I think that this is the *right* Beetle, Jack Brown."

And then I kiss him.

# Epilogue

LIFE GOALS
Emma Beaufort Taylor
Age 30 and 364 days

1. Move in with Jack. Live with him forever.

2. Have Jack's babies. But not yet, I have a career to pursue.

3. Have dinner with lovely friends at Chez Nous every Sunday night.

4. Make monthly donations to aid Human Rights and World Peace. Although I also like the idea of buying more livestock for Third World villages.

5. Get a new roof for Jack's house. Of course, if I got a Tiffany's engagement ring, that would be lovely. But he really needs the new roof before winter.

**6 A.M.**

Radio alarm clicks on. I blearily open my eyes and remember that it's my birthday. I will not obsess just because I am thirty-one.

And then I remember that I'm in Jack's house. In Jack's bed . . . Heaven!

"And now," comes the voice of the morning DJ on my favorite classic rock station, "we have a very special dedication. This is for Emmeline Beaufort Taylor, from her boyfriend Jack. Emma, babe, the next song is just for you."

It's Led Zeppelin's "Whole Lotta Love."

Oh, how lovely.

I've never had a more romantic gift in my life.

And as I snuggle back toward Jack so I can give him all of *my* love, his arm comes around me and pulls me toward his morning erection.

"Don't get any ideas about breakfast in bed, old lady," Jack tells me, nibbling my shoulder.

And then, quite a long time later, he tells me something else, too.

"Emmeline," he says. "Naked is a great look for you."

# AVON TRADE... because every great bag deserves a great book!

Paperback $13.95
ISBN 0-06-056277-3

Paperback $13.95
($21.95 Can.)
ISBN 0-06-056012-6

Paperback $13.95
ISBN 0-06-053437-0

Paperback $13.95 ($21.95 Can.)
ISBN 0-06-051237-7

Paperback $13.95 ($21.95 Can.)
ISBN 0-380-81936-8

Paperback $13.95 ($21.95 Can.)
ISBN 0-06-008166-X